HELLION

KAREN LYNCH

For my nieces and nephews:

Ashley, Daniel, Hailey, Noah, Abby, Travis, Oliver, Joseph, Devon, Ryan, and Philip

Follow your dreams

ACKNOWLEDGMENTS

So many people have helped me over the years to realize my dream of being an author. Thank you to my family and friends for your love and support, and to my readers for giving my books a chance and sticking with me. And thanks to the indie community that gave me so many wonderful friends. I couldn't imagine doing this without you all.

PROLOGUE

1 *1 years ago, San Francisco, CA*

I lifted the bottom corner of the plywood that covered the window and slipped through the opening. Inside the building, it was dark, and I took a minute for my eyes to adjust before I moved away from the window.

A shiver went through me. I didn't mind the dark, but it was chilly in here and my coat was thin. I was going to have to find something warmer to wear before the weather turned cold.

My stomach rumbled painfully, reminding me I hadn't eaten since yesterday. Spurred by hunger, I made my way down a hallway to what had once been the lobby of a small hotel. Here, the sun shone through a higher window that hadn't been boarded up, providing enough light to see my surroundings.

I headed for a large square patch of sunlight in a corner, grateful for any warmth I could find. Sitting cross-legged on the dirty floor, I listened to make sure I was alone. The other kids I shared this building with rarely came back until dark, but I'd learned to be careful.

I had been living on the street since I ran from my foster home three weeks ago, and it hadn't taken long to learn to trust no one. Out here, everyone was trying to survive from one day to the next, even if that meant stealing from the new girl.

Hearing nothing, I opened my small backpack and pulled out the turkey and cheese sandwich I'd lifted from a deli an hour ago. My mouth watered at the smell of bread and mayo, and I could barely wait to get the plastic off before I took a huge bite. I had to force myself to chew slowly despite the gurgling sounds coming from my stomach. If I ate too quickly when I was really hungry, I'd end up throwing it up and I would be back to where I'd started.

"Whatcha got there, J?"

My heart leaped into my throat, and I nearly choked on the food in my mouth as a red-haired boy entered the room. *Shane.* I cringed inwardly because he was the last person I wanted to see. I made a point of avoiding him as much as I could.

At fourteen, Shane had four years on me, and he was at least a foot taller. He was scrawny like most of the kids I'd met out here but tough from years on the street. And he was a bully.

I flicked a nervous glance behind him. He also didn't go anywhere without his little group of friends. The four of them said they owned this building, and they bossed everyone around. If I could find another safe place to sleep, I wouldn't stick around here.

"Just a sandwich." I wrapped it in the plastic again. No sense lying because he'd already seen it.

"You gonna share?" he asked, his eyes never leaving my hands.

I tucked the sandwich inside my backpack. "No."

Shane scowled and lifted his gaze to mine. He wasn't hungry. I'd seen him and his buddies eating hot dogs two hours ago. He just didn't like someone telling him no. Well, too bad. I worked hard to get this sandwich, and I was so hungry I could cry. Not that I'd ever cry in front of him.

He took a menacing step toward me. "You know this is my place. You want to squat here, you got to pay. That's the rule."

I was on my feet before he could get any closer. Dropping my backpack behind me, I clenched my fists as fury erupted in me and a familiar growl filled my head. The voice was angry. It didn't like most people, but it hated anyone who tried to hurt me.

Shane snickered as I tensed for his attack. "You going to fight me, J?"

"If you don't back off, I will."

"Just give me half the sandwich, and I'll consider it fair payment."

"No," I shot back, almost shouting this time. "It's all I have to eat. Get your own food."

He drew himself up to his full height, towering over me. But as big as he was, he didn't scare me. He'd get in a few punches, but I'd taken my fair share of hits over the years. I had learned from an early age to either suck it up or fight back. I fought back. I'd beaten up the son of my last foster mom for trying to touch me, and he was a year older than Shane.

"Just for that, I'm taking the whole thing," Shane snarled before he lunged at me.

I was ready for him, and as soon as he was within reach, my foot landed between his legs. The breath left him on a high-pitched squeak, and he doubled over, cupping himself in his hands.

More, growled the voice that was still seething with anger.

As if someone else was moving it, my arm drew back and my fist plowed into Shane's eye. The blow hurt my hand, but it made the voice crow with glee. It liked to fight. Sometimes, I could stop it, but mostly it was too strong. It didn't care that it got me kicked out of every home I'd lived in. I should hate it, but having it inside me made me feel like I was never really alone.

Shane fell to his knees, wheezing with hatred blazing in his eyes. He was in no shape to hurt me now, but once he was better, he and his friends would gang up on me. I could take on one of them but not four. I needed to disappear before the rest of them came back.

Snatching up my backpack, I ran back the way I'd come. Voices up ahead brought me up short, and I swallowed hard when I recognized Shane's friend Lana. She might be a girl, but she was almost as mean as Shane. And she had a crush on him, which meant she would be mad when she found out what I'd done.

I ducked into the first doorway I found and hid in the dark room as quiet as a mouse. I held my breath as Lana and the others walked past my hiding place, talking and laughing. As soon as they reached the end of the hall, I slipped out of the room and raced silently toward the way out.

I was almost at the window when I heard shouts and running feet. My heart thundered in my ears as I shoved my backpack through the opening and followed it. It would take a few minutes for them all to get through the window. If I could get far enough, I might make it out of this.

A pair of hands latched onto my ankle when I was halfway out, and I let out a small scream.

"I got her!" yelled Kevin.

I kicked out hard and felt my foot connect with soft flesh. Kevin let out a muffled *oomph* and released my leg, sending me crashing to the ground. My shoulder took the worst of the fall, and I knew I'd have a nasty bruise later. But I was free.

Scrambling to my feet, I grabbed my backpack and took off. I ran for at least an hour, up one street and down another, putting as much distance between me and Shane's gang as I could.

I was panting when I finally stopped behind a small strip mall. There was a patch of grass at the back of the parking lot, and I sank down wearily, mostly obscured from view by a large dumpster. Feeling safe for the moment, I pulled out the bottle of water I kept in my bag and downed the contents. Then I unwrapped the squished sandwich with trembling hands and devoured my well-earned meal.

I wiped my mouth with the back of my hand when I finished. I didn't feel full, but at least my stomach was no longer hurting. It would have to be enough until tomorrow.

I had a bigger problem than hunger. I couldn't go back to the hotel, so I'd have to find a new place to sleep tonight. There was safety in numbers, which was why I'd stayed at the hotel. Now I was alone, and it was more than a little frightening.

There had to be other groups of kids like me. I just needed to find them before it got dark in a few hours. I couldn't sleep outside. I'd seen some scary things my first few days on the street, like those two short guys with the cat eyes and horns I'd watched breaking into a butcher shop. I didn't know what they were, but no way were they human.

A shudder went through me when I remembered the strange creatures emerging from the shop with a bucket of blood. I knew it was blood because I'd watched them drink the stuff. That was an image I wouldn't soon forget.

The thought of spending the night out here alone drove me to my feet. I brushed off my jeans and put my water bottle into my pack as I walked across the parking lot toward the street. Someone had said a lot of kids liked to hang around the mall. I'd go there and try to make some new friends. It was the only thing I could think of right now.

I was walking past the dumpster when I discovered I wasn't alone. Shane and Lana stepped out from where they'd been hiding on the other side of the dumpster, and their smiles told me I was in trouble. I didn't see Kevin and Ash, but they were here somewhere. Shane knew I could take him alone, so he'd bring his whole gang. I was pleased to see his right eye was almost swollen shut.

"Well, hello, J. Fancy meeting you here," Shane drawled in a smug voice.

I held my chin up, hiding my fear. "I don't have any food left if that's what you're after."

He sneered at me. "I don't want your crappy sandwich. I'm here to teach you that you don't mess with me and get away with it."

"You messed with me first."

"You were in my building," he said as if that made it okay.

Lana huffed. "Can we just do this so we can go get a pizza?"

Shane turned his head to say something to her.

I ran.

I made it to the end of the strip mall before Ash leaped out in front of me, shoving me to the ground. He was twelve, overweight, and stronger than he looked. I'd wondered how he didn't lose all that weight living on the street. We didn't exactly get three square meals a day out here.

I rubbed the back of my head, which had hit the pavement. It hurt so much that tears pricked my eyes. I blinked them away, refusing to cry.

Footsteps approached. Shane and Lana loomed over me, grinning.

Shane kicked me in the thigh, and I couldn't stop the small cry of pain that escaped me. His grin widened, and Lana laughed.

The voice in my head growled like an alligator I once saw on a nature show. It was madder than ever, but I didn't think it could help me this time.

Lana bent down and snatched up my backpack, which had fallen off my shoulder. "Let's see what you have in here."

"Give that back," I demanded. There was nothing of value in the bag, just a change of clothes, a toothbrush, and my water bottle, but it was all I owned in the world.

Ignoring me, she dumped the contents of my pack on the ground, making sure to step on my toothbrush and grind it with her foot.

"Junk," she muttered. "Not even a few dollars."

Shane crossed his arms, wearing a triumphant look. "Tell me you're sorry, and beg me to let you go. I'll go easy on you this time."

"No," I said defiantly.

"Suit yourself. But this is going to hurt."

I glared at him, refusing to be cowed. "You're nothing but a bunch of sissies who have to gang up on people. One of these days, I'll be big enough to kick all your asses."

The three of them laughed, and Shane kicked me in the leg again, harder this time. He stared at me expectantly, but I refused to cry out again.

"What's going on over there?" called a woman's voice.

Shane, Lana, and Ash turned toward the street. I couldn't see what they were looking at, but I heard them swear under their breaths, and Shane hissed, "Let's get out of here."

The three of them took off running, and I eased myself into a sitting position on the ground. My leg and head hurt, and I could feel a bad headache coming on. On top of that, my change of clothes were on the ground and Lana had made off with my backpack.

The tears I'd been holding back threatened again, and I swallowed past a lump in my throat. Why did everything have to be so hard?

"Are you okay, sweetheart?" asked a gentle voice.

My head jerked up in surprise, and I stared at the woman I hadn't even heard approach. She was tall and pretty with kind blue eyes and long blonde hair in a ponytail. She wore jeans and black boots, and I thought I could see the hilt of a knife peeking out of the top of one boot.

I didn't speak as I watched her come closer until she was only a few feet away. I let out a soft gasp when a strange sense of recognition filled me. I'd never felt anything like it before, but I knew instinctively that it was something big.

The woman's eyes widened, telling me she felt it, too. She crouched in front of me. "I'm Paulette. What is your name?"

"Jordan," I whispered, unsure of why I was telling a complete stranger my name. But something about her told me I could trust her.

"How old are you?" she asked gently.

"Ten."

Shock flashed in her eyes before she smiled again. "Where's your family, sweetheart?"

"Got none," I replied defensively. My mom had given me up when I was four, and none of her family had wanted me. As far as I was concerned, I had no family.

If Paulette was surprised by my answer, she didn't show it. "How long have you been living on the street?"

I shrugged. "Not long. A few weeks."

She laid a hand on my foot, and a strange emotion that felt like joy surged in me. I knew in that moment Paulette was like me.

"Do...you have a voice inside, too?" I asked her breathlessly.

Her smile grew brighter. "Yes, I do."

My chest tightened. All my life, people looked at me like I was crazy when I mentioned the voice. Paulette acted like it was perfectly normal. And she said she had a voice, too.

"Do you want to know something else?" she asked softly.

I nodded.

"I'm from a place where everyone has a voice in them, just like you and me. And we have children your age. Would you like to live there?"

I chewed the inside of my cheek. Paulette seemed nice, but every adult I'd met had acted like I was crazy and shoved me in one awful home after another. I'd rather take my chances on the street than go back to living like that.

"Is it a foster home?" I asked.

"No. It's kind of like a little town. There's a playground and a school, and you'll have your own room in a nice house."

"I don't like school." I rubbed my hands on my jeans, remembering the fights, the taunts, the suspensions.

She smiled. "I think you'll like this school. It's a special one where you'll learn all kinds of cool stuff, and you'll train to be a warrior like me."

My whole body perked up at that. "A warrior? For real, like with a sword?"

"Would you like that?"

I nodded eagerly. "Yes!"

"Good." Paulette stood and held out a hand to me.

I stared at it for a long moment before I put my smaller hand in hers and let her help me up. I stumbled when I put weight on my sore leg, but she caught me and kept me from falling.

I looked down at my pitiful possessions strewn across the pavement. Maybe I could get new clothes and a toothbrush where I was going.

Paulette squeezed my hand. "We'll get you all new things when we get home."

"And a sword?" I asked hopefully.

She chuckled. "I think we'll start you out with a practice one. But I can already tell you're going to be a fine warrior, Jordan."

I beamed at her. "I'm going to be the best warrior ever."

1

"What do you say we hit up Suave tonight?"

Mason grunted. "Can we discuss this later? Little busy here."

"*Pfft.*" I swung my sword, the blade slicing cleanly through the throat of one of the two vampires I was facing off against. Her eyes took on that shocked, angry look vampires always got when they realized their worthless life was over, and she crumpled to the floor.

Behind me, a vampire shrieked in pain, and I knew Mason was holding his own.

"Don't think you're getting out of it again," I said, turning my attention to my remaining opponent. "You promised to hit the club with me."

Mason groaned, and I smiled at the male vampire whose gaze was darting between me and the nearest doorway. He was calculating whether or not he was faster than I was.

"Go for it." I waved my free hand at the door. "I'll even give you a head start."

He didn't think twice. He bolted for the door, and true to my word, I didn't run after him.

"What are you doing?" Mason asked incredulously. "You're letting him go?"

"Please." I scoffed and drew the knife strapped to my thigh. A flick of my wrist sent the weapon into the back of the fleeing vampire. He screamed as the silver blade burned him from the inside out, but he kept staggering forward.

9

I sighed as I went after him. I really had to work on my throwing skills. I'd been at least an inch off his heart.

The vampire stumbled past the concession stand, where the smell of stale popcorn and butter still hung in the air even though the movie theater had been closed for over a year. I caught up to him near the entrance to one of the theaters and plunged my sword into his back, making sure to hit his heart this time. He gasped and collapsed, his body sliding off my blade.

"Heads-up, Jordan and Mason," Raoul called over the comm. "Two coming your way."

I straightened and spun to see two vampires sprinting toward Mason from the opposite direction. I ran to intercept. "On it."

Mason was still fighting his opponent, so I engaged the newcomers alone. Their speed told me they were young, like most vampires we encountered, though still a little faster than I was. It annoyed the hell out of me that I'd have to wait years to build up the speed of the older warriors like Raoul. Whose brilliant idea was it to create a race of vampire hunters that took a century to reach their full strength?

The vampires snarled and came straight at me. I gripped my sword, ready for them. What I lacked in speed, I made up for in combat. I had better be good after sparring regularly for months with Nikolas Danshov. I'd also trained briefly with Desmund Ashworth. They were two of the best swordsmen alive, and I was going to join their ranks one day.

The first vampire took a swipe at me, and I relieved him of one of his hands. He screamed and clutched his bloody stump.

"What?" I quirked an eyebrow at him. "It's not like you're going to need it."

If there was one thing I knew about vampires, it was how badly they reacted to taunts. He bellowed and lunged at me. I removed his head. A little messy but effective.

Running feet drew my attention to the second vampire, who was making an escape. I shot a look at Mason and saw he didn't need my help finishing off his kill. Then I set off in pursuit.

The vampire disappeared through a door, and I yanked it open to see him racing up a flight of stairs. The building had three floors, and we were on the bottom. My gut told me he was headed for the roof. We were close enough to the neighboring buildings for him to make his escape that way.

I sped up the stairs, my eyes on the figure two flights above, frantically trying to kick down a door.

"Jordan, where are you?" Mason asked over the comm.

"Stairs," I replied. "Have one going for the roof."

Raoul cut in. "Wait for your partner, Jordan."

The door above me crashed open, and a rush of cool night air hit me.

"My partner better get his ass in gear because I'm not letting this bastard get away."

I could hear swearing on the other end as I ran through the roof access door that now hung on its hinges. I caught sight of my quarry as he leaped to the roof of the next building.

"He's jumped to the bakery roof," I informed the team as I went after him.

I landed on the other roof as the vampire sped to the opposite edge to jump again. Obviously, no one had told him he could survive a three-story fall, or he wouldn't be making it so easy for me to follow him. I'd survive three stories, too, but not without some bruises, and he'd most likely get away.

The next roof was a story lower. This time, the vampire jumped down to the alley between the buildings.

I followed suit, wincing as the shock of the landing traveled up my legs. Maybe it was time to invest in more practical boots for work. Heels were hot, but combat boots were a lot better for jumping off buildings.

The vampire sped away, and I put on a burst of speed to close the distance between us. He ducked through a door into another building. I went in after him.

I came up short when I found myself in what looked like a storage area of some kind. The room didn't hold my interest as much as the three vampires I was suddenly facing.

The one I'd been chasing smiled, showing off his snakelike fangs. "Looks like you're outnumbered. Your friends won't save you now."

I shrugged. "That whole damsel in distress bit is not really my thing anyway. So, who wants to go first?"

"Me." The biggest one, who looked like he'd been a thirtysomething biker when he was changed, licked his lips. "I'm going to rip your guts out and eat them while you watch."

I made a face. "Someone's been watching *The Walking Dead* too much."

"You won't be cracking jokes when I'm done with you," he said as the three of them spread out, trying to surround me.

I kept my back to the door so the most they could do was form a semicircle. Holding my sword in a relaxed grip, I waited for them to make the first move.

My friend from the theater and the third vampire, who looked like he'd been a computer nerd in his former life, rushed me from either side. Twisting, I ran my blade through the stomach of Nerd Guy and sent a high kick to the throat of the other. It was a move I'd been practicing for weeks, and I was kind of bummed no one was there to see it.

Both vampires went down, and I turned my attention to the ex-biker as he charged. He swung a clawed hand at me, and I ducked, coming up behind him. Before he could turn around, I drove my sword into his heart.

The vampire with the gut wound writhed on the floor, so I went after the other one. He'd recovered from the blow I'd given him, but instead of helping his friends, he was running for the door. Bending, I whipped a blade from my boot and threw it. He let out a choked cry, and I did a fist pump because my aim had been perfect this time.

A whimpering sound behind me reminded me my job wasn't done. The last vampire seemed almost happy to be put out of his misery when I went to kill him.

Feet pounded on pavement, and I looked up as Raoul filled the doorway with Mason and Brock behind him.

Raoul's lips pressed together as he took in the scene. "You turned off your radio?"

"Of course not." I patted the inner pocket of my jacket where I carried the small device, but the pocket was empty. Crap.

I gave Raoul a sheepish smile. "It must have fallen out when I jumped off the laundromat."

He sighed and rubbed his forehead.

"You jumped off a two-story building in those boots?" Brock gave me a lopsided smile. "Hot."

Raoul shot him a warning look. "Do not encourage her." He cocked his head as if he was listening to something. Then he said, "Copy that," before he looked at us. "All clear."

"How many in total?" I asked.

"Fourteen," Raoul replied. "And six humans recovered."

"I'd call that a good night's work." I tallied up my kills in my head as I wiped my blade on the jeans of one of the dead vampires. Six out of fourteen. Not bad at all.

"And since Jordan had the most kills, she gets the honor of writing up the report," Raoul announced.

The smile fell from my lips, and I didn't try to hide my dismay. There were few things I detested more than writing up field reports. It was so tedious and boring. But the Council was a stickler for record keeping. One of these days, I was going to tell them what they could do with their reports.

Raoul patted my back. "It should only take an hour, two tops."

Mason snickered, and I fixed my gaze on him.

"Don't worry. It will still give us plenty of time to go out tonight," I said sweetly.

He looked like he was in pain. "Wouldn't you rather find some other girls to go out with?"

"I don't know any other girls here, so you're my new BFF."

"I miss Beth," he grumbled.

I missed Beth, too. And Sara. I didn't make female friends easily, and it figured that my two best girlfriends had gone and settled down with mates. They were ridiculously happy, and I was happy for them. But I missed having them around. Mason was fun to hang with, even when he pretended not to like it, but it just wasn't the same.

Maybe it was time for a visit. I talked to Sara and Beth all the time, but we hadn't seen each other since the week I spent at Westhorne for Christmas, and that was five months ago. The two of them, along with Nikolas and Chris, were in Chicago now, setting up the newest command center.

Sara was six months pregnant – something I still found hard to believe – and whenever we talked, she complained that Nikolas wouldn't let her do anything fun. I bet she would love a visitor.

The more I thought about it, the more I liked the idea. I loved Los Angeles and my job, but every girl needed a little vacation once in a while.

I didn't realize I was smiling until Mason waved a hand in front of my face.

"What's so amusing?" he asked warily.

I winked as I walked past him. "I'm just thinking about how much fun we're going to have tonight."

"How long do we have to stay here?" Mason complained as he leaned back against the bar, wearing a bored expression.

"We've barely been here an hour."

"And that's an hour of my life I'll never get back."

I nudged him with my shoulder. "Come on. It's not that bad. Maybe if you moved away from this spot, you'd enjoy yourself. God knows there are enough girls wanting to dance with you."

One corner of his mouth turned up. "Jealous?"

A laugh burst from me. "I can barely keep from throwing myself at you."

"You wound me," he said with a sad face that might have been believable if not for the gleam of amusement in his eyes.

"I'll make it up to you." My gaze moved past him to the hordes of women nearby, some of whom were staring greedily at my friend.

"What are you doing?" he asked as I studied the faces around us.

Ignoring him, I continued my perusal. There were a lot of gorgeous women here, but most of them weren't his type. Mason was pretty laid back, and the majority of these women looked too high-maintenance for him. No, he needed someone more like...

I smiled when my gaze landed on a trio of blondes. Two of them were dressed in short tight dresses that showed off their toned bodies and enhanced breasts. The third one wore a dress, too, but she was trying to discreetly tug on the hem when she thought no one was looking. She was as pretty as her friends, but her whole demeanor told me she felt out of place here. She kind of reminded me of Sara when I used to drag her out clubbing with me.

The girl's two friends said something to her. She shook her head, and they walked to the dance floor and started dancing with each other.

"Back in a sec," I said to Mason as I left him and walked over to the girl.

I gave her my most winning smile. "Hi. Love your dress."

"Thanks." She shyly returned my smile. "I like yours, too."

I leaned in to speak in her ear. "Hey, do you see that tall, hot guy behind me in the gray shirt?"

She glanced around me, and her eyes widened when they found Mason. "Yes."

"That's my friend Mason. I made him come with me tonight, and this is not really his scene. I think he'd feel better if he had someone other than me to talk to."

She shook her head. "I... He doesn't look like he needs help meeting people."

"He's shyer than he looks," I lied. "You want to meet him?"

"Me?"

"You have a nice face," I told her honestly. "I have a good feeling about you."

"Oh." She stole another peek behind me. "Okay."

"Great! I'm Jordan, by the way."

"I'm Emily," she replied as I led her over to the bar. Mason watched me curiously as I approached with my new friend in tow.

"Mason, this is Emily. Emily, Mason." I smiled at them, ignoring his questioning look. "You two get to know each other. I'll be right back."

Before either of them could say anything, I split, disappearing into the crowd. When I got to the other side of the club, I looked over to see Mason and Emily deep in conversation.

Called it. I gave myself a mental pat on the back as I searched for someone to dance with. I was always bursting with energy after a job, and dancing was one of my favorite ways to burn some of it off. My other favorite way required a bit more privacy than this place offered.

I checked out the men around me and got more than a few interested looks in return. I passed on them because in my heels I was over six feet, and I didn't like dancing with someone shorter than I was. It cut down on my options, but a girl wants what she wants.

The crowd parted, and I found what I was looking for. Standing at around six-four with wide shoulders and a trim waist, he was perfect. He looked my way, and I took in the black hair and olive skin that gave him an exotic appearance. I smiled in appreciation. *You'll do nicely.*

I walked up to him, and neither of us spoke when I took his hand and led him to the dance floor. Pressing my back to his chest, I lifted my arms above my head, and began to move. His hands settled on my hips, and he ground against me in a sensual dance that sent heat to all the right places in my body.

By the end of our third dance, I didn't need to feel his arousal to know he was as into me as I was into him. I could smell the lust coming off him in waves. We still hadn't spoken, but no words were necessary. I wanted him, and he wanted me.

I turned in his arms and leaned in close enough for my lips to brush his ear. *Mmmm.* He smelled good. "Want to get out of here?"

"I thought you'd never ask," he said in a deep, husky voice that sent a thrill through me.

I glanced in Mason's direction and found him still at the bar, talking to Emily. Smiling, I looked at my companion. "Don't go anywhere. I have to tell my friend I'm leaving."

I was going to get an earful from Mason about forcing him to come with me and then ditching him. But I'd offer to go surfing with him this week to make up for it. I'd done it a few times, and it was kind of fun. I was a California girl through and through.

I'd barely gone two steps when a girl stumbled into me, dumping the contents of her glass down the front of my dress. I swore as a pink stain spread across the white fabric.

"Oh, shit! I'm so sorry," she slurred.

Waving her off, I turned toward the restrooms to clean up as best I could. I bypassed the small line outside, and a few women complained until I turned to face them and they saw my dress. They waved me in ahead of them. Not that it mattered. The dress would require a professional cleaning to get the stain out.

I grabbed some paper towels and started blotting up the liquid, barely paying attention to the people around me. My mind was on the man waiting for me and how I planned to spend the rest of my night. The way he'd held me against him and his unhurried movements told me he was good at more than dancing, and I was looking forward to getting him alone.

The sound of retching in one of the stalls pulled me from my pleasant thoughts. In the mirror, my eyes met those of the girl at the next sink. Her lips pressed together, and she looked a little green as she hurriedly finished washing her hands. I went back to cleaning my dress. I'd seen and heard worse things than some drunk girl puking.

"Oh, my God. What is that smell?" someone choked out a second before a putrid odor filled the air around me. My nose twitched, and I nearly gagged on the foulness that smelled like a mix of sewage and blood.

Stall doors were flung open, and women ran for the restroom door without stopping to wash their hands. In a matter of seconds, I was the only one left in the room. Well, me and the unfortunate woman who was still throwing up.

"Hey, are you okay in there?" I called, figuring someone had to check on her.

She moaned and started sobbing between bouts of retching. I stared at her bare legs visible beneath the stall door, unsure of what to do. Aside from Sara that one time, I hadn't been around many sick people in my life. I put a hand over my nose. Was it normal for it to smell this awful?

The woman began making a gagging, choking sound. Afraid she might be dying in there, I banged on the stall door. "Hey, are you –?"

My question was cut off by the sound of something hitting the water in the toilet with a loud plop. That in itself was alarming enough. And then a squelching, splashing sound came from the toilet.

"What the fuck?"

There was a soft thump as the woman collapsed on the floor. Bending down, I grasped her foot, which was jutting out beneath the door, and dragged her from the stall. Her dark hair was plastered to her face, and a greenish black sludge covered her mouth and the front of her red dress. It left a trail on the floor, and it smelled even worse up close, if that was possible. I checked the pulse at her throat and found a faint heartbeat. She was alive but barely.

More sloshing came from the toilet. It didn't take being a warrior to know that puking up something that moved was a very bad thing.

I reached for my clutch on the vanity and pulled out my phone to send off a text to Mason. **Trouble in restroom. Human down. Call for backup.**

His reply came thirty seconds later. **On my way.**

Stuffing my phone back into the clutch, I grabbed the folded karambit I carried when I went clubbing. My dresses didn't leave any room for concealed weapons, but I'd seen enough in my life to know I'd have to be an idiot to go out unarmed.

The curved silver blade was only three inches long, but I could do damage with that. Gripping it in one hand, I placed myself between the unconscious woman and the stall. I wanted to know what that thing in the toilet was, but my main priority was to protect the human until backup arrived.

Water splashed again, followed by a scraping sound. Before I could register that the thing was trying to climb out of the toilet, I heard a wet plop on the tile floor.

An ominous silence filled the room. I didn't breathe.

Out of the corner of my eye, I caught movement, and I jerked my head to the right in time to see a black tentacle appear under the neighboring stall door.

I barely had time to react before the creature came flying at me. I side-stepped the attack, and the thing crashed hard into the mirror, sending glass raining down on the vanity.

A shapeless black glob landed in one of the sinks. I raised my knife and took a step toward the vanity. At the same time, the restroom door started to open. I shouted a warning as the creature launched from the sink toward the door.

My arm moved without conscious thought, and my knife sailed across the room. The blade struck the creature and pinned it to the wall, inches from Mason's startled face. Impaled on the blade, the thing thrashed violently and went still as smoke poured from its body.

Mason hurried into the room and shut the door, his eyes never leaving the creature. "What the hell is that?"

"No idea, but my guess is it's a demon."

He scanned the room, taking in the damage. "Where did it come from?"

I pointed to the woman on the floor. "It came out of her."

His eyes went wide. "Shit. Is she dead?"

"She was alive last I checked, but God knows what that thing did to her." I studied the demon that had stopped moving, but I couldn't make out a shape.

It was a blob with tentacles. I saw a curved black claw on the end of one tentacle.

Someone banged on the door, and Mason put his hand against it to prevent them from coming in. He looked at me. "I called for backup, but we won't be able to keep people out of here for long."

His meaning was clear. We had to get rid of the demon before the humans saw it. It was too big to flush, and I had a feeling Raoul was going to want to see this one. I could stuff it in the garbage, but what if it wasn't dead and it attacked someone else? Or one of the humans found it?

I grimaced when I realized there was only one place I could hide the thing so we could get it out of here. I dumped my phone and cash from my clutch and carried it over to the door. Grasping the handle of my knife, I yanked it out of the wall and dropped the demon into the purse. I had to use paper towels to get all the tentacles inside because no way was I touching that thing if I could help it. It was a tight squeeze, but I managed to squish the demon into the clutch.

Once the demon was safely tucked away, I handed my knife to Mason, and he put it in his pocket. Then I motioned for him to stop blocking the door.

A bouncer in a black club T-shirt was the first one to enter the room, and he came up short at the sight before him. "What's going on in here?" he demanded, no doubt wondering why Mason was in the women's restroom.

I put one hand to my chest and pointed to the unconscious woman with the other. "She was throwing up, and then she went into convulsions and broke the mirror."

Moving past Mason, the bouncer crouched to check on the woman. "What is this black stuff? And what is that god-awful smell?"

"I think a toilet backed up," I said innocently. I hoped he didn't push the matter because I had no good answer for him.

He stood and spoke into a wireless radio attached to his ear. "Call nine-one-one. We have a possible OD."

More club staff poured into the room, and I motioned to Mason that we should leave. We slipped past the crowd outside the restroom and exited by the club's rear door. Before I left, I looked back and found the man I'd danced with. He was still where I'd left him and looking at his watch. I felt a stab of disappointment as I turned away and followed Mason outside.

Raoul and Brock were the first to arrive, and they met up with us in the parking lot of the building next to Suave. I gave them a rundown of what had happened in the restroom, and Mason added the part where he'd come in.

By the time we'd finished recounting our story, a white van pulled in and

Jon's team got out. I used to share a safehouse with them when I first came to Los Angeles, so we knew each other well.

Jon, a big blond Norwegian whom I'd nicknamed Thor, grinned at me. "Why am I not surprised to see you? Causing trouble again?"

"Just saving the world. Same old, same old." I waved at the van. "You have a cleanup kit in there?"

"Yah, what do you need?" he said.

I held up my clutch. "Something to store this thing in."

He eyed the purse. "What is it?"

"Dead demon. At least, I think it's dead."

That got everyone's attention, and they came closer as Jon reached into the van and lifted out a large bin. From the bin, he took a thick plastic bag, which he held up to me. I walked over to him and unclasped my purse, dumping the demon into the bag. Jon immediately sealed it and placed it inside a silver mesh sack as an extra precaution. If the demon was playing possum, it would not be able to break free of its confinement.

Raoul took the bag from Jon, turning it over in his hands and staring at the demon for a long moment. "This came out of the woman?"

"Yes." I waited for him to say something else, but he just continued to study the demon.

"Do you know what it is?" Mason asked him.

Raoul wore a puzzled expression when he looked at us. "It looks like a Hurra demon, but that's not possible."

I looked from Raoul to the demon. "Are they not usually found in North America?"

He frowned. "They aren't found anywhere on Earth because they were eradicated three centuries ago."

"Whoa." Mason's eyes rounded, and I'm sure his shocked expression mirrored mine.

Raoul rubbed his chin. "We need to get it back to the lab for identification before we report this."

"And if you're right about what it is?" I asked him.

His eyes met mine. "Then we have a serious problem."

2

_____

"Any word yet?" I sank down on one of the visitor chairs in Raoul's office. Mason took the other chair.

Raoul looked up from his laptop. "Should hear something soon."

Once we had gotten back to the command center, we'd taken the demon to the medical ward that had been set up in the old guesthouse. At any given time, there could be up to two dozen warriors in southern California, so the powers that be had seen the need for a full-time medical staff at the house. We had two healers who also ran a small lab in the ward. The lab wasn't as sophisticated as one you'd find at a stronghold, but it worked in a pinch. Like now. Instead of having to send the demon to the nearest stronghold for identification, the healers could run a genetic test in our very own lab.

I tapped my fingers on the arms of my chair. "While we're waiting, can you tell us what a Hurra demon is? Must be bad for us to kill them all off." I decided not to point out that we'd obviously failed in that endeavor.

Raoul leaned back in his chair. "A Hurra demon is a parasitic middle demon. Outside of the demon dimension, it can only survive inside a human host."

"Like a Vamhir demon," I said.

"Or a Mori," Mason added.

Raoul nodded. "Closer to a Vamhir demon. A Hurra demon takes control of the host, and it feeds off the flesh of other humans. But unlike a vampire, the host body will deteriorate and die within a year of infection, so the demon has to find a new host."

I made a face. "A demon zombie. Nice."

Raoul nodded. "It's actually where some of the zombie lore started. Fortunately for us, the Hurra can't reproduce outside of their dimension, which made it easier to wipe them out."

So how did this one get here? I wondered. Demons couldn't just pass from their dimension to ours. About two millennia ago, something happened to create a hole in the barrier between Earth and the demon dimension, and thousands of demons escaped to our world. According to our legends, angels fixed the breach and created the Mohiri to hunt the more dangerous demons, like vampires. But by then, the demons had started multiplying and there was no way to get them all.

The only way a demon could cross the barrier now was by a summoning ritual performed by magic wielders such as warlocks and shamans. Only upper demons could be summoned, and only in non-corporeal form. Physical matter could not pass through the barrier.

The demon I'd bagged tonight had definitely been in solid form. If it was in fact a Hurra demon, then we obviously hadn't killed them all off.

I voiced my thoughts and Raoul nodded gravely. "Good question. Maybe I'm wrong."

"You're not wrong," said a voice from the doorway.

I looked over my shoulder at the red-haired healer standing there. George, who usually wore a pleasant smile, was as serious as I'd ever seen him.

He stepped into the office. "Leslie and I ran a DNA sample against the database and found a match. It's a Hurra demon. We're sending it off to the lab at Valstrom for further analysis."

Raoul nodded and reached for his phone. "I need to notify the Council immediately."

"Wait." I held up a hand to stop him. "I don't understand. If a Hurra demon stays in a host until it's worn out, why did that girl throw up this one? She looked pretty healthy...except for the whole puking thing."

"I think I know the answer to that," George said. "I spoke to one of my contacts at Cedars where they took the girl. He said she had lupus. I don't know how she came in contact with the demon, but I believe her body rejected it."

"She didn't make it?" I asked.

George shook his head. "She died in the ambulance."

I slumped in my chair. That poor girl. What a horrible way to go.

"Jordan," Raoul said almost apologetically. "I know it's been a crazy night, but the Council is going to want a thorough account of what happened at the club. Can you write up the report while I make this call?"

I sighed and pushed up out of the chair. "Yeah. I'll get on it right away."

"I'll help," Mason said, following me.

I shot him a grateful smile as we left the office and entered the main control room. We pulled up chairs to an available workstation, and I opened a blank report.

"What do you think the Council will do?" Mason asked in a low voice.

"I have no idea," I admitted. "But we probably won't like it."

"What do you mean?"

I turned to look at him. "A demon they tried to wipe out hundreds of years ago suddenly popped up in a nightclub in L.A. Mark my words. In twenty-four hours, this place will be taken over by one of the Council's special investigative teams."

"And that's a bad thing?"

I huffed softly. "Mason, the Council interferes in my life enough as it is. The last thing I want is them stepping in and telling me how to do my job."

He bumped me with his shoulder. "I don't know. It might be fun to watch someone try to tell you what to do."

A smile tugged at my lips as I focused on the report again. *They can try.*

I was wrong. The Council didn't send someone in twenty-four hours. Their people showed up less than eight hours after Raoul made his call. They hadn't even reacted this fast when they found out we had an active Lilin in Los Angeles, which made me suspect there was more going on here than the discovery of a supposedly extinct demon.

When I entered the control room the next morning, I found a blonde female and two dark-haired males I didn't know sitting around the small conference table with Raoul. They stood as I approached them.

"Jordan Shaw, this is Vivian Day, Aaron Lee, and Eugene Harris," Raoul said. "They were sent by the Council to investigate the Hurra incident."

Vivian held out a hand to me. "It's good to meet you, Jordan," she said in an English accent. "Raoul's told me all about you."

I slid my gaze to Raoul as I took her hand. "I'm not sure whether to be flattered or worried."

Raoul chuckled, and amusement lit up Vivian's eyes.

"It was all good," she said. "Although, now I'm thinking he might have left out some things."

I merely smiled and turned to greet her two companions. I had a feeling I was going to like Vivian Day, but she *was* here on behalf of the Council. I decided not to disclose too much until I got a better feel for her.

After the introductions had been made, we all sat and the three investigators got down to business, drilling me about last night.

"How did the victim look when she first entered the restroom?"

"How many strikes did it take to kill the Hurra?"

"Would you say it moved quickly or slowly?"

"Did you observe any other humans displaying similar symptoms?"

I held up a hand after I'd answered half a dozen questions. "All of this is in the report I wrote up last night."

Vivian smiled. "We like to get a firsthand account of these things."

"Why did I spend over two hours working on a report when no one is going to read it?" I asked irritably, thinking of the countless hours I'd wasted doing reports since I came to Los Angeles. Did anyone even read those?

"Reports are mainly used for research material in future jobs," Eugene said unhelpfully. "And they allow the Council to keep track of statistical data such as how many vampire kills took place in a geographical area in one year."

I wanted to tell him I already knew this, but a warning look from Raoul kept me quiet. These were Council investigators, and I was going to have to play nice with them. For now. Hopefully, they'd wrap up their job here in a day or two and be on their way.

Vivian wore an amused smile. "You remind me of Nikolas. He always hated doing reports, too."

"You know Nikolas?" I asked, and then I did a mental eye roll. Of course, she knew Nikolas Danshov. Who didn't?

Her smile grew fond. "Since we were children."

"Wow." She was the first person I'd met who had known Nikolas that long, and I bet she had some stories to tell.

"About the reports," Eugene cut in.

"Yes." Vivian got back to business. "We read your report, and we appreciate the level of detail in it. But memory can be tricky, especially when it comes to situations like this. Asking the right questions might help you recall something you didn't think of when you wrote up the report."

"Okay," I conceded because what she'd said made sense.

Over the next hour, I answered every question they asked. Eugene took notes while Aaron mostly nodded thoughtfully at every answer. Vivian did most of the talking, and I found myself appreciating the way she filtered through the details, focusing on what she clearly thought were the more important ones.

"I think we have everything we need," Eugene said at last. "Thank you, Jordan."

It sounded like a dismissal. A polite one, but a dismissal all the same, and I felt my hackles rising again.

I looked at Vivian, who appeared to be the leader of their team. "Now that we've told you what we know, why don't you tell us something?"

Her expression was open and friendly. "What would you like to know?"

"I get that finding a live Hurra demon is a little exciting, but there seems to be more behind your questions. This isn't an isolated incident, is it?"

A glance at Raoul told me he thought the same thing. Unlike him, I wasn't content to let the Council take over without pushing for answers.

Vivian exchanged a look with Eugene and Aaron, and then she shook her head. "We've had two other incidents, one in Florida a week ago and one in Alaska three days ago. The Florida one was a Hurra demon. The one in Alaska was a Geel."

I sucked in a sharp breath and heard Raoul do the same. A Geel was the kind of thing you'd find in your worst nightmares. It was a lower demon that attached itself to its victim's face and laid its eggs in their throat while they were fully conscious. It took two days for the eggs to hatch, and then the offspring consumed the victim.

Resembling large worms, Geel lived in the deserts of Africa because they could only survive in a hot, dry climate. Even if someone had captured one and taken it to Alaska, it would die within a day.

"Was the Geel alive?" Raoul asked.

"Yes." Vivian clasped her hands on the table. "And it was already attached to a host when our people got there. We were able to extract it and save the human. Fortunately, we were also able to erase his memory of the attack. No one should have to live with that."

"Christ," Raoul muttered.

I folded my arms across my chest. "Time for the sixty-four-thousand-dollar question. How does a desert demon end up in Alaska, of all places?"

"That is what we are trying to find out," Vivian replied. "The Council's lead investigator is there now."

"You're not the lead investigator?" I asked.

"No. I was called in to assist on this one until he is free. As you can imagine, these incidents are troubling and of great concern to the Council."

It all made sense. No wonder the Council had jumped on this so quickly. "So, what happens now?"

"Our next plan of action is to look into the victim..." Vivian glanced down at a notepad on the table. "Chelsea Head. We'll check out her home and try to retrace her steps over the last few days to see if we can discover how and where she came into contact with the Hurra demon."

I leaned forward eagerly. I might not be the Council's biggest fan, but this was definitely not an ordinary investigation. I was more than a little curious.

Vivian picked up on my interest, and she gave me a knowing smile. "If Raoul can spare you, you're welcome to come with us."

"Really?"

"You bagged the demon, so it's only fair that you get to be on the job," she said. "But we'll take the lead."

"Sure," I agreed readily. "When do we start?"

Vivian laughed. "I've been traveling all night, so I'm going to freshen up and eat something first. We'll head out at noon."

"Are you staying here?" I asked her as we stood.

"If you have room. I normally stay at hotels, but I thought it would be better to be at the command center for this job."

"We can sleep on couches if there are no available beds," Aaron offered. I figured that in his job, he'd probably slept in a lot less comfortable places.

"We have one bedroom available," Raoul said. "Vivian, you take that. Aaron and Eugene, we have couches or some army cots you can use."

"I'll show you where it is," I told her.

We left the control room and walked to the main entryway to grab her bags. I grinned when I saw the large suitcase and a smaller carry-on. Unlike most warriors, Vivian Day apparently didn't like to travel light. I might have found a kindred spirit in her.

I led her to the other end of the Spanish-style villa where the bedrooms were. One room was Raoul's, and next to it was mine. I'd moved into Sara and Nikolas's old room after they left because this place was a lot less crowded than the safe house.

Brock and Mason shared a room with twin beds since they were hardly ever here. Those two lived like college kids, and all they cared about, outside of being warriors, was surfing. If it had been safe to sleep on the beach, I think they would live there.

I showed Vivian to the room across from mine and left her to settle in. An hour later, I found her in the kitchen making a cup of tea.

"I always carry some Earl Grey with me," she said as she added milk and sugar to the cup. "You never know if you'll be able to find good tea."

"I guess not." I sat at the breakfast bar, resting my elbows on the granite counter. "So, you knew Nikolas when you were kids? What was he like back then?"

"I met him when we were sixteen, and we trained together. We were very competitive with each other, and I think that's how we became such good friends."

I tried to imagine Nikolas as a boy in training. "I wish I could have been there."

Vivian smiled over the top of her cup. "I have a feeling you would have given us both a run for our money back then." When I raised an eyebrow, she chuckled softly. "I read your file on the way here. You already have an impressive record for such a young warrior."

I tried to hide my surprise. I didn't like the idea of the Council having a file on me, but they probably had one on every warrior, even Nikolas.

"I started younger than most." I grinned. "Thanks to Sara."

"Nikolas's mate? I've heard a lot about her, and I'm looking forward to meeting her." She sipped her tea. "I work mostly overseas, and every time I plan to visit them, a new job comes up."

"You'll love Sara. I can honestly say there is no one like her."

Vivian set her cup down on the counter. "I believe you. It would take a very special woman to claim Nikolas's heart. Seems like only yesterday we were setting out into the world, and now he's mated with a baby on the way."

I made a face. "Having seen the way he is with Sara, I can't wait to see how protective he'll be over his daughter. If we could go gray, I think this would do it for him."

Vivian burst out laughing. I wasn't sure what it was about her, but I liked her. I could see how Nikolas had liked her, too. She had to be very good to work directly for the Council, but she wasn't as serious as Aaron or Eugene.

"So, this is what you do, traveling all over the world to investigate for the Council?" I asked her. "Sounds like you're not settling down anytime soon."

"Lord, no." She wore a look of mock horror. "Although, don't say that to my mum. She wants grandchildren, but I'm perfectly content with my life."

"Me, too," I declared. "I have enough people trying to tell me what to do without adding some overbearing male to the mix."

Vivian raised her cup to me in a toast. "Amen to that."

"What was it like on your first official Council investigation?" Mason asked.

"First and only," I corrected him. "And it was interesting."

I took a bite of my hot dog and chewed slowly as I watched people walk by on the boardwalk in Venice Beach. It was good to be back on patrol after spending the last two days tagging along with Vivian's team. I hadn't lied when I said the work was interesting, but I much preferred to be in the action instead of observing.

I had to admit, the Council investigators were nothing if not thorough in their work. We'd started with Chelsea's apartment in Burbank, which she had shared with her boyfriend of three years. He'd told us the night she died, she'd gone out with some girlfriends to celebrate a birthday. He was adamant she had never done drugs even though that was the official cause of death. The poor man was devastated, but there was nothing we could do to make it better. Neither the Council nor the human officials wanted the public to know a woman had died throwing up a parasitic demon. It would cause a panic, and that was something we didn't need.

After going through her home, we'd checked out her workplace, a dental practice where she'd been a hygienist. That turned up nothing, as did the interviews with Chelsea's friends who'd gone to the club with her. We'd gone through Chelsea's neighborhood, visited her favorite coffee shop, and even scoured the little park where she walked her dog.

While the investigation had turned up nothing, Vivian and I had hit it off and she'd entertained me with stories about the jobs she'd done over the years. She led an exciting life, traveling all over the world, staying in five-star hotels, and driving fast cars. Not to mention the things she'd seen. The life-style held more than a little appeal for me, except for the part where she worked directly for the Council.

A phone rang nearby, and I peered past Mason at Brock as he answered the call.

"Yeah. We're not too far from there. We'll check it out," he said to the caller before he hung up and looked at us. "Command picked up a nine-one-one call from a woman who claims a giant spider tried to eat her dog. The police aren't taking her seriously, but Raoul wants us to have a look."

"A giant spider?" It didn't sound like any creature or demon normally found here, but anything was possible after the Hurra incident and the Geel appearance in Alaska.

"How big is giant?" Mason asked as we tossed our food wrappers and walked to our bikes.

Brock picked up his helmet. "As big as the woman's collie."

It took us less than ten minutes to reach the address Raoul had given Brock. The elderly woman looked surprised to see us instead of the police, and Brock told her we worked for animal control. That seemed to appease her, and she told us she'd been walking her dog like she did every evening, when that thing came out of nowhere and went after her dog. She described a brown, furry creature with six or eight legs and pincers for a mouth. Brock asked how she'd gotten away from it, and she proudly showed us the stun baton she carried on her walks.

She told us where she was when the attack happened, and we left her to investigate. When Brock found several drops of blood on the street, we started searching from there. It didn't take long for me to find a broken basement window in what looked like an empty house. The glass fragments outside the window indicated it had been smashed from the inside.

I alerted Brock, who made short work of the lock on the back door, and we quietly entered the house, weapons drawn. The door opened into the kitchen where we discovered an assortment of pewter bowls, candles, and packets of brown and red powder. I knew without asking that these items were used by warlocks in spells. But what kind of spell, and where was the person who had cast it?

"Stay together," Brock whispered. He led us from the kitchen and into a living room that looked untouched. A search of the first and second floors turned up nothing, but we needed to make sure there were no humans in the house.

As soon as Brock opened the door to the basement stairs, the stench of blood and sulfur hit us, and I had to put a hand over my mouth. The grim look on Brock's face when he shut the door again told me it was bad.

"What is it?" I asked, following him back to the kitchen.

"Looks like a summoning gone wrong," he said as he pulled out his phone and called Raoul.

I suppressed a shudder. Warlocks summoned upper demons and held them captive to strengthen their magic. Summoning was dangerous because it required a powerful spell to pull a demon through the barrier. More than one warlock had ended up dead – or wished they were – because they'd messed up the spell and lost control of the demon. Just because summoned demons weren't in their physical bodies, it didn't mean they couldn't inflict a lot of damage and pain.

Brock hung up and looked at us. "Raoul and the Council team are on the way."

"Why would Vivian's team care about a summoning?" I asked. As dangerous as they were, summonings were commonplace among magic users, and not something the Council bothered with. Unless, they thought this was more than a normal summoning.

Mason leaned against the doorframe. "You think that spider thing is a summoned demon that got loose?"

"Not possible," Brock and I said together. He smiled at me and continued. "Even if the spell went wrong, the demon wouldn't have an actual body. It could possess the summoner, but it would look human. That spider might have come from this house, but it wasn't summoned."

"Well, there goes that theory." Mason's brow creased. "By the way, shouldn't we be out there looking for it?"

Brock nodded. "We'll go out after Raoul gets here. He wants us to sit on this place until then."

Over thirty minutes later, an SUV pulled into the driveway. Los Angeles traffic is a bitch unless you're on a motorcycle that can maneuver easily around the other vehicles.

Not exactly the most patient person, I was pacing when they entered the house.

"Have you been down there?" Vivian asked Brock.

"No. Raoul said to wait for you."

"Good." She turned to Mason and me. "Ever been to the site of a failed summoning?"

Mason answered for us. "No."

She smiled grimly. "It can be messy, and there might be residual magic, depending on what happened. We'll go first, and once we give the all clear, you can come down."

"Got it." I watched Eugene set a metal box on the counter. He opened it and pulled out a rectangular device, which he switched on. Seeing my curiosity, he said. "It's warlock-made, and it detects magic so we don't accidentally walk into a spell."

"Handy device." I'd never seen one before, and I wondered if it was new technology they were trying out. I thought about how Sara could see through glamours, detect magic, and neutralize spells. Maybe our tech guys were trying to replicate that ability in a device.

Raoul opened the basement door, and Eugene went first, holding the device in front of him. Raoul and the others followed, leaving Mason and me alone.

I was more than happy to stay up here for now. It wasn't that I had a weak stomach around dead bodies. I detested magic. A warlock named Orias had bound me with magic once, a few years ago, and I hated how helpless it had made me feel. The only magic user I trusted was Sara because I knew she would never use her power against me.

"Crazy shit, huh?" Mason said.

I kept my gaze on the open door to the basement. "At least it never gets boring."

He snorted. "I swear I've seen more action since I came to L.A. than most new warriors see in ten years."

"You picked the right assignment."

"Actually, L.A. was Beth's idea. If I'd had my way, we would have gone to Westhorne."

"Really?" Why would anyone want to go to a stronghold over a place like Los Angeles? Sure, Westhorne was home to Tristan and Nikolas, but nothing beat being in the field.

He smiled as if he'd read my mind. "I wanted to go there to work with Nikolas, but Beth refused to go because of Chris. We all know how that worked out."

"What about now?" I asked. "You still think about going to Westhorne?"

"And give up all of this? And surfing?" He gave me a look of mock horror. "Not a chance."

"All clear," called Raoul.

Mason and I hurried down the stairs. I braced myself for whatever was waiting for us. As a warrior, you had to have a strong stomach, but I'd heard how gory a failed summoning could be. I prepared to see blood and body parts everywhere.

I reached the bottom of the stairs and looked around the open basement in surprise. There was a body and some blood, but it wasn't as bad as I'd expected.

A large circle was painted on the concrete floor in what looked like dried blood. Outside the circle, symbols had been drawn with a crystal placed in the center of each one. At the center of the circle was a smaller one done with more crystals. The inner circle was broken by the body sprawling across it. Based on the white robe he wore, he was most likely a warlock. Or he had been before his chest had been ripped open.

My eyes took in the trail of blood from the circle to the broken window. Could the warlock have been killed by the thing that had attacked the woman and her dog? And what kind of creature was present at a summoning? My gut told me it was a demon – maybe even a new one – despite what we'd said to Mason about it being impossible to summon a physical demon.

I shivered at the thought. Our people had spent a millennium identifying and documenting every species of demon on Earth. We knew their strengths and weaknesses, how they killed, and more importantly, how to kill them. If someone had figured out how to bring new demons out of their dimension, the implications were too great to consider.

I went to inspect the window. I had no experience with summonings, but I knew how to kill things, so I focused on that. Demon or not, that thing was clearly a threat to humans, and we needed to hunt it down before it killed again.

"Raoul," I called. When he joined me, I pointed at the window. "You guys have this situation under control. I think Mason, Brock, and I should track down whatever broke out of here. I'm guessing it's the same thing that attacked the woman and her dog earlier."

He stared thoughtfully at the window for a moment before he nodded. "I'll go with you. Vivian can handle this."

"I will hunt the demon," said a deep, accented voice from behind us.

Raoul and I turned at the same time to face the newcomer, and my stomach gave a little flutter.

"Hamid," Raoul said. "It's great to see you again."

3

I didn't speak as my eyes drank in the most magnificent male specimen God had ever created. Standing at over six and a half feet with shoulders broad enough to make an ogre jealous, Hamid Safar was the biggest warrior I'd ever seen. And the sexiest. The Egyptian warrior had intense ice-blue eyes, thick eyebrows, high cheekbones, a close-trimmed beard, and luscious full lips. His black hair that used to be tied back, was short now, but he was every bit as hot as I remembered. Even his scowl made my girly parts melt.

It had been over three years since I last saw Hamid, not that we had been friends or anything. He'd been all business the few times our paths had crossed, barely even looking my way. Sadly, his lack of interest hadn't stopped me from lusting after him. It wasn't something I was proud of, but could you really blame me?

Last I'd heard, he and his brother were somewhere in South Africa, and I had figured it would be many years before our paths crossed again, if ever. What was he doing in Los Angeles, and here at this house in particular? And what did he mean he was going to hunt the demon?

That last question snapped me out of my thoughts. Raoul and Hamid were talking, and I'd missed part of their conversation. Tearing my gaze from Hamid, I looked at Raoul, who was speaking.

"One of our teams will go with you," Raoul told him.

"I need no team," Hamid replied brusquely, already turning toward the stairs.

"Hold up," I said.

Hamid paused and turned back. His piercing gaze held mine, making me almost forget what I wanted to say.

I cleared my throat. "How do you know it's a demon? And why are *you* going after it? We're already on the job."

"This falls under the Council's authority, so I am assuming command," he said without answering my first question. I'd obviously missed the part where he said he was working for the Council.

"Why would the Council care about a summoning?" I'd suspected something was off when Vivian and her team showed up here, and Hamid's comments confirmed there was more to this whole thing than they were letting on.

Hamid's scowl deepened. Normally, that would be a turn-on, but I was pissed he was going to take this hunt from me.

"That is not your concern," he said with the air of someone who was not used to being challenged. He might as well have waved a red flag at me.

Hands on hips, I glared at him. "I'm the one who bagged the Hurra demon, and I found this house. That makes it my concern."

"You killed the Hurra?" he asked with a note of disbelief that only fueled my anger.

"What? Like it was hard?" The arrogance of this guy.

He narrowed his gaze on me. "You are barely out of training."

Oh, no, he did not.

"Jordan –" Raoul began.

My hands clenched into fists. "I don't know how they train warriors where you're from, but by the time I finished training, I'd already killed at least a dozen vampires. I've lost count of how many kills I've had since then, but I'm sure you can read all about them in the records. You might be older, but you're not the only one here who knows how to use a weapon."

Hamid folded his muscled arms across his chest. Any other time, I'd take a moment to appreciate the sight. Right now, I was too busy trying not to lose my cool.

"Are you done?" he asked as if he were talking to a child.

"No." I gritted my teeth, wondering if the others could see steam coming out of my ears. "You called the thing that broke out of here a demon. What kind of demon is it?"

"I will know once I find it."

I folded my arms, mimicking him. "You have no idea what it is or what it can do, and you're going after it alone? What if you can't handle it by yourself?"

If I hadn't known better, I would have sworn I saw the tiniest flash of amusement in his eyes.

"Fine. You may accompany me...if you can keep up," he said a second before he disappeared in a blur.

"Argh!" I threw up my arms and turned furious eyes on Raoul. "Can he do that? Just come in here and take over?"

Raoul shrugged. "He's the lead investigator for the Council. He can do anything he wants."

I looked at Vivian, who was standing nearby, watching me with open curiosity. "Is that true?"

She nodded. "Anything within reason that he deems necessary to solve a case."

"That's not fair," I burst out, wanting to stomp my foot in frustration.

Vivian smiled. "Most Council investigators work with the local teams like we are doing. Hamid prefers to do his own thing most of the time."

I huffed. "How the hell do you put up with that?"

"Hamid's very good at his job, and he doesn't talk much." She chuckled. "Come to think of it, I've never heard him say that many words together at one time."

"Don't I feel special?" A new thought occurred to me, and I turned back to Raoul. "You said he can do what he wants. Does that mean he can take over the command center and start bossing us around? Because I'm telling you right now, that's not going to work for me."

Raoul sighed. "No, he won't take over, but you need to play nice and cooperate with the investigation."

"I'd never jeopardize an investigation." I was insulted he would even think that.

He gave me a pointed look. "And you'll play nice?"

I stuck out my chin. "I will if he will."

Brock snorted, and Mason muttered, "Is it too late to get reassigned to the East coast?"

I was having the most delicious dream when a loud noise dragged me from my sleep. I stared blearily at the ceiling, still caught between the dream and reality, silently cursing whatever had awoken me.

"Jordan, wake up, damn it," Mason called as he rapped on my door. "You don't want to miss this."

I glanced at the bedside clock and swore when I saw it was just after five in the morning. I'd been so wound up last night after my argument with Hamid that I'd had to run for an hour to burn off my anger when we got back. And it had still taken me forever to fall asleep.

Kicking the tangle of sheets off me, I rolled out of bed and went to open the door. "I swear, if you woke me up at this ungodly hour to go surfing, I'm going to beat you with your board."

Okay, so maybe I was more of a night owl than a morning person.

Mason, however, looked disgustingly chipper, considering how late we'd been up last night. He grinned boyishly at me. "No surfing. I figured you'd want to see the demon Hamid just brought in."

Suddenly, I was wide awake. "He caught it?"

"Killed it." Mason turned away from my door. "Come on. He took it to the lab."

I hurried after him, eager to get a look at the demon. It was dark out, but the house was lit up and buzzing with activity.

In the living room, we ran into Brock, who smirked when he saw me. "Nice jammies."

I looked down at my matching sleep shorts and camisole. In my excitement, I hadn't even taken a moment to slip on shoes.

I covered a yawn with my hand. "It's more than I normally wear to bed."

His eyes widened, and I hid my grin as I moved past him to the French doors that led to the backyard. Across the yard was the guesthouse, and I headed straight for it. The front door was open when I reached it, and I could hear voices coming from within.

Entering the house, I followed the voices to the bedroom that used to belong to Mason. Now it was a small lab with cabinets along the walls and a metal worktable in the center of the room.

People crowded around the table, blocking it from my view, and I moved around the room until I could see what they were all looking at. My jaw sagged when I saw the creature that took up half the table. Brown and covered in spiky fur, it had a rounded body and eight legs that dangled over the edge of the table. Even dead, it had a menacing appearance. That old woman must have nerves of steel to have saved her dog from this thing.

"Do we know what it is?" Vivian asked. Like me, she looked like she'd recently woken up, but she'd managed to pull on jeans and a shirt.

"Yes and no." George wore a serious expression as he tapped the screen of the tablet in his hand. "It's a demon, but preliminary tests don't match anything in our database."

A collective gasp went through the room.

Raoul studied the demon. "How accurate are the tests?"

"Ninety-nine point nine percent," the healer replied. "We'll send it to Valstrom, but I doubt they'll find anything different."

Eugene picked up one of the demon's legs and examined the black claw at the end. He was wearing protective gloves, and he held the leg away from him.

I inched closer to the table for a better look. "An undocumented demon? What does that mean?"

"It means this demon is new to our world," said a gruff voice that could only belong to one person.

I lifted my gaze to Hamid, who stood just inside the doorway, towering over everyone else. His hair was wet, and he'd changed his clothes. I watched as his eyes moved up my body to meet mine, and goose bumps spread across my skin as if he'd physically touched me.

Heat blossomed in my stomach, but it was immediately doused by a wave of irritation when I remembered the arrogant way he'd dismissed me last night.

"Are you saying that dead warlock was able to summon a demon in solid form?" Brock asked, drawing Hamid's attention away from me.

"It wasn't summoned," Vivian said, and it was the most serious I'd seen her since we met. "They would have had to open the barrier to bring it through."

Everyone started talking at once, while I just stood there trying to grasp the implications of her statement. There was no one – human or otherwise – on Earth that should be able to open the barrier to the demon dimension. It was that way for a very good reason. There were supposedly billions of demons on the other side of the barrier, enough to overrun the earth if they ever found a way out of their dimension. A breach in the barrier between our worlds could end life as we knew it.

"Does the Council know?" I asked loud enough to be heard in the noisy room.

"Yes," Hamid said.

When it was apparent he wasn't going to elaborate, I said, "What happens now?"

Vivian answered for him. "They'll start reaching out to the most powerful warlocks to see if anyone can shed light on this."

Raoul walked over to where Hamid stood. "If there's anything you need while you're here, let me know."

"Thank you."

I stared at the dead demon and pretended not to listen to Raoul and Hamid's conversation. Of course, this discovery meant the Council people would be sticking around. Nothing was as important as maintaining the integrity of the barrier, and I wouldn't be surprised to see more warriors arriving today.

"Excuse me, everyone," George called. "I hate to kick you out, but we need to get the demon packed and shipped to Valstrom, ASAP. Council's orders."

I was at the farthest point from the door, so I had to wait for the rest to file out before I could leave. When I got to the living room, there was no sign of Hamid, Vivian, or Raoul.

Knowing it was no use trying to go back to bed after this, I returned to my room to dress before I sought out Raoul. Things were going to get crazy here, and I wanted to know where we fit into all of this.

I was disappointed, but not surprised, to learn that Raoul was holed up in his office with Hamid and Vivian, no doubt on a call with the Council. I'd never been a patient person, but this whole situation had me more wound up than usual. I spent the time working out and sparring with anyone who was within reach. It didn't matter that most warriors here were older and faster than I was. I liked to push myself hard in training.

I was dripping with sweat and feeling pleasantly drained when I finally left the gym several hours later. A glance at the closed office door told me Raoul was still tied up, and I huffed out a breath as I headed to my room to shower. How long was this going to take?

There was still no sign of Raoul when I emerged from my room thirty minutes later. Unable to sit still, I grabbed my keys and went for a ride to the gourmet coffee shop that Sara and Beth used to frequent when they lived here. I wasn't as fond of espresso as my friends were, but I liked to indulge every now and then.

Leaning against my bike, drinking my coffee, I had a sudden flashback to the first time I'd drunk the stuff. I'd been in my second year of training at Westhorne, and Liv had convinced me to try it at lunch. I had spent the entire afternoon session using up my excess energy on my fellow trainees. I smiled as I remembered how Liv and Mark had begged me to never drink coffee again.

Olivia and Mark. My smile fell away, and the old pain pricked my chest. Before Sara had come along, the closest friend I'd ever had was Olivia. At first, it was because she'd been the only other female my age at the stronghold, but she'd been the kind of person who made it impossible not to like her. I'd liked Mark, too, but I'd never taken the time to really get to know him. I regretted that now.

Three and a half years ago, vampires had done the unthinkable and attacked Westhorne, trying to get to Sara. Five people had been killed, including Olivia and Mark. I'd watched Olivia die at the hands of a vampire, and even though Sara and I had killed him, nothing would ever erase the memory of Olivia's and Mark's lifeless faces as they lay side by side in the snow.

For months after, I'd dreamed about them every night. I'd see the vampire latched onto Liv's throat, but no matter how fast I'd run, I could never reach her in time. If I'd only been a little faster, a little stronger, I might have saved her. I'd felt so helpless watching her die, and I had vowed I'd never feel like that again.

I took a large gulp of my cooling coffee, trying to shake off the melancholy that had stolen over me. I could go days now, sometimes a week, without thinking about Olivia and Mark, and then some small thing would trigger a memory of them. Olivia used to joke about how I lacked sentimentality. She'd have a field day if she knew a cup of coffee made me miss her silly laugh.

Tossing my now empty cup into a garbage can, I mounted my bike and drove back to the house. I found Raoul in the kitchen making a sandwich.

"All done with your Council business?" I asked as I sat on one of the stools at the breakfast bar.

He grimaced. "Days like this, I wish my biggest concern was where to ride on patrol."

"That bad, huh?"

I was dying to ask him what had been said in the hours-long call with the Council, but I wasn't sure how much he could tell me. This morning's discovery was bigger than anything we'd ever dealt with, and I had no idea what would happen next.

He piled deli meat on his bread. "The Council is putting all of their resources on this, so expect to see more of our people in Los Angeles."

My pulse quickened. "Does this mean we'll be working on the investigation, too?"

"No," Hamid said in a clipped tone as he entered the kitchen.

I peered at him over my shoulder, wondering why he was angry this time. Or maybe that was how he always sounded and I just hadn't noticed it before now. Come to think of it, had I ever seen him smile?

Hamid moved to a spot where I could see him easier, and I had to suppress a sigh. It was almost criminal for someone who looked that fine to be in a perpetual bad mood. My girly bits mourned for what might have been.

"Okay, then." I shot Raoul a wry smile as I stood. I couldn't say I was surprised Hamid didn't want me involved, but I was bummed I was going to miss out on what was shaping up to be the biggest investigation in history. "I guess I'll go see what Mason and Brock are up to."

"They're not here," Raoul said. "They just left to take their stuff to the Glendale safe house."

I stopped in mid-turn and spun back to him. "Why would they do that?"

Raoul was unconcerned by my outburst. "It makes the most sense for Hamid to stay here since he is heading up the investigation. Mason and Brock offered up their room to him."

I avoided looking at Hamid as I silently cursed my friends for not telling me what they were doing and for abandoning me here with Oscar the Grouch. Not to mention all the other Council warriors who were sure to be filling this place up soon. Suddenly, the command center seemed too small and crowded for my taste.

"I should do that, too." I pulled my phone from my back pocket. "Jon and the guys will make room for me at their safe house."

"That will not be necessary," Hamid said briskly. "You will stay here."

I swung my gaze to him, bristling at his imperious tone. "Excuse me?"

His expression hadn't changed, but his eyes seemed a shade darker. "The other investigators have already filled the available spaces in the safe houses. There is no need for you to leave here."

"Maybe I want to," I challenged. "Besides, I wouldn't want to be in the way of you guys doing your job."

"I'm sure we'll all be getting in each other's way for the next few weeks," Raoul said to me in a conciliatory tone. "But we'll make it work. It will be business as usual for the rest of us."

Hamid shook his head. "Until we know what we are dealing with, it might be best if the young warriors are pulled from patrols."

"What?" Blood pounded in my ears. Where the hell did he get off? He might be some big shot with the Council, but no way was he coming in here and telling me I couldn't do my job.

"I don't think we'll need to take such drastic measures," Raoul said in a rush, shooting me a *I've got this* look.

Hamid did not look convinced. "We don't know what kind of demons could show up next. She is weak and might not be able to defend –"

I started around the breakfast bar toward him. "Listen here, you –"

Raoul intercepted me, physically holding me back. "Okay. Obviously, you two don't see eye to eye on things."

"You think?" I bit out. I pushed against Raoul, but he was determined and a lot stronger. I nearly growled my frustration.

"What's going on?" asked Vivian as she entered the living room.

"Just a small difference of opinion," Raoul told her.

I scoffed.

Vivian looked from me to Hamid, and a knowing smile curved her lips. "Making friends again, Hamid?"

Raoul blocked my view of the big Egyptian, but I heard a soft snort. The bastard was enjoying this.

Vivian looked like she was trying to hold back a laugh. "Well, I hate to break up your fun, but Hamid and I have a meeting with Orias in half an hour. We need to leave now if we want to make it in time."

Hamid grunted something that sounded like, "Let's go," and the two of them exited the kitchen through the door to the garage.

Raoul waited until the door shut behind them to release me.

"Why did you stop me?" I demanded.

He went back to his sandwich. "You're no match for Hamid, and you know it. And I can't have you trying to punch the Council's lead investigator in the face."

"I wouldn't have aimed for his face," I retorted hotly, not adding that the other parts were more within my reach.

Raoul sighed. "Am I going to have to call a time out for you two?"

I crossed my arms. "Only if he tries to stop me from doing my job. I'll stay clear of their damn investigation, but I'm not going to be treated like some untrained child."

"I know. And I'll talk to him." He picked up his sandwich.

"Good." I sat again and let the anger drain from me. "I didn't know Orias was in town."

Orias lived in the desert outside of Albuquerque. We hadn't exactly hit it off, what with him binding me with his magic and all. He was an arrogant jerk, but he was a powerful warlock, and he'd helped out the Mohiri on more than one occasion. Last I'd heard, he had rebuilt his place that had been destroyed after a vampire attack, and he was back in New Mexico.

"Orias likes to keep a low profile these days." Raoul grabbed a glass from the cabinet and poured some water from the fridge. "I'll probably have to work with Hamid some of the time, so I'll rearrange the patrol teams to make up for my absence."

"Does this mean I won't be confined to the house like a bad little girl?" I asked dryly.

He smiled. "As long as you promise not to slug Hamid."

I made a face. "I can't promise you that. I swear he gets his kicks from seeing how far he can push me. A girl can only take so much before she snaps."

40

"He certainly knows how to push your buttons. I've never seen anyone rile you up that easily. He hasn't been here for twenty-four hours, and you're ready to do him bodily harm."

I hated to admit it, but Raoul was right. I'd dealt with arrogant males before, but none of them had aggravated me as much as Hamid did. Maybe it was because I'd built him up in my head since the first time I saw him, and the real version didn't live up to the fantasy. Physically, he was perfect, but his personality put a damper on any physical attraction I had to him.

I shrugged. "I guess some people just don't mesh."

Raoul took a long drink of water. "I know it's not an ideal situation and Hamid can be a little abrasive, but he's the best at what he does. Do your job and stay out of his way, and he'll be gone soon enough."

A little abrasive? I wanted to laugh at Raoul's description of Hamid. Instead, I nodded. This investigation was far more important than my bruised ego or Hamid's overinflated one. I'd take Raoul's advice and steer clear of our visitor so he could focus solely on his job. The less I saw of Hamid Safar, the happier I would be.

I killed my bike engine outside the garage and pulled off my helmet, grimacing when my hair stuck out in all directions. I could only imagine how bad it looked after the last few hours. I ran my fingers through it and groaned at the tacky wetness clinging to some of the strands. Vampire blood was a bitch to get out once it started to dry.

Dismounting, I laid the helmet on my seat and walked through the garage toward the door to the kitchen. Normally, the house was quiet at night, except for whomever was manning the control room. I was surprised when I entered the kitchen and saw Vivian sitting at the dining room table, working on a laptop. I hadn't spent any time with her since Hamid had arrived three days ago. The downside of avoiding him was that he was usually with Vivian, so I didn't get to see much of her either. He might be a colossal butthead, but I liked Vivian.

Vivian looked up when I walked in. Her eyes widened, and then she let out a burst of laughter.

I tossed my keys on the counter. "That bad, huh?"

"I'd hate to see the other guy," she said, grinning.

I smiled back. "The other guy is now a pile of ash, along with his three friends."

Male voices drifted from the other side of the house, and I looked in that direction as Raoul entered the living room with Hamid and Orias. They stopped walking when they saw me, all wearing different expressions. Raoul was amused, Orias looked surprised, and Hamid's forehead was creased. Was that concern in his eyes? Surely not. I blinked, and it was gone.

Orias hadn't changed a bit in the three years since I'd last seen him. He wore a dark blue suit, minus the tie, and his long black hair was tied back at his nape. I was pretty sure he was Native American, but we'd never gotten around to discussing our ancestry.

His dark eyes narrowed on me as recognition set in. "Still wreaking havoc, I see," he drawled.

I tipped my chin at the satchel he carried over one shoulder, which contained the demon he used to strengthen his own power. "Still have your little pet, I see."

Vivian looked from me to the warlock. "You two know each other?"

"Orias and I go way back," I said.

"Indeed." He harrumphed and placed a hand protectively over the satchel. "In one visit to my place, you and your friends managed to wreck my reception area, scare away half a dozen clients, and kill another. And then I had to rebuild my home after Price's followers came for retribution."

"We didn't start that fight," I argued. But we sure as hell had ended it.

"Wait." Vivian stared at me. "*You* killed Stefan Price?"

"Regretfully, no. I helped, but Sara did most of the work."

Stefan Price was an old vampire, over one hundred and fifty years old, who had been very good at evading our warriors. During our first visit to Orias, Price had shown up and attacked Sara. She and I had faced him down, but she'd been the one to kill him. Someday, I'd encounter another vampire like Price, and that kill would be all mine.

Vivian nodded appreciatively. "Going up against a vampire that strong is impressive for such a young warrior."

"Actually, I was still a trainee then." I could feel Hamid watching me, and I resisted shooting him a smug look. I made a point of ignoring him as much as I could, not an easy feat with someone whose presence seemed to fill any room he entered.

"You really are a young Nikolas," Vivian said, making her my new favorite person.

Raoul waved at me. "Do I want to know?"

I glanced down at my clothes, which were covered in blood. "We found four vampires lurking around outside a homeless shelter. Probably thought they'd find an easy meal. As you can see, they didn't go without a fight."

He glanced at his watch. "You've had a busy night already, and it's barely ten o'clock."

"Yep. I only came back to clean up because I can't ride around looking like this. I'm meeting up with Mason and Brock again in an hour."

"There are only three of you on your team?" Hamid asked in a disapproving tone.

Forced to acknowledge him, I met his eyes. "We never patrol in full teams." As if he didn't already know that.

"These are not normal circumstances," he said. "Young warriors should be on teams with seasoned warriors."

"Like you?" I retorted.

"Yes."

His gaze swept over me, taking in my bloody, disheveled appearance. I cursed my traitorous body when warmth unfurled in my stomach despite my dislike for the warrior.

"Thanks, but we're good. And Brock has more than enough experience," I said with a hint of innuendo, enjoying the flash of annoyance in his eyes.

"Besides," I continued, "we haven't seen anything out of the ordinary since you brought in that spider demon." *The one that should have been my kill.*

"Kraas demon," he corrected me.

I gave the others a questioning look. "I thought we had no record of it on file."

"We don't," Raoul said. "Kelvan searched the demon archives and found several entries about the demon based on the description. It's a lower demon in the same class as a bazerat or Lamprey demon."

"Way to go, Kelvan." Who knew that a reclusive Vrell demon living alone with his cat would become one of our most valuable allies? "Then it's a species of demon we overlooked?" I exhaled in relief. If the demon archives had a record of the Kraas demon, it hadn't come through the barrier as we'd feared.

"The demon archives include species that have never left their dimension," Raoul said, killing my happy moment. "According to Kelvan, the Kraas demon is one of them."

I frowned. "So, aside from knowing what it's called, we're back to where we started."

Vivian nodded. "Pretty much."

"Then I guess I'll leave you to it." I turned toward the hallway that led to my room.

"Did you know you have a big rip in the back of your jeans?" Vivian asked.

"Yes, and these were my favorite pair. They made my butt look great." I put my hand over the tear that bared half my ass and looked over my shoulder at her. "This job is hell on the wardrobe."

Everyone laughed, everyone except Hamid, that was. I glanced at him, expecting to see his usual glare, but instead I found his gaze fixed squarely on my backside. His eyes lifted to mine, and my breath caught at the heat that flared in his for several seconds.

What do you know? I'd been starting to wonder if there was actually a robot beneath that handsome exterior. Looked like he was a red-blooded male after all. I lifted one corner of my mouth in a half smile that let him know I'd caught him checking me out. He answered with a scowl.

I left feeling like I'd finally won a round against him. It was a small victory, but I'd take it.

4

I stared at the blank report on the monitor with distaste before I began the boring task of recording the incident at the homeless shelter last night. Brock, Mason, and I had drawn straws to see who would get stuck writing up the report today, and I'd lost. I suspected those two had cheated because Brock was good with that sleight of hand stuff. I couldn't prove it, so here I was.

The door to Raoul's office opened, and I heard the rumble of a deep voice.

"Until we know what we're dealing with, I think it would be best," Hamid said as he emerged from the office.

Raoul walked out behind him. "That might be a bit drastic, and we don't exactly have a need for a day patrol."

Day patrol? I stood so fast I nearly turned my chair over in the process.

"What are you talking about?" I demanded, even though I had a damn good idea what Hamid was suggesting.

"It's nothing," Raoul said calmly.

"I heard you mention day patrol. You can't be serious." Patrolling during the day would be like going to an amusement park when all the rides are closed. Boring as hell and a waste of time.

Hamid faced me. "I believe we haven't seen the last of the demon activity here, and I think it would be safer to keep new warriors off night patrols for now."

"I don't think so," I said as angry indignation flooded me.

He continued as if I hadn't spoken. "I plan to make the recommendation to the Council today."

I clenched my jaw so hard it hurt. "You can send it to them tied up with a pretty bow for all I care. But the only way you're keeping me here at night is if you shackle me to my bed."

His nostrils flared, but I was fuming too much to care if I pissed him off.

Mason's laugh came from the door that led to the garage. "We've only been gone a few days, and you guys have resorted to shackles."

I turned my glare on him and Brock. "You won't find it funny when you're spending your nights in here playing solitaire."

His grin faded as he took in our serious faces. "What do you mean?"

I pointed an accusing finger at Hamid. "He wants to put you and me on day patrol."

Mason's mouth fell open in dismay. "What?"

Brock shook his head. "That makes no sense. It's a total waste of manpower."

I folded my arms across my chest. "Exactly. And I didn't train for years just to sit around and do nothing when there is work to be done."

Hamid maintained his infuriatingly impassive expression. "Most new warriors spend the first few years at a stronghold, or they are given less dangerous field assignments. They rarely work in cities like Los Angeles."

"Rarely, but not always," I countered. "Most new warriors don't have as much experience as I did by the time I finished training. Plus, Tristan doesn't have a problem with me being in L.A."

"Neither does the leader of Longstone, who sent me here," Mason added.

"This is not a normal situation," Hamid said. "We have no idea what we are up against here or what new dangers we could encounter out there. You are not prepared for this."

I breathed deeply through my nose, trying to keep my temper in check. "No warrior knows what they'll have to deal with from one day to the next. When Nikolas Danshov was captured by a Master, his age and experience didn't help him. Neither did Desmund Ashworth's when he got attacked by a Hale witch. And Chris Kent got taken down by a Hale witch...at Westhorne of all places. Last year, we had a Lilin running around California, and you know who killed him? A warrior, two years out of training."

Hamid didn't respond, which was just as well because I wasn't done.

"I get that you've been around a while and you're probably a badass like Nikolas. I even respect that. But you don't know me or what I can and can't do. You've already established I'm not as fast as you, but have you ever seen me fight? No. You don't like me, fine. I'm not trying to win a Miss Popularity contest. But do not dismiss me because I don't measure up to your impossible standards."

For the first time since I'd met him, Hamid's expression softened to something that wasn't quite a scowl. Was that admiration?

Right. And next he'd go down on one knee to profess his undying love for me.

I pressed my lips together, done arguing with him about this. Too riled up to sit and work on a report, I turned to Brock and Mason. "You guys up for some sparring?"

Mason eyed me warily. "I don't know. How much is it going to hurt?"

"Wuss," Brock barked behind a cough.

"Really?" Mason shoved him. "I don't hear you offering to go first."

Brock chuckled. "That's because I'm older and smarter than you. And I was her pin cushion the last time she was in a bad mood."

"Yeah, but you also heal faster," Mason said.

I tapped my foot impatiently. "Are we doing this or not?"

Vivian entered the control room. "I'll spar with you."

"Okay," I said eagerly, feeling a rush of adrenaline. Vivian had told me how competitive she and Nikolas were back in their training days, so she would be very skilled with a sword. And I needed a challenge to burn off all the negative energy bouncing around inside of me.

She smiled. "Give me a minute to change into some workout clothes."

"I'll go warm up," I called to her back as she left the room.

"This should be fun," Mason said to Brock. "Want to place bets?"

I scoffed at them and headed to the gym. As I passed Raoul, he mouthed, *I'll handle it.*

A tight smile curved my lips. I should have known he'd have my back.

I ignored Hamid, who hadn't spoken since my little speech. Good. I had nothing more to say to him. He was too set in his ways to change his mind, and I wasn't going to back down, ever.

I'd meant it when I said they'd have to shackle me to keep me from doing my job. Since the day I'd learned what I was, all I'd ever wanted was to be a warrior. No one and nothing was going to take that away from me.

"I swear to God I'm going to end up strangling him if he stays here much longer," I ranted into my phone as I paced around the edge of the pool. "It'll be justifiable homicide. No one who knows him could blame me."

Laughter came from the phone, and I stopped walking to glare at it. "This is not funny, you guys."

"It so is," Beth said before dissolving into giggles.

Sara made a sound that was between a laugh and a cry. "Oh, God. I think I just peed myself."

That sent the two of them into another fit of laughter, and I had to wait a full minute for them to stop.

"Beth, you're now on my shit list," I grumbled.

"Me?" Beth choked out. "What about Sara?"

I sat on one of the loungers and scowled at the evening sky. "She gets a pass this time because she's preggers and she's susceptible to bouts of insanity."

Sara sniffled. "Being pregnant doesn't make you crazy."

"I don't know," Beth said. "Only a crazy person would eat that nasty moulis."

"Moulis?" I asked.

"It's a Fae water plant," Sara explained. "Eldeorin gave me some to help with morning sickness."

I put an arm behind my head. "What's wrong with that?"

"What's wrong is it looks like slimy seaweed and smells like dirty socks." Beth made a gagging sound.

"If you ever carry a Fae baby, we'll talk food choices." Sara groaned softly. "I can't believe Faerie pregnancies last a whole year. I already look like I have a soccer ball under my clothes."

Beth laughed. "She does not. She looks adorable."

"You're feeling okay, though?" My own woes suddenly seemed insignificant. "No problems with the baby?"

"The baby and I are great," Sara rushed to reassure me. "Eldeorin said she's strong and healthy."

I exhaled in relief. "Good."

"So, back to your hot Egyptian warrior," Beth drawled. "I want to hear more about him."

I let out a humorless laugh. "He's not my warrior."

Sara snickered. "I remember when all you could talk about was his *big sword*."

"That was before he showed up here and decided to ruin my life."

It had been two days since our argument about patrols, and thankfully, the subject hadn't come up again. That didn't stop Hamid from annoying the hell out of me in other ways.

I ground my teeth together when I remembered my sparring session with Vivian. I had been doing great and feeling pretty good about it until Hamid had come to stand in the doorway and watch. His glowering presence had unnerved me, and I'd messed up several times. After our match, Hamid had the nerve to point out my mistakes and to offer to help me with my technique. As if I needed him to show me how to properly use a sword.

"I guess this means there will be no future hookup for you and him," Beth said.

I snorted. "Are you kidding me? He'd probably criticize my performance, and then I'd be looking for a place to hide the body."

The two of them started laughing again, and this time, I joined in.

"Man, I miss you girls," I said when we were laughed out.

"We miss you, too," Sara replied. "When are you coming for a visit?"

"Yeah, like a permanent one," Beth chimed in. She'd been trying to get me to go work with them ever since they left Los Angeles.

"I might do a short visit." The more I thought about it, the more I liked the idea. I'd get to hang out with my BFFs and put a lot of miles between Hamid and me. I could work just as easily in Chicago as I could here, and by the time I came back, the Council's investigators should be gone. Perfect.

"When?" Sara and Beth asked in unison.

"Soon. I need to run it by Raoul, but I don't think he'll have any problem with me leaving."

Through the French doors, I saw Raoul approaching. Speak of the devil.

He opened the door and came outside. "Going on a call. Want to ride with me?"

"Sure. Give me one minute." I put the phone to my ear again. "Duty calls, girls. Talk to you soon."

"Bye," they called together.

Standing, I stuck my phone in my back pocket. "What's up?"

"We got a call from a night janitor at Fisher Middle School in Compton. He said he heard suspicious noises coming from the gymnasium."

"Why would a janitor call us instead of the police?" I asked as I walked toward Raoul. "How would he even know about us?"

Raoul stepped aside to let me enter the house. "He's a Vrell demon."

"Ah." Vrell demons were one of the few demon species who could blend in well with humans, as long as they hid their tiny horns and fangs. Sara's work with the demon community had built up their trust in us so they were less afraid to call us when they needed help or to report suspicious activity.

"Grab your stuff," Raoul said. "Brock and Mason are meeting us there."

"You sure the Council's people don't want to handle this?" I asked when I met up with Raoul in the garage. "I wouldn't want to step on any delicate toes."

He grinned as he pulled on his helmet. "Hamid and the others went to San Diego today with Orias, so their toes are safe."

I frowned. "What's going on in San Diego?"

"I don't know. I haven't been briefed on it yet."

I shook my head as I mounted my bike. Of course not. Why keep us in the loop?

Mason and Brock were waiting for us when we pulled into the school parking lot. Raoul decided it was best for us to stay together, considering recent events, and we walked to the front door as a group. On the other side of the glass door, a nervous Vrell demon visibly relaxed when he saw us.

"Thank you for coming," he whispered, running a shaky hand through his curly brown hair.

Raoul introduced us, and the demon said his name was Kaden. Then Raoul asked him to tell us what was going on.

"First, I could only hear voices, and I thought some kids had snuck into the school. But then I heard someone speaking in demon tongue."

I paused in adjusting the leather harness that held my sword against my back. Demon tongue was the language common to all demon species, although most spoke English. We had scholars who spent their lives trying to understand the complex language. Whoever was in the gym was definitely not human.

"What did they say?" Raoul asked him.

Kaden wrung his hands. "I don't know. My family doesn't speak the old language, so I only know a few words. But it has a very distinct pronunciation."

Raoul nodded gravely as he pulled out his phone and made a call. "Hamid, are you still in San Diego?" Pause. "We're in Compton, and we might have a situation here." He went on to relate what Kaden had told us, and the two of them talked for another minute before Raoul ended the call. The thin line of his mouth told me I wasn't going to like what he said.

"Hamid and the others are twenty minutes out. We'll wait for them."

"Why are we waiting?" Mason asked before I could.

Raoul darted a glance at Kaden and motioned for us to walk a short distance from the Vrell demon before he answered Mason.

"The Council wants Hamid to take the lead when there is suspicious demon activity."

Annoyance pricked at me, but I kept my mouth shut for once. Raoul was stuck between doing his job and following the orders of the Council. I didn't envy him, and I wouldn't make it harder for him by complaining about something he had no control over.

I paced in front of the doors like a caged animal. I was armed to the teeth and ready to fight, yet I was forced to stand by and wait for the cavalry. My Mori's excitement fueled the energy coursing through me, making me feel like I'd touched a low-voltage wire.

When something clattered to the floor behind me, I spun with knife in hand and scared the hell out of a wide-eyed Kaden, who had dropped his phone.

"S-sorry," he stammered as he retrieved the phone with a shaking hand.

I sheathed my knife. "It's okay. I'm just –"

A man's agonized scream echoed down the hallway.

Raoul raced past me in the direction of the sound, with Brock close at his heels. Mason and I took up the rear, but we couldn't keep up with the two older warriors. By the time he and I reached the gym, the door was open and I could see Brock and Raoul a few feet inside, their faces bathed in light as they stared at something.

Quietly, I slipped in behind them and came up short at the scene before me. In the middle of the gym floor, a large red circle was painted with a smaller one inside, just like the one we'd found in the basement of the house. Whereas the other circle had been inactive, this one was lit by the glowing crystals around the perimeter.

Standing at the center was a tall figure in a gray robe, his face hidden beneath a hood, holding another man in a white robe by the throat. The smaller man's hood had fallen, and I could see the terror etched on his face as he clutched at the hand choking him.

I took a step forward, but Raoul grabbed my arm and held me back. "You can't enter an active summoning circle," he said in a low voice. "It will kill you."

I stopped pulling against him, berating myself for the rookie mistake. I knew not to mess with magic, especially a powerful summoning spell.

The gray-robed man began chanting in a deep, gravelly voice. Beside me, Raoul inhaled sharply.

"What is it?" I asked, my eyes still on the two people inside the circle.

"Demon tongue."

I tore my gaze from the circle to stare at Raoul. "He's a demon?" There were no demon warlocks, so how could a demon be performing a spell only used by warlocks?

Before Raoul could answer me, the tempo of the demon's chant increased. The crystals' glow intensified, and the air began to crackle with electricity. I gripped my sword handle as a sense of dread settled over me.

The demon's voice rose until it reached a crescendo. I could only watch in shock as he punched his hand into the chest of his captive. I heard the crunch of ribs breaking and the sickening wet plop as his bloody hand reappeared, holding a still beating heart.

"Jesus," Mason whispered in horror.

The demon released the dead man, and the body crumpled to the floor at his feet. Holding the man's heart in both hands, he raised it above his head, still chanting. A wave of magic pulsed outward from the circle, and I gasped as it stung my skin like tiny needles, driving us back several feet.

"What is that?" Brock pointed, and I followed his gaze to a shimmering crack that had appeared in the air six feet off the floor just outside the larger circle. The crack began to widen, revealing nothing but blackness on the other side.

When the hole was a foot wide, the demon lowered his hands to his mouth. I couldn't see his face beneath the hood, but I could hear the sound of teeth tearing at meat. I had to fight my gag reflex. I'd seen plenty of ghastly things, but this one topped the list.

The demon shouted something. Then he drew back his hand and threw the heart into the fissure.

Seconds ticked by. I was starting to think the spell had failed when the hole widened another foot, revealing a murky reddish glow on the other side. A faint howling, like the wind whistling through a cave, came from the hole. There were other sounds, too, but they were distorted and impossible to make out.

Then I saw movement inside the hole. A scaly hand appeared, followed by a second one. Something gripped the edges of the hole and prepared to squeeze through.

One look at the long black claws and barbed knuckles told me what was coming out of the hole before the scaly head made its appearance. A Drex demon. The demon looked like an upright crocodile, complete with a long snout full of razor-sharp teeth. Its body was covered in venomous barbs that couldn't harm a Mohiri, but the venom could incapacitate a human and make them easy prey.

A thrill went through me. I'd only seen one Drex demon up close, and Sara had killed it. My body tensed in anticipation of my first fight with one of these reptilian demons.

The Drex demon growled as it forced its large body through the small hole. A few seconds later, it landed on the floor with a loud thump and a scratch of claws against hardwood. Standing, it looked at the robed demon before it swung its beady gaze to us and bellowed. I wanted to answer its challenge, but it was still inside the circle and the magic kept us at bay.

A hissing sound drew my attention back to the hole in time to see a second demon push through. It was a Kraas demon like the one Hamid had killed, and its appearance rocked me back on my heels. There was only one place that thing could come from. We were looking at a window to the demon dimension.

"What do we do?" I asked Raoul as a third demon started emerging from the hole. My voice cracked, and I wasn't sure if it was from excitement or fear. Maybe a bit of both. Only a crazy person could witness this and not be afraid.

"We wait for Orias," he said, not taking his eyes off the demons. "He's the only one who has a chance against this magic."

As if on cue, a door on the other side of the gym opened, and in strode the warlock, followed by Hamid, Vivian, Aaron, and Eugene. The warriors hung back as Orias walked toward the demons, chanting in a language I didn't know. He held out one hand as he walked the perimeter of the circle, and his other hand lay on the bulge in the satchel he carried.

Orias seemed unaffected by the power in the room, and as he neared us, I felt the stinging magic lessen until I was able to take a few steps forward. Whatever he was doing, it was counteracting the robed demon's spell.

The demon clearly knew this because he turned to face Orias, throwing up his arms and starting a new chant. Undaunted, the warlock squared off against him, and little by little the crystals around the outer circle dimmed. I'd known Orias was powerful, but this display of power was incredible.

Inside the weakening circle, demons continued to climb from the hole in the barrier. There had to be at least ten of them, and the only ones I recognized were two Drex demons. What would happen when the robed demon's spell failed completely and they were able to leave the circle?

"What is Orias doing?" I whispered to Raoul so I didn't distract the warlock.

Raoul shook his head. "I think he's trying to bind the demon's magic with his own."

I looked at the hole. "Will that seal the barrier?"

"I don't know," he said grimly.

Orias moved closer to the circle, his words growing louder and more forceful. Hope flared in me when I saw the demon falter, looking unsteady on his feet for the first time.

The demon bellowed in rage. Dropping his hands, he whispered something that set off a flash of purple light. In the time it took for me to blink, he was gone, vanished into thin air.

I looked at the window in the barrier, expecting it to have disappeared with the demon who had opened it, but it was still there. My eyes widened as

I watched a thick gray tentacle lined with barbed suckers reach through the hole. I considered myself a brave person, but I really didn't want to see what was on the other end of that thing.

Orias turned his full attention on the hole, just as the crowd of demons rushed from the circle in every direction. All eight warriors in the gym leaped into action.

I went for the demon closest to me, which looked like a mutant red porcupine the size of a Great Dane. Every time I tried to get near it, the quills stood on end and I was sure I was about to be skewered.

"Screw that," I muttered, pulling one of my knives free. I aimed for the demon's throat, which looked like a vulnerable area. The blade hit its mark, and the demon rolled around on the floor, squealing as smoke poured from it.

I took the opportunity to move in and finish it off with my sword. I left my knife buried in its throat, not wanting to get too close to those quills. Our scientists were going to have a field day with this one.

I looked up from the dead demon to see all the warriors engaged in battle. Orias was still chanting at the hole, which looked half its size now. Relief welled in me. Whatever he was doing was working.

A growl tore my gaze from the warlock to the Kraas demon that was stalking toward him. Orias was so focused on his spell that he didn't see what was coming at him. If that thing attacked him or broke the spell, we were all in trouble.

I leaped over the dead demon at my feet and raced to intercept the Kraas demon before it got to Orias. It turned its head and stared at me with glassy black eyes. Hissing, it sped up, and I matched its speed. Five feet from Orias, I threw my body between him and the advancing demon.

The demon reared back and opened its pincers to show off a mouth lined with three rows of teeth.

I grinned back, brandishing my sword. *Come and get me.*

Something snarled off to my right at the same moment the Kraas demon jumped at me. Before I could react, an arm wrapped around my waist. I was pulled back against a hard body and spun away from the demon as a sword flashed over my head.

The demon impaled itself on the long blade, and its heavy body slammed into me and my rescuer, sending the two of us stumbling backward.

In the next instant, there was a bright flash as a loud bang shook the gym. I closed my eyes against what felt like an explosion. An icy tingle spread through me, and I gasped for breath as the air was sucked from the room.

5

I must have blacked out for a few seconds, because when I came to, I was lying on the floor with a heavy weight pressing down on me. My ears were ringing, and I couldn't see or move. God, had the whole roof fallen on me?

I pushed against the thing on top of me and was surprised to feel a warm body instead of roof debris. "Hey," I wheezed.

The person above me shifted. I found myself caged between two muscled arms and staring up into dazed blue eyes. Without his usual surly expression, it took me a few seconds to recognize Hamid. Why was he staring at me like that?

"Can you get off me?" I pushed at him again, but he didn't budge.

His lips moved, but I couldn't hear him over the ringing in my ears.

"I can't hear anything." My voice sounded muffled, but at least I knew I wasn't deaf.

What I didn't know was why he was still on top of me and staring at me like he'd never seen me before. This close, his irises were the most stunning shade of blue with little flecks of gold in them. A girl could drown in those eyes. And his lips. Wow. My mouth watered, and I was overcome by the urge to close the few inches between us and run my tongue across that full lower lip.

Whoa. I swallowed and closed my eyes. Was the school on fire? Because it had suddenly gotten hot in here.

I peeked at Hamid, who was still acting all kinds of strange. It was starting to freak me out. Maybe he'd taken a blow to the head in the explosion. That was the only thing I could think of to explain his odd behavior.

"Are you hurt?" I raised my voice in case he was having trouble hearing, too. "Can you move?"

He shook his head slowly but didn't speak. Was he saying he wasn't hurt or that he couldn't move? I shoved at him again to no avail.

Turning my head to one side, I yelled, "Hello, is anyone else alive? If so, can you help me before I'm crushed over here?"

The ringing had subsided a little, so I could hear muffled voices. A pair of feet in dark shoes appeared, and the person knelt beside us. Orias. He said something, but it was garbled.

"My ears are messed up," I shouted. "Can't hear you."

"Don't move," he said in a louder voice I could just make out.

I would have huffed if I could have taken a deep breath. "I *can't* move. In case you haven't noticed, I'm kind of stuck here." Orias didn't respond, and I said, "What are you doing? Get this brute off me, will you?"

The warlock leaned down until I could see his face. "At least we know you are unharmed," he said dryly. "You and Hamid were hit by my spell, and I need to ensure you're okay before I allow the others to come near you."

Ah. That explained the explosion and my hearing loss. Hamid must have taken the brunt of the spell, which was why he was being all weird.

I kept my head turned to avoid Hamid's unsettling gaze. I wished I could ignore him completely, but that was out of the question with his big body covering mine and the soft caress of his warm breath against my cheek.

Orias went back to his knees and said some words I couldn't understand. For several seconds, Hamid and I were encased in a soft blue light. It faded, and Orias stood.

A minute later, booted feet appeared in my line of vision, and someone tapped Hamid's shoulder to get his attention. I breathed a sigh of relief when he pushed off me and stood.

I looked up to see Raoul's worried face. "I'm fine," I assured him, and his grin told me I was still talking too loudly.

He reached down to help me up. Suddenly, Hamid was there, nudging Raoul aside none too gently and lifting me to my feet.

I was so surprised by his actions that for a moment, I just stood there with my hand in his larger one. When I came to my senses, I tried to pull my hand away, but he refused to let go.

I looked up to ask what his problem was, and the words died on my tongue when I saw the way he was staring at me. The confusion was gone from his eyes to be replaced by what could only be described as possession.

Orias's magic must have addled his brain. That was the only logical explanation.

"Hamid," Raoul said with a note of concern in his voice. "You okay?"

Hamid blinked, and his grip loosened, allowing me to escape from his hold. I immediately backed up, putting several feet between us. Hamid replied to Raoul, but with my reduced hearing, I couldn't make out what he said.

Orias spoke to Hamid, and I used that opportunity to move away from them. I'd let Raoul and Orias sort out whatever was going on with Hamid. I located my sword, which had flown from my grasp when Hamid had tackled me, and got my first look at the gym.

The place looked like a war zone with dead demons everywhere, some of them in pieces. Black demon blood coated everything, and the smell of death was thick in the air. A quick scan of the room told me all our people were okay.

My eyes sought out the hole in the barrier, but there was no trace of it, hopefully sealed forever by Orias's spell. That display of power had given me a whole new respect for the warlock. If his magic could seal a tear in the barrier to the demon dimension, it was no wonder Hamid was acting all wonky after being hit by it. I was feeling out of sorts, too, and he'd blocked me from the worst of it.

I glanced at Hamid who was still talking to Orias. I hoped he was okay. I didn't like him, but I'd never wish him any harm. It bothered me that he might have been hurt protecting me.

As if he sensed my eyes on him, Hamid's gaze shifted from Orias to me, and my stomach quivered at the intensity of his stare. No male had ever looked at me that way, like he owned me, body and soul. It angered me and excited me at the same time.

I spun away, breaking eye contact with him, and came face-to-face with Mason, who looked like he'd bathed in demon blood.

"Damn, what happened to you?" I asked him.

He grinned at me. "Why are you shouting?"

I lowered my voice. "Sorry. My ears are still ringing from Orias's spell. Why are you covered in blood?"

"Drex demon. I had no idea those things bled so much."

Envy tugged at me. "You killed a Drex?"

"Yeah. Brock got the other one." His eyes gleamed with excitement. "What a night, huh?"

I rubbed at my temple where a dull throbbing had started. "You can say that again."

Mason laid a hand on my shoulder. "Hey, you okay? You got pale all of a sudden."

"It's just a headache. I'm sure it'll pass soon."

"Hold on. I'll get you some gunna –" He broke off and stared at something over my shoulder. Whatever he saw made him take a hasty step back.

"What?" I turned to find Hamid standing behind me, his expression dark and unreadable.

"You're hurt," he said stiffly.

I frowned, confused by his attention. "I have a small headache. It's nothing."

"You should see one of the healers."

"I don't need a healer." If either of us needed one, it was him. Whatever was wrong with him was freaking me out.

I was about to call Orias over when Hamid moved forward into my space. Before I could back away, one of his hands came up to cup my cheek with a gentleness I did not expect from the big warrior.

I gasped as a warm tingling sensation radiated through me, and my heart began to thump so loudly I could feel it in my ears. My body thrummed with a strange energy, and it felt like I was experiencing the biggest adrenaline rush of my life.

Suddenly, the headache was gone, along with the ringing in my ears. That was when I felt the odd fluttering in my mind that seemed to be coming from my Mori. This was something I'd never felt before, and I wondered if my demon had also been affected by Orias's magic. Maybe Hamid was right and I should see a healer after all.

Reaching up, I gently pushed Hamid's hand away from my face, and then I stepped backward with a hand in front of me to keep him at bay. I'd never been shy or uncomfortable with male attention, but I was more than a little flustered by his proximity and his touch. It made me feel weak and vulnerable, and I didn't like it one bit.

"You're kind of creeping me out right now, big guy," I said as kindly as I could. "I never thought I'd say this, but I'd like to have the old Hamid back, please."

Confusion clouded his eyes, lending to my suspicion that he was suffering some ill effects of the spell. The Hamid I knew would be staring down his nose at me and telling me how this was no place for a young warrior. Blah, blah, blah. He definitely wouldn't be hovering over me and touching me like I was a piece of glass that might break.

"Orias," I called loudly when Hamid didn't respond to my comment. "Can you come here?"

The warlock appeared at my side. "Yes?"

I turned to him. "Are you sure that spell didn't cause any damage to us?" I asked with a meaningful tilt of my head toward Hamid. "Maybe you should do some more tests."

Orias narrowed his eyes thoughtfully as he looked from me to Hamid. "I would not be surprised if you were both feeling a bit off after that. I can do another spell to see if there is any lingering magic."

"Great," I blurted. "You can start with Hamid."

I literally shoved the warlock at the silent warrior and hurried to where Raoul was on his phone, probably calling in a cleanup team. We'd need a big one for this mess.

He hung up and gave me a questioning look. "What's up with you and Hamid?"

"Your guess is as good as mine." I waved a hand at the carnage before us. "What do we do now?"

"Tristan's calling the governor and mayor as we speak, and the Council is already assembling a team of scientists to send here. They want us to leave the scene untouched until they arrive."

"Won't the humans be suspicious if a school closes for no reason?" I asked.

Raoul shrugged. "The mayor's office will handle that. I'm sure they'll have some plausible story."

I watched Vivian, Aaron, and Eugene, who were talking as they walked the perimeter of the larger circle. Now that it was all over, it was hard to believe that a few minutes ago, I'd seen someone tear a hole in the barrier to the demon dimension. It should not have been possible, yet I'd seen it with my own two eyes.

Mason came to stand beside us. "How's your head, Jordan?"

"You hurt your head?" Raoul asked. "Why didn't you say something?"

I heaved a sigh, tired of people fussing over me. "My head is fine. I had a little headache, but it's gone."

I decided not to mention the way my Mori was acting up out of fear Raoul might confine me to the house for a few days. The last thing I wanted was to be stuck in close confines with Hamid, especially in his current state.

My Mori did that fluttering thing again, and a wave of excitement came from it. Like steel to a magnet, my gaze was drawn to the warrior who was deep in conversation with Orias on the other side of the gym. The two men stopped talking as Vivian approached them. She said something and smiled at Hamid.

My body stiffened involuntarily as a growl filled my head along with a single word.

Mine.

Shock rippled through me, and I swayed on my feet as the truth slammed into me with the force of a Mack truck.

Raoul steadied me. "Are you alright?"

"Yes." I laughed to cover the tremble in my voice. "Been a crazy night."

Mason chuckled. "That's an understatement."

Solmi, my Mori said fiercely.

My mind began to race as panic set in. *No, no, no! No way. This is not happening.*

The voice in my head became more insistent. *Solmi.*

Shut up! I tore my gaze from Hamid, trying to silence my demon, but it was too late. The damage had been done.

It was no wonder Hamid was acting so weird. I'd thought the spell had screwed up his head, and all along it had been the bond.

Our bond.

Fear and denial made my stomach roll. I couldn't be bonded. I didn't want a mate, least of all *him*. I didn't even like him, and he barely tolerated me.

Oh, God, this was so messed up.

The air in the gym thickened until I found it hard to breathe. I needed to get out of here, to get away from him.

"You sure you're okay?" Raoul asked me. "You look a little pale."

I schooled my expression. "Actually, I think I could use some fresh air after nearly being fried by Orias's magic and almost crushed to death by Hamid."

Raoul studied my face. "Why don't you head back to the house and have one of the healers check you out? Just to be safe. The rest of us can manage here."

"I just need a few minutes outside." I wanted to get as far from Hamid as possible, but I wouldn't leave in the middle of a job. And there was absolutely nothing a healer could do to help me now.

Raoul smiled, but his voice was stern. "I'm pulling rank on you and ordering you to go see the healers. You can come back once they give you the all clear."

"Fine. But don't think you can start bossing me around."

He laughed. "Wouldn't dream of it."

I left by the door we'd come in, and though I kept my gaze averted from Hamid, I could feel his eyes on me until I exited the gym.

I found Kaden in the hallway, looking scared and confused, and I told him he could leave if we had his contact information. He gave me a jerky nod of relief and hurried away. I didn't blame him for wanting to get away from there, although I had a completely different reason.

As soon as the main door of the school closed behind me, I doubled over and took large gulps of the cool night air. Panic threatened to overtake me, and I forced myself to calm down, calling upon the meditation breathing techniques I'd learned years ago.

I was almost back in control when my Mori started to flutter, reminding me why I'd been close to hyperventilating a minute ago. The fluttering grew stronger, and my Mori's growing excitement told me Hamid was coming toward me. He was the absolute *last* person I wanted to see in my current state.

I ran to my bike, sheathed my sword, and took off without even bothering to don my helmet. I barely registered it rolling across the pavement behind me as I sped out of the parking lot. I didn't have to look back to know Hamid had come outside and stood there watching me ride away. I could almost feel the heat of his gaze burning into me.

I forced myself to slow down once I could no longer feel Hamid's presence. It wouldn't do to crash my bike, and I needed time to clear my head before I reached the house. If I arrived in this state, there'd be no hiding that something was wrong, and I was in no mood to answer questions.

I'd managed to evade Hamid for now, but eventually he'd come looking for me. We'd bonded, and he was going to want to talk about that. Under normal circumstances, I'd expect him to break the bond, but he was not acting like himself tonight. The way he'd fussed over me and touched my face was how a male behaved with his mate. I had no doubt that getting blasted by that spell was the reason for it.

"Argh!" I shouted into the wind. This was all Orias's doing, and I wanted to go back and punch him in the throat for my troubles.

The logical side of my brain knew the warlock wasn't at fault. If he hadn't performed that spell, God only knew what would have happened tonight. But my emotional side, which was a hairsbreadth from losing it, needed someone to blame.

I managed to calm down by the time I reached the command center, and I went straight to the guesthouse to see the healers. I knew Raoul would ask them if I'd been to see them, and he'd give me hell if I hadn't.

Once Leslie gave me a clean bill of health, I debated whether or not to return to the school. I'd never left a job unfinished, but the thought of seeing Hamid made a pit form in my stomach. I went to the control room where Caleb and Will were manning the computers tonight. They'd already heard from Raoul about what had happened at the school, and they peppered me with questions, which I answered as well as I could.

When I could stall no longer, I told them I'd see them later and headed back to my bike. I was about to start the engine when Caleb caught up to me.

He laid a hand on one of my handlebars. "Do you have to go back to the school right away?"

"No, why?"

"We just got a call about a possible vampire attack in Malibu. You want to ride with me to check it out?"

"Sure," I said, hiding the relief that filled me.

Caleb went to his bike. I quickly dialed Raoul to let him know I was responding to a call with the other warrior, and I wouldn't be coming back to the school.

"Did you see one of the healers?" Raoul asked.

I rolled my eyes even though he couldn't see me. "Yes, Dad."

"Okay." His voice lacked his usual amusement. "I don't need to tell you to be extra vigilant after what went down here tonight."

Coming from anyone else, that comment might have annoyed me. But Raoul and I had been friends for three years, and I knew he wasn't questioning my abilities. The events at the school had everyone rattled, and he was just worried about me.

"I will." I heard Caleb's bike come to life. "Gotta go. Catch you later, boss man."

"How long is this going to take?" I asked as I stared up at the living room ceiling in the guesthouse. I was lying on the rug where the coffee table used to be, while Orias walked around me, chanting and waving his hands over me.

Orias stopped walking and shot me an exasperated glare. "It will go a lot faster if you keep still and stop asking questions."

I huffed loudly and scowled at the light fixture above me. For the last hour, I'd had to lie here while he ran his magical tests on me to see if there were any side effects from his spell. I tried to forget I was the one who'd suggested he test Hamid and me to figure out why the warrior had been acting so un-Hamid-like last night. Of course, that was before I knew the real shitstorm I had landed in.

My traitorous Mori did that annoying little flutter again to remind me said warrior was close by, probably outside waiting for Orias to finish with me. The situation at the school had kept Hamid and the other Council investigators busy last night, which meant I hadn't seen him since we'd bonded. I grimaced. Just thinking about bonding with anyone, let alone him, made me want to throw up my breakfast.

"Hmmm," Orias murmured.

I tilted my head to one side to look up at him. "Hmmm, what?"

"I'm detecting some residual magic around you that shouldn't be there. Interesting."

"What the hell does that mean?"

He stroked his chin. "I'm not sure yet. It might be nothing."

I sat up and glowered at him. "It *might* be nothing? That's all you can say?"

He peered down his hawk nose at me. "This is not an exact science. There are many nuances to magic that can make it difficult to identify."

"But it's *your* magic."

Orias let out an exaggerated sigh, as if I should already know what he was about to tell me. "You and Hamid were caught in the crossfire between my binding spell and the one used to open the barrier. When two magics merge, they become something new."

Caught between two spells? A chill ran across the back of my neck when I remembered the hole appearing in the barrier. If magic could do that, what would it do to Hamid and me?

"So, what now?" I asked him.

"I'll know more once I test Hamid again and see if I find traces of the same magic. For now, you may go."

"Thanks," I muttered, standing.

I walked to the door and opened it, feigning surprise when I saw Hamid leaning against the wall with his arms folded across his chest. The dark blue Henley he wore did little to hide the muscles underneath, and I wondered briefly if the shirt was custom made. Did they even make clothes big enough for shoulders that wide?

My Mori quivered, and warmth flowed through me.

Gah! Stop that.

I hid my body's reaction to Hamid behind a mask of annoyance. "If you're waiting for Orias, he's all yours."

I'd barely taken two steps away from the door when his hand captured my arm and turned me to face him. His face was hard, and I couldn't tell if it was anger or determination or some other emotion burning in his eyes. Whatever it was, it made my entire body tingle with awareness of him.

"We need to talk," he said brusquely.

"About what?" I yanked my arm from his grasp, and surprisingly, he let me go.

He stared at me as if I'd spoken another language. "About what happened last night."

"You were there, and you saw the same thing I did," I replied in a voice that belied the apprehension building in my chest. "If you need anything else, you can read it in the report."

His eyes narrowed. "I'm glad to hear that, but I want to talk about what happened between you and me."

"Between us?" I frowned. "Oh, I get it. You want me to thank you for saving little old me from the big bad demons."

Hamid's eyebrows drew together, and it was a struggle not to squirm under his sharp perusal. "Why do you pretend?" he asked with a note of impatience.

"Pretend what?"

"That our Mori did not bond last night."

I let my mouth fall open, and my eyes go wide in feigned shock. "You're out of your mind," I said with as much incredulity as I could muster without being over the top.

The hard lines of his face softened. "I understand this upsets you, but denying it won't change the fact that we are bonded."

"Stop saying that," I snapped.

"Why?" he challenged. "It is the truth."

"It's not," I persisted stubbornly.

During my sleepless night, I'd come up with the brilliant plan to just deny everything. My plan didn't feel so brilliant now that I was face-to-face with him. But it was the only one I had, so I was sticking with it.

He reached out and took my hand, his strong fingers closing around mine so I couldn't pull away. My Mori went nuts at the contact, and my heart began to pound against my ribs.

"I know you feel what I feel," he said huskily. "I can see it in your eyes."

A delicious shiver went through me, and I caught myself before I could lean into his touch. I swallowed dryly. "You're seeing what you want to see."

His eyebrows rose. "You think I wanted this?"

I shoved hard at his chest with my free hand. "Screw you. You're an ass."

The door opened beside us, and Orias looked from Hamid to me. "Good. You're still here, Jordan. I had a thought about the magic I sensed on you, and I need both of you to test my theory."

"What magic?" Hamid asked, still holding my hand despite my attempts to pull free from his grasp.

64

If Orias noticed the quiet power struggle taking place between us, he didn't mention it. He gave Hamid the same explanation he'd given me about the two magics merging, and asked us to come inside so he could do an illumination spell on both of us at the same time.

"It will allow me to see if you two have the same magic residue and give me a better picture of what the magic looks like," he said.

"Why is that important?" I didn't want to spend a second longer with Hamid than I had to.

The warlock's eyes gleamed. "If I can get a feel for the structure of the magic, I might be able to separate mine from the other. Isolating the other magic could help us learn how it was used to open the barrier."

I stared at him. "You can do that?"

"I've done it before, though not with magic this advanced," he admitted. "I will certainly give it my best effort. If anyone knows what is beyond that barrier, it's me, and I do not want that unleashed on the world."

Hamid nodded. "What do you need from us?"

Orias stepped aside and waved us into the house. "Just a few minutes of your time to perform the spell."

"Okay. Let's do this." I tugged my hand from Hamid's, and he released me so I could enter the house ahead of him. Once inside, Orias instructed us to stand in the middle of the living room, facing each other a foot apart but not touching. Laying a hand on each of our shoulders, he muttered a string of words that sounded like gibberish to me. He removed his hands, and a yellow misshapen bubble formed around Hamid and me, blocking out all sounds, except our quiet breathing.

Trapped inside the bubble with Hamid, I was hyperaware of his nearness. Thankfully, our height difference meant I couldn't look him in the eye without tilting my head, so I focused my gaze instead on the hollow of his throat. But it was impossible to ignore him, especially with his delectable male scent surrounding me. It made me think of exotic spices and hot desert breezes, and it was all I could do not to close my eyes and breathe him in.

Minutes ticked by. Hamid was as still as a statue, but I soon began to shift from one foot to the other. What the hell was taking so long?

Finally, Orias raised his hand. With a faint popping sound, the bubble disappeared. As much as I wanted to get away from Hamid, I stayed where I was until the warlock said I was free to move. I did not want to have to repeat the spell.

"I think I have what I need," Orias said. "You're free to go."

I moved back several paces. "How long will it take you to isolate the magics?"

"Several days, at least." He smiled. "Then the fun begins. The magic that opened the barrier was the strongest I've ever encountered. It will take a bit longer to study it and break it down."

"We appreciate your help on this," Hamid told him as the three of us walked to the door. "We'll be waiting to hear from you."

"I'll be in touch as soon as I know something." Orias opened the door. "In the meantime, try to stay away from other magic until the remnants of the spell wear off. It should be gone in a week or so.

"Thanks." I walked outside and started for the main house without a backward glance. I needed to find Raoul and make some plans before the day got any older.

"Where are you going?" Hamid called.

"Things to do," I said over my shoulder.

"Whatever it is, it can wait. We are not finished here."

Bristling at the command in his tone, I spun back to face him. "Oh, we're finished alright."

He frowned. "Are you forgetting we are bonded?"

"Not anymore. I hereby release you from the bond."

"Release me?" he repeated the words as if they made no sense to him.

"That's right. Since neither of us wants a mate, there's nothing else to talk about." I turned my back on him again. "Have a nice life, Hamid."

6

I pulled off my helmet and stared at the two-story industrial warehouse that sat on a large fenced-in lot in the middle of Chicago. From my spot in front of the building, I could see a bunch of security cameras mounted around the property, and I waved at the nearest one. No doubt, someone was watching me at one of the workstations in the control center.

Kicking down my stand, I got off my bike and stretched out the kinks from three days on the road. I could have flown here from Los Angeles and had the Ducati shipped, but I'd been in a desperate hurry to leave after my encounter with he-who-shall-not-be-named. And I'd needed some time alone to clear my head before I got here. Nothing was better for head clearing than riding a fast motorcycle across the country.

I grabbed the duffle bag I'd rushed to pack after letting Raoul know I was taking a trip to Chicago. He'd been surprised I wanted to leave with all the excitement in Los Angeles, but I'd reminded him there wasn't much for me to do with the influx of warriors and scholars sent by the Council. It would be better if I gave up my room to one of them and used the opportunity to visit Sara and Beth. When he'd asked how long I planned to be gone, I'd given him a vague answer. The truth was I didn't know. How long did it take for a new bond to dissolve?

My Mori whined unhappily. It had been doing that a lot since I set out from Los Angeles three days ago. I'd gone through several bouts of what felt like depression, for which I blamed my sullen demon. It wasn't handling the bond-breaking very well, and I wished it would just get over it already. We hadn't even been bonded for twenty-four hours for Christ's sake.

I started walking to the small door next to the loading bay and stopped when a wave of light-headedness hit me.

Standing still, I waited a moment for it to pass before I continued walking. It was the second time that had happened in the last two days, and I wondered if it was a side effect of breaking the bond. I wished I had someone to ask about these things, but no way was I telling a soul that I'd bonded with Hamid Safar. I'd take that secret to my grave.

I reached the door and eyed the electronic keypad mounted there. But before I could wonder how to gain entry, the door was flung open and a screaming blonde threw herself at me.

Beth hugged me so hard I could barely breathe. "It's about time."

I wheezed out a laugh. "Great to see you, too."

She pulled back to grin at me. "We've been waiting all afternoon since you told us you'd get here today. Come on. I can't wait to show you around."

I followed her inside and found myself in the large loading bay that now served as a parking area for motorcycles and SUVs. I'd expected the interior to be dimly lit, but it was well-illuminated by high windows and skylights that Beth informed me had been installed during the renovations.

She led me down the center of the building, pointing at rooms that had been constructed on either side of the wide main area.

"Gym, weapons room, interrogation, holding cells," she said as we passed several doors.

I stared at the last door. "You have holding cells here? Have you used them yet?"

"Not yet. We're still not one hundred percent up and running. Right now, we have a skeleton staff, but when we're done, this place will be able to function as well as a stronghold."

I let out a low whistle. "I'm impressed."

Beth smiled. "The Council is sparing no expense on these command centers. Whatever they can think of, they are giving us. We even have a massive generator behind the building in case of a power outage...or the apocalypse."

I chuckled. "Nice."

"That's the control room." She pointed at a closed door but didn't stop. "We'll show you that later. Right now, I'm under orders to find Sara before we do anything else. I have a pretty good idea where she is."

We passed through a pair of double doors at the end of the building into a large open living area comprised of a living/dining room and a modern kitchen. The place looked inviting and comfortable, and I could definitely see a feminine touch in the light colors and furnishings. There were plenty of couches and rugs and a long wooden table that could seat at least a dozen people.

The best sight, however, was the petite brunette standing at the island in the massive kitchen, chowing down on a mountain of spaghetti. Sara stared at me for several seconds with the fork halfway to her open mouth before she let out a squeal and dropped the utensil.

"You're here!" she cried, running toward me.

I hadn't seen Sara since Christmas, and my eyes widened at the sight of her rounded belly. It wasn't the size of a soccer ball as she'd claimed, but there was a noticeable bump under her sweater. Wow. My best friend was having a baby. It hadn't felt real until that moment.

She was also glowing as she neared me, and not in the way pregnant women do. A soft bluish-white aura surrounded her, and I could see tiny blue sparks flickering in her dark hair.

"Sara." Beth waved her arms to get Sara's attention. "You're doing it again."

Sara skidded to a stop and looked down at her body. She sighed and placed her hands on her belly, speaking softly to the baby she carried.

"Settle down, little one. I know we're excited to see Auntie Jordan, but we don't want to accidentally zap her, do we?"

I watched in amazement as the glow around Sara faded and a smile of pure joy lit up her face. She gently rubbed her belly. "That's my good girl. Now, let's go say hi to Auntie Jordan."

"Auntie Jordan?" I asked with a silly grin when Sara looked at me again.

Sara shrugged. "You and Beth are like sisters to me, so of course, you're her aunts."

Warmth filled my chest. "And I'm going to be the coolest aunt ever. I'll teach her everything I know."

Beth laughed. "Maybe not *everything*."

"No corrupting my daughter," Sara said with mock severity as she reached out to hug me.

Orias's warning repeated in my head, and I backed up before she could touch me.

Sara frowned. "It's safe now."

"That's not it," I assured her. "Did you guys hear about what happened at that school?"

Sara gave me an *are you kidding* look. "Yes. It's all anyone can talk about these days."

"So, you know Hamid and I got caught between the two spells?"

Sara and Beth nodded.

"Orias tested us to make sure we're okay, and he said we have some trace magic clinging to us. It should disappear soon, but he warned us not to come into contact with other magic until then. We don't know exactly what this magic can do, so I don't think we should risk it with the baby."

Undaunted, Sara held a hand out toward me, close enough to feel the magic I spoke of but not to touch me. Immediately, her hand began to glow and sparks rolled across her skin.

She yanked her hand away. "Did Orias tell you it was demon magic?"

I recalled everything the warlock had told me. "No, but that makes sense because it was a demon that cast the spell to open the barrier."

Sara pursed her lips. "I don't think it can harm me or the baby. I'm more concerned about what our power might do to it."

"Doesn't Fae magic cancel out all other magics?" Beth asked her.

"Yes, but it's not that simple. The magic isn't just clinging to Jordan. It's attached to her. My power might not be able to tell the difference and..."

"And no more Auntie Jordan," I finished for her. Then I realized what else she'd said. "What do you mean it's attached to me? Orias never mentioned that."

Sara motioned for me to follow her to the kitchen. She picked up her fork and ate a mouthful of spaghetti before she answered me.

"Sorry. I'm always hungry these days." She wiped her mouth with a paper napkin. "Fae power is a lot stronger than warlock magic, and it's very sensitive to demons. I'm able to see the magic around you more clearly than Orias can, now that I'm looking for it."

"Lovely." I hopped up to sit on the granite countertop a safe distance from Sara. "This isn't exactly how I wanted to start off my visit with you guys. I can't even go near you."

"I'm sure it'll be gone soon. Orias might not be as strong as I am, but he really knows his stuff." Sara spoke through another bite of spaghetti. "The main thing is you're here."

Beth grabbed three bottles of water from the fridge and handed me one. "We want to hear all about what's going on in Los Angeles. Reading reports is not nearly as good as a firsthand account. I still can't believe you actually witnessed someone opening the barrier. What was it like?"

"It was...surreal. And scary." *In more ways than one.*

Sara drank from her water bottle. "Tell us everything."

I took a deep breath and launched into the story about the events in the gym, adding every detail I could remember. When I got to the part about

Hamid tackling me, the girls oohed and aahed in delight. I made sure to leave out any mention of his strange behavior and the fact that he and I had bonded.

Beth made a silly swooning sound. "He rushed in to save you."

"I didn't need saving," I grumbled. "I was doing fine on my own until he decided to go all alpha male on me."

"Alpha male, huh?" Sara said with a sly little grin. "I've never seen Hamid in action, but I do remember thinking he was a little scary the first time I saw him. And I believe you said he was perfect."

I made a face. "Don't remind me."

"What happened next?" Beth asked.

"Not much," I lied. "I had a bit of a headache from the magic, so Raoul sent me back to the house to see the healers. I planned to return to the school, but Caleb asked me to go on a job with him."

Sara eyed me curiously. "Since when do you pass up something like that to go out on a routine job?"

I lifted a shoulder. "Raoul told me they would just be keeping the place secure until the other Council teams arrived. There was nothing for me to do there, and you know I hate sitting around doing nothing."

"True." She laid down her fork with a contented sigh.

I shook my head at her now empty plate. "Is there even enough room in your stomach for all that food?"

Sara laughed. "You know how fast our metabolism is. It's double that when you're pregnant. And when you're growing a Fae baby, it's double that again."

My eyes rounded. "Damn."

She took her plate to the sink to rinse it. "Eldeorin and Aine said Fae pregnancies don't usually make the mothers this hungry, but I'm half Mohiri so that changes things."

"I guess that makes sense," I said. "And what's with the glowing thing you were doing when I got here? It kind of reminded me of when you used to glow before you went into liannan."

"Oh, that. She can feel whenever I get happy or excited, and she reacts the only way she knows how," Sara said, motioning for us to go to the living room.

"Is that normal?" I sat on one of the leather armchairs, and Beth took another.

Sara sat on one end of a couch with her feet up. "Yes. And Eldeorin said as far as he can tell, she's healthy and happy."

I tapped the arm of the chair with my fingers. "As far as he can tell? He's their best healer, right? Shouldn't he be able to see everything that's going on in there?"

Sara laid a hand over her belly again, something she seemed to do a lot. "You remember when Eldeorin put me in the deep sleep to help my body adjust to liannan? He said I put a wall around my Mori to protect it from my Fae power. Well, this little one takes after her mama. She seems to be protecting her Mori from my power and Eldeorin's. I can feel her there, but I can't see her and neither can any other Fae."

"Wow."

"My thoughts exactly," said a male voice I knew well. I looked up to see Nikolas enter the room.

He smiled at me and went directly to Sara, leaning down to kiss her lightly on the lips. Then he lifted her legs and sat beside her with her feet on his lap. I'd seen him be affectionate with Sara plenty of times, but there was a new gentleness to his actions that hadn't been there before.

"Glad you could visit us," Nikolas said to me as he rubbed Sara's feet.

"Me, too." I stared at him. "How is the baby not zapping you?"

"Are you kidding?" Laughing, Sara took Nikolas's hand and placed it on her belly. "She absolutely adores her daddy."

I rolled my eyes. "I'm going to die from cuteness overload around you guys."

Nikolas arched his eyebrows at me, but I noticed he didn't remove his hand. He was so busted.

"How long will you be in Chicago?" he asked me.

"Trying to get rid of me already?"

He smiled. "You're welcome to stay as long as you want. Although, I'm surprised you chose now to visit with all that's going on back in Los Angeles."

I scoffed. "That city is practically swarming with Council investigators now, and you know they aren't going to let me anywhere near this one. They want me to stand on the sidelines like a good little girl. No thanks."

It was all true. I just left out the part about me bonding with the most infuriating warrior alive and then breaking the bond. Small details that they didn't need to know. Ever.

"Well, we have plenty for you to do here," he said. "You can take a few days to visit before you start."

"God, no." I made a face. "Put me to work, please."

The last thing I wanted was to hang around here doing nothing. I needed to be busy doing stuff that would occupy my mind and keep me from thinking about things I'd rather forget. Apparently, declaring your intention to break a bond didn't wipe all thoughts of the other person from your mind, an important fact that had been left out when I'd been taught about bonding.

Nikolas let out a deep chuckle. "Okay. You can start patrols tomorrow."

"So, this is a wrakk," Beth said a week later, as she and I walked toward a seemingly deserted red brick building. There were a handful of vehicles parked outside, and the only sounds came from the planes taking off and landing at the nearby airport.

"It doesn't look like much, but wait'll you see the inside." I smiled, remembering my first visit to a demon marketplace in San Francisco. I'd gone there with Chris on my first job, and we'd ended up in a standoff with eight Gulaks until Sara had shown up to even the odds. Good times.

Today's visit was not official business, however. We were here as a favor to Sara, who had been asked to help find a runaway teenage Mox demon from Detroit who had been spotted here. Sara couldn't come to the wrakk with her power acting up, so she'd asked us to come in her place.

I opened the door and entered the quiet building. Two steps inside the door, it was like someone had flipped a switch to turn on the sound, and I knew I'd passed through the demon wards that protected the building. The wards were meant to keep out non-demons, and they also muted all sounds from the place.

We walked down a short entranceway and into the wide marketplace area that was a maze of tiny shops and booths, selling everything from produce to clothes to medicines and housewares.

Some of the shops we passed had skewers of meat you couldn't have paid me enough to try. I was adventurous, but demons had a very different palate. I'd probably spew if I found out I was eating Lamprey, which some demons considered a delicacy.

The wrakk was alive with activity. Vendors called out their wares as demons of every shape and size walked by. Adults mingled and shopped while trying to keep an eye on the children running about.

Beth and I got more than a few curious stares as we made our way through the place because Mohiri didn't normally frequent wrakks.

A few years ago, those stares would have been wary, even hostile, but that was before we had started building relationships with the demon community, thanks to Sara. It amazed me how far we'd come in three years, and the changes had proven beneficial to us and the other demons. We'd gained a ton of new allies and informants, and they could come to us when they needed help, like in the case of runaway teenagers.

"This place is a lot bigger than I expected," Beth said after we'd covered at least half the market. "There are a ton of places a kid could hide in here."

"Maybe we should ask if anyone has seen her." I craned my neck to scan the area, and a tiny shop caught my eye. It had colorful fabrics decorating the open front, and racks of clothes were visible from where we stood. At the back of the narrow shop, a female Mox demon knelt on the floor, placing pins in the hem of a long dress worn by another of her kind.

I walked up to the store. "Excuse me."

The female on the floor stood and brushed off her long blue skirt. "May I help you?" she asked hesitantly.

"I hope so." I stepped inside the store. "I'm Jordan, and this is Beth."

The shopkeeper smiled timidly. "I am Terra. Were you looking to buy something?"

I shook my head. "We're actually looking for a missing Mox teenager, and we heard she might be around here."

Terra's brow furrowed, and I could see the suspicion in her eyes. Not that I blamed her. Mox demons were a docile race and were often preyed upon by stronger demons, so they weren't all that trusting of strangers. Luckily, I'd come prepared for this.

"We're here on behalf of *talael esledur*," I said in a low voice. All I needed was for the whole place to hear me.

My words got the desired reaction. Both Mox females gasped and placed their hands over their hearts, their faces lit with excitement. *Talael esledur* was the name given to Sara by the demon community after she'd made it her mission to save every demon she met. The good ones, anyway. In demon tongue, it meant "kind warrior," which was a pretty apt description of Sara.

"The girl's name is Lia, and her parents contacted a Vrell demon named Kelvan who works with Sara," Beth explained. "Kelvan tracked Lia from Detroit to Chicago and to this wrakk. Normally, Sara would come herself, but she is...working on a special project and couldn't get away."

Terra clasped her hands. "Of course. How can I help?"

"You can tell us if you've seen any new teenagers here this week," I said.

Mox children didn't normally go out on their own like human kids because of the dangers to them. Chances were, most Mox teenagers hanging around here were accompanied by an adult relative. A girl on her own would stand out.

Terra thought for a moment. "No, but I've barely left my shop this week except to go home. I can ask around for you."

Beth touched my shoulder. "I don't think that will be necessary."

I followed her gaze to a slight figure with long white hair emerging from between two stalls less than a hundred feet away. The girl glanced around furtively before she adjusted the backpack on her shoulder and started walking casually in our general direction. She kept her eyes down and her pace slow, clearly trying not to draw attention to herself.

I waited until Lia was abreast of Terra's shop to call softly to her. Her head jerked in our direction at the sound of her name, and fear filled her eyes. And then she ran.

I sprinted after her, keeping her in my sight as we weaved through the shops and stalls. Twice, I almost had her, but she was a nimble little thing, and she managed to swerve out of my reach each time.

She ducked under a cart full of vegetables, and I barely avoided knocking the whole thing over, leaving an angry vendor shouting in my wake. Instead of being annoyed, I grinned. I hadn't had this much fun on a chase in forever.

Up ahead, I saw a flash of blonde hair as Beth ran around the corner of a bakery shop to head us off. Lia let out a small cry of dismay and looked around frantically. Then she was gone, slipping into an impossibly narrow space between two stores in the center of the market where neither Beth nor I could follow. Shit!

I pointed, and Beth nodded. The two of us separated in an attempt to corner Lia again. I had to take the long way around the row of shops to get to the other side. By the time I reached the place she would have emerged from, she was nowhere in sight.

Hands on hips, I was scanning the area, trying to decide my next move when a girl screamed. I raced toward the sound, hoping she'd run into Beth and not something worse.

Definitely worse, I thought as I rounded a shop and found the struggling girl thrown over the shoulder of a tall, scaly, winged demon with a single horn in the middle of his forehead. I sighed. A visit to a wrakk wouldn't be complete without at least one Gulak to cause trouble.

The other demons in this part of the market stood back fearfully. Some of them wore angry expressions, but it was clear none of them was brave enough to go up against a bigger demon known for its brute strength. Gulaks were the thugs of the demon community, and they lived up to their name, running drugs and slaves and whatever else made them money.

"Let her go," I called as I strode toward them.

The Gulak looked me up and down, and his lizard-like lips curved into an ugly leer. "It must be my lucky day. You'll fetch a lot more than this puny thing."

"Funny, I was just thinking it was *my* lucky day. I hear Gulak hide suitcases are all the rage now."

He showed me his teeth. "You're gutsy for a human."

"And you're stupid for a…never mind."

I stopped ten feet away from him and reached behind me to unsheathe the short sword I wore under my coat. It was a smaller version of my favorite katana and custom made for me. Some women liked to accessorize with jewelry. I had a weapon for every outfit.

The Gulak blinked in surprise and backed up a step.

"We can do this one of two ways," I said evenly. "You can release the girl and walk out of here, or I take her from you and you leave in a body bag."

I hoped he was smart enough to go with the first option. I could take him, but I didn't want to risk the girl getting hurt.

The crowd parted, and two more Gulaks stepped out into the open. I should have known he'd brought friends with him. These guys didn't go anywhere alone.

"Or you can drop the weapon and come along quietly," said one of the newcomers as he walked over to stand beside the one holding the girl.

I fingered the hilt of my sword as I sized up the situation and wondered where Beth was. I could handle two Gulaks, but three might be messy.

The third Gulak laughed. "Got nothing to say now?"

I smiled. "I'm just thinking about that new luggage set I'm going to have made."

Someone in the crowd tittered, and the three Gulaks growled.

The Gulak with the girl bared his teeth menacingly at the bystanders. "Any one of you could be next. Remember that."

The place fell silent except for the sound of running feet. I looked past the Gulaks to Beth, who had stopped a few yards from them, holding what looked like a wooden staff.

"Sorry I'm late," she said to me.

I grinned. "You're just in time."

The Gulaks shifted nervously as they looked from me to Beth, not quite so sure of themselves now. That was the thing with bullies. They were all bluster when they faced a weaker person or they had backup. The moment they had to face a stronger opponent, they'd turn tail and run. The question now was would they give up the girl or try to run with her.

"What's it going to be?" I asked when they were quiet for a full minute. "No one has to get hurt here today if you give up the girl."

The three Gulaks exchanged looks, and the one holding the girl scowled. One of the others whispered something to him, but he shook his head and tightened his hold on her, making her cry out. This made the third Gulak whisper and gesture wildly at him. His response was to punch the guy in the face.

The wounded Gulak bellowed in pain as blood poured from his nose. With one hand trying to staunch the flow of blood, he cast a sour look in my direction and stomped off toward the exit.

Beth shot me a questioning look, and I nodded. If he wanted to leave peacefully, I wouldn't stop him. Besides, it made our job easier with one less opponent to fight.

I turned my attention back to the remaining two Gulaks, who were arguing in harsh whispers while keeping an eye on Beth and me. They seemed to come to some agreement because the one holding the girl pulled her off his shoulder and held her in front of him with an arm around her waist. His free hand grabbed the cutlass he wore at his hip, and he brandished it at me. I focused all my attention on him and the girl. Beth could more than hold her own against the other one.

"Stay back if you don't want the female to get hurt," he snarled.

"Using a child as a shield?" My lip curled in disgust, and I let my gaze drop to the front of his pants. "Are you sure you even have a pair in there? Maybe we should get you a skirt instead."

He shook with rage as my barb hit home. Gulak males were misogynistic to a fault. They saw females as weak, and they treated their own like possessions whose sole purpose was to bear their offspring. Questioning his manhood was an insult he couldn't ignore without losing face in front of his friend.

He threw the girl off to one side, where she landed on her hip with a cry of pain. There was no time to make sure she was okay because he rushed me with his sword raised.

Oh boy, he was pissed. I could see the blood lust in his reptilian eyes as I sidestepped his clumsy attack and hooked my blade beneath his to disarm him. His sword slid across the floor to disappear beneath one of the stalls.

He stumbled past me and righted himself, staring at his empty hand with a stunned expression. For a moment, the only sounds were the thwack of a staff hitting flesh somewhere behind me, followed by a grunt of pain.

Hushed whispers came from the crowd, and I saw some of their shocked faces. No doubt seeing someone take down a Gulak was a foreign sight for most of them. It irked me that they didn't stand up for themselves more. I got that they were smaller, but they didn't have to be weaker. Anyone could learn to fight. ·

The Gulak bellowed and lumbered toward me with all the grace of a drunken sailor.

I raised my sword to meet his attack when I caught sight of two Vrell boys pushing their way to the front of the crowd, their eyes shining with awe. I guessed them to be in their early teens, around the same age I'd been when I started my formal training.

Dodging the attack, I ran over to the boys and laid my sword on the floor at their feet. "Keep this for me, will you? Just don't touch it."

"But...how will you fight the Gulak?" one of them stammered.

I winked at him. "Watch."

I turned back to the Gulak, who was already coming at me again. This time, he held a knife he must have had tucked inside his clothes. He grinned triumphantly when he saw I no longer had my sword.

I waited until the last second and ducked out of his reach. He spun and tried again and again, and each time, I evaded his attacks.

"Lesson one in how to fight a bully is try not to get hit," I said to the wide-eyed boys after the Gulak's fourth failed attempt to reach me. "Most bullies, like this guy, are stronger than you, so a good blow from them could be all it takes to defeat you."

The Gulak came at me again. He was persistent, I'd give him that, even if he was a terrible fighter. This time, my foot hooked his as he went past, and he flailed wildly trying to stay upright.

I smiled at the boys. "Lesson two. You're smaller and faster, so make him chase you. He'll tire himself out eventually."

"Gonna gut you, bitch," the Gulak panted.

I wagged a finger at him. "Language. There are children present."

A few people laughed, which only made his face twist in fury. But it was clear to everyone that he was in no shape to follow up with his threats.

"Lesson three," I said loudly enough for all to hear. "Words are just words. They're meant to frighten and intimidate, but they can't hurt you."

I moved in, going on the attack for the first time. My foot connected with his knee, and he howled in pain. Not letting him recover, I came around and wrenched the knife from his slack grip, tossing it on the floor beside my sword.

I grinned at the boys, who looked more excited than afraid now. "Ready for lesson four?"

Their heads bobbed in unison.

"Lesson four," I called as I circled the Gulak, who was limping now. "Fight dirty and make your hits count. You punch a Gulak in the chest and all you'll get for your trouble is a broken hand. A good kick to the knee is much more effective as you can see. A throat punch works, too, if you can get one in. But if you really want to bring the pain..."

I struck fast, my booted foot catching him right between the legs. He let out a high-pitched whine and sank to the floor, where he lay on his side with his hands cradling his groin.

"Go straight for the jewels." My gaze swept the gawking crowd. "Any questions?"

The boys' hands shot up, and I was surprised to see a few adults raise theirs as well. I nodded at a Mox male who looked to be in his thirties.

"You make it look easy, but you're a trained warrior." He waved a hand at the Gulak. "How can one of us hope to defeat the likes of him?"

"Anyone can learn to fight," I told him. "Look at humans. They take martial arts or self-defense lessons all the time to learn how to fight bigger and stronger opponents."

"But we cannot walk into one of those places for lessons," he said.

"That's true." I turned my head to look at Beth, who stood over the other defeated Gulak. He was facedown but still breathing. She smiled and gave me a thumbs-up.

I faced the Mox demon again. "What you need is to have your own self-defense classes."

He shook his head. "Most of us here are quiet people who abhor violence. We know nothing of fighting or self-defense."

I bent to pick up my sword. "And that's why Gulaks will always prey on you. They know you won't fight back."

"I-I want to fight back," one of the Vrell boys declared as I straightened.

"I do, too," his friend said earnestly. "Will you teach us?"

His question gave me pause. When I'd suggested they learn to fight, I'd assumed there had to be someone among them who could teach them. I hadn't even considered me taking on that role. I'd just been having fun at the Gulak's expense and making an example of him. I'd be a terrible teacher.

"I'm only in Chicago for a short visit," I told them, although that wasn't exactly true. As long as Hamid was in Los Angeles, I couldn't go back there. Chicago was as good a place as any to spend my self-imposed exile.

"Oh," said one of the boys as their faces fell.

The Gulak groaned behind me and tried to stand. I walked over and put a foot on his back to keep him down until I decided what to do with him. I didn't want to kill him in front of children, but if I let him go, he'd most likely come back another day to cause more trouble.

I shot Beth a questioning look, and she shrugged to let me know she was leaving the decision to me. She'd probably let them go if it was up to her.

I released the Gulak and leaned over him. "Looks like this is your lucky day. I'm going to let you live. You and your pal have exactly thirty seconds to clear out of here before I change my mind."

He muttered something I couldn't make out and stood on wobbly legs. Still holding his injured groin, he hobbled over to his friend, who was slowly getting to his feet. They were a sorry-looking pair as they limped away.

Beth walked over to me, grinning. "Not a bad day's work. We found our girl and kicked some Gulak ass."

The girl. I'd almost forgotten our main reason for coming to the wrakk, and I looked around now for Lia. She was standing beside Terra, who had a protective arm around the girl's shoulders.

"Did he hurt you, Lia?" I asked the girl, who looked down timidly as I approached them.

She shook her head without looking up. "I am okay."

"You don't have to be afraid. You're safe with us," I told her. "But I hope you see how dangerous it is for a girl your age on the streets."

"Yes." She sniffled. "I-I don't like it here."

I thought back to the weeks I'd lived on the streets when I was even younger than Lia. I remembered the gnawing hunger and the cold, the loneliness even when I was around other kids, and the constant fear of being attacked for what little I had. I'd chosen that life because it was safer than my foster home. But I would have given anything for a loving family who cared enough to search for me. My foster mother probably hadn't even reported me missing just so she could keep collecting the checks.

"Are you ready to go home?" Beth asked kindly.

Lia wiped her eyes and lifted her head. "I defied my parents, and they must hate me now."

"It was your parents who asked for our help to find you," I said. "I'm reasonably certain they wouldn't do that if they hated you."

Hope filled her eyes. "Really?"

"Yes." I looked at Terra as I pulled out my phone. "Would it be okay if Lia stays with you until her parents get here?"

Terra hugged the girl to her side. "Of course."

"Thank you." I walked a few feet away and called Sara to let her know we'd found her runaway. I left out the part about the Gulaks because it would be more fun if Beth and I shared that story in person.

"Oh, that's such a relief," Sara said. "Lia's parents left to drive to Chicago as soon as Kelvan told them he found Lia. They should be there in an hour or so."

Hanging up, I relayed that information to Lia and Terra. Smiling tearfully,

Lia thanked us for saving her from the Gulaks before letting Terra lead her away.

Beth smiled at me. "This was fun. I missed doing stuff like this with you."

"Me too. The guys are cool, but I need my girl time, too."

"Mason still hates going to night clubs?" she asked with a knowing grin.

I scoffed. "You'd think I was dragging him to the dentist. Not that we've ever been to one, but you know what I mean."

She laughed. "I tell you what. There's a new night club here that opened a month ago. I've been meaning to get Chris to go with me. Why don't we check it out tomorrow night?"

"It's a date. I left most of my clothes in L.A. though, so you'll have to go shopping with me tomorrow. I'm in the mood for something slinky."

"Ow. Stop twisting my arm," she said with a pretend grimace. "And I know just the place."

"Perfect."

She glanced around. "Do you think we should stay here until Lia's parents arrive?"

"Wouldn't hurt to hang out for a while," I said.

Beth tilted her head toward the two Vrell boys who were still standing by my sword. "I think you made some fans today. Maybe you can teach them a few moves while we wait."

I looked from the boys to her and let out a breath. "Only if you agree to be my assistant."

"I'd love to." She grinned wickedly. "Let's go teach these boys how to kick some ass."

7

Approaching the command center, I clicked the new fob on my keychain that activated one of the bay doors. As soon as the door was high enough, Beth and I rode inside and parked our bikes. I hit the button, making the door come down again.

I pulled off my helmet and smoothed down my hair, trying to figure out why I suddenly felt out of sorts again. In addition to occasional bouts of light-headedness, I'd also started getting these weird mood swings in increasing frequency. One minute I was fine, and the next I was cranky and irritable. I hoped I didn't have to deal with these until the bond completely dissolved.

"It was really nice of you to offer to give self-defense lessons at the wrakk," Beth said as she dismounted her Harley. "Lem and Jal already idolize you, and I think some of the adults do, too."

I shrugged. "It was more fun than I expected it to be, and I figure I might as well do some good as long as I'm here."

"And how long do you plan to be here?" she asked for the umpteenth time.

"Long enough for you to get sick of me."

"Never!"

I laughed, and we started toward the kitchen, where we were most likely to find Sara. The door to the control room opened, and Nikolas stepped out followed by Chris.

Suddenly, my Mori started to go haywire.

A second later, I found out what was wrong with my Mori when a third person came into view. I stopped walking abruptly as my stomach clenched. "What the hell is *he* doing here?"

Beth's gaze followed mine, and it took her all of two seconds to figure out who our visitor was. "Oh my, is that Hamid?" she asked in a hushed voice.

I think I answered her. My mind was racing, and I thought about hopping on my bike and getting the hell out of there. But I didn't move as Hamid strode toward me with long purposeful strides.

I glared to let him know exactly what I thought of him showing up here. Had I not made it clear enough that I wanted nothing more to do with him? He didn't want the bond either, so what was he thinking coming here without warning me? He had to know that distance was essential to dissolve this thing.

"What are you doing here, Hamid?" I bit out. "Shouldn't you be in Los Angeles heading up the investigation?"

"You and I need to talk," he said without his usual gruffness.

"I'm pretty sure we said all we needed to say before I left." I swallowed dryly. This non-scowling side of him was throwing me off kilter. It didn't help that my Mori was practically doing flips at having him there.

"There's been a new development."

I frowned. "What does that have to do with me?"

"I will explain when we talk." He waved at the small exit door. "We can do it outside or in the office."

"What?" I stared at him as heat suffused me.

"Where would you prefer to talk?" he asked, and there was no mistaking the gleam of amusement in his eyes.

"Outside." I wanted to take no chances of my friends overhearing a word of this conversation.

I spun on my heel and walked briskly to the door, wanting to get this over with. I'd been having such a good day. Leave it to Hamid to ruin it for me.

I exited the building and walked a dozen paces away from the door before I turned to face Hamid, who had followed me. He was watching me silently with an almost apologetic look in his eyes. My stomach knotted with apprehension. Hamid never apologized, especially to me.

"Alright, spit it out. What is so important that you had to come here to talk to me?"

He walked toward me, stopping a few feet away. His nearness was unsettling, but I stood my ground, not wanting to reveal that he had any effect on me. There was no denying the physical attraction I had for him, which had only intensified with the bond. But it was the warmth in my chest that really threw me. There was no way I was happy to see him. Not unless hell had frozen over and no one had bothered to tell me.

"Orias has been doing more tests on me as part of his study of the demon's magic," Hamid said. "Last night, he made a discovery that complicates things."

"If you mean the magic isn't going away like he said it would, I already know that." Sara had been checking daily to see if the magic was still there, and according to her, it hadn't faded at all since I arrived.

"It's more than that." He exhaled slowly, looking almost reluctant to continue. "The magic he detected isn't remnants of the two spells. According to Orias, when you and I got caught in the crossfire, we became a part of the new spell that sealed the tear in the barrier."

Alarm coursed through me. "What the hell does that mean?"

"Orias confessed he didn't know exactly how he managed to close the barrier, which was why he was so keen to study the magic. He believes it might have been the addition of a third element that made the spell work."

"What third element?" I asked, more confused than ever.

"Us."

I narrowed my eyes at him. "That's ridiculous. What's so special about us? We have no magical ability."

For the first time since I'd met him, Hamid actually looked uncomfortable. "Our Mori bonded as the spells hit us, and Orias thinks the bond somehow strengthened the spell."

"What? No," I croaked in denial. "How would he even know about that?"

Hamid stuck his hands in his jeans pockets. "I told him."

"Why would you do that?"

"Orias said the combined magics should have killed us. He wanted to know every detail of what happened, and I felt that was too important to leave out."

I started pacing. "Lovely. So, what happens now? Will the spell wear off on its own, or does Orias have to take it off us?"

The thought of going back to Los Angeles with Hamid, even for a day, did not sit well with me. Just by coming here, he'd undone a week's progress in breaking the bond, and I was going to have to start all over again. Great.

He didn't answer me, and I stopped pacing to look at him. My stomach pitched when I saw him watching me with an expression of unease. "Hamid?"

"The spell cannot be broken," he said.

I waved a hand dismissively. "Maybe not by Orias, but Sara could undo it without batting an eye. In fact, let's go ask her."

"No." He grabbed my wrist as I walked past him toward the door. His next words hit me like a punch in the gut. "If the spell is broken, the hole in the barrier could reopen."

I stumbled. "W-what?"

Hamid loosened his grip but didn't release me. "The new spell sealed the barrier, but we don't know what damage was done before Orias was able to stop the breach. He believes that breaking the spell might reopen the barrier and possibly destabilize it."

I stared at him as I tried to wrap my head around what he was saying. "What happens to the spell when we break the bond?"

He glanced away, and when his gaze returned to me, it felt as though all the oxygen had been sucked out of my lungs. "We can't break the bond."

Roaring filled my ears, and I swayed on my feet, dimly aware of him taking hold of my other arm to steady me. I heard him speaking, but it came from a long way off. Everything was drowned out by the five words on repeat in my head.

We can't break the bond.

We can't break the bond.

"Jordan."

I jolted as Hamid's sharp tone cut through the fog around my mind. I looked up to see him watching me with worried blue eyes. The last thing I needed from him was kindness or concern. I wanted to see the arrogant, brooding warrior who never spoke to me unless it was absolutely necessary.

I pulled out of his hold and put several feet of space between us. "What?"

"I understand why you're upset," he said calmly.

"I don't think *upset* is the right word for how I feel. And why don't you look upset about it?"

His expression did not change. "I've had half a day longer than you to accept it."

I crossed my arms. "If you think I'm going to accept this, you're delusional. I'm not taking a mate...*ever*."

I had plans for my future, and they did not include a male breathing down my neck and cramping my style. I had nothing but respect for Nikolas and Chris, but I'd witnessed their overprotectiveness for Sara and Beth enough to know I didn't want that for me. Hamid didn't like me or want the bond, but eventually it would start to rule his emotions and turn him into a testosterone-fueled, raging pain in my ass. Hell no.

Fury replaced my shock, and I closed the distance between us to poke him hard in the chest. "This is all your fault! If you hadn't rushed at me like some bloody Neanderthal, we wouldn't be in this mess. There'd be no bond and no spell tying us together."

Hamid frowned and captured the hand jabbing him. "You are being irrational."

"I think I'm entitled to be irrational," I yelled at him.

If Orias's spell hadn't worked, who knows what would have happened to the barrier. Millions of lives might have been at risk. I knew this, but the logical side of my brain was at war with the emotional side, and right now my emotions were winning.

"The Council is already assembling a team of scholars and magic users to study the magic," Hamid said as if I hadn't just gone off on him. "They will work together to try to create a stronger spell to replace this one."

"Oh." I took a deep breath, almost giddy with relief. We had some brilliant minds among our scholars, and Orias wasn't the only powerful warlock in the world. Between them all, they should be able to figure out a solution to this.

"We will have to be patient and work together until this is resolved." His warm hand squeezed mine, and my Mori practically swooned.

I yanked my hand from his. Why did he keep touching me? It was hard enough to think straight without him making my demon go crazy.

"Patience is not one of my virtues," I replied dryly as I went back to pacing. I needed to do something to work off this nervous energy. "And we don't need to work together or even see each other. We just have to agree not to break the bond...for now."

Hamid raked a hand through his hair. I caught myself staring and remembering how much I'd wanted to run my fingers through that hair when I used to lust after him. Disgusted with myself, I tore my gaze away and waited for him to speak.

"There is another reason why I came to see you," he said as if he was reluctant to share it. I was about to ask him what could be worse than the news he'd already given me, when he said, "Orias consulted with some of his colleagues. They are concerned that due to the nature of our bond, the spell could weaken the longer we are separated."

I fought to keep my anger in check. "You have got to be kidding me. You don't honestly expect us to live and work together?"

"We are warriors. We will do what is required of us," he stated like it was as simple as that.

"We're also *bonded*," I said through clenched teeth. "You know as well as I do that the more time we spend together, the more the bond will grow. I've seen enough bonded couples to know how that ends."

His calm mask slipped, and for several seconds, all I could see was the frustration and pain in his eyes. It hit me then that I was making this all about me, but it couldn't be any easier for him. Maybe even worse because males were always affected more deeply by the bond. He was going to start feeling things for someone he didn't want, and there was nothing he could do to stop it. And when we finally broke the bond, he would suffer the most.

Another thought struck me. What if there was someone else, some other female he'd already given his heart to? He'd never talked about his personal life to me, but even he couldn't work all the time.

Most of the anger drained out of me. "Can I ask you something?"

"Yes."

I licked my suddenly dry lips. "Is this bond going to hurt someone in your life?"

His brows drew together until understanding dawned in his eyes. "There is no one else."

"At least, there's that," I said, relieved no one else would be hurt by this.

Neither of us spoke for a long moment, and then he asked, "And you?"

I let out a short laugh. "God, no. I like to have my fun, but I usually never see them again."

Hamid's nostrils flared, and I wondered what I'd said to annoy him this time. I thought back over my last words, and it took a few seconds for realization to set in. Bonded males didn't like to hear about their females with another male. His female. Ugh. Just thinking it made me want to run as far and as fast away from him as possible. At the same time, a tiny, dangerous part of me wanted to be his, for him to be the only male who touched me.

"Okay, then," I said in a rush. "If we're going to do this, we need to set some ground rules."

"Ground rules?"

I took a deep breath. "Yes. We can't break the bond, but we can take measures to keep it from growing too quickly. Maybe at the end of this, we'll both come out of it with our sanity intact."

He folded his arms across his chest. "I'm listening."

Encouraged by his willingness to get on board with this, I continued. "We might have to be near each other, but we don't have to spend every second of the day together. I think we should limit our time together as much as possible."

"What else?"

"Absolutely *no* touching, for any reason whatsoever." I backed up a step to make my point.

There was a moment of silence before he said, "No touching, unless I need to save your life."

I shot him a dark look. "In case you're forgetting, that's how we got here in the first place. And who says *I* won't be the one doing the saving?"

His mouth curved into the tiniest of smiles. It was so out of character for him that all I could do was stare.

"Is that everything?"

His question brought me back to my senses. "There's one more thing. None of our mutual friends know about the bond, and I want to keep it that way."

"How will that help?" he asked.

"It will help me. People get weird around bonded pairs, and I don't want the looks or the questions. This is between you and me. And the Council," I added sourly.

Hamid nodded. "As you wish."

I eyed him suspiciously. He was being awfully agreeable.

He stared back. "Is something wrong?"

I pointed at him. "You're being too nice to me. That has to stop."

This time he did more than smile. He let out a deep chuckle that made my stomach flutter and my nether regions tighten.

"Stop that!" I threw up my hands and spun away, shaken by my body's reaction to him. If he could affect me like this now, what was it going to be like in a few weeks or a month?

I took a steadying breath. They would figure out how to replace the spell before then. I just had to keep telling myself that.

"I shouldn't be nice to you?" Hamid asked, amusement evident in his voice.

I turned to glower at him. "No. Back in L.A., you were cold and patronizing toward me. If you start acting differently, people are going to figure out something is up with us."

"I see. I promise I will do my best to treat you with cold indifference." He wiped the smile from his face, but he couldn't hide the sparkle of laughter in his eyes.

My jaw clenched. I didn't know which Hamid annoyed me more: the arrogant one or the one before me now. It was hard to believe they were the same person.

Hamid's tone became more businesslike. "If we are finished discussing your ground rules, we should inform your friends that you will be returning to California with me."

I let out a resigned sigh. I wasn't ready to leave Sara and Beth, but

Hamid's place was in Los Angeles, and I had to go where he went. His investigation was bigger than us and our problems.

"Let's get this over with," I said flatly, starting toward the door.

"I'm sorry you have to leave your friends," Hamid said, and I could hear the sincerity in his voice.

I opened the door. "It's like you said. We're warriors, and we do what's required of us."

I felt him come up behind me. He reached for the heavy door to hold it open for me, but he made sure our bodies didn't touch. Not that it mattered. His nearness and his scent were enough to make my skin tingle with awareness of him.

Assuming the annoyed expression I usually wore around Hamid, I entered the building. I wasn't surprised to see Sara and Beth lingering outside the living area, waiting for our return.

Hamid headed for the control room, most likely to talk to Nikolas and Chris, and I walked toward my friends.

"What's wrong?" Sara asked before I'd even reached them.

I gave her a rueful smile. "Looks like I'm going to have to cut my visit short."

Beth reacted first. "No! Why?"

I waved at the door to the living area. "Let's go sit, and I'll explain it to you."

Once the three of us were comfortably seated, I told them what Hamid had said about the two of us being a part of the spell that had closed the barrier.

I left out the part about the bond for obvious reasons. I felt a twinge of guilt over my lie of omission, but I knew they wouldn't hold it against me. Bonding was intimate and personal, and they understood that better than anyone. Plus, I was a private person when it came to certain aspects of my life. I joked around about men and sex, but I wasn't a kiss-and-tell kind of person. Not that there would be any kissing going on here.

"So, you have to go wherever he goes?" Sara asked when I finished.

I made a face. "You make it sound like we'll be joined at the hip. We have to be in the same house, but if I'm lucky, I won't have to see much of him."

Beth made a little swooning sound. "It's like something out of a romance novel. Two people who secretly want each other are forced to spend time together, and they fall madly in love."

"Whoa." I held up a hand. "You need to lay off watching the Hallmark channel. There is nothing even remotely romantic about this situation."

Beth snickered and leaned in closer to Sara. "Did you notice she didn't deny they secretly want each other?"

Sara laughed, watching me the whole time. "I did."

"Ugh!" I threw a small pillow at them. "To think I was going to miss you two."

Their smiles fell, and Sara said, "Do you have to leave tonight?"

"Hamid didn't say. I guess I should ask him."

Hamid's voice came from the doorway. "Ask me what?"

I looked over to see him enter the room with Nikolas and Chris.

"Whether or not we're leaving tonight," I said.

He looked like he was about to say yes, but he surprised me by shaking his head. "Tomorrow morning."

Beth smiled at me. "At least we have you for one more night. But it's too bad we never got to go shopping for that slinky new dress you wanted."

I lifted a shoulder. "I'll go shopping when I get back and buy something special for when I come to visit again. Hopefully, that will be soon."

I could feel Hamid's gaze on me, but I avoided it. I didn't need to look at him to know he was also hopeful this nightmare would be over soon and he'd be free of me. I just had to keep reminding myself he wasn't the bad guy here. But I wondered if he would have jumped in to save me if he'd known we'd end up bonded and in this predicament.

Who was I kidding? With his arrogance and sense of duty, he would have considered it a worthy sacrifice and all in a day's work.

"The boys are going to be so disappointed that you can't continue their lessons," Beth said. "They had a blast with you today."

"Boys?" Chris asked.

"Two Vrell teenagers we met at the wrakk. I agreed to give them self-defense lessons." I smiled at the memory of the boys' enthusiasm as I'd taught them a few simple moves today. I was surprised by how much I enjoyed working with them, and I was a little bummed I had to give it up.

Chris laughed. "You gave self-defense lessons to demon kids? How did that come about?"

"Beth and I gave some Gulaks a little beatdown and sent them on their way, and I –"

"Gulaks?" Chris's gaze shot to Beth.

She shrugged it off. "It was nothing. They snatched the Mox girl we went there to find, and we got her back." Her eyes met mine, and she grinned as she told them about my self-defense demonstration with the Gulak.

"You laid down your weapon to fight Gulaks unarmed?" Hamid asked with a hard edge to his voice.

"One Gulak," I corrected him. "And Sara fights better than he did."

"Hey." Sara gave me a look of indignance.

I smirked at her. "Sorry, girl, but I've seen you training. I'm amazed Nikolas still has all his limbs."

Everyone laughed, everyone but Hamid. It was a relief seeing him back to his usual surly self, and some of the tension from our talk left me.

"Anyway, after the Gulaks left, the boys asked if I would help them learn to defend themselves. It's not like they have someone else to teach them, so I agreed to give them lessons as long as I was in Chicago."

Sara pressed her hands to her chest. "That was so sweet of you."

"I feel bad that I'm going to let them down." I looked at Beth. "Before I leave tomorrow, I'll drop by the wrakk to tell them."

"I can continue the lessons for you," she said. "Until you come back."

"Thanks." I leaned back into the cushion with a sigh. Staring at the skylight above me, I sent up a silent prayer that I'd be able to come back very soon.

The next day, Beth and I went to the wrakk to tell the people there that I had to leave town but that Beth would continue the lessons for anyone who wanted them. The two boys were disappointed at first, but after Beth did a demonstration with a staff, they quickly warmed up to the idea of her as their instructor.

We got back to the command center ten minutes before Nikolas and Chris were supposed to drive Hamid and me to the airport. But when we entered the building, there was no sign of any of them. We found Sara in the state-of-the-art control room that could probably rival NASA's.

"They left half an hour ago to drive to Detroit to check out some suspicious activity," she said when I asked where they were.

"Suspicious like what happened in L.A.?" I asked. Detroit was almost five hours away, so it had to be important for Hamid to drive there and delay our flight.

She stood and stretched her back. "All I know is it has something to do with a summoning. Hamid said to tell you that you guys would be staying another day."

I frowned. Hamid had my phone number. Would it kill him to call and tell me this himself? Then I remembered he was the last person I wanted calling me.

"We get you for another night." Beth gave me a one-armed hug. She looked from me to Sara. "Who's up for lunch and shopping?"

Sara declined in favor of a nap, so Beth and I spent the afternoon shopping. When we returned four hours later, Sara informed us Nikolas had called to tell her they'd be late getting back that night. He'd also let her know it had been a false alarm. The Detroit team had overreacted when they found the scene of a failed summoning, and they'd called it in. Everyone was a little tense these days, not that I could blame them with all the craziness going on in L.A.

Sara, Beth, and I enjoyed a pleasant dinner together, followed by a few hours of quality girl time. At ten, Sara yawned and bid us good night. She could barely stay up past that these days. Mohiri females didn't get tired this early in their pregnancies, but apparently, growing a Fae-Mohiri baby was exhausting.

As soon as Sara was gone, I stood and looked at Beth. "I need to get out of here and ride for a while. Feel like doing a patrol with me?"

"Sure."

The two of us patrolled for hours, but it was a quiet night and we didn't see anything suspicious. I was so used to Los Angeles where you couldn't travel five blocks without coming across some vampire or demon up to no good. For all its size, Chicago didn't have the activity of places like New York City or Los Angeles.

It was just after 1:00 a.m. when Chris called Beth to let her know they were back. Since there was nothing going on out here, we headed to the command center.

We pulled into the parking bay, and it was like déjà vu when I saw Hamid striding toward us. Only this time, he looked angry and I was at a loss as to why.

"You went out without a team," he said in a harsh tone that had my hackles rising.

I took my time getting off the bike and setting my helmet on the seat. "We've been over this before. We don't patrol in full teams."

He stopped a few feet from me. "You do now."

"Excuse me?" I said slowly.

Beth cleared her throat. "Um, I'll just leave you two to talk." She shot me an apologetic look before she hurried away.

I turned back to Hamid and spoke with as much civility as I could muster. "Please, explain."

He glanced around then pointed at the open gym door. "Let's talk in there."

"You expecting this to come to blows?" I asked when we had entered the room.

He shut the door. "No, but I believe this room is soundproof."

My mouth fell open. Did Hamid just make a joke? I stared at him, but his face gave nothing away.

"I'm adding a new ground rule," I said when he faced me. "No acting like an overbearing bonded male, and definitely no bossing me around."

He leaned against the door. "This has nothing to do with the bond, except for its connection to Orias's spell. If anything happens to one of us, the bond will break and the spell could fail. That is why we must minimize risks."

"Wait. If that were true, the Council would have whisked us away to some safe location." Not that I would have stayed there for long.

He didn't answer right away. I didn't like it when he was slow to respond. Turned out I was right to be wary.

"Most of the Council members want to send us to a high-security facility," he said.

I sank down on a weight bench. I'd go crazy confined to a stronghold for weeks or even months on end. Not to mention the little problem of being in close proximity to Hamid for that long. At least out here I could get away from him for a few hours at a time.

"I can't do it," I said, feeling my freedom slip away.

"Tristan argued against it. He said you'd refuse to stay there unless they locked you up, and he would not do that to you."

Hope flared in me. "And the Council listened to him?" *Please, please, say yes.*

Hamid sat on a metal bench near the door. "Not until I convinced them I could keep you safe."

I gaped at him. "You?"

"I have no wish to be confined to a facility any more than you do." He rubbed his short beard. "We need all our best people on this investigation, and where I go, you go."

"I get that, but how exactly do you plan to keep me safe?" If he mentioned day patrols again, we were going to find out how sound proof this room was.

"By taking some extra precautions and having you agree to a few conditions," he said.

Indignance filled me. "Why am I the only one who has conditions?"

"I'm not the one with a reputation for being reckless and having a problem with authority." His eyes held mine as if challenging me to disagree. Which of course, I did.

"I don't have a problem with authority. I just don't like the Council always being up in my business."

He wore a wry smile. "They said you'd say that. You've made something of a name for yourself in your short career."

"Really? What's that?" I asked even though I was pretty sure I already knew the answer.

"The warriors in Los Angeles call you *Hellion*. A fitting name from what I've seen."

I held his mocking gaze without blinking. "I will take that as a compliment."

"Which is why I am setting out terms you must agree to." He was back to being serious again. "The first is that you go where I go, which we have already agreed upon. The second is that you no longer go off alone while on a job, and no patrolling without a full team. You also agree to wear a tracker whenever you go out, day or night."

I pressed my lips together. Those terms would definitely cramp my style, but I could live with them if it meant keeping my freedom. It wasn't like I had much choice in the matter. I nodded tersely. "Okay."

"The Council will be monitoring the situation closely. If they think we are not doing enough to keep you safe, they will send a security detail for us."

My lips curled in disdain. "Bodyguards?"

"I don't like it either, but it'll be that or protective custody. It's up to us to make sure it does not come to that."

I lowered my head into my hands and let out a groan of frustration. My life was turning into a three-ring circus. If I ended up with bodyguards, Brock and Mason would never let me live it down.

"Kill me now," I mumbled into my hands.

Hamid coughed, and it sounded suspiciously like a laugh. I jerked my head up to glare at him, but he wore no trace of a smile.

I narrowed my eyes. "Why am I just hearing this now? You didn't mention any of this yesterday."

"You were distressed by the news about the bond and the spell, and I didn't want to upset you further," he replied. "I was going to wait until we got back to Los Angeles to tell you the rest."

"I wasn't distressed. I was angry." His choice of words made me sound like a helpless little girl. "From now on, I'd prefer if you didn't hold anything back to protect my feelings. I don't like being kept in the dark about things that concern me."

"I will try to remember that," he said.

"Good." I stood wearily. I was normally a ball of energy, but my body suddenly felt like it was dragging. I knew it was an emotional drain, not a physical one, but that didn't make me any less tired.

Hamid opened the door for me, and as I passed him, he laid a large hand on my shoulder. "I am sorry for all of this."

"Yeah, me too." I shrugged off his hand. "Rule number two, no touching."

"I will write down your rules so I don't forget them," he said, and I could have sworn I heard a smile in his voice.

Too tired to stop and glare at him, I called over my shoulder, "You do that."

8

I shifted in my seat in the back of the private jet, wondering why it was taking so long for us to take off. When we got here an hour ago, I'd boarded the plane, leaving Hamid speaking to someone on the phone. Based on the few sentences I'd heard as I walked away from him, he was talking to the Council. I had no idea how he was able to deal with them on a daily basis, but he chose to work with them.

My phone vibrated with a text from Sara. **Our house is yours if you need some extra space.** It was followed by a heart emoticon.

I frowned at the odd message and started to type a reply when I heard someone enter the plane. Looking up, I saw Hamid walking toward me, his mouth set in a hard line.

He stopped and rested his hands on the seat on either side of him. "There's been a change in plans. We are going to Westhorne."

"What? Why?" I fought to keep the panic out of my voice. Had the Council changed their minds and decided to send us to a secure location? Westhorne was well fortified, and the whole valley was protected by Fae wards, so it made sense to send us there. It was the place I considered home, but even Westhorne would slowly suffocate me after a while.

The slight softening of his face told me I hadn't been successful in hiding my fear. "We'll be there a week, two at the most. The Council's team of scholars and magic users is meeting at Westhorne, and they want us there so they can interview us and run some tests."

My shoulders dropped in relief, making me realize how tense I was. "Wouldn't it be better to do that in L.A.?"

"Orias and two of his peers have already examined the summoning sites and say there is nothing more to learn from them. The team wants to focus on the spell and our part in it. Westhorne is secure and large enough to accommodate all of us."

Hamid's expression told me he didn't like this any more than I did, and I found that oddly comforting. I hated the thought of spending a week or two being studied by a bunch of warlocks, but if there was a chance of them freeing me from the spell, I'd do it without argument.

I let out a heavy sigh. "When do we leave?"

"In a few minutes." He turned and went to the cockpit, I assumed to let the pilot know about our new destination.

The flight to Boise was uneventful. Hamid sat in the front row and spent most of the trip on the phone. I couldn't hear his conversation, just the low rumble of his voice. I alternated between texting with Sara and Beth and staring out the window at nothing.

A few weeks ago, I'd been living it up in Los Angeles and my only worry had been how to get out of doing field reports. How had my life gone from that to this mess so fast?

When we taxied into our private hangar at the Boise airport, I wasn't surprised to see my favorite Irish twins waiting for us beside a black Escalade. But even Seamus's and Niall's playful grins couldn't bring me out of my funk. My mood got even darker when Hamid informed me I couldn't ride my motorcycle to Westhorne.

"Why the hell not?" I'd just spent hours on a small jet with him. Was it too much to ask that I have a few minutes to myself?

"Because I don't have a motorcycle here and you are not to travel alone," he said patiently as if he were speaking to a child.

I threw up my arms. "Oh, for fuck's sake. It's barely an hour's drive, and I'll even stay in sight of the SUV the whole time."

He gave a stubborn shake of his head. "Not tonight."

I growled in frustration, and Niall stepped forward. "Why don't you ride together? Hamid's big, but if you squeeze, you should fit."

Seamus flashed me a suggestive smirk from behind his twin, and I was mortified to feel heat creep into my cheeks. I was not a blusher and it took a lot to embarrass me, but apparently, being bonded changed all the rules. Just the thought of being pressed against Hamid's body made my skin feel flushed despite the cool evening air.

"Forget it." I avoided looking at Hamid as I marched to the SUV and threw my duffle bag in the cargo area. Without another word, I opened the back door and got in.

No one said much during the drive. Seamus and Niall tried to strike up a conversation, but it was soon apparent that neither Hamid nor I was in the mood to talk. After a while, the brothers fell silent. I was positive I heard them both exhale in relief when we passed through the tall iron gates of Westhorne. Not that I could blame them. Hamid and I weren't exactly fun to be around today.

I smiled for the first time that day when we pulled up to the front door of the main building and I saw Tristan standing on the steps. He came down to the SUV and hugged me as soon as I exited the vehicle.

"It's good to have you home, Jordan, although I wish it was under different circumstances," he said when he released me.

"You and me both." I attempted a smile, but it came off as more of a grimace.

The look Tristan gave me was so full of kindness that my chest squeezed painfully. There were few people I looked up to more than the leader of Westhorne, and he had a way of making you feel like he could handle any problem. I knew he couldn't fix mine, but just being near him made me more hopeful for a happy outcome.

He held out a hand to Hamid, who had walked around the car to join us. "Hamid, welcome to Westhorne."

Hamid clasped his hand, and the smile he gave Tristan spoke volumes of his regard for the other warrior. "It's good to see you again. Have the others arrived?"

"All but one of them. She'll get here later tonight." He led us into the main hallway. "The rest of the team is eager to meet with you, but I told them it can wait until tomorrow."

"Great," I said without an ounce of enthusiasm.

Tristan smiled. "You missed dinner, but I can have the kitchen prepare something for you."

"That would be great. Thanks." I glanced toward the stairs that led to the upper floors of the north wing. "Is my old room still available?"

He looked surprised by my question. "This is your home, and the room is yours until you say otherwise."

Again with the tightness in my chest. I resisted the urge to rub at it. This bloody bond was turning me into a sentimental fool.

Tristan turned to Hamid. "I had one of the rooms in the south wing prepared for you."

"Thank you," Hamid said, but his gaze was on me. Was he waiting for me to say something?

I hoisted my duffle bag onto my shoulder. "I'm sure you two have a lot to talk about. If you don't mind, I'm going to head up to my room. I have a feeling tomorrow is going to be a long day."

Tristan nodded. "I'll have some food sent up to you shortly, and we'll talk more tomorrow."

Wishing them both a good night, I jogged up the stairs, eager to put as much distance between Hamid and me as I could. I was immensely grateful to Tristan for putting us in separate wings, but it wasn't like I could have said that without being rude.

Sometime in the last few days, I'd stopped trying to make Hamid the bad guy in all of this, and I'd come to accept that he was as much a prisoner in our situation as I was. But that didn't change the fact that we were bonded, and the last thing we needed was to spend more time together than necessary.

My room was on the third floor, and I let out a relieved sigh when I opened the door and saw everything just as I'd left it. Leaving my bag on the floor, I flopped down on my stomach on my bed and buried my face in the pillow. I stayed there until a knock came at the door, and one of the kitchen staff entered carrying a covered tray that smelled heavenly of grilled steak and baked potato.

After I'd devoured every morsel of food on my plate, I took a long, hot shower and climbed back into bed to answer the half dozen texts I'd gotten from Sara and Beth since I arrived. I assured them I was fine and that I'd let them know how it went tomorrow, and then I turned off the light and tried to sleep.

Sleep, however, did not want to come to me. I'd grown used to the sounds of the city, and I'd forgotten how quiet it was here at night. Rooting through my bag, I found my earbuds and started listening to the playlist that always helped me relax.

An hour later, I threw the earbuds across the room in frustration. I glanced at my phone and groaned when I saw it was barely midnight. If I didn't find some way to relax my mind and body, it was going to be a long, sleepless night.

I rolled out of bed and dressed in some of the old training clothes I'd left in my closet. Pulling on a pair of running shoes, I left my room and quietly made my way downstairs. I didn't expect to run into anyone, but I also didn't want to take the chance of alerting my self-appointed protector that I wasn't tucked snugly in my bed.

The first floor of the north wing was the training area, and I moved through the darkened hallways with practiced ease until I came to the door that opened to a small courtyard. I slipped outside and eased the door shut behind me. The cold night air felt good as I set off across the lawn at a light run and followed a narrow gravel road into the trees.

The woods were quiet except for the light scuffs of my feet hitting the road and the occasional rustle of a small animal in the brush. My breath steamed the air, and it was so dark I had to enhance my sight to see the pale outline of the road as it curved through the trees.

Once my eyes became accustomed to the dark, I increased my speed. In lieu of a heavy sparring session, a brisk run should help burn off my excess energy. Tomorrow, I'd find someone to train with so I wouldn't have to do this in order to sleep.

Five minutes later, I saw the faint glimmer of the lake up ahead that signaled the end of the road. When Nikolas had built their gorgeous log home out here last year, he'd had the road put in to make it easier for Sara to travel between the lake and the stronghold. There was nothing that man wouldn't do for his mate.

I was barely winded by the time I reached the clearing that was used for parking, and I knew it was going to take a few more roundtrips to get me tired enough to sleep. Resigned to that fact, I made a U-turn to retrace my steps.

I almost yelped when I saw the tall figure standing in the road. That was also when I realized my Mori was doing that strange fluttering thing, which should have alerted me to his presence. I was still getting used to the oddities of the bond, but this one I should know by now.

I stalked toward him. "Are you following me?"

"I saw you run into the woods, and I came to check on you," he replied. "What are you doing out here at this hour?"

I waved a hand at my workout clothes. "What does it look like I'm doing? And since when do I have a curfew?"

Hamid shot me a disapproving look. "You don't have a curfew, but you should not be out alone in the woods in the middle of the night."

"I am not going to get into everything that is wrong with that sentence," I said with more restraint than I'd thought I had. "I will remind you that we are on a road, not in the woods, and still on Westhorne grounds."

"No place is impervious to attack."

I let out a short laugh. "Are you serious right now? You know this place is under Fae protection, not to mention our own security and…"

I trailed off when I saw two pairs of glowing red eyes in the darkness a few yards behind him. Anywhere else, such a sight would have me reaching for a weapon, but here, I knew exactly what those eyes belonged to.

"And what?" Hamid took a step toward me.

Two menacing growls froze him in his tracks, and he turned slowly toward the sound, putting his big body between me and the creatures. I grudgingly admired how calmly he reacted in the face of an unknown threat. Well, unknown to him. Just imagining his expression as he got his first look at Sara's little pets had me grinning like an idiot.

I peered around him to see the two massive hellhounds that took up the whole road when they stood side by side. "Hey, boys! How are my favorite hell beasts doing?"

The hounds stopped growling to pant happily at me. Everyone knew hellhounds were territorial of their home and the people who lived there. I'd been around these two enough times to feel safe with them. They wouldn't harm Hamid either unless he tried to hurt me.

But he didn't know that.

Hamid shifted his weight from one foot to the other, and the hellhounds growled again.

"I wouldn't do that if I were you." I walked around him, fighting to keep my expression serious. "Hugo and Woolf are very protective of Sara and her friends."

At the mention of Sara's name, both tails began to wag. I walked over to the nearest hound and scratched his head, which came almost to my shoulder. "Such a good boy," I crooned. "You'll keep me safe from the big, mean warrior, won't you?"

"Jordan," Hamid said in a warning tone, and I had to keep my head down so he couldn't see me trying not to laugh.

I gave the hound one last pat on the head. "Okay. Go patrol, and try not to eat anyone."

The two of them barked and took off into the woods. They'd stay out here all night until Sahir came to feed them in the morning. I wasn't sure how they stayed within the borders of our land, but they never strayed.

I smiled at Hamid, who looked like he wasn't sure what to make of the last few minutes. "And *that* is why it's safe for me to be out here at night. Now, if you'll excuse me, I'd like to finish my run."

He didn't respond, and I didn't wait for him to think of something to say. I spun on my heel and started running back toward the stronghold, feeling lighter than I had in days.

Back on the grounds, I decided I didn't need another lap after all. I headed up to my room where I took my second shower of the night and lay on the bed, replaying the scene with Hamid and the hellhounds. I think I was still chuckling when I fell asleep.

"I always knew you'd come back to us," said a familiar voice the next morning as I was filling a plate in the dining hall.

I looked up from the buffet to see a grinning black warrior with short black hair and hazel eyes. "Someone had to make sure you weren't going soft here," I retorted lightly.

Terrence laughed and tossed a grape, catching it in his mouth. "Come sit with us, and tell us about all the excitement in L.A."

"You heard about that?"

He snorted. "Who hasn't? And I don't think a single person here was surprised to hear you were smack dab in the middle of it all."

I walked with him to his table, where a smiling blond warrior greeted me. I should have known Josh would be here. He and Terrance had been as thick as thieves since our first year of training, and one would never leave without the other. They'd been stationed at Westhorne since they completed their training six months after I did.

"Is the old gang getting back together?" Josh joked when I sat next to him.

Silence fell over the table, and I didn't need to look at their faces to know we were all thinking about the same thing. There had been six of us in training, not counting Sara, and only three of us remained. Olivia and Mark were dead, and Michael, the traitor who had betrayed us to vampires and caused our friends' deaths, was locked in some facility for mentally unstable kids in India.

Sara said Michael was sick and shouldn't be held responsible for what he'd done. She was a bigger person than I was because I could find no forgiveness in my heart for him.

Josh coughed uncomfortably. "Sorry. I wasn't thinking."

"Don't worry about it," I told him. I'd left here after Olivia and Mark died. and I'd only come back for visits. I didn't know how Terrence or Josh had been able to stay here, surrounded by so many memories of our fallen friends. I couldn't have done it.

"Tell us about what's going on in L.A.," Terrance said. "It's all anyone can talk about here."

"I'm not surprised." I told them what I could, and they bombarded me with questions.

"Man, that must have been something," Josh said when I'd finished telling my story.

Terrence nodded. "Did you really bag a Hurra demon by yourself?"

I laughed. "Have you ever seen a Hurra demon? It's a little blob with tentacles and nothing to write home about. If it weren't for the fact that it was supposed to be extinct, no one would be making a big deal of it. You should have seen the Kraas demon Hamid killed. That was a lot more impressive."

Speak of the devil. My Mori began to flutter, and a few seconds later, Hamid entered the dining hall with a warrior I didn't know. The two of them looked deep in conversation until Hamid's gaze landed on me. I felt the intensity of his stare from across the room, and I wondered if he was still annoyed about last night.

Josh leaned over until our shoulders were touching. "Damn. Who's the goliath?"

"That would be Hamid," I said, my eyes still on the big warrior.

Hamid's eyes narrowed as they shifted to Josh. It took me a moment to clue in to the fact he wasn't happy about the other male being so close to me. I'd known this could happen, but I'd hoped we could get out of the bond before it got to this point.

I shifted in my seat to gain his attention again, and when I had it, I sent him a pointed look that said to knock it off. For a moment, his expression didn't change and I thought he was going to come over and cause a scene. But then he looked away, and my body relaxed.

Hamid and the other warrior stopped at the buffet for food and walked to a table on the far side of the room. As they passed, I could hear giggles from three girls at the next table. I watched the girls' eyes follow Hamid and heard their dreamy sighs. I caught myself scowling at them and wondering if I'd been that silly the first time I saw him. The thought made me cringe inwardly.

"Trainees," Josh said, seeing where my attention lay. "Can you believe that was us only a few years ago?"

I smiled. "Sometimes it feels like a lifetime ago, and sometimes it feels like just yesterday."

We spent the rest of our breakfast catching up, and they told me they were being assigned to one of the new command centers in a few months. They didn't know which one yet, but they'd both asked to go to the same one. I'd been to all of the command centers, though I'd spent the most time in Los Angeles, and I was happy to answer all their questions.

I was carrying my dishes to one of the bus bins when I felt Hamid come up behind me. Setting my plate in a bin, I turned to face him.

"The team is assembled in the arena and waiting to talk to us," he said.

"Okay." A little ball of dread formed in my stomach. I was eager to get this spell off me, but I didn't like magic or the idea of being the subject of anyone's tests.

We left by the main exit and walked across the grounds to the arena. Made of stone with a glass domed roof and tall windows, the arena was used mainly for training and sporting events such as dueling. It made sense that they were holding the meeting out here. The building was private and had plenty of room to perform spells and such.

Hamid opened the door for me, and I reluctantly entered the building. I walked down the short hallway that opened into the main room where Orias and four people I didn't know waited for us. Two of them were warlocks like Orias, and the other two were scholars.

A Mohiri female stepped forward and took my hand in a firm grip. She had dark hair, fair skin, and an English accent. "Charlotte Wright. It's lovely to meet you."

"You too," I said before the next one, a red-haired warrior named Marie Blast, introduced herself.

Orias introduced me to his peers, who appeared to be around the same age as him. Ciro was a quiet, serious-looking warlock with dark skin and a pleasant smile. Bastien was shorter than the other two and what I would call portly. His hair and skin were so white he looked like an albino, and he spoke with a thick French accent.

"There are no female magic users on the team?" I asked them.

"Witches use Earth magic, not demon magic," Orias explained. "They have no experience with summoning spells."

"It figures only males would screw around with this shit," I said, earning a glare from Orias and a chuckle from Charlotte.

Another thought occurred to me. "What about faeries?" I got the impression the Fae weren't overly concerned about what happened in our world, but Eldeorin and Aine would help if Sara asked them to.

"We can't have a faerie near the spell and risk them breaking it," Ciro said. "And we certainly don't want them anywhere near a hole in the barrier."

I frowned. "Why not?"

Bastien gave me an indulgent smile. "The barrier is made up of elements from both dimensions. What do you think would happen if a faerie got too close to an opening in the barrier and exposed it to their magic? The whole thing could become destabilized."

"I guess I never gave much thought to what the barrier is made of," I admitted. To be fair, I'd had little reason to think about the barrier before the start of all of this. I already knew more about it than I ever wanted to.

After all the introductions were out of the way, we sat and the team got down to business. For the next two hours, they asked question after question about the night we'd been caught in the spell. Every detail seemed important to them, from the exact sequence of events down to what we were wearing at the time. I answered them all until Marie asked if I had been in my fertile cycle at the time.

"What does that have to do with anything?" I demanded.

"In some cultures, females are believed to be more receptive to magic during their fertile time," she explained.

Avoiding Hamid's eyes, I said, "No. I wasn't in my fertile cycle."

The scholar nodded, but she almost looked disappointed. Thankfully, someone else started a different line of questions.

After the questions came the tests. They mainly consisted of Hamid or me or both of us standing in the center of the room while the warlocks took turns "examining" the magic, much like Orias had done in Los Angeles. Even though none of the tests were invasive, I was more than ready to get out of there when Charlotte called for us to break for lunch.

I headed to the dining hall, where I found myself the subject of many curious stares. It seemed that everyone knew about the magical testing going on in the arena today and that I was one of the guinea pigs. Uncomfortable with the scrutiny, I grabbed a bottle of water and went to my room. Back in my training days, I used to love being the center of attention, but I was coming to learn that not all attention was good.

I changed into my running clothes and ran laps back and forth to the lake. Hardly anyone used the road when Sara and the others weren't at home, so I had the place to myself. That suited me just fine because I was in no mood for company.

When the time came to return to the arena, I had to force myself to go back to my room to shower and change. Not surprisingly, I was the last one to arrive. The look Hamid gave me when I entered the building told me he had been expecting to have to go search for me.

He met me halfway across the floor, concern etched on his face. "Are you okay?"

"Peachy," I said with forced lightness.

His brows drew together. "If you need a longer break, you don't have to –"

"I don't need to be coddled," I replied more sharply than I meant to. Softening my tone, I said, "If you're ready, so am I. Let's do this."

The sooner we got this over with, the sooner I could get out of here. Over lunch, I'd decided to take Sara up on her offer to stay at their house, and I was already looking forward to a peaceful night alone at the lake.

Hamid and I took our places at the center of the room and endured another round of magical tests. As the afternoon wore away, so did my patience, until I was sure I'd snap the head off the next person who tried to perform a spell on me.

"I think that will be enough for today," said Charlotte, who appeared to be the unofficial team leader. "We'll spend the night going over our results from today and reconvene tomorrow morning."

"Awesome," I muttered, already turning for the exit.

"I'd like to perform one more test, if you don't mind," Bastien called.

I closed my eyes for several seconds before I came around to face them again. "Can't it wait?"

The warlock gave me an apologetic smile. "This will only take a few minutes, I swear, and it could prove very helpful in our discussion tonight."

"Fine." We were all here for the same reason – to create a new spell to replace the one on Hamid and me. If Bastien's test could help them figure things out, I wouldn't say no.

Bastien instructed Hamid and me to stand with our backs to each other, holding each other's hands behind us. Even though I couldn't see Hamid, it felt too intimate having him hold my hands this way. Every nerve ending in my hands seemed to tingle at the physical contact, and my heart gave a weird little flutter. It was like nothing I'd ever experienced before, and it made me want to lean into him and run away at the same time.

The warlock walked around us, laying crystals on the floor in a circle with us at the center. When he was done, he came to stand in front of me. "This spell will attempt to map the magical connection between you two. It won't replace the existing spell, but we can study it and potentially use it as a blueprint for a new spell."

"Got it," I said.

Bastien stepped back and started to chant, and within a minute, the crystals were giving off a bright white glow. It reminded me a little of the crystals from the summoning ceremony, and my fingers flexed nervously around Hamid's. He didn't speak, but his thumbs began stroking the backs on my hands in a slow reassuring pattern. Unable to pull my hands away, I stood there and told myself I wasn't at all soothed by his touch.

I winced when a sharp pain lanced through my head. It was gone in a second, but it had been bad enough to make my eyes close against the pain.

The second time the pain struck, it was stronger, and I sucked in a sharp breath. Again, it was gone in an instant, but I tensed as I waited for the next one.

"Argh!" I cried as white-hot pain burst in my head. It was like someone had driven a knife right through my eye socket. My whole body sagged, and the only thing holding me up was Hamid.

"Stop it now," Hamid snarled viciously. Seconds later, he released my hands and spun to catch me before I collapsed in an undignified heap.

"It's over," he said gruffly against my ear. "I'm sorry. Had I known it would hurt you, I wouldn't have allowed him to perform the spell."

I nodded, but it was a minute before I could speak or stand on my own. I had no choice but to stand there with my back pressed to Hamid's chest and his arms wrapped around me. If I'd thought holding hands was intimate, that had nothing on the sensations flooding me now.

As soon as I was able to move, I stepped out of his hold. My eye narrowed on Bastien. I closed the few feet between us, hauled off, and slugged him.

He staggered backward with his hands over his gushing nose, and I followed him. Before I could land a second blow, Hamid grabbed me from behind and pulled me away from the moaning warlock.

"Let me go," I yelled as I fought his hold to no avail.

Hamid turned us until I could no longer see Bastien. "Calm down."

"You have a hot poker shoved into your eye and see how calm you are," I said through gritted teeth.

His body stiffened. "That's what it felt like?"

I stopped struggling since it was no use. "I'll take that to mean you didn't feel any pain."

"There was some pain, but nothing like you described."

"Lucky you," I said sourly. "Now, can you please let me go?"

"Do you promise not to attack Bastien?" he asked, not loosening his hold on me.

"Not unless he comes near me again."

"I will see that he doesn't." Hamid's voice took on a hard edge that made me believe he meant what he said. He let his arms drop, releasing me.

I straightened my shirt and faced everyone. "If you'll excuse me, I'm done being your lab rat for today."

Casting Bastien a scathing look, I spun and strode toward the door. I barely made it six feet before I was yanked backward.

I turned with a snarl on my lips to ask Hamid what the hell he was doing. But he was exactly where I'd left him, his brows drawn down in confusion as he stared at me.

I took another step toward the door – or I tried to. It felt like something was holding me back, but when I looked over my shoulder, I saw nothing but the group of people looking at me like I'd lost my mind.

"What the hell is this?" If they thought they could force me to stay here for more tests after what had just happened, they were the ones out of their minds.

"What's wrong?" Orias asked, walking toward me.

I shot him a dark look. "I can't leave. That's what's wrong. This better not be another one of your goddamn tests, or so help me..."

Orias shot me a droll smile. Holding out a hand, he muttered a few words, and I gaped at the silvery thread forming in the air before me. One end of it was attached to me, and the other was attached to Hamid, who seemed to have been struck mute.

"What is that?" I demanded, hating the shrillness in my voice.

"That," Orias said slowly as he studied the thread, "is the map created by Bastien's spell. It appears to have tried to replicate my spell."

Ciro came over for a closer look at the thread. "Fascinating. Look at the composition of the bond. You can see how it has filaments of the original spell woven into it."

Orias nodded. "Yes, but the magic is incomplete in places. See there?" he pointed at a section of the thread. "That is where he stopped the spell."

I crossed my arms, mostly to keep from punching someone else. "If you two don't mind, I'd like to leave. Will one of you please get rid of that thing?"

"I'm afraid that's not possible," Ciro said, still staring at the thread.

"What do you mean it's not possible?" My heart sped up as fury and fear crowded my chest until I was on the verge of hyperventilating. *This cannot be happening.*

9

Hamid came to stand beside me. A large hand engulfed one of mine, and for once, I didn't try to pull away. I was ashamed to admit it, but his nearness soothed the storm of emotions inside me.

"Explain," he ordered harshly.

"What he means is that we can't destroy the new connection without risking my spell," Orias said calmly. "But Bastien's spell is incomplete, so it will dissolve on its own in a few days without harming the original spell."

I found my voice again. "You mean we are stuck in this building until that thing dissolves?"

"No, you may leave," Orias replied. "You just won't be able to go far from each other. Based on what I've seen, I'd say no more than a few feet."

"Are you serious?" My voice grew louder. "You expect us to be stuck together like this for days?"

"As the spell weakens, you should be able to move farther apart," Ciro said as if that would make things better. "And this might be a good thing for us to study. If we could just –"

I turned away from them, pulling Hamid with me by the hand. Not that I could have forced him to leave against his will but I think he knew how badly I needed to get out of there.

As soon as we left the arena, I dropped his hand, and neither of us spoke for a minute. The full extent of my dilemma didn't hit me until we neared the main building and I realized I couldn't go off to be by myself once we got inside. Neither was I going to have my night alone at the lake. I was literally stuck with Hamid until we were free of this thing.

"God, this just keeps getting worse," I muttered more to myself than to him.

"I'm flattered to hear you think this is worse than our bonding."

"I'm glad at least one of us can joke about it." I stopped walking to scowl at him.

Hamid gave me one of his almost smiles. "Getting angry about it will not change our situation, and it will be an uncomfortable few days if we dwell on our misfortune."

I rolled my eyes. "If this investigative thing doesn't work out for you, you really should think about a career in the greeting card business."

"I will take that into consideration," he said with a straight face.

I let out a heavy sigh, and we resumed walking.

"Are you feeling better?" he asked.

"Not as good as I'd feel if you had let me punch Bastien again."

His deep chuckle did funny things to my stomach. "Didn't anyone ever tell you it's not wise to pick a fight with a warlock?"

I huffed. He was right, but I'd never admit it. "I'll try to remember that the next time one of them makes me feel crippling pain."

I said it in a joking tone, but there was nothing humorous in Hamid's reply. "None of them will hurt you again, you have my word on that."

We entered the main hall, and I hesitated, unsure of what to do now. Hamid took the decision from me when he steered us toward the dining hall.

"I'm not that hungry," I lied.

"You didn't eat lunch. You can't miss dinner as well."

"How do you know I missed lunch?" I asked as we walked into the noisy dining hall. Had he been following me again?

"I saw you return from your run, and something told me you'd needed to work off your frustration from the morning's tests."

He went to the steaming buffet, and I had no choice but to follow him. I was already starting to feel like one of those children's pull toys.

I filled a plate with baked salmon, rice, and vegetables and looked around for a free table while I waited for Hamid. When he'd finished piling his plate with enough steak to feed a human family of four, we sat at the end of one of the longer tables.

"You need to eat more," he chided as he cut into his steak.

"That's why they invented seconds," I retorted. This was just the first course. I already had my eye on the baby back ribs. I'd probably follow that with the six-layer chocolate cake for dessert.

Neither of us said much for the first half of our meal, and surprisingly, it wasn't an uncomfortable silence. I did see curious looks sent our way, but I figured if he could ignore them, I could, too. They were probably staring at him anyway; he didn't exactly go unnoticed in a crowd.

"How did you end up working for the Council?" I asked as I dug into my dessert. It was something I'd wondered about when he first showed up in Los Angeles. When I'd seen him three years ago, he and his brother were working together as partners, and from what I'd heard, they were very close.

Hamid looked surprised by the question, and for a moment, I thought he wasn't going to answer.

"The Council tried to recruit me many times, but I was content to work with my brother, Ammon. Two years ago, we were on a job in South Africa and Ammon found his mate. She is English, and they are living at Hadan Castle now. When the Council approached me again, I decided to work for them for a few years."

I licked chocolate icing from my fork. "You must miss working with your brother."

"I do," he admitted. "But he and Alice are very happy, and that is all that matters to me."

"Do you get to see them often?" I asked, curious about his family life. I told myself I was just making conversation since we were stuck together, but who was I kidding? Hamid had always been a mystery to me, and I couldn't resist this opportunity to learn more about him.

He wiped his mouth with his napkin. "My work with the Council has kept me busy the last two years. Once our...investigation is over, I plan to visit them."

I heard his brief pause and wondered if he'd started to say "Once our bond is broken." The thought of never seeing him again filled me with a fleeting sense of wrongness. I shifted uncomfortably in my chair. *It's just the bond.*

"And you?" he asked.

"What about me?"

"Do you see your family often?"

"I don't have a family," I said. At his questioning look, I added, "I was an orphan."

He leaned back in his chair, wearing a frown. "They didn't do the DNA test to find your sire?"

"They did, but I didn't want to meet him."

We had a central DNA database that held records for every Mohiri alive at the time testing started about thirty years ago. Since then, the DNA of all newborns were added to the database, along with the DNA of orphans when they were found. The database was more for identification should a warrior be killed in a way that made it necessary, but it was also used to match orphans with their Mohiri family.

I'd been tested a week after I was found, but I'd chosen not to meet my father. I knew his name, that he was Austrian, and that he'd been visiting the US when he met my human mother. I also knew he'd never checked up on her to see if their brief union had resulted in a child. If he had, I wouldn't have spent the first ten years of my life scared and alone.

Hamid eyed me thoughtfully. "What of the people who raised you when you were brought in?"

I shrugged. "I never really got close to them."

His eyes darkened. "Did they neglect you?"

"Of course not." I was shocked he would even ask. Mohiri children were sheltered and cosseted, and orphans were treated with the same care. "They're good people, and it wasn't for lack of trying on their part. But after ten years of being abandoned and mistreated by adults, I wasn't exactly the trusting type when I was brought in."

I wasn't sure why I was telling him all of this, because I rarely talked to anyone about that time in my life. It was something I didn't like to think about.

He blinked in surprise. "You lived among humans until you were ten?"

His reaction was one I was used to. A child's Mori started asserting itself at a young age, usually around three or four. Without a parent or guardian to teach the child how to control their Mori, the demon grew stronger and more dominant until the child eventually became mentally unstable. It was rare to find an orphan older than six who wasn't suffering from some psychological issues. At ten, I'd been the oldest orphan ever brought in, until Sara. But she was in a category all her own.

I grinned. "I'm your classic overachiever."

"One of my finest trainees," said Tristan, whom I hadn't heard approach. He smiled at me then looked at Hamid. "I just stopped by to tell you we had to move tonight's conference call from nine o'clock to eight."

Hamid's gaze flicked to me and back to Tristan. "About that. Jordan will be joining us for the call."

"Jordan wants to speak to the Council?" Tristan gave me an incredulous look.

I made a face. "Um, no, she doesn't."

"What I mean is that she will have to accompany me." Hamid filled Tristan in on the spell that had backfired.

Concern creased Tristan's brow. "I'll talk to Charlotte. They were given permission to interview you and do tests, but nothing that would harm you."

"That won't be necessary. It will not happen again." There was a hardness in Hamid's voice that hadn't been there a minute ago, but his eyes didn't reflect his tone when they met mine. "I'm sorry, but I have to take this call. It shouldn't take more than an hour."

I gave a small nod. "No need to apologize. But if you really want to make it up to me, you can let me hit Bastien again."

Tristan laughed. "Never pick a fight with a warlock, Jordan."

Hamid shot me a smug look, and I resisted the childish urge to give him the finger. Just because we had this temporary truce while we were stuck together, didn't mean either of us was going to change our ways.

We accompanied Tristan to his office, where I tried to occupy myself with browsing the Internet on my phone while Hamid and Tristan had their conference call. I wouldn't have minded if the call had been interesting, but it was ninety minutes of planning where each of the Council's investigative teams would go next. I was half asleep in my chair by the time the call finally ended.

It was only ten o'clock when we left Tristan's office, but my body felt like it had been up for days. Being poked and prodded with magic for hours had that effect on you.

"It's been a long day," Hamid said when he caught me stifling another yawn. "We should try to get some sleep."

"Okay." I started to tell him good night, but the words died on my tongue as I realized we had a new problem. We were going to have to sleep in the same room until Bastien's spell wore off. Hamid's expression said he'd already thought of it and had been waiting for me to catch up.

"I'll sleep on the floor," he said before I had time to work myself up over it. "We can go to your room if you prefer. It doesn't matter to me."

The thought of us alone in my room made my stomach dip. Something about it felt far too cozy for my comfort, and the last thing we needed was intimacy at a time like this.

"Your room is probably bigger, and it'll be more comfortable for you," I said. "I just need to grab something from mine to sleep in."

Hamid standing just outside my bathroom doorway while I brushed my teeth for bed was definitely one of the more surreal moments of my life. He looked larger than life when I came out of the bathroom, and I wore a rueful smile as I dug through my sleepwear drawer for a soft T-shirt and matching shorts. There'd been a time not so long ago when being alone in a bedroom with the big warrior was my number one fantasy. That hadn't exactly turned out liked I'd imagined it.

We were both lost in our thoughts during the walk to Hamid's room on the second floor of the south wing. I changed into my sleep clothes while his back was turned, and then I helped him lay out blankets and a pillow on the floor. I felt guilty when I climbed into his king bed and heard him stretch out on his makeshift one, but every time I'd offered to take the floor, he'd refused to hear of it.

I turned off the lamp, sending the room into darkness, and lay back on the bed. Moving around until I found a comfortable position, I closed my eyes and tried to sleep. But just like last night, it was impossible to turn off my mind. It didn't help that Hamid's scent lingered on the pillow or that I could hear his soft breathing a few feet away.

I tried not to disturb him whenever I shifted positions, because one of us might as well get some rest. At one point, I thought about going for another run since that had helped last night. Then I remembered I wouldn't be going anywhere without him, and I let out a quiet sigh.

"Can't sleep?" His voice startled me because I'd assumed he was asleep.

"Sorry. I'll try to stop moving around."

"Do you always have trouble sleeping?" he asked.

I stared at the ceiling. "Sometimes. I guess I'm still a bit wound up from today."

I didn't tell him that sometimes when I couldn't sleep, I liked to ride my bike through the city, or I found an all-night club and a partner to dance my cares away. On nights I patrolled or was out on a job, I had no problem falling asleep when I got home.

"Would you like to go for a run?"

"Yes," I answered without hesitation.

Sitting up, I flipped on the lamp and blinked as light filled the room. My eyes strayed to the floor, and I stared at Hamid lying shirtless on top of the blankets. *Sweet baby Jesus.* He'd left on a pair of sweats, but the sight of his muscled shoulders and chest and ripped abs was enough to make me forget everything else.

Hamid's eyes met mine, and I looked away, but not before I saw the hint of a smile on his lips. I waited for him to stand up and pull on a T-shirt before it felt safe to glance at him.

"I'll have to get some running clothes from my room," I told him, hoping he wouldn't think it was too much of a bother and change his mind.

He sat on the bed to pull on a pair of Nike runners. "You might as well grab enough clothes for the next day or two so you don't have to keep going up there to change."

He said it so offhandedly, but nothing about this felt casual to me. First, we had to sleep in the same room, and now, I would be bringing my things over here. For two people trying not to strengthen a bond, we were moving into dangerous waters.

It didn't take long to get the stuff I needed from my room and drop it off in his. I changed into my workout clothes, and we left the building by the main door, jogging across the lawn to the lake road.

As we neared the woods, I glanced to my right and saw lights on in the arena. The team must be in there going over their findings from today. *Or planning new ways to torture us tomorrow*, I thought with a shiver.

I put the team and their tests out of my mind when we entered the woods. Hamid didn't try to talk to me, which suited me fine, and we ran in companionable silence. At the lake, we turned without stopping and headed back to the stronghold.

By the end of our fourth round-trip, I felt pleasantly tired and a sheen of sweat coated my body. "I think I'll be able to sleep now," I told Hamid when he looked at me to see if I wanted to go again.

He nodded, and we went inside. We made a detour to the dining hall for bottles of water before we climbed the stairs to his room.

Back inside his room, I discovered another problem when I grabbed my bag and made it a few feet in the direction of the bathroom before I could go no farther. I stood in the middle of the room, frustration eating at me.

"I'll stand outside the door while you shower," Hamid said from right behind me. Startled, I looked over my shoulder at him. How could someone his size move so quietly? Or maybe I had been too caught up in my pity party to notice.

We took turns showering while the other person stood near the bathroom door. It was a good thing the bathroom wasn't much larger, or we would have had to both be in there at the same time. As curious as I was to know if Hamid's lower half was as impressive as his upper half, being around each other without clothes was asking for trouble.

Lying in bed a little while later, I listened to Hamid settle down on the floor. After he'd stopped moving, I spoke into the darkness. "Thank you for that."

"Do you think you can sleep now?" he asked.

"Yes."

"Good." There was a long moment of silence then, "Sleep well."

"Thank God that is over, at least for today," I said as Hamid and I walked away from the arena after our second day of tests. I was starting to forget what it was like to not be constantly surrounded by magic, and it wasn't a pleasant feeling.

He slowed his stride to match mine. "You handled it better today."

"I'm a great actress. I was one spell away from losing it." I gave him a sideways look. "I don't know how you always look so calm in there. I still feel like I have bugs crawling all over me from that last one."

"I've had more exposure to magic because of my work with the Council. And I am older and stronger than you."

I scoffed lightly. "So you keep reminding me."

He smiled, something he'd started to do more often since we'd gotten to Westhorne. It was a good look on him. Based on the dreamy expressions from the two girls we passed, I wasn't the only one who thought so. Not that I cared if someone else found him attractive. The flare of anger from my Mori told me it didn't share my feelings.

My steps faltered when I saw we were headed to the main building. Except for my runs, I'd spent most of my time inside since we'd arrived, and I wasn't looking forward to another long evening and night of the same. I longed to go for a long ride on my Ducati, but I couldn't even do that until Bastien's spell wore off.

Hamid slowed with me. "Is something wrong?"

"Do you mind if we stay out here for a little while? I'm not used to being cooped up inside this much."

"I could use some fresh air myself," he admitted readily. "I haven't seen much of Westhorne since I arrived. Would you care to show me around?"

I smiled gratefully. "Yes, but I warn you there's not a whole lot to see."

We took our time walking around the grounds, and I explained what each of the outbuildings was. He was curious when I pointed out the menagerie, so we went inside. All the cages were empty, but we found Sahir cutting up what looked like half a cow for the hellhounds' dinner. He looked after Hugo and Woolf, as well as Sara's cat and imps, whenever she was away from home. We talked to him as he worked then helped him load plastic bins of beef into his truck to take to the lake.

After that, Hamid and I walked to the river, where I told him about the night Sara and I had jumped into the water to escape vampires during the attack on Westhorne.

"The water was freezing, and I would have died if not for Sara. She used her magic to keep us warm and afloat, and she brought us to this exact spot." I pointed to the embankment below us. "And right there is where two kelpies jumped out of the water to kill the vampires that had us cornered."

Hamid's eyebrows shot up, and I laughed. "I'm not lying. You won't believe some of the stuff I've seen just being around Sara."

He stared thoughtfully at the rushing water. "I heard about the attack, but I didn't realize you were here for it."

"Sara and I were smack in the middle of it. All of the trainees were..." My smile faded as the memories of that night played in my head. Standing here where it had all gone down made the images more vivid and the pain more intense.

"What is it?"

"Two of my friends were killed that night. We were too late to save them, and we watched Olivia die." I breathed in deeply and pushed the grief down. "But Sara and I got the vampire that killed her and Mark."

I couldn't look at him as I spoke, so I wasn't expecting the hand he laid on my shoulder.

"I'm sorry for your loss."

I opened my mouth to tell him he was breaking rule two again, but instead I said, "Thank you." He let his hand fall back to his side, and for a moment, I felt cold and strangely bereft.

Shaking off the feeling, I faced him. "That's pretty much it for the grounds, and you've already been to the lake."

"Thank you for the tour. Would you like to eat dinner now?"

I would have preferred to stay outside longer, but dusk had fallen and there wasn't anything else to show him. I nodded, and we walked to the main building.

In the dining hall, we filled our plates, but instead of sitting alone, we joined Tristan and Callum, one of my old trainers. I'd never eaten at Tristan's table, and I felt out of place sitting there now. I ate quietly while the three of them talked, only joining in when someone asked me a question.

Tristan and Callum excused themselves after the meal, leaving me alone with Hamid once again. A few days ago, it would have annoyed me to have to spend any time with him, but I was getting used to having him around. I spent the rest of the meal asking him about jobs he'd done and places he'd seen.

"Is it true you and Nikolas hunted a Master together in Spain?" I asked as I dug into a big slice of apple pie. "And that you stole his bike when yours got run over?"

Hamid smiled devilishly. "Yes, and he has not yet forgiven me for that."

"For the bike or for beating him to the kill?"

"A little of both, I think."

I ate a bite of pie thoughtfully as I tried to imagine hunting with two powerhouses like Hamid and Nikolas. It would be many years before I was strong enough to even think of going after a Master. But someday, I'd get my chance, and I would be ready for it.

"Was that your only Master kill?" I asked him.

"That was my first. I killed another near Beijing, five years ago. She was much older, and it took six of us to defeat her." He gave me a play-by-play description of the fight. "I was the fortunate one who was in position to make the kill."

"Wow." I knew I must have looked a little awestruck, but I didn't care. A story like that deserved it.

"Jordan," Terrence called, walking over to our table. "Josh and I are off tonight, and we're thinking about hitting a few clubs in Boise. Thought you might like to come with us if you don't have plans."

I perked up at the mention of clubbing, but my excitement fizzled when I remembered I couldn't leave Hamid. I could ask him to go with us, but I didn't think it was wise for us to be socializing that way.

"Can't tonight," I told Terrence, who looked disappointed. "Maybe next time if we're still here."

"It's a date," he said with a grin. Then he looked at Hamid, and unease crept into his eyes. "Um...you're invited, too."

I didn't need to look at Hamid to know he was being his usual charming self. Terrence's hasty goodbye and departure were conformation enough. When I glanced at Hamid, I was not expecting the icy glare he was shooting at my friend's departing back.

"You have any Council business to take care of tonight?" I asked, bringing Hamid's attention back to me. It was early, and I had no idea what we were going to do to pass the hours until bed.

"Not tonight. Is there something you wanted to do?"

I thought about it. "I wouldn't mind a good sparring session, but that would probably bore you."

He rested his arms on the table. "Why is that?"

I laughed even as the thought of training with him sent a shiver of excitement through me. "As you have so *eloquently* pointed out on several occasions, I'm a new warrior and you've been around for... Exactly how old are you?"

His lips quirked. "One hundred and eighty-six."

I lifted my hands and let them fall. "Exactly."

"I will try to take it down a notch," he responded playfully, standing.

I was a little breathless as I followed him to one of the training rooms. We selected swords from the large rack along one wall and faced off against each other.

As I'd expected, sparring with Hamid was like going up against Nikolas, Chris, or Desmund. He was so fast that even when he didn't engage his Mori speed, he made me look like I was moving in slow motion.

After a few minutes, he deliberately slowed his movements until we were evenly matched in speed. I was good with a sword, but I had to admit Hamid was a masterful swordsman. His strikes and parries were concise and effortless, and he moved with a smooth agility that surprised me.

As with the time he'd watched Vivian and me sparring in Los Angeles, he critiqued some of my moves. But his appraisal didn't piss me off now, and I asked him to show me how to improve any weak areas.

Once we'd smoothed out my rough spots, we sparred again, and he didn't hold back as much, making it more challenging for me. He pushed me until I was dripping with sweat and fighting at a level I had never reached before. It was beyond exhilarating, and I didn't know how I'd be able to go back to practicing with Brock and Mason after this.

Clapping came from the doorway when we finished, and I was surprised to see we'd drawn a small audience. Seamus stood there along with a male trainee and one of the girls I'd seen in the dining hall yesterday. The two trainees stared at Hamid in awe, and I hid my smile. A few years ago, that had been me watching Nikolas fight.

I received another shock when I glanced at the clock on the wall and discovered we'd been in the training room for over two hours. I hadn't even noticed the time passing.

"Do you want to run before bed?" Hamid asked as I downed a bottle of water in the dining hall.

"No, I think that two-hour session should do it." I'd probably sleep better than I had in ages after that workout.

We went to his room and took turns showering like we had the night before. While he was in the bathroom, I tested the magic connection between us and made the happy discovery that I could now move about ten feet away from him. I hadn't said it out loud, but I'd secretly been worried the spell might not wear off like the warlocks had promised. It wasn't that I hated Hamid's company; it was just best if we put some space between us. He never mentioned it, but he had to feel the same way.

As we had the previous night, I got into bed and Hamid stretched out on the floor. I turned off the light and closed my eyes, but I couldn't stop thinking about how much I'd improved my sword skills tonight. My body was tired, but I was already itching to go another round with him.

"Are you having trouble sleeping again?" Hamid asked, sounding as wide awake as I was.

"No, just...thinking." I rolled to face in his direction. "How long did it take you to get that good with a sword?"

"Many years. You are already more advanced than I was a few years out of training."

Warm pleasure flooded me. I'd been around him long enough to know he did not give praise unless he meant it.

I moved to the edge of the bed so I could peer down at him. "Since we're both stuck at Westhorne and there's not a whole lot to do here, do you think we could –?"

"Yes."

"Thanks."

"Now get some sleep. You'll need your rest because I won't go as easy on you next time." His face was stern, but I heard the smile in his voice.

I fell onto my back, grinning. "I wouldn't expect anything less."

10

I felt Hamid arrive before he entered the dining hall. We'd been bonded for three weeks, and I was starting to get used to being able to sense him nearby. It was still a little unsettling to have that kind of connection with another person, but it no longer filled me with the urge to run away from him. Not that running would solve anything. I was resigned to being bonded until Orias's spell could be broken without damaging the barrier.

So far, no real progress had been made on creating a new spell, and the team reminded me daily that something this complicated could not be rushed. Easy for them to say. Hamid and I had been subjected to so many tests over the last week that my skin seemed to be constantly tingling from the magic.

Since Bastien's spell had worn off four days ago, I didn't see much of Hamid outside of the arena and our nightly sparring sessions. We'd decided it was best if we stayed away from each other. Well, I'd decided it, and he hadn't disagreed. The times we were in each other's company, we maintained the camaraderie we'd developed during the days we'd been stuck together.

Hamid's gaze met mine as he started toward me. We had another thirty minutes before we had to be at the arena, so I knew I wasn't late.

"What's up?" I asked when he reached my table.

"Grab your stuff. We're leaving in fifteen minutes." His expression and tone were serious, and he didn't resemble the man I'd gotten to know. This was the old Hamid, closed off and all business.

KAREN LYNCH

He turned and strode away, and I hurried after him. In the main hall, I grabbed his sleeve to force him to stop and look at me. In getting to know him during our eight days at Westhorne, I'd learned that when he was intensely focused on work, he tended to be abrupt and closed off. I tried not to take it personally, but sometimes I still had the urge to slug him.

"Are you going to tell me where we're going?" I asked, not put off by his brusque manner.

"Nikolas called," he said at last. "One of his teams found a summoning site that matches the two in Los Angeles."

A sliver of dread worked its way into my chest. After witnessing the barrier being opened and seeing what had come through it, I was half afraid to ask what else they'd found.

"Do they know if the summoning worked?"

Hamid nodded grimly. "They found a Hurra tentacle at the site."

"I'll be packed in five minutes." I raced up the stairs to my room and threw my things into my bag. Ten minutes later, we were in an SUV, headed for Boise. Behind us, two other vehicles carried the Council's team who were accompanying us to Chicago.

Hamid spent most of the drive on the phone with Nikolas, who was overseeing the investigation until we arrived. When we boarded the plane, Hamid switched over to a call with Tristan and the rest of the Council. I found a seat at the back of the plane, stuck in my earbuds, and ignored the excited conversations around me for the three-hour flight.

It was noon when we landed at O'Hare, where two SUVs waited to take us directly to the summoning site. As soon as we entered the building that had once been a Chinese restaurant, the stench of sulfur and death in the air made me want to turn around and leave.

Warriors guarded the exits and pointed us to the kitchen, where Nikolas and Chris were waiting to give us a quick rundown of the situation.

"We've kept everyone out of the site since we found the Hurra tentacle," Nikolas told Hamid. "Based on the condition of the human's body, the summoning happened less than twelve hours ago."

I could practically feel the warlocks' excitement at the opportunity to examine a fresh site. I, on the other hand, had zero interest in seeing another one of those.

"I'm going to wait outside," I said when Hamid noticed I wasn't going with them. "I've been exposed to enough magic to last me a lifetime."

The air outside the restaurant didn't smell the best, but it was an improvement over the sickening smells inside. I chatted with two of the warriors on guard and started a slow sweep of the area, mainly for something to do. Nikolas and Chris were thorough. If there was anything of interest out here, they would have found it.

The sound of coughing led me to an elderly homeless man huddled on a bench half a block away from the restaurant. My lips pressed together at the sight of his frail body and the thin coat that was no protection against the cold. I'd only spent a few weeks on the street, but I would never forget the constant hunger, the worrying about where my next meal would come from. It was no way to live.

There was a convenience store nearby, so I went in and bought a couple of their pre-made sandwiches and a large coffee. It wasn't a nice hot meal, but it was food, and the coffee would help warm him for a little while.

As I approached him, I made enough noise so he wouldn't be startled. It was scary enough on the street without someone sneaking up on you while you were asleep.

The man jerked awake and sat up with some difficulty. His face was gaunt and ashen, and his eyes looked feverish as he watched me warily. I had to bite my lip to keep from swearing. What was wrong with society that they would allow an old man to suffer? It was times like this that I wondered why I fought so hard to protect humans when they wouldn't help their own.

"It's pretty cold out here today. I thought you might like something hot to drink," I said as I set the coffee and sandwiches down on the end of the bench farthest from him.

He didn't speak or move to take the food, not that I expected him to. Kindness from strangers probably wasn't something he saw much, and he was most likely wondering what I was up to.

I walked away and made it five feet before a shuffling sound alerted me he was behind me. I turned to see what he wanted and caught him as he lunged at me, eyes crazed and mouth foaming.

He was surprisingly strong for the shape he was in, but still no match for me. I easily subdued him, pushing him back and down on the bench as I wondered what to do with him. He was obviously suffering from some form of dementia, and I couldn't leave him here alone.

Distracted by my thoughts, I loosened my grip on him and paid for it when he sank his teeth into my hand. I had to pry his mouth open to force him to let go, and he snapped at me like a rabid dog.

I looked at the crescent-shaped bite mark on my hand and shook my head. I'd fought countless vampires without one of them getting a single bite, and one little old man had managed to get the drop on me.

"What am I going to do with you?" I asked, more to myself than to him.

The only thing I could think of was to take him to the nearest hospital and let them care for him. I held him with one arm and tried not to breathe in his rank odor as I pulled out my phone to call for a pickup.

The man grunted and tried to buck out of my hold.

"Damn, you're a slippery old guy." I adjusted my grip on him.

He growled.

It was such an unhuman sound I nearly dropped my phone in surprise. I turned him until I could see his face and sucked in a breath. The eyes that had been a watery gray a minute ago were now solid black. Something told me I'd just found the Hurra demon that was missing a tentacle.

I held him down while I dialed Hamid's number.

"I think I might have found your Hurra demon," I said when he answered.

Surprise filled his voice. "Where?"

"About half a block away from there." I gave him directions to where I was.

"Why did you leave the building?" he asked harshly. "You should not be –"

"Doing my job? Walking around in broad daylight?" I countered dryly. "Can't you just once say 'Good job, Jordan' and leave it at that?"

I hung up, grumbling.

The man growled.

I nodded. "You can say that again."

I didn't have long to wait for Hamid. He showed up less than a minute later with Nikolas, and I was quite happy to hand the man off to Hamid as I filled them in on what had happened.

Nikolas called for a pickup, and we took the old guy to the command center. They strapped him down in the medical ward, and Xavier, a blond healer with a polite British accent, went to work on him. We had to confirm there was a demon inside him before we could take any actions to remove it.

"It's a Hurra demon," Xavier said when he'd finished his examination. "Unfortunately, the man's body is too frail to survive the extraction. I can try, but I don't want to put him through that if he's only going to die."

I looked at the old man, who was lying on the exam table, growling at the ceiling. "What about Sara?"

Hamid looked at me in confusion. "Sara?"

"She can kill a Vamhir demon without hurting the host. Can't be much different from a Hurra demon."

Nikolas shook his head. "She's pregnant and –"

"And?" Sara asked from the doorway. She smiled at me as she entered the room. "Welcome back."

Nikolas walked over and put a protective arm around her. "And you passed out the two times you did that. You shouldn't take any risks with the baby."

"He's right. I wasn't thinking." I was sorry the man wouldn't make it, but I wouldn't put Sara or her baby in danger for anyone.

Sara laughed and shrugged off Nikolas's arm. "I think you guys are forgetting I'm growing a Fae baby. Between her power and mine, I could light up a stadium right now."

She walked over to the table. As soon as she got within two feet of the man, he started to make a strange screeching sound and struggle violently against his binds.

"You poor thing," she murmured soothingly as she took in the man's condition. "Let's see if we can't make you feel better." Reaching out, she barely grazed his hand with one fingertip.

The man seized like he'd been electrocuted. His mouth stretched wide, and without warning, the demon shot out of his body.

And straight at me. Seriously, what was it with me and these things?

Before I could react, Hamid was in front of me. He caught the demon in one hand, mindless of the claws that embedded themselves in his forearm.

Nikolas came over with a glass specimen canister, and Hamid deposited the demon inside after he'd pried it from his arm. It was a totally badass move and a bit of a turn-on. Not that I'd *ever* admit that to anyone.

"How is he?" Sara asked Xavier, who was checking on the man.

Xavier smiled. "Unconscious, but alive. I think he'll make it. Good job, Sara."

I gave Hamid a pointed look. "See how he did that? He told her she did a good job, and his head didn't explode. Try it sometime. You might like it."

"*She* did not go off on her own the minute my back was turned," he said, sounding more exasperated than angry.

Sara and I looked at each other and burst out laughing. Nikolas shook his head before he went back to studying the Hurra demon squirming in the canister.

Hamid scowled, but all it did was make us laugh harder.

Sara wiped her eyes. "I'm so glad you're back. I missed you."

"Missed you, too. Westhorne is not the same without you."

"I want to hear all about it." She started for the door. "I was just about to have lunch. Hungry?"

I followed her. "God, yes. We left before I could finish breakfast."

"Good thing I made extra."

We entered the living area, and the smell of tacos made my mouth water. Instead of sitting at the table, we ate at the island where everything was laid out.

"This is so good," I mumbled around my first mouthful. "Have I told you lately how much I love you?"

Sara grinned. "I could stand to hear it again."

It wasn't until I devoured my second taco that I slowed down enough to tell Sara all about my visit home. We'd texted while I was gone, but I'd saved all the good stuff to tell her and Beth in person.

"I miss Hugo and Woolf," she said longingly after we'd laughed at my story of Hamid's first encounter with them.

"Why not go home then?"

She drank some water. "Because I get to hang out with you and Beth here. And I want to finish this job. Once the baby comes, we don't plan to take any big jobs for a few years."

"Speaking of Beth, where is she today?" I asked, reaching for my fourth taco.

"She's at the wrakk, doing the self-defense class. She should be back soon."

I was surprised to feel a little jealous that Beth was teaching the class I had planned to give. Before Hamid had shown up and changed everything, I'd actually been looking forward to training the Vrell boys. Maybe I could teach the class with her for as long as I was here.

Sara pushed away her plate with a happy sigh. "That was good. I've been craving tacos all week."

I made her go sit in the living room while I cleaned up from our lunch. I couldn't sense Hamid, so I figured he and Nikolas had gone back to the restaurant.

Sara was watching me with a curious expression when I joined her in the living room. "So," she began after I made myself comfortable. "You and Hamid seem to be getting along a lot better. Did anything happen that you haven't told me about?"

I snorted. "You call *that* getting along a lot better?"

She shrugged. "When you left here, you could barely stand to be in the same room with him."

"Well, being magically bound to someone twenty-four-seven will do that. It's too exhausting being angry all the time. My face started to cramp from all the scowling." I made a face, and she laughed.

Hellion

"Admit it, though, you like him."

I thought about it. "I will say that there's more to him than I saw in L.A., and he can be nice when he wants to be. I respect him, but I wouldn't exactly call us friends."

She wrinkled her nose. "Will the real Jordan please come out now?"

"What?"

"He's nice? You respect him?" She rolled her eyes. "I know you. Tell me you didn't think once about hooking up with him while you were there."

My mind immediately conjured an image of Hamid coming out of the bathroom in nothing but a towel on our third day sharing a room. I'd stared at him for a good ten seconds before I came to my senses. If it hadn't meant giving up my freedom and binding myself to a mate for life, I would have given that man a night he'd never forget.

I smiled slyly. "Maybe once, but I didn't want to ruin him for other women."

She chuckled. "Or you didn't want him to ruin you for other men."

"That too," I admitted honestly. Something told me that even without the bond, sex with Hamid would be off the charts. That man didn't do anything halfway.

"Do you know if you guys will be staying here?" Sara asked with a hopeful expression. "Nikolas said he wasn't sure, but he thought Hamid might want to stick around for a few days at least."

"I haven't had a chance to talk to him since we left Westhorne, but I can't see him leaving soon. He'll need to be where the action is, and nothing's happening in L.A. that we know of. Even Vivian left to go on another job in France."

"Good." Sara rubbed her belly.

"Everything okay?"

She smiled. "Yes. The little one is just letting me know she's happy you're here. Either that or she really loved the tacos."

I draped my legs over the arm of my chair. "They were really good tacos, so I won't hold it against her."

Sara and I hung out until I couldn't sit still any longer, and then I went for a long run to work off my excess energy. After a week at Westhorne, I was itching to get back on regular patrols, but Hamid had made it clear that I could no longer go off and do my own thing. I had to follow his rules or suffer the humiliation of having my own security detail. Some things were infinitely worse than wearing a tracker.

Beth was there when I returned from my run, and the three of us spent the rest of the day together. Nikolas, Hamid, and Chris didn't show up until after the dinner dishes had been cleared away.

Orias and the rest of the Council's team were still at the restaurant running tests and were expected to stay there all night. I was glad to be free of them. Hopefully, now that they had a new summoning site to play with, they'd forget about doing tests on me for a while.

I wasn't sure if Hamid and I would continue our training sessions after we left Westhorne, so I was secretly thrilled when he asked if I wanted to spar with him. I'd already improved so much in the short time we'd been training together.

"Enough for tonight?" he asked when I reached for my water bottle after an intense two-hour session.

I nodded and took a long pull on my water. I was going to miss these workouts when we were finally able to go our separate ways. Hamid pushed me like no one else ever had.

"Do you know how long we'll be here?" I asked him as we walked to our rooms.

"At least a week, unless I'm needed elsewhere."

I brushed my damp hair out of my face. "I want to start patrolling again. I'll go crazy here if I don't."

He nodded. "I already spoke to Nikolas about it. He'll put you on a team tomorrow."

I was too surprised to answer at first. I had expected more of a fight to get back on patrol. "Thanks."

We reached my room, and I opened the door. "Good night."

"Good night." He started to walk to his room, which was next to mine. When he stopped and looked back at me, he wore a hint of a smile. "Good job today, Jordan."

"That's it for today, folks," I said to the five kids and three adults who were practicing their stances with the new staffs I'd brought for them today. Beth and I had been taking turns giving the self-defense class at the wrakk, and we'd decided our students were ready to learn to use a weapon. Used properly, a staff could be as deadly as a sword.

"Can we take these home with us?" asked Jal, one of the Vrell boys.

I picked up my leather jacket. "Those are yours, and I expect you to practice with them at least an hour a day."

He smiled broadly. "I will. Thanks!"

"See you in two days," I called to them as I headed to the exit.

Over the last week, my days had fallen into a new pattern. Hamid worked with the Council team on the investigation, and I'd gone back to regular patrols. Nikolas had assigned me to a team with three seasoned warriors, and I followed Hamid's rules and didn't go off alone. It wasn't ideal, but it was better than the alternative.

Outside of our training, I didn't see much of Hamid. After the night he'd walked me to my room, I'd realized I was getting too comfortable with him. That coupled with the things Sara and I had talked about made me see how much my feelings toward him had changed in the last few weeks. I'd gone from barely tolerating him to enjoying his company.

And I couldn't deny my physical attraction to him was growing. I'd always found him incredibly sexy, but more and more, I'd been imagining what it would be like to explore every inch of his muscled body. I wanted to blame my increased desire on the bond, but I couldn't lie to myself anymore.

Sara called me as I walked to my bike. "Are you still at the wrakk?"

"Just leaving. Why?"

"Perfect. Would you mind stopping by the grocery store on the way home. I'm dying for some Ben & Jerry's, and we're all out."

"How much do you want?" I asked, laughing. I was used to her food cravings and crazy appetite. Two days ago, she'd eaten a bunch of bananas and a whole jar of peanut butter in one sitting. And that had been her midmorning snack.

"You are an angel," she gushed. "Two tubs of Chocolate Fudge Brownie should tide me over until we can do a grocery run."

I got to my bike and rooted in my pocket for my keys. "I'll get four tubs, just in case."

The sound of a van door sliding open drew my attention to the large blue cargo van parked on the other side of my bike. A lot of the vendors here used vans, so I didn't pay much heed to it until a Gulak jumped out. He was quickly followed by five more, all carrying clubs and knives.

In a matter of seconds, I was surrounded.

"Jordan, you still there?" Sara asked.

I kept my eyes on the Gulaks. "Um, I may be in a wee bit of trouble."

"What kind of trouble?" Alarm filled her voice.

"The Gulak kind," I answered flippantly as I reached for the sword strapped to my bike. "You might want to send in the cavalry for this one."

I hung up and slipped my phone into my pocket. I couldn't afford any distractions, and Sara knew where to send backup – if anyone was close enough to get here in time. Something told me these guys weren't going to play around.

"I'm going to enjoy this," one of the Gulaks said, and I turned slowly to find the speaker.

"Do I know you?" I asked, although I already suspected he was one of the Gulaks Beth and I had fought here a few weeks ago.

He sneered. "You don't remember me?"

"Sorry. You guys all look the same to me."

A laugh rumbled from him. "I'll fix that. After I'm done with you, you'll never forget my face."

The soft scuff of a boot hitting a pebble alerted me to the first attack. I spun as a club swung at my head.

I ducked and brought my sword up, slicing a shallow gash across the Gulak's stomach. If he'd been a vampire, that strike would have gutted him. Damn Gulaks and their scaly hides. It was enough to make him howl in pain and back off, but there were five more ready to step in and take his place.

My years of training had prepared me to fight against the odds, and I employed every technique I'd learned from Hamid. For several minutes, I held off my attackers, letting them feel the sting of my blade when they got too close. But they just kept coming, and I knew I couldn't hold them back indefinitely. All it would take was one slip for them to get past my defenses. Gulaks were strong bastards, and they could do a lot of damage.

The first blow took me by surprise, even though I'd been waiting for it. The club slammed into the side of my knee so hard I could hear the bone crack. I struggled to find my balance as the sharp stabbing pain tore a cry from my lips.

The Gulaks didn't waste time moving in, and the second blow was to my sword hand. My fingers went numb, and my sword slipped from my grasp.

I grabbed the knife sheathed at my hip with my good hand, but it was no match for six Gulaks with clubs.

The third strike shattered my cheekbone and made the world go black for several seconds. I hit the pavement hard, and my sight returned in time to see a club coming down in what, to my pain-addled brain, looked like slow motion.

The club slammed into my side, and I gasped as pain ripped through me. I tried to take a breath, but the fire in my lungs told me at least one of them had been punctured by a rib.

Blows began to rain down on me, and all I could do was cover my head with my arms. Not that it would matter soon. The viciousness of the attack told me these guys weren't going to be satisfied until I was dead.

I was teetering on the edge of consciousness when an enraged roar pierced the fog of pain surrounding me. The sound pulled at me, refusing to let me slide into the dark abyss.

Shadowy shapes moved above me. I blinked, and my vision cleared enough to see the flash of a sword as it took the head off a Gulak. Hot blood sprayed my face, but I couldn't move either of my arms to wipe it away. All I could do was watch Gulak body parts fall around me as ice spread through my body.

The coldness reached my chest, and I let out a slow rattling breath. So, this was what death felt like. I'd always expected to go out in a blaze of glory. This was such a disappointment.

Gentle hands touched my face, and I heard Beth's desperate voice from a long way off. "Jordan, stay with me." Then she shouted, "She's not breathing!"

Someone knelt beside me, and even with the life draining from my body, I knew it was him. The touch of his hand on my throat sent a flicker of warmth through me like a beacon in a storm. My Mori was too weak to call to his, but we knew he was here with us.

Hands tilted my head back, and a mouth covered mine. Warm air flowed down my airway, filling my lungs. It hurt so much when they expanded, but pain meant I was still alive, so I welcomed it.

Over and over, he forced air into me, and with each push, I felt the coldness recede a little, until I could finally draw a breath of my own.

"That's it," he said gruffly, his face so close I could feel his warm breath against my cold skin. "Fight for it, Jordan. You're too stubborn to give up."

I pulled in a shallow breath and then another. As long as I didn't take in too much at once, my lungs could handle it.

I tried not to think about the fact that I couldn't move my arms or legs or open my eyes. And one side of my face was completely numb. After the blow I'd taken to it, that was probably a blessing.

I couldn't speak either, something I discovered when I attempted to form words. All that came out was a garbled sound.

"Don't try to talk," Hamid said. "The healer will be here soon."

"Can't we give her gunna paste?" Beth asked.

Chris answered her. "We can't take the risk of her choking on it. Xavier will help her."

I think I passed out then. The next thing I remembered was being jolted awake as I was lifted into a van, strapped to a gurney. I knew Hamid was with me before I heard him order the driver to get us back to the command center.

"I'm going to give her something to help her sleep now," Xavier said in a low voice.

The thought of going under again terrified me. I tried to move and cry out, but I was incapable of doing either. I hated feeling so completely helpless.

"You're not alone," Hamid said into my ear as a needle pricked my arm. "I'll stay with you as long as you need me."

11

A beeping sound woke me. My eyes were dry and scratchy, and it took some effort to open them and stare at the white ceiling. Carefully, I turned my head to one side to discover I was in the medical ward at the command center. The lights were low, and I could hear nothing except the heart monitor I was hooked to.

I tried to lift one arm and then the other, but they lay on top of the sheet as if they belonged to someone else. My body should have healed itself.

Oh, God, was I paralyzed? Or maybe I really had died and this was my hell.

"Hello?" I rasped, fighting to keep the panic from my voice.

A chair creaked beside the bed, and Hamid's face appeared above me. His eyes were dark with concern, and he looked like he hadn't slept in days. "How do you feel?"

"Can't...move," I said through gritted teeth. "What's...wrong with me?"

"It's just the drugs. You were in bad shape, and Xavier had to immobilize you to help your spine heal."

I swallowed dryly. "How bad?"

He ran a hand through his hair as he listed my injuries. "Fourteen broken bones, including four ribs, fractured spine, punctured lung, ruptured kidney, fractured skull and cheekbone."

"That explains why I feel like death warmed over," I croaked.

A shadow passed over his face, and I realized what I'd said. I'd stopped breathing, and he had literally breathed life back into me.

"S-sorry." I coughed. "Water."

He held a cup with a straw in it to my mouth, and I drank greedily.

"More?" he asked when I had drunk it all.

"No." I licked my dry lips.

He set the cup on a table. "Are you in pain?"

I took stock of my body. My head hurt, but from the neck down, there was nothing. Panic threatened to suffocate me again, and I had to remind myself it was temporary.

"No." I stared at the ceiling so he couldn't see my weakness. "How long?"

"A day and a half. Xavier said you're healing well, but you'll be in here for a few more days."

"Great," I muttered, already feeling the drugs pulling me down again. I fought against them.

"The more you sleep, the faster you'll recover," Hamid said. "I'll stay with you."

"You don't have to stay," I murmured, even though his presence soothed away the fear that clung to me. I tried not to think about what that meant.

He didn't respond. I heard him sit, and though I couldn't see him, I could feel him there.

I sighed and let sleep take me again.

The next time I awoke, sunlight shone in through the high windows and I could hear the murmur of male voices somewhere in the room.

I turned my attention to my body and made two discoveries. The first was that I could move my arms and legs. The second was that moving hurt like a son of a bitch. I pressed my lips together against the pain but a small grunt slipped out.

Hamid and Xavier appeared beside the bed.

"It's good to have you back," Xavier said with a smile. "Don't try to move. I've started cutting back on the drugs to allow your Mori to take over the healing, but you're not in any shape to move around yet."

I grimaced. "So I've noticed."

"Xavier will give you something for the pain," Hamid said.

"Don't need anything," I lied. I coughed, and it felt like someone was stabbing me in the chest. I bit my lip to keep from crying out.

Hamid took my hand in his. "You've been through a lot. Crying does not make you weak. And neither does taking something for the pain."

I scowled and tried to pull my hand from his. "I don't cry."

He smiled, and for a moment, I completely forgot the pain.

"It's good to see you haven't lost that stubborn streak," he said.

I huffed and tried again to extract my hand from his. "Don't you have something better to do with your time than hanging out here?"

"No."

I turned my head to watch Xavier, who had gone to a cabinet and returned with a syringe of pale blue liquid. "What's that?"

He injected the stuff into my IV. "Just something to help with the pain."

"I said I don't need anything." I blinked as drowsiness hit me, making my words slur. "God damnit. I'm going to kick your ass when I get out of this bed. Both of you."

Hamid chuckled. "I'm looking forward to it."

My retort died on my tongue as I succumbed to the drugs.

It was dark outside the windows the next time I opened my eyes. I turned my head, expecting to see Hamid in the chair, but it was empty. There was no sign of Xavier either. I must be doing a lot better if they'd both felt it was okay to leave me here alone.

I tentatively moved my arms and legs and let out a relieved sigh when I felt no pain. The IV had been removed, too. Good. Maybe I could get out of this room now.

It was a struggle to sit up. The pain might be gone, but I was as weak as a newborn kitten.

I swung my legs over the side of the bed and stopped moving as a wave of dizziness hit me. I would have lain down again, but my bladder suddenly decided it needed emptying. Not to mention I felt like I hadn't bathed in a week. I was also starving, but that could wait until I took care of more pressing matters.

I was a mess, but God, it felt great to be alive.

I managed to stand and started making my way to the bathroom in the ward, using the wall for support. It took a few minutes, but I got there. I didn't have a change of clothes, but I found clean hospital gowns and towels in a linen closet next to the bathroom. Score.

The bathroom had a large walk-in shower stocked with shampoo and soaps. I let out a blissful moan when I stepped under the spray of hot water. I was in heaven.

The dizzy spell hit me the second I took my hand from the wall to stand on my own. I leaned against the tile, taking slow deep breaths as black spots floated before my eyes.

When my legs began to wobble, I swore in frustration. There was no way I was making it back to the bed without falling flat on my face.

I hung my head in defeat. *Not one of my more brilliant ideas.*

I didn't register Hamid's presence until the shower door opened. Before I could protest, he turned off the water and stepped into the stall.

"You shouldn't be out of bed." He wrapped an arm around me and bent to slip the other one behind my knees.

"I stink," I whined as he picked me up. "I just wanted to get clean."

He set me on my feet again, and with one arm around my waist, he reached out and turned on the shower. He moved us under the spray, unmindful of the fact that he was fully clothed, and began to lather my hair with shampoo.

"What are you doing?" I asked and then moaned when his strong fingers massaged my scalp. God, that felt amazing.

He didn't answer as he continued his ministrations.

"This is a serious violation of rule number two," I murmured, earning a chuckle from him.

He finished washing my hair and turned us so he could rinse out the shampoo. The arm around my waist moved, and his hand grazed the under-side of my breast. Heat shot to places that should be nowhere near this man without several layers of clothes between us.

When he shifted us so he could shut off the water, my hand brushed against him and I discovered I wasn't the only one affected by our close contact. Need coursed through me, and it was all I could do not to turn around and pull his head down to mine. It was a good thing I was too weak to do much, or I'd be in serious trouble right now.

Hamid opened the shower door and lifted me out of the stall. Sitting me on the vanity, he grabbed a thick white towel and dried me off. He was tender, but surprisingly, there was nothing sexual in his actions despite what I'd felt in the shower. I studied his face, but he was as unreadable as ever.

Once I was dry, he helped me into a clean gown and used the towel on my hair. Then he stripped off his wet shirt and carried me back to the ward. Instead of laying me on the bed, he sat me in the chair and proceeded to strip my bed and make it up with clean linens. I tried not to watch the ripple of his muscles as he moved, but I couldn't tear my eyes from him.

"You'd make a great nurse," I said after he had settled me back in bed and adjusted it so I was sitting up.

He walked over to the neighboring bed and picked up a tray of food I hadn't noticed because I'd been too preoccupied watching him. He laid the tray across my lap, and my mouth watered at the smell of chicken and alfredo sauce.

"Eat slowly. You haven't had solid food in three days." He went to the door. "I'll be back soon. If I find you out of bed, you'll be getting those bodyguards."

"It's not nice to threaten a patient," I called after him.

My stomach growled painfully, and I dug into my meal. By the time Hamid returned, wearing a change of clothes, I'd cleaned my plate, and I was resting comfortably against the pillows he'd propped behind me.

"Where is everyone else?" I asked when he lifted the tray from my lap. I was surprised I hadn't seen Sara and Beth by now.

He set the tray on the other bed. "They've been here a few times while you slept. I expect you'll see them tomorrow."

I couldn't think of any other way to ask my next question, so I just came out with it. "Why are you here with me instead of one of them? Don't they need you on the investigation?"

"They do, but you needed me more. Your Mori was weakened and in distress, and having mine close by calmed it. It's common among bonded pairs."

He said it so casually, as if his presence here was for a medical purpose only. But then, if I died, Orias's spell could fail and the barrier might be reopened. That made my health pretty important to a lot of people and probably put me before their investigation.

To my dismay, my throat tightened. I didn't want him having any tender feelings for me, so his answer shouldn't bother me.

Get a grip, Jordan, I scolded myself. I was just being emotional after what I'd been through. Being nearly beaten to death would affect anyone, right?

"Thanks for everything you did," I said quietly. "I don't think I'd be here if not for you."

His jaw clenched, and for a fleeting moment, I saw anguish in his eyes. It told me better than words how close I'd come to dying. Even if he didn't want to be mated, his Mori must have been upset when mine almost died. That couldn't have been easy on him.

"You don't have to thank me for that." He looked a little put out. I didn't try to understand why; I just accepted it as a Hamid thing.

"Yes, I do. And since I think we can safely say I'm on the mend, you don't have to stay with me. I'm sure you have more important things to do besides sitting here watching me sleep."

"I like watching you sleep. It's the only time I know you won't argue with me," he said without missing a beat.

My eyebrows shot up. I'd never heard him joke around like that.

Hamid moved to stand beside my bed. "Do you want to talk about what happened?"

"I thought I could shower on my own. No big deal."

"You know that's not what I meant."

I twisted the blanket between my fingers. "They got the jump on me, and I wasn't strong enough to fight them off."

He sat on the foot of the bed. "You were outnumbered six to one. It had nothing to do with your strength."

"You would have been able to fight them."

His gaze held mine. "A little over eight years ago, my brother Ammon and I were with a team that was cleaning out a big nest in Bolivia. I got separated from the others, and I was ambushed by five mature vampires that were just as fast and as strong as I was. My strength and speed were no advantage against the five of them. If Ammon hadn't found me, I probably would have died that night."

"You can't compare mature vampires to Gulaks," I argued.

"Yes, I can," he said. "One-on-one I was a match for those vampires, but not all of them at once. It's the same for you and the Gulaks. You could easily go up against one or two of them, and they knew it. It's why they came at you as a group."

Logically, I knew he was right, but mentally, I felt like I'd failed somehow. I couldn't help going over the attack in my head and looking for ways I could have changed the outcome.

"It's normal to doubt yourself after something like this," he said as if he'd read my mind. "But don't let doubt weigh you down. You're one of the finest young warriors I've ever met, and I think you know it."

A smile played at the corners of my mouth. "Can I get that in writing?"

His laugh warmed me all the way to my toes. "No. But I will let you prove how good you are the next time we spar."

"How generous of you?" I stifled a yawn as a pleasant lethargy swept over me.

He moved to lower the head of my bed. "For now, you need to sleep."

"But I just woke up," I protested.

"And you're still recovering from serious injuries." He picked up the tray and walked to the door. "Unless you want Xavier to keep you in here for another day, you better get some rest."

That shut me up. I was so over the whole patient thing. I wanted out of this ward and hospital gown and back into my own clothes.

"Fine," I called after him. "But no more watching me sleep. It's creepy."

Hamid said something I couldn't quite make out, but it sounded suspiciously like, "See you soon."

Xavier released me from the medical ward the next morning, but only after I showed him I could stand for five minutes and walk across the room without support. I was still weak, so he offered to take me to my room in a wheelchair. He laughingly rescinded the offer after I not-so-sweetly suggested where he could put his wheelchair.

The building was quiet when I walked slowly to the sleeping quarters, and I was grateful no one was around to see me like this. I'd planned to get a shower, but I was so tired by the time I got to my room that I had to lie down and rest for an hour first. I'd never been sick or badly injured before, and I wasn't used to my body not doing what I needed it to. It frustrated me to the point I wanted to punch something – if only I had the strength to do it.

Showering was a slow process, but at least I was able to do it without assistance. As I lathered up my hair, I couldn't help but remember the way Hamid had held me against his hard body, the feel of his hands on me as he'd washed me. I'd been with men before, but that had been the single most erotic experience of my life.

I felt more like myself once I was showered and dressed in my most comfortable jeans and a soft sweater. Leaving my room, I followed the delicious smell of pancakes to the kitchen, where I found Sara and Nikolas eating a late breakfast.

Sara's face lit up when she saw me. "You're up!" She started to stand but stopped, her brow furrowing unhappily. "I can't even hug you."

We'd been careful to keep a safe distance from each other ever since she discovered it was demon magic attached to me. She wasn't allowed to come within two feet of me out of fear of her power destroying the magic of the spell.

"It's the thought that counts," I told her as I took a seat at the table. "You can make it up by feeding me."

She and Nikolas laughed, and he went to get a plate for me. He piled pancakes on it and set it in front of me. "Good to see you back on your feet again."

"Thanks. If I never see the inside of a medical ward again, it will be too soon." I poured maple syrup over my pancakes and ate a large bite. "Mmmm, this certainly beats the intravenous diet."

Sara shoved a plate of sausages at me. "Here. You must be starving."

"I am." I helped myself to a few sausages. "Where is everyone this morning?"

"I believe Chris and Beth are in the gym," Nikolas said. "Hamid and the Council team left early to investigate another summoning site."

"Another site?"

Nikolas nodded. "One of the patrols found it late last night. It's an older site, and we don't know yet if it was a normal summoning or an attempt to open the barrier.

I was about to ask if they had any idea who was behind this, when Beth and Chris came in. Beth looked like she'd been running for an hour, and Chris wasn't even sweating.

"Look who decided to get out of bed," Chris teased.

Beth's smile was huge. "You look great."

"A few days of drug-induced beauty rest does wonders for the body," I joked. "But I wouldn't recommend it."

She looked down at her damp clothes. "I'm going to hold off until after my shower to hug the crap out of you. Don't go anywhere."

She took Chris by the hand and tugged him after her. He gave me a little wave and let her lead him away. Knowing those two, it would be a long shower.

An image of Hamid in the shower with me came to mind, and I quickly banished it. Gah! I had to stop thinking about him like that.

We finished our breakfast, and Nikolas ordered Sara and me to sit while he made short work of cleaning up.

"There is something incredibly sexy about a big, strong warrior doing dishes," I said to Sara in a whisper loud enough for him to hear.

Nikolas laughed, and Sara gave me a playful glare. "You checking out my man?"

"Never," I declared dramatically.

After he'd finished cleaning the kitchen, Nikolas left us to catch up.

Sara kept shooting me glances like she wanted to say something. I didn't question her about it. I expected my friends to act strange around me for a day or two after what had happened.

We had just moved to the couches when Beth joined us. She hugged me until I begged for mercy.

"Don't ever scare us like that again," she ordered as she let me go.

"Trust me, it's not something I want to repeat." I thought back to the attack, but everything after I started to black out was a blur. "What happened after I talked to you, Sara?"

Sara hugged a pillow to her chest. "I ran like a bat out of hell to the control room to send out a distress call. Thank God Chris and Beth weren't too far from you. Hamid was a little farther out, but he actually got to you first."

"Hamid completely lost it," Beth said, her eyes wide with the memory. "He cut those Gulaks to pieces, all six of them. We got there as he killed the last one, and it was a gruesome sight. You were lying in the middle of all of it, covered in blood, and I thought..." Her voice hitched. "I thought you were dead. I ran to you, and Chris tried to calm Hamid down before he killed anyone else."

"Who else was there?" I asked, trying to piece together the bits of my memory from that day.

"Some of the demons from the wrakk came outside when they heard the noise. They were too terrified of Hamid to move. I don't blame them. I've never seen anything as scary as he was that day. His eyes were black, and he was growling like a wild animal."

She shivered at the memory. "I think he would have leveled the place if I hadn't yelled that you'd stopped breathing. He pushed me out of the way and did CPR on you, and he wouldn't let anyone else near you until Xavier got there. At first, he wouldn't let Xavier touch you, but Chris told him you were in a lot of pain."

"He wasn't much better when they got you back here," Sara said. "I thought Nikolas and Chris were going to have to restrain him while Xavier worked on you. Once Xavier had you stabilized, Hamid went in, and we felt it was best to leave him alone with you. I didn't go to see you until the next day, but you were still out. He didn't leave your side for the first two days, not until Xavier said you were past the worst of it."

I didn't speak as I processed everything. Hamid had gone into a full rage over me, something only a bonded male would do. Everyone here knew that, which meant my secret wasn't a secret anymore. I avoided Sara and Beth's gazes, but I could feel their eyes on me as they waited for me to speak.

I sighed heavily and looked at them. "Go ahead and ask me."

"How long?" Sara asked softly.

"Since the night we got hit with the spell. It was the first time we touched."

Their eyes grew round, and Beth said, "But that was a month ago. You didn't say anything."

I shrugged. "Neither of us wanted the bond, so I told him I was breaking it and left to come here. I didn't think it was worth mentioning when I wasn't going to see him again."

"Then he came here and..." Sara put a hand to her chest. "He told you about the spell and that you had to stay near each other."

"Yeah." I dragged out the word. "It's actually worse than that. Orias thinks we bonded at the moment the spell hit us and our bond somehow became part of the spell. That means if we break the bond, we break the spell."

"Oh, Jordan," Beth breathed.

"We agreed to some ground rules to keep the bond from growing. No touching and only spending time together when we absolutely have to. It was easy at first because I couldn't stand to be in the same room with him.

"And then Bastien put that new spell on us and we were stuck together for days." I inhaled deeply. "It's hard to be around someone that much and not talk. We got to know each other, but it never got physical between us. And outside of training, we hardly talk since we came back here."

Sara and Beth exchanged a glance I couldn't decipher.

"What's that look for?" I asked.

Sara hesitated before she answered me. "Are you sure Hamid doesn't want the bond?"

"Yes. He told me so himself back in L.A."

"Back when the bond was brand new," Beth said. "But you two have spent a lot of time together since then and gotten closer. He might not be around much, but I've seen you guys in the gym. It's like there is no one in the world but the two of you."

I laughed at what she was implying. "We love to spar, and he enjoys teaching me new stuff. That's all it is. Like I told you, we got to know each other and decided we didn't hate each other after all. But he doesn't want a mate any more than I do. Trust me on that."

"And the rage?" Sara asked.

I picked at a loose thread on my sleeve. "We both knew the bond would grow no matter what we did to slow it down. All I can say is he acted like any bonded male would in such an extreme situation."

Neither of my friends was convinced. They were looking at this as happily bonded females, and they could only see the romantic side of bonding with the happy ending. But that wasn't for everyone.

I ignored the tiny pang of longing in my chest. "Anyway, that's all of it. I'm sorry I lied to you guys, but it's not something I wanted to talk about."

"You have nothing to apologize for." Sara's green eyes were full of compassion. "Bonding is very personal, and you don't have to explain your feelings to anyone."

"But if you want to share, that's what we're here for," Beth added. "Especially for the juicy stuff."

I snorted indelicately. "What happened to the girl who used to blush when I brought up sex?"

"She mated the sexiest man alive," she replied with a lusty sigh.

Not quite the sexiest. Chris was hot, but Hamid was in a league of his own. And that wasn't the bond talking. I'd known it since the first moment I saw the fierce warrior with the intense blue eyes and the sexy scowl. No man before or after had measured up to him. It depressed me to think that no one ever would.

12

"I thought we were done with the tests," I said as I settled into one of the chairs in the conference room a day later.

Orias sat in front of me, his expression that of an adult who was tired of explaining something to a child. "I don't recall you complaining this much when we first met."

"That's because I wasn't being used as a lab rat back then," I retorted. "It took me days to recover from all those magic tests at Westhorne."

He placed his hands on either side of my face. "This one won't take long. We need to make sure your brush with death didn't weaken the spell."

Resentment flared in me. "God forbid anything should happen to your spell. I'd hate to inconvenience you all with my death."

"I would be a little put out if you left us." Amusement flickered in his eyes. "You're entertaining for a lab rat."

Bastien chuckled, and I glared across the table at him. I still hadn't forgiven him for that binding spell he'd put on Hamid and me.

Orias started chanting, and I felt magic crawl across my skin. It was a test he'd performed daily at Westhorne so I was used to it, but I still hated it. I closed my eyes and counted down the seconds until it was over.

When I opened my eyes, I saw the rest of the team had entered the room and taken seats around the table. Ciro wasn't among them, so I asked where he was.

"He went to Atlanta to check in on his protégé," Orias said as he pushed his chair back and faced the table.

"You guys have protégés?" There was a lot I didn't know about warlocks, but they seemed to prefer working alone most of the time. I couldn't imagine Orias being a mentor to anyone.

It was Bastien who answered me. "It takes years of training and guidance to master our spells, and to summon the right demons to enhance our power. Once we reach our full power, we take on apprentices, usually one at a time. I recently took on a new one."

I looked at Orias. "What about you? Do you have one?"

"Not at the moment. I'm having more fun with you," he said dryly.

"Funny guy."

My Mori fluttered, letting me know Hamid was approaching. I looked up as he entered the room, and his eyes briefly met mine as he walked around the table to sit on my other side. The last time I'd been this close to him was when I was in the ward, and my body warmed now at his nearness.

I wasn't allowed to do anything strenuous for the next few days, which meant no working out. I couldn't decide if I was more bummed about not being able to spar or not being able to spar with him.

"How do you feel?" he asked in a low voice.

I turned slightly toward him. "All better. Just waiting to get my strength back."

He studied my face as if he wasn't sure I was being honest. He knew me well enough by now to know I'd say just about anything to stay out of the medical ward.

He looked satisfied by what he saw. "Are you eating enough to help build up your strength?"

I resisted the urge to roll my eyes. "Don't worry. Sara has that covered. She's been feeding me nonstop."

"Good."

Charlotte spoke, pulling our attention to her. "Before we start the meeting, I want to say how happy we are to see you've recovered from your injuries, Jordan."

"Thanks." I started to stand. "I'll get out of here so you can have your meeting."

Charlotte smiled. "You're welcome to stay. This investigation affects you as much as anyone else."

I paused, halfway out of my chair. I'd never been included in their meetings, outside of the tests, and I'd been happy to stay away from anything to do with the Council. But I was interested in the outcome of this one, and honestly, I was bored out of my mind just hanging around the command center.

"Okay." I sank back into my chair.

The first ten minutes of the meeting was spent discussing my health, or actually the health of the spell. Orias informed us my close call hadn't weakened the spell. On the contrary, it looked a little stronger than the last time he'd checked it a week ago.

I wondered if anyone else was thinking the same thing I was. If my bond with Hamid was part of the spell, then any strengthening of our bond should theoretically strengthen the spell. I kept my musings to myself. I was not going to discuss my bond with a bunch of warlocks and scholars as if it was just another part of this investigation. Plus, they might get it into their heads next that completing the bond would make the spell unbreakable and keep the barrier safe.

That thought led to a rather X-rated one about how Hamid and I would complete the bond. I shifted in my chair as I tried to put the image from my mind. Ever since that night in the shower, I'd been having these fantasies, each one more graphic than the last. To make matters worse, I couldn't even find relief for all this pent-up sexual tension, because the thought of touching another male repulsed me.

Thanks for nothing, demon.

Solmi, it grumbled resentfully. At least, I wasn't the only unhappy one. Misery loves company and all that.

"The only demon with enough power to open the barrier is an archdemon," said Marie, yanking me from my thoughts.

Bastien clasped his hands on the table. "Impossible. If there was an archdemon on this side of the barrier, we would know it."

An involuntary shudder went through me. An upper demon was powerful, but an archdemon was virtually indestructible. In its physical form, an archdemon was said to be impervious to earthly weapons, and not even a faerie could kill one of them. The only weapon that could destroy an archdemon was an archangel's sword, and I didn't see any angels walking around here.

I raised a hand to get their attention. "Could an archdemon have opened the barrier first from the other side and come through it?"

Charlotte shook her head. "The barrier can only be opened from this side."

"How do you know that for sure?" I asked.

"It was created that way," she replied. "The original breach only happened because someone on this side opened the barrier."

"If an archdemon could open the barrier from their side, they would have done so long before now," Orias explained.

"True." I thought back to my demon studies and realized we'd only scratched the surface of that subject in school. It was no wonder our scholars dedicated their lives to it, because it would take a lifetime to understand it all.

"The only way a demon can cross the barrier without opening it is through a summoning, but that leaves them without a body," I said more to myself than anyone else. "If the summoning is done incorrectly, the demon could possess the warlock, and that would give them a body."

"To an extent," Orias said, interrupting my thoughts. "The human body could house the demon, but the demon wouldn't have all its strength and power without its own body."

"Would it be strong enough to open the barrier?" I pressed.

Bastien's smile was patronizing. "An upper demon cannot open the barrier."

I rested my arms on the table and leaned in. "What would happen if a warlock summoned an archdemon?"

All chatter around the table stopped, and everyone stared at me as if I'd started speaking in tongues.

Orias cleared his throat. "No warlock would attempt such a thing. It would be suicide."

"Our spells can control an upper demon, but containing an archdemon would be like trying to stop a volcano from erupting," Bastien said. "It cannot be done."

I looked from Bastien to Orias. "You're saying a warlock wouldn't try to summon one, not that they couldn't do it."

Orias pursed his lips. "It takes a very complex and powerful spell to summon an upper demon and bring it through the barrier. Using that same spell to summon an archdemon would be like a human sitting in a rubber dinghy and trying to catch a great white shark with a fishing rod. If they somehow managed to hook it, they wouldn't be strong enough to reel it in."

"What if the shark decided it wanted to come to the boat?" I asked.

He cocked an eyebrow. "Ever watch *Jaws*?"

"I see your point."

The conversation shifted to persons of interest in the Chicago area they wanted to interview. Orias mentioned a local witch named Seraphine who had deep ties to the Chicago underworld. They'd been trying to set up a meeting with her, but she was distrustful of other magic users and hated warlocks.

It was decided that Hamid would talk to her if they could get her to agree to a meeting. He wouldn't be my first choice to send to talk to someone who was skittish around most people, but what did I know? He was lead investigator for a reason.

I stayed in the room until the conversation returned to their favorite topic – the spell. There was nothing I could contribute to the discussion, so I excused myself from the meeting before they decided they wanted to do more tests.

I could feel Hamid's eyes on me as I left the room, but I didn't look at him. Other than asking me how I was feeling, he hadn't spoken to me in the meeting. His absences and lack of interaction made it obvious he was pulling back and distancing himself from me. It was probably for the best, but I couldn't help feeling a little melancholy. I was going to miss our sparring sessions.

Beth came out of the control room as I approached it. "What's with the long face?"

"Meeting with the Council team," I said, hoping she'd leave it at that. "Where are you off to?"

She hesitated before she said, "Chris and I are going to the wrakk to do the self-defense class."

"He's going with you?"

She grimaced. "He doesn't want me going there alone after what happened."

"I don't think any of those Gulaks are coming back," I joked.

"Yeah, but your attack freaked him out more than he wants to admit. He keeps saying it could have been me. I don't want to stop doing the class, but I hate having him worry over me. So, he's been coming with me." She bit her bottom lip. "The boys asked when you'll be back. I can tell them you –"

"Tell them I'll see them soon and I hope they've been practicing with the staffs I gave them."

Her smile returned. "I'll let them know. I'd better go. Chris is waiting for me."

"Have fun."

I watched her walk away, envy gnawing at me. I wanted to be the one going to the wrakk today, not just to do the class but to stand on the spot where I was attacked and show the world that I was back and I wasn't going out that easily.

"But it's been three days since I left the medical ward, and I feel fine." I stood in the doorway of Nikolas's office and gave him a pleading look. "Come on, Nikolas. I'm going crazy, and I need to be on patrol."

He sat on the corner of the desk with his arms crossed and an unyielding expression. "I'm sorry, but Xavier said you need at least five days before you can go back to work. I won't risk your safety by letting you return too soon."

"What about my mental health? Because I'm going to lose my mind if I have to be cooped up here much longer."

I wasn't exaggerating. Not only did I hate being idle, this forced "rest" was wreaking havoc on my sleep schedule. I couldn't work out or do anything strenuous enough to burn off all the restless energy building up inside me, so it was taking me hours to fall asleep. Every morning, I crawled out of bed feeling unrested and in a worse mood than the day before.

He smiled sympathetically. "I know this has been hard for you, but it's just two more days."

I groaned and slumped against the doorframe. "You're killing me. I thought you liked me."

"I'll tell you what. I could use a break from these reports. Why don't we take the bikes out for a run?"

My head shot up. "Don't toy with me, Nikolas. I'm a woman on the edge."

He chuckled and reached into his jeans pocket to pull out the key to his Ducati. "I'll meet you at the bikes in five minutes."

I nearly ran down two warriors in my haste to get to my room and change. Nikolas was waiting for me when I entered the loading bay a few minutes later, nearly jumping up and down in my excitement. It was crazy how I'd taken things as simple as riding my bike for granted. I'd never realized how much I enjoyed the freedom it gave me until it was taken from me.

Nikolas and I rode for a little over an hour. I would have stayed out all afternoon if he had let me, but I didn't argue when he said it was time to go back. I planned to ask him to let me ride again tomorrow. Being difficult now wouldn't win me any favors.

"Thanks for that," I told him after we parked our bikes. "I really needed it."

"Hang in there. You'll be back wreaking havoc in no time."

I laughed. "You know it."

We parted ways at the door to the control room. Nikolas went inside, and I continued on to the living area. The room was empty except for a warrior named Rory who was reading on a tablet. I'd never been a big reader, and I wished now that I was. Anything to pass the time and break up the boredom of my current existence.

I wandered over to the tall bookcase in the living room to see if anything looked good. Sara had added it, saying it made the place feel homier and that everyone should have books in their lives. I shook my head in amusement when I saw the selection. Leave it to Sara to fill the thing up with mostly classics.

"Now this is more my style," I murmured when I found a series of manga comics on the bottom shelf.

My hand paused reaching for the comics when my Mori did that annoying flutter to alert me that Hamid was nearby. I hadn't laid eyes on him since the meeting two days ago, and I was surprised he was here in the middle of the day when he seemed to be going out of his way to avoid me.

"Where have you been?" he demanded from behind me.

I looked over my shoulder to see him standing in the doorway. His hard stare and drawn brows said he was angry, but I was at a loss as to why.

I stood unhurriedly. "I've been here. Where else would I be?"

"You weren't here for the last hour," he said.

"How do you know that?"

He strode toward me. "I received a notification from the tracker on your motorcycle that it was moving. Why were you out riding around the city when you should be resting?"

I planted my hands on my hips. "Why are you getting alerts from my tracker?"

The tracker was one of the conditions I'd agreed to in order to keep some semblance of normalcy in my life. I had one on my bike and one I carried with me. But he had said nothing about me being under constant surveillance, and definitely nothing about him getting alerts.

He stopped a few feet from me. "I am responsible for your safety. Since I cannot be with you throughout the day, I configured your trackers to let me know where you are."

"I'm not an invalid who will fall and break a bone if I'm left alone," I argued. I wasn't sure if I was more annoyed that he was treating me like I was helpless or that he'd disappeared for days, only to show up now all concerned about me. "And you don't get to tell me when I can come and go from here. That was not part of our arrangement."

A muscle ticked in his jaw. "You are recovering from a near fatal attack and under the healer's orders to not overexert yourself. What if you'd had a relapse out there with no one to help you?"

I breathed through my nose, trying to keep my temper in check. It was on a short fuse these days, and he was dangerously close to igniting it.

"I was not alone. Nikolas was with me, and he is more than capable of *protecting* me if I need it."

"Nikolas rode with you?" he asked. "He knows you are –"

"He knows I am going out of my mind here," I almost yelled at him. "He knows there is more to a person's health than their physical well-being, something you obviously have no clue about. Maybe you would have seen that if you'd been around instead of monitoring your goddamn trackers."

Hamid looked taken aback by my outburst. "What do you need? Tell me, and I will give it to you."

I crossed my arms, hating the way my heart squeezed a little when his expression softened. I was starting to feel things for him beyond the physical attraction, and it scared me. I needed him to go back to being the arrogant warrior who stirred nothing but my anger. It was the only way I was going to come out of this intact.

"I don't need anything from you," I said coldly. "Go back to your investigation."

I met his gaze, refusing to back down or look away. He looked like he wanted to say something else, but then he turned on his heel and left. I glanced over at Rory, but he was no longer there. He must have slipped out while I was arguing with Hamid.

Sinking down on the couch, I rubbed at the ache in my chest, which had only worsened. I didn't understand. I'd gotten what I wanted, so why did it hurt so much?

Solmi, my Mori whispered sadly.

For the first time, I didn't have it in me to argue with it.

I shifted in my bed for what felt like the hundredth time tonight. Groaning, I threw off the covers and sat up. I didn't need to look at the clock to see that it was after 3:00 a.m. because I'd been checking the time every half hour since I'd come to bed.

It was no use trying to sleep. This was my reality until I was allowed to do the things that helped me burn off my endless store of energy. Resigned to my fate, I quietly dressed and left my room, not wanting to disturb anyone else's sleep.

I slowed at Hamid's room, although I already knew he wasn't inside. I hadn't seen him or felt his presence since our argument that afternoon, and I didn't expect to after the way I'd told him to leave me alone.

Shame pricked me when I thought about the harsh words I'd said to him. He had been expressing his concern in his own way, and I'd taken my frustrations out on him. I had lashed out because if I couldn't stop my feelings for him, I'd drive him away. It was immature and not one of my finer moments, and it had plagued me ever since.

I passed through the quiet living area and headed to the gym. Closing the door behind me, I went to the wall where the throwing knives were hung and selected a set. I positioned myself in front of the target and began unleashing all my aggression. It wasn't as satisfying as sparring, but it would have to do.

I was on my fifth round when my Mori alerted me that Hamid was nearby and coming closer. Hoping he'd see the closed door and keep on walking, I went back to my throwing. I knew I had to apologize to him, but I wasn't sure how to explain why I'd been such a bitch after all he'd done for me. Obviously, the truth was out of the question.

The door opened. I didn't look because I knew it was him. For a minute, he stood there watching me throw knives at the target.

When I finished, I moved to retrieve my knives, but he walked over and pulled them from the target, where they were embedded up to the hilt.

"I'm not overexerting myself," I said to his back.

"I know." He faced me, the corner of his mouth tilted up. "I feel safer talking to you when you're not holding weapons."

"Smart man." I bit back a smile.

He lost his teasing tone. "Can't sleep?"

I nodded, because I couldn't pretend with him. He'd spent enough time with me by now to know my sleep habits.

"Anything I can do?"

"No. A sedentary lifestyle doesn't agree with me, and I've been pent up here a little too long. I'll be okay once I can get back to a normal routine."

His eyes grew troubled. "I'm sorry. I should have known how hard this would be for you."

"Stop." I held up a hand. "If anyone should apologize, it's me. I've been in a foul mood, and I took it out on you today."

Hamid hefted one of the knives. "Does throwing these help you sleep?"

"Not really. But it's better than staring at my bedroom ceiling."

"Then we need to make it more interesting." He came to stand beside me. "Closest to the center wins."

"What do I win?" I asked, taking the knife he offered me.

"You can name your prize *if* you win," he said with a cocky lift of his eyebrows.

I narrowed my eyes at him. "Fine. But no engaging our Mori. That way the playing field will be a little more even."

"I accept your terms." He stepped aside and waved me over. "Ladies first."

I moved into position, took aim, and threw. As soon as the knife left my hand, I knew it was one of my best shots. It hit the target almost dead center, and I had to resist the urge to let out a whoop.

"Not bad," he said as he took my place.

"Not bad? That was a nearly perfect throw."

He drew back his arm and released his knife without stopping to take aim. I could hear the scrape of metal on metal as the tip of his blade sank into the target next to mine. I didn't need to walk over to the target to know he'd beaten me by a fraction of an inch.

"Show-off," I muttered.

He handed me another knife. "Best two out of three?"

We threw three knives each. I could have thrown two dozen knives, and I still wouldn't have bested Hamid. The man was a machine, never missing his mark once.

I slanted a look at him. "Are you sure you're not engaging your Mori?"

"Are you calling me a cheater?"

"No," I grudgingly admitted. "Will you show me how you can throw so well without even aiming?"

He chuckled. "I was waiting for you to ask."

Over the next hour, Hamid patiently demonstrated his knife throwing technique, and I practiced until I felt comfortable with it. When we finished, I challenged him to another contest, and this time, it was my knife that took the center spot.

"Yes! Do you see that?" I jumped up and down. "I could kiss you right now."

I turned to face him and stumbled into his hard chest. His arms wrapped around me, and I tilted my head up to give him a sheepish smile.

"Sorry, I –"

My words were cut off when his mouth came down over mine. Every nerve ending in my body fired when his tongue swept possessively across the seam of my lips, demanding entry. I opened to him eagerly as my hands went to the back of his head, holding him against me. There was nothing gentle about this kiss. It was hungry and hard, and it stoked my desire for him into an inferno.

Without breaking the kiss, I pushed him, and he moved backward until he came up against the weight bench. He sat, and my lips stayed fused with his as I climbed onto his lap to straddle him. His arousal pressed against me through our clothes, and I moaned into his mouth. Needing more, I rocked against him, and he growled deep in his chest. Dear God, that was the sexiest sound I'd ever heard.

My hands slid down his back to slip beneath his shirt and glide over his hot skin. His breath hitched, and he made a tortured sound when my fingers traced the muscles of his abdomen. I'd seen him shirtless, but nothing compared to the feel of his hard body under my hands. He was perfection.

One of his large hands moved under my top to cup my breast, and I moaned at the heat of his touch through my bra. I shifted restlessly on his lap, aching to feel all of him without the barrier of clothes between us.

The sound of the outside door opening vaguely registered in my lust-drunk mind. It wasn't until I heard footsteps coming toward us that I came to my senses and broke the kiss. I stared into Hamid's eyes, which were drugged with desire, and reality hit me like a bucket of ice water.

What am I doing? I started to climb off his lap, but his arms tightened around my waist like a vise.

"Stay," he said in a gravelly voice that made me want to do whatever he asked of me. And that realization terrified me more than anything ever had.

"I can't," I whispered hoarsely. "Let me go."

Frustration crossed his face, and for a moment, I thought he wasn't going to release me. But then his arms loosened, and I was able to move away from him.

I couldn't look at him. He'd made the first move, but it was I who had been all over him, getting both of us worked up and so close to losing control. If someone hadn't come along, how far would I have gone? Would I have stopped at all?

A weak "I'm sorry" was all I could manage before I ran from the gym and fled to my room.

13

"Hey, there you are." Beth looked up from the computer she was working on as I entered the control room two days later. "I was just about to go look for you."

"It's a little early for patrol," I joked, excitement rippling through me. I had finally been cleared to go back to work, and tonight I was going out with Chris, Beth, and Rory. Something told me Chris was going to be keeping an eye on me for my first day back, but I didn't care. I was so full of energy after my convalescence that it felt like I would burst out of my skin if I didn't see some action soon.

She smiled. "Nikolas asked me to find you. He said to send you to his office."

I made a face. "Called to the office on my first day at work. This can't be good."

Nikolas's door was closed, which was my first clue that something was up. He never closed it unless he was on a call with Tristan or someone else equally important.

I knocked, and he called for me to enter. My smile disappeared when I opened the door to see that Nikolas was not alone. Hamid was seated in one of the visitor chairs.

It was the first time I'd seen Hamid since that night in the gym, mainly because I'd been doing everything I could to avoid being in the same room with him. Call me a coward, but I didn't know how to face him after that kiss.

Holy Mother, that kiss. My skin heated just remembering the taste of his lips, the feel of his body under my exploring fingers.

My eyes briefly met his stoic gaze before I looked at Nikolas. "You wanted to see me?"

"We did. Come in."

My stomach knotted as I took the chair next to Hamid's. I did not have a good feeling about this.

I gave Nikolas an expectant look, but it was Hamid who spoke.

"The team and I are needed in Atlanta. We leave in two hours."

I wasn't sure why he felt the need to tell me this when we weren't even on speaking terms these days. But I was curious all the same. "Is it another summoning?"

"No. Ciro contacted us an hour ago to say he uncovered something and he needs us to go there immediately. He said it was related to our investigation and of the utmost importance. That is all I know." Hamid's eyes were unreadable, betraying nothing of what he felt about me now. It was almost as if the kiss had never happened and we were nothing more than two warriors working on the same job.

"Oh." I rubbed my palms on my thighs, not sure what to say next. "How long do you think you'll be gone?"

He looked confused for a few seconds. "We will be several days at least. You will want to pack enough clothes for that."

"Me?" I looked from him to Nikolas, who seemed happy to sit back and let us talk. "I don't think Ciro needs me there."

Hamid nodded. "I am needed there, and where I go, you go."

"But..." I started to say I wanted to stay here where I would be useful, but nothing was more important than this investigation. My wants did not matter as long as the person responsible for all of this was still out there.

I nodded and stood. "I'll go pack."

Ten minutes later, I sat on my bed staring at the packed duffle bag on the floor and wondering how I was going to be around Hamid for several days after what had happened between us. He appeared to have moved past it, but I couldn't put it out of my mind. I was starting to think the spell had messed with our bond. How else could I explain why I was obsessing over him while he was composed and indifferent? Had it only been a heat-of-the-moment thing for him?

I let out a pitiful groan and flopped back on my bed. *Why me?*

I stayed there until Beth knocked on my door to tell me it was time to go to the airport. I picked up my bag and set my shoulders before I went to join the others.

One good thing about traveling with the team was that I didn't have to be alone with Hamid or talk to him unless it was necessary. I couldn't get out of riding in the same vehicle as him, but I took the seat farthest from his on the plane. When we landed in Atlanta, he was so focused on the job that he barely looked at me as we piled into the waiting SUVs.

We found Ciro at a modest two-story house in Edgewood. From the outside, the house looked like any other on the street, but as soon as I passed through the front door, my skin prickled almost painfully from the magic inside. I rubbed my arms as I walked down a short hallway, trying to get rid of the pins and needles sensation.

"It's a ward," said Bastien, who had followed me in. "The effects will fade soon."

Ciro was waiting for us in the living room, and his grave expression told me whatever he'd found was not good. Dread coiled in my stomach as I waited for everyone to join us. For him to call the whole team here instead of telling them this over the phone, his discovery had to be huge.

"Thank you for getting here so quickly," he said as soon as the last person entered the room. "This is the home of my protégé, Kai. I came here to check in with him because I haven't heard from him in two months, but he wasn't here. It's not like Kai to go off for this long without telling me."

"You suspect foul play?" Hamid asked, his eyes already scanning the room for clues.

My gaze followed Hamid's and landed on a framed photo of Ciro with a thin man with dirty blond hair, who looked to be in his mid-thirties.

"No." Ciro clasped his hands in front of him, and I noticed tightness around his eyes and mouth. "Kai is quite gifted and powerful for a young warlock. But I was concerned by his absence, so I searched his house, looking for clues to where he might have gone. This morning, I found something hidden in his workroom. It's an old parchment covered in Arabic, of which I only know a few words, but I believe it's a spell. That along with something I read in one of Kai's journals convinced me I had to bring you here as soon as possible."

He waved at a door on the other side of the hallway. "Please, follow me."

I started forward with everyone else, until Hamid grabbed my wrist, holding me back. I looked up at his serious face.

"We're entering a wizard's workroom, and there is no telling what magical traps we'll find inside," he said. "Stay near me, and do not touch anything until the wizards tell us it's safe."

"Okay." Revulsion twisted my stomach at the thought of coming into contact with more magic, but warriors did not let their aversions or fears stop them from doing their job. This would not be the only time in my career that I would have to deal with magic, and the sooner I learned to handle it, the better.

I followed him through the door that led to the basement. I was expecting a dank, dark room filled with potions and magical instruments, and I was surprised to find just the opposite. Kai's workroom was clean and well-lit, and there wasn't a potion in sight. Along one wall was a workbench with cabinets above and below it, and there were two full bookcases and a large stuffed chair that looked worn from use. A woven rug covered the center of the stone floor and the windows were covered with blackout curtains. On a small table beside the chair, a book was open facedown, as if the owner planned to return any moment.

It could almost pass for a normal room if not for the lingering magic that made the hairs on my arms stand up. A month ago, I probably wouldn't have felt the magic at all, but that was before I'd become a guinea pig for a bunch of warlocks.

The team was crowded around a table in a corner of the room, making it impossible to see what they were looking at. If it was the parchment, I'd be of no help to them anyway. I was almost fluent in Spanish, and I knew enough Mandarin to order at a Chinese restaurant, but I wouldn't know Arabic from Russian.

Orias looked over his shoulder at us. "Hamid, can you translate this?"

Hamid ushered me toward the table, obviously not trusting me enough to leave me alone. I went willingly because despite my conflicting emotions over him, I respected his knowledge and experience. If he had concerns about this place, I wasn't going to challenge him.

People moved aside to let us through, and I was able to see what had them all so captivated. On the table lay a piece of parchment between two sheets of glass. The stained parchment was so old it was crumbling around the edges and the writing was faded from age.

Hamid leaned down and studied the document before he began to read the words aloud in English. I couldn't make much sense of what he was saying, but Orias and the other warlocks hung on every word. They interrupted Hamid half a dozen times to ask him to repeat a phrase, and then they'd all nod thoughtfully and go back to listening. When he came to a section he had trouble with, he explained that the language was ancient Arabic and some of the words did not translate well.

"Is it a spell?" Charlotte asked when Hamid finished.

Orias stroked his chin. "It's a summoning spell, but not like anything I've seen."

"Parts of it resemble the spell we use," Bastien said. "But this one has many more layers to it. It's more complex than any spell I know of."

Ciro moved closer to touch the edge of the glass with a finger. "I believe we might be looking at one of the original summoning spells."

Everyone started talking at once until Charlotte called for quiet. She looked at Ciro. "The breach was over two thousand years ago. How could this document have survived that long?"

"Magic maybe. I don't know, but the evidence does not lie," the warlock said.

I held up a hand. "Will one of you please tell me what the original summoning spells are?"

Orias turned to me. "You have heard the story of the great breach and how the archangels supposedly sealed it."

I nodded, and the scholars in the room huffed.

"Not supposedly," Charlotte said.

He ignored her. "The breach didn't happen on its own. It's said that three warlocks created spells that, when used together, tore open the barrier."

"And you think this is one of those spells?" I asked him.

"Yes," Ciro said with a certainty that sent a chill down my spine. "I wasn't sure until I read the last few pages in Kai's journal. It's mostly scattered thoughts, but one word is written several times. Alaron."

I had no idea what Alaron was, but based on the horrified faces around me, it wasn't good. A pit opened in my stomach when I saw the expression mirrored on Hamid's face. If just a mention of this Alaron got such a reaction from him, things were far worse than I'd thought.

"What is Alaron?" I asked, already dreading the answer.

I wasn't sure whether to be reassured or afraid when Hamid moved so close to me our arms were touching. What did he think to protect me from?

"Alaron is an archdemon," he said grimly. "His name is known to us because he tried to come through the barrier during the breach and was driven back by the archangels."

I swallowed dryly. "You think Kai is using this spell to try to create another breach and bring an archdemon through?"

Ciro exhaled deeply. "This spell alone cannot open the barrier. I think Kai tried to summon Alaron with the intent to contain him."

I remembered Orias's analogy about the fisherman and the great white. There was no way Kai could have contained an archdemon, which meant he was dead or...

"Are you saying there could be an archdemon walking around in the body of a warlock?" I asked, the question sounding ludicrous to my own ears.

"It's highly improbable," Bastien said.

"But not impossible," Orias added. "We can't know for sure unless we locate the summoning site." He turned to Ciro. "Do you know where Kai would perform a summoning?"

Ciro nodded. "He owns a small warehouse in an industrial park. I went there yesterday but saw nothing out of the ordinary. No one has been there in months."

"If he was going to summon Alaron, he'd want some place more private." Hamid pulled out his phone. "What is Kai's full name? We'll have our people dig around and see what they can find. I'll inform the Council."

"Bradley," Ciro said weakly.

"What does all of this mean?" I asked the group after Hamid stepped aside to make a call. "You said an archdemon has enough power to open the barrier. Is he trying to create another breach?"

Orias looked at the parchment again. "If Kai did manage to summon Alaron and Alaron possessed Kai's body, it won't be enough for him. He'll try to make a hole large enough to bring his physical body through."

Marie made the sign of the cross. "God help us if he succeeds. In his true form, he could destroy the barrier completely."

My head spun as I tried to come to grips with what they were saying. Everyone I loved would die if the barrier fell. Not even the Fae could protect us from what was on the other side of it.

I looked at Orias, who seemed to know the most about this. "Can Alaron be killed without his body?"

"Yes. His magic is strong, but the body he is possessing is still human."

I let out a breath. "That's something at least."

Ciro's face seemed to have aged ten years since we arrived. "I've known Kai for fifteen years. How could he have done this without me seeing that something was wrong with him? You don't decide overnight to summon an archdemon. This would have taken months, maybe years of planning."

"Why would he do it?" I asked. "What could he hope to achieve by calling Alaron?"

"Power," Orias said without hesitation. "A warlock is only as powerful as the demon he commands, and an archdemon would make him invincible."

I looked at the parchment. "If this spell is so important, why would he leave it here?"

"It's too fragile to carry with him," Ciro said. "Kai put a spell around the parchment that is strong enough to preserve it but not to travel with it. A more powerful spell might damage the document."

Hamid joined us again. "The Council is putting people on finding everything there is to know about Kai Bradley. In the meantime, we need to go over every inch of this place and the warehouse."

Ciro nodded gravely. "Kai has magical wards all over the house, and some might be harmful to you. It would be safest if you warriors split up with us."

"I'll take Jordan," Orias said, surprising me. To Hamid he said, "I will keep her safe."

Hamid glanced at me, and I could tell he was not happy about us separating. But what Ciro said made sense.

The group split up with Orias and me on the third floor. I suspected he took me there because it was the least likely place to find anything dangerous. I didn't need to be a genius to see he was protecting me while the others searched the rest of the house.

"Are you strong enough to kill Alaron if we find him in time?" I asked as Orias rifled through drawers in the master bedroom.

Orias didn't stop what he was doing. "Not alone."

I sat on the foot of the neatly made bed. "What happens when you kill the host body? Does the demon die, too?"

This time, Orias looked at me. "He will return to his own dimension. Summoned demons can't be killed as long as their physical body is still alive."

My eyes went to the satchel he always carried that held his demon. "Do you keep the same demon forever, or release them after a while and get a fresh one?"

He raised an eyebrow.

I shrugged. "What? It's a valid question."

"It depends on the warlock. I've had my demon for about fifty years." He went back to poking around in the dresser. "Now, stop asking questions, and let me work."

It was almost midnight when we finished searching the house, having made no other significant discoveries. After some discussion over what to do with the parchment, it was decided that Charlotte and Marie would hold it until it could be sent to our archives in England for study and safekeeping.

Hamid said we would wait until the next day to go to the warehouse, so we left to find accommodations and food since the house could not sleep us all. Orias felt it would be better if we all stayed together, and Hamid agreed. He booked us rooms on the top floor of the Ritz-Carlton, and we headed over there.

I stood back talking to Charlotte while Hamid checked us in and got our room keys. Then we piled into two elevators and went to the top floor where he handed out the key cards. I waited for mine and frowned when I didn't get one.

"Where is my key?" I asked him when the others headed off to their rooms.

Hamid held up the remaining key card. "You and I are sharing."

My stomach fluttered wildly despite my dismay. "Why do we need to share? No one else is sharing."

"No one else needs my protection," he replied. "And it's not like we haven't shared a room before."

He turned to walk down the hallway, but I stayed rooted to the spot. How could I be alone in a hotel room with him after what had happened a few nights ago?

Hamid stopped walking when he realized I wasn't following. He looked back at me. "If it bothers you that much, I will sleep outside the door."

"You can't sleep in the hallway." He needed his rest, and I wouldn't be able to sleep knowing he was out here on the floor.

I let out a sigh. "We can share – but just for tonight."

He waited for me to catch up to him, and we walked past two more doors until we came to ours. He unlocked the door, and I walked in ahead of him. I came up short at the sight of the king bed in the middle of the room.

I swung back to him. "You couldn't get one with two beds?"

"They were out of double rooms on this floor, and I wanted us all to stay together," he said, dropping his long duffle bag on the bed. The soft clink of metal told me the bag was probably half full of weapons.

If he'd been any other man, I might not have believed him. But Hamid was above such deception. If he'd gotten a room with one bed on purpose, he would have told me.

"I'm taking a shower," I said angrily, heading to the bathroom with my bag.

I took an extra long shower, not in any hurry to go back to the room. When I finally opened the bathroom door, I found Hamid eating a large burger in the sitting area. My stomach growled at the smell of food, and I dug into the burger waiting for me.

"Thanks," I mumbled between bites. "I was starving."

"I apologize for not stopping for dinner. I'm used to skipping meals when I'm on a job."

I licked ketchup off my lip. "It's okay."

Neither of us said much after that. We finished our late dinner, and Hamid went to shower. I sized up the sleeping situation and got butterflies when I thought of sharing the bed with him. My gut told me it was a very bad idea, but I couldn't ask him to sleep on the floor again. I knew he would refuse to allow me to take the floor, and the couch was too short for either of us.

I pulled back the covers on one side of the bed and got in as close to the edge as I could. I left one light on for him and figured he'd work out where to sleep. Closing my eyes, I tried to will myself to sleep before he came out of the bathroom.

I should have known it wouldn't be that easy. Even after a long day full of travel and excitement, my body refused to shut down.

When the bathroom door opened, I kept my eyes closed and my body turned toward my side of the bed. I listened as Hamid walked into the room and set his bag down on the floor. There was a pause, and then the light went out.

A second later, the bed dipped as he got in. I had to force myself to take slow even breaths and not think about him lying a few feet away – and how easy it would be to roll over and touch him.

I thought I was doing a good job of feigning sleep until he said, "We can go down to the hotel gym if you need to."

I smiled to myself. "I'm good. Thanks. It's just been a crazy day."

"Do you want to talk about it?"

"I think you guys explained it all pretty well. If Alaron gets his body, it'll be the end of life as we know it."

"We'll find him before that happens," he said confidently.

"How can you be so sure?"

"If he could have done it by now, he would have." Hamid sounded a lot more relaxed than I felt. "He might not be strong enough in the human body to bring his own body through. Whatever the reason, we still have time."

I rolled over to face him, and I could see the outline of him on his back with an arm behind his head. "How do you do it? How do you focus on the job, knowing what's at stake if we fail?"

He was quiet for a moment. "It comes with experience. Once you've been doing this as long as I have, you lose the fear you had as a young warrior."

"I'm not afraid of dying. I'm afraid for Sara and her baby, who might never be born if this goes wrong, and for all of the people I love."

He turned his head toward me. "You take that fear and channel it into your work. It's the person with the most at stake who will fight the hardest."

I thought about his words long after his breathing had evened out. I envied him lying there so peacefully while my mind whirled with what-ifs. I had the insane urge to slide across the bed and take comfort from being close to him, but I refused to act on it. Things were already complicated enough between us.

The sound of a phone ringing woke me from a deep sleep. I must have totally passed out, because I felt groggy and the last thing I wanted to do was get up. God, this bed was comfortable. How had I not noticed that last night?

The phone started up again. I groaned and stretched...or I tried to, only to find myself trapped by a male arm around my waist. I froze as my body registered the chest against my back, the warm breath tickling my ear, and the muscled thigh tucked between my legs.

I shifted slightly, and the feel of a hard length pressed against my bottom made my belly clench. I closed my eyes against the exquisite torture of being so intimately close to the man I wanted more than anything and couldn't have.

I held my breath and slowly lifted his arm to slide away from him. If I could get up without waking him, he'd never know about our little spooning session.

A guttural sound of protest came from behind me. The next thing I knew, I was on my back with Hamid hovering above me. His weight rested on his forearms while his lower half was nestled snugly between my legs.

I drew in a sharp breath and stared up into heavy-lidded, ice-blue eyes that were anything but cold. I wasn't sure if he was fully awake, but parts of him definitely were. The hungry determination on his face told me I had to move before this went somewhere I couldn't come back from.

"Thanks for the wakeup call," I said with forced levity as I pushed against his chest with both hands. "I think I'm awake now."

He lingered for a few more seconds before he rolled off me. I got out of bed and grabbed my bag without looking at him. Locked in the bathroom, I splashed cold water on my face and tried to get my heart back to its normal rhythm.

A knock came on the bathroom door as I was changing. "Yes?"

"We're checking out," Hamid said through the door. "Take your stuff with you when you leave."

I paused buttoning my jeans. "We're not staying in Atlanta?" After yesterday, I'd assumed we'd be here for a least a week, retracing Kai's steps.

"Our guys found a house near Tallahassee that Kai Bradley rented for six months. We're leaving for the airport in half an hour."

"Okay. I'll be out in two minutes," I called.

When I left the bathroom, Hamid was standing by the window, waiting for me. His duffle was on the couch, and he picked it up and walked toward me. His expression was all business, and there was no trace of the man I'd woken up next to. How did he do it? I wished I felt as composed as he looked.

We met the team in the lobby, and judging by their barely concealed excitement, they already knew why we were leaving. I gave Charlotte a grateful smile when she handed me a couple of breakfast sandwiches and a bottle of water from the hotel restaurant. God only knew when we'd get another chance to eat today.

The flight to Tallahassee was less than an hour. We didn't have a safe-house there, so Hamid arranged ground transportation for us during the flight. Two hours after he'd told me we were leaving Atlanta, we were driving down a gravel road to the property rented by Kai.

It was clear Kai had chosen this place for its isolation. The area was heavily wooded, and the farmhouse he'd rented was on twenty acres of land, with the closest neighbor a mile away. It was the perfect location for a warlock who didn't want anyone to know what he was up to.

The two SUVs stopped at the bottom of a long driveway that ran up a small hill. The house was hidden from the road, so we had no idea what was up there.

"Ciro, Bastien, and I will go in first in case Kai has the place warded or booby-trapped," Orias said after we'd all exited the vehicles. "Once it's clear, the rest of you can come in."

Hamid, Charlotte, Marie, and I armed ourselves while we waited. I wasn't sure how good our weapons would be against magic, but I felt better having my favorite sword in my hand. It was a featherlight samurai sword that I'd gotten from the weapons stash of an arms dealer in Los Angeles a few years back. Sara had paid the guy well to let me choose what I wanted from his secret store, and it had been love at first sight when I saw this sword.

Hamid's phone rang. He answered it and hung up almost immediately. "Orias said we can go up now. Jordan, you stay with me."

I nodded and fell into step beside him. At the top of the hill, we slowed and took in the white two-story farmhouse. The paint was peeling in a few places, but otherwise, it looked intact. The fields beyond the house were overgrown, telling me this place hadn't seen crops in a long time.

The barn off to one side looked like it could use some work too, and even from here, I could see a few holes in the roof. The whole place had a sad, deserted air about it.

Orias waited for us at the front door of the house. "We had to neutralize some powerful wards. It's clear he wanted to keep people out of here."

Hamid glanced at me and back to Orias. "Is it safe?"

"The house is. Ciro and Bastien are checking the barn now."

We entered the house, which looked like it had been built in the early twentieth century. The rooms were small, except for the kitchen, and there was no way a summoning could have been done here.

The food in the fridge and takeout containers in the garbage told us the house had been used as recently as a few days ago. Kai's body would still need human food even if he was possessed by a demon.

"Orias," Bastien called from the door. "We found the site."

We followed the warlocks to the crumbling barn. The large doors had been thrown open to provide more light, allowing us to see the summoning circle painted on the wooden floor.

I'd only seen a couple of summoning sites, but I could pick out differences between this one and the others. There were more symbols than usual painted around the circle, and they covered the walls as well. And there was no mistaking the scorch marks and dried blood in the center of the circle.

"What can you tell us?" Hamid asked Ciro, who was studying one of the symbols on the far wall.

The warlock's mouth pressed into a severe line. "These are containment symbols, but they have been altered. Kai must have thought he could use them to hold Alaron."

"We can detect traces of magic," Bastien added. "Orias will be able to tell if it's the same magic from the summoning you witnessed in Los Angeles."

I watched from the doorway as Orias walked the outside of the large circle with one hand out. He appeared to be mumbling something under his breath, and every now and then, the air inside the circle rippled. He did two trips around the circle before he stopped and nodded. "It's the same demon magic. We'll need to do more extensive tests, but I believe Alaron was summoned here."

"I don't get it," I said to the warlocks. "If Kai is the one opening the barrier, why would he do it in L.A. and other places if he has this secluded spot all set up for it?"

It was Ciro who answered me. "Some believe a demon can sense when their physical body is close to the barrier. It's possible that Alaron might be performing the spell in locations where he can feel his body the strongest."

"And that's not creepy at all." A shiver went through me, and I backed up. "If you all don't mind, I'm going to stay out here." The last thing I needed was to come into contact with more of that demon magic. Who knew what it would do to the spell on Hamid and me?

Hamid followed me. "You can help me search the house."

I suspected he was using the house as a reason to keep me near him, but I didn't mention it. Being in this place where an archdemon had most likely been summoned gave me a giant case of the willies. I'd never been faint of heart, but this wasn't like any foe we had ever faced. Even without his body, an archdemon on the loose was a terrifying thought.

"Where should we start?" I asked Hamid when we entered the house.

He led me down the narrow hallway. "The kitchen looks like it's been used the most, so we'll start there."

He entered the kitchen ahead of me. A second later, there was a flash of light and a robed figure appeared in the middle of the room.

I gasped at the misshapen face of Kai Bradley. His cheekbones and chin jutted out cartoonishly, and his grayish skin was stretched across the bones. The eyes were solid black, and two horns curled against his temples. *Horns?* I couldn't see the rest of his body beneath the robe, but he was big, maybe even bigger than Hamid.

Hamid and I drew our swords at the same time.

The next thing I knew, Kai grabbed Hamid by the throat and lifted him off the floor as if he weighed nothing. He muttered a few words in demon tongue and threw Hamid across the room, where he lay on the floor, gasping for air.

14

Something dark and feral came roaring to life inside of me. A growl issued from my throat as I ran to Hamid and stood between him and Kai. I felt Hamid's hand on my leg, and I took strength from the contact.

Kai threw back his head and laughed maniacally like a villain in one of those superhero cartoons.

I snarled in response and lifted my sword. Demon or not, he'd have to go through me to get to my mate.

The warlock flung out his hands in my direction. I staggered as magic hit my blade, sending a shockwave through me.

The stunned expression on Kai's face told me the spell was supposed to do a lot more damage. He threw it again, and like last time, I stayed on my feet.

He bellowed in rage and let loose another spell. This time, the impact sent pain shooting through my sword hand and down my arm. It was all I could do to keep my grip on the hilt. I didn't think I could sustain another hit, but I'd die before I let him touch Hamid.

Orias's deep booming voice filled the kitchen, followed by Ciro's and Bastien's. The three warlocks chanted in unison, and the air sizzled with their combined magic.

I dropped my sword and fell to my knees beside Hamid, who was no longer struggling to breathe. He tried to sit up, but I pushed him back down out of harm's way.

"Stay down," I ordered firmly.

Surprise crossed his face, but he didn't fight me on it. Instead, he pulled me down beside him as magic crackled in the air above us.

The chanting grew louder as the powerful warlocks spread out, trying to surround Kai. I held my breath as a shimmering sphere began to form around Ciro's protégé. If they could take him down, this would all be over.

Kai let out a growl that made the hair on my body stand on end. He cast an enraged look at me, and then he disappeared before my eyes.

I moved to get up, but Hamid held me down. "What were you thinking, putting yourself in front of me like that?"

"If I hadn't, you'd be dead," I shot back.

"Never endanger yourself for me," he said harshly.

"You don't get to make that call."

Orias cleared his throat. "When you two are done bickering, we'd love to hear how Jordan was able to deflect those spells thrown at her."

"I have no idea." Pulling away from Hamid, I got to my feet. I looked for my sword and sucked in a breath. The blade looked like it had been cleaved in two along its length.

"Don't touch it," Orias barked when I leaned down for a closer look. He came over and crouched beside the sword, holding a hand over the blade. A minute later, he stood. "It's clean."

I felt a pang of sorrow when I picked up the destroyed sword. It was probably silly to get emotional over a weapon, but this sword and I had been through a lot together.

"Jordan?" Orias called.

I tore my gaze from the sword to look at him. "What?"

He didn't look happy to have to repeat himself. "I asked what it felt like when the spells hit you."

"It hurt but mostly because of the force of the blow. My sword took the worst of it."

"There is nothing special about that sword. I would have detected it," he said.

I lifted a shoulder. "I don't know what to tell you. Maybe the spells weren't that strong."

The three wizards looked at me like I'd said the sky was green.

"Those spells came from an archdemon," Ciro said as if speaking to a mentally impaired person. "They should have obliterated you."

I threw up my hands. "Listen, I have no idea why I'm still alive. Maybe after all the bloody tests you guys have done on me I'm becoming immune to magic."

Orias stroked his chin thoughtfully.

I rolled my eyes. "I was joking."

"Yes, but there may be a grain of truth in what you said." He looked at Ciro and Bastien. "The spell attached to Jordan and Hamid is made of my magic and Alaron's."

Ciro's eyes grew round with excitement. "Of course! A demon cannot harm itself with its own magic. The magic in the spell protected her from the brunt of his power."

I held up a hand. "Great theory, but Alaron or Kai, or whatever we're calling him, was able to choke Hamid with his magic."

The warlocks considered this, muttering among themselves for several minutes.

Orias looked from Hamid to me. "Were you two touching when Alaron used his magic on Hamid?"

"No, I was still in the hallway when he grabbed Hamid," I said.

"And what about when Alaron went after you?" Bastien asked me.

My brow furrowed as I tried to remember. It had all happened so fast. "I'm not sure."

"Yes, we were," Hamid spoke up. "I had my hand on Jordan's leg the whole time."

The three warlocks smiled triumphantly.

"That's it then," Orias said. "When you are physically touching, you are protected from his magic."

Hamid and I exchanged a disbelieving look before he turned back to Orias. "How confident are you about this?"

"Very confident based on what we witnessed. The only way to know for sure is for you to face off against Alaron again."

"I'll take your word for it." I thought about Kai's misshapen face and body. "Is it normal during a possession for the body to start looking like the demon?"

"No," Orias said. "But Kai is possessed by an archdemon, and we can only guess what will happen to the body."

Ciro looked at me with sad eyes. "Our bodies are not strong enough to host an archdemon. Kai's body will deteriorate until it can no longer hold the demon. When that happens, Alaron will be forced to go back to his own body."

"That's something, at least." We just needed to thwart the demon's plans long enough for that to happen.

"It looks like we were correct in our assumption that Kai has been using this place for a home base," Ciro said. "But it's highly unlikely he will return now that he knows we have found it."

Orias nodded. "I agree. Still, it would be wise if Hamid and Jordan stayed together and near one of us while we are here."

We spent the remaining daylight hours going through the house and barn for any clues about what Kai was up to and where he might go now. The warlocks spent the time either running tests on the barn or discussing their findings with the rest of the team in excited whispers. At least someone was enjoying this little excursion.

Hamid was on edge after our showdown with Kai, and he didn't let me out of his sight all day. I drew the line when I tried to go to the bathroom and he insisted I leave the door open. I got that he was being protective, but a girl needs her private time.

When dusk came, he suggested he and I drive into town to get dinner for everyone. I hoped the time away from the farm would help him relax a bit. It did until we returned with the food. As soon as the farmhouse came into view, he tensed up again.

We worked late into the night. When the team said they wanted to stay there overnight, Hamid vetoed it immediately.

"We don't know for sure that Alaron won't come back here, and I will not take that risk," he said in a tone that brooked no argument. "We should all stay together while we are in this area."

Everyone darted glances at me. We all knew I was the reason Hamid refused to stay here, but no one mentioned it. Before we left, the warlocks placed multiple wards on the farm that would hopefully trap Kai if he returned. And then we all drove to a hotel in town.

I didn't argue when Hamid told me we were sharing a room again. After the way he'd been acting all day, I wasn't going to push it. I relaxed when we entered the room and I saw the two queen beds. At least, there would not be a repeat of this morning.

He was quieter than usual as we took turns showering. I sat on my bed and waited for him to come out of the bathroom to talk about it.

"Are you okay?" I asked him as he turned down his covers.

"Yes," he said without looking at me.

"Liar."

He got into bed without answering me, but I wasn't about to let this go. If he insisted on sharing a room with me, he could put up with my questions.

"Are you still mad because I got between you and Kai?"

He turned his head toward me, and I could see the anger in his eyes. But there was also something else. Fear.

"You put yourself between me and an archdemon," he corrected me tersely.

I huffed out a breath. "What was I supposed to do? Let him kill you?"

"You could have run for help."

"Right. And I'm sure he would have spared your life until help arrived." I crossed my arms. "I won't apologize for what I did because I'm right, and you know it. Any other warrior would have done the same."

He looked up at the ceiling and scrubbed his jaw with a hand. "It's impossible for me to treat you as any other warrior," he admitted.

We'd been bonded over a month, and his protective instincts had to be riding him hard, especially after I'd nearly died a week ago. I'd gone a little crazy myself today when he was in danger, so I understood what he must be feeling. But I couldn't allow him to treat me like some fragile thing to be bubble-wrapped and handled with kid gloves.

"I know this isn't easy for you. It's not fun for me either," I said. "But I'm not going to stop being a warrior, so we have to find some middle ground we can both live with."

He frowned. "I am not good with compromise."

"There's a shocker," I joked lightly.

"You must promise not to take unnecessary risks," he said. "And I will try to give you more freedom."

I smiled. "I'll watch where I'm stepping, but I won't promise not to jump in again if I see you in trouble. You may be a pain in my ass most of the time, but you've grown on me."

He arched his eyebrows.

"Don't let it go to your head," I said wryly. "Do you know how hard it is to find a good sparring partner?"

He grew serious again. "I'm sorry about your sword. I know you were attached to it."

"How do you know that?"

"I saw how well you cared for it, and you were rarely without it," he said, surprising me. He'd noticed that?

"It was a gift from Sara." I told him the story of how I had come to own the beautiful sword. "Anyway, it's not like it was a *Muramasa*, and it's silly to get sentimental over a weapon."

"You are familiar with Japanese swordsmiths?" He rolled to face me with an interested gleam in his eyes.

"I've read up on them a bit, but I'm no expert." I laid on my side, facing him with my head propped on my hand. "How about you?"

"I spent a year in Japan a long time ago, and I met a swordsmith who enjoyed teaching me about his craft."

"That must have been amazing," I said eagerly. "I plan to go to Japan someday and train with one of our samurai warriors. Did you ever train with them?"

"Yes, for almost a year."

"What was it like? I hear their training regime is a lot stricter than ours is."

Hamid smiled. "It is. They start physical training at a young age, as soon as they learn to control their Mori. They have a strong spiritual discipline and a code of ethics that is as much a part of them as being a warrior."

He went on to tell me about his time in Japan while I listened with rapt attention. I asked him a ton of questions, and he answered them all.

"I think we should try to get some sleep," he said some time later.

"But you haven't told me about the swordsman." I didn't want our conversation to end. I loved hearing his stories.

He chuckled and reached for the light. "Tomorrow."

The room plunged into darkness, and I lay back with a troubled sigh. Talking to Hamid tonight had brought two things into clarity for me. The first was that if there really was a perfect match for each of us, mine lay a few feet away from me. The second was that it was going to hurt like hell when I had to let him go.

We stayed in Tallahassee for three days while the team went over every inch of the farm. Hamid kept busy going between calls with the Council and consulting with the team, but there wasn't a whole lot for me to do. I soon grew so bored that I almost hoped Alaron would show up again just for some excitement. Then I remembered how he'd hurt Hamid, and I felt shame for my selfish thoughts.

Hamid and I continued to share a hotel room, although we only went there to sleep. Each night, we lay in our separate beds and I asked him questions about his travels. He asked about my life among the humans, but I didn't like to talk about that part of my past. I always found a way to steer the conversation back to him.

The more we talked, the more I looked forward to the end of the day. I told myself it was a bad idea to spend time alone with him, but a loud inner voice insisted I should enjoy it while it lasted. So what if the moment he turned out the light, my chest squeezed painfully and I lay there berating myself for my weakness?

On the fourth day, Hamid informed me we were returning to Chicago. I was happy to leave Tallahassee but sad to see the end of our late-night talks, even though I knew it was for the best.

Upon our return, we fell back into our old routines. I went on patrols, and he did his own thing. We still sparred every evening, but that was the extent of our interaction.

That all changed on our third day back in Chicago.

I was in the control room writing up a report from the night before when Nikolas called to me from the office doorway.

"Jordan, have you heard from Hamid today?"

"No, was I supposed to?"

Nikolas frowned. "He told me he was going to talk to Seraphine and he'd be back for a Council call at two. It's not like him to miss a call."

I glanced at the time on my monitor and saw it was almost four o'clock. Nikolas was right. This wasn't like Hamid.

"Did you call him?" I asked.

"Half an hour ago, and I got his voice mail."

I picked up my phone and called Hamid. It rang three times and went to voicemail. I hung up without leaving a message and stood. "Let's go."

"I thought you might say that." Nikolas held up a slip of paper. "The address."

We met up with Sara as we were leaving the control room. "Where are you two off to in such a hurry?" she asked.

Nikolas filled her in, and she said she was coming with us.

"Maybe it would be best if you stayed here," he said.

Sara hit him with a hard stare. "Don't you try to pull the pregnancy card on me. I barely leave here as it is. And if Seraphine has done something to him, who else here is qualified to deal with her?"

My jaw clenched. If that witch hurt Hamid, she was going to need a lot more than magic to protect her.

I rode my bike, and Nikolas and Sara took one of the SUVs. Twenty minutes later, we pulled up to a small blue bungalow, and I didn't know whether to be relieved or concerned when I saw Hamid's bike in the driveway. It was possible his interview with Seraphine had run long, but there was no way he'd ignore calls from Nikolas and me.

We parked on the street and walked to the front door. Sara and I stood a few feet back while Nikolas rang the doorbell. I could sense Hamid inside, but when I heightened my hearing, I couldn't pick up any sound.

Nikolas turned to me with an odd expression on his face. It wasn't alarm, but it caused a tiny knot of apprehension to form in my stomach.

"What?" I asked him.

He put a hand on the doorknob. "I'm going in. You two stay here until I give the all clear."

"I should go first." Sara moved to stand beside him.

"That won't be necessary," he said. "I think this is something I should handle."

He glanced at me, and I saw it again. That look. What was he not telling us?

A sense of foreboding filled me, and I knew I had to see what was happening inside. I pushed past Nikolas, who didn't try to stop me, and turned the knob.

The door opened to a small entranceway from which I could see right into the kitchen and living room. I stood frozen to the spot when my gaze took in the sight before me.

Hamid was sitting on the couch, shirtless, with a woman straddling his lap. Her long red hair fell to the small of her back, but it could not hide her nudity from the waist up. His hands were on her breasts, and he and the woman moaned as they kissed deeply. They were so wrapped up in each other they were oblivious to the fact they were no longer alone.

Pain tore through my chest, stealing my breath. Hamid was kissing another female, touching her intimately the way he'd touched me. I'd always heard bonded males couldn't be with other women, but that didn't seem to be a problem for him.

Now I knew why Nikolas hadn't wanted me to come in here. I wished I'd listened to him.

"You bastard," I choked out. My pain gave way to the anger bubbling up inside me, and my next words were shouted. "You fucking bastard."

I was across the room in a heartbeat. My fingers grabbed a fistful of red hair, and I ripped the bitch off his lap, sending her crashing into a curio cabinet. I heard glass shattering and shouts, but I was too focused on *him* to give a shit about her.

Hamid's face twisted in anger, but my outrage eclipsed his when my eyes fell on the open button of his jeans. I drew back my fist and punched him so hard in the jaw that pain shot through my wrist. I welcomed it. It was better than the other kind of pain.

"You son of a bitch," I spat at him. All he did was stare at me as if he hadn't done a thing wrong.

Nikolas's arm wrapped around my waist, pulling me backward. "Calm down, Jordan. This is not what you think."

I laughed harshly. I was no innocent, and I knew exactly what this was. I sent Hamid a look of pure loathing. "You come near me again and I'll castrate you."

I wrenched out of Nikolas's hold, and he let me go. Storming out of the house, I ignored Sara's calls for me to wait. I was driving away when she ran out onto the front step, but I didn't stop. I had to get away from this place before I lost it.

Solmi, my Mori wailed.

"He's not your goddamn mate, and he never will be," I ground out.

My phone rang when I was a few blocks from the house. I reached into my pocket and turned it off without checking to see who was calling. There was no one I wanted to talk to, not even Sara or Beth.

I rode around the city for hours with no destination in mind. No matter how long I rode, I couldn't get the image of Hamid and that woman or the sound of their moans out of my head.

When I spotted a neon sign for a dive bar, I pulled in, intent on finding someone to help me forget for a few hours. If he could do it, why couldn't I?

I shut off my bike, but that was as far as I got. Just the idea of touching another male made my stomach turn. I swore in frustration and rode off.

Night fell, but I couldn't bear the thought of going back to the command center. I started patrolling, itching to find someone to take out my aggression on. I didn't care that I wasn't supposed to patrol alone. Hamid, the Council, and their rules could all go to hell.

Lucky for me, the underworld denizens were active tonight. When I came across two Gulaks dragging a teenage girl into an alley where a moving van was parked, I smiled in vicious glee. I'd always despised the scaly demons, but now my hate for them was tenfold.

I didn't utter a word as I drew my sword and went after them. They didn't see me coming, so I was able to cut the first one down before they knew what was happening.

The second one drew his short sword and brandished it at me. I laughed coldly before I relieved him of his sword and then his head.

I looked around for the girl, but she had run off during the fight. After I checked the van to make sure it was empty, I tossed the dead Gulaks inside, and then I was on my way again.

An hour later, I was cruising down by the port when I heard a man scream. By the time I found the source, the man was dead, but the vampire was still there finishing up her meal and drunk on the fresh blood.

She was a few years old and more of a challenge than the Gulaks, but a good fight was just what I needed. I came away from it with a few claw marks and another vampire kill. I left the bodies behind a dumpster and made a mental note to send someone later for cleanup.

I was riding away when I felt a faint trickle of awareness that told me Hamid was nearby. The anger I'd been working hard to burn off flared to life again. There was no way he was here by accident. If he thought I was going to let him track me down and take me back with him, he had another thing coming.

As soon as I could no longer sense him, I pulled off the road and removed the tracker from my bike and the other from my coat. I tossed them into a garbage container and took off again.

Part of me wanted to jump onto the closest interstate and just ride until I had to stop. But duty kept me from following my instincts. I couldn't stomach the thought of seeing Hamid, but I couldn't leave either, not without jeopardizing the integrity of the spell. Too many lives would be at risk if the barrier did reopen, and I couldn't live with the knowledge I was responsible for that.

I was trapped like a rat in a maze. I could run around this city all I wanted to, but I couldn't leave. And eventually, I was going to have to go back.

But not tonight.

Around midnight, I had my second vampire kill of the evening outside a movie theater. People leaving late movies were easy targets since they were usually still caught up in the movie and not paying attention. Lucky for the girl, who was more interested in texting than watching her surroundings, I spotted the vampire lurking around the corner of the building. Unlucky for the vampire who should have been paying better attention, too.

After the movie theater kill, my body reminded me I hadn't eaten since lunch. I sought out an all-night food truck and amazed the vendor with the number of tacos I could consume. I'd managed to wipe the blood from my kills off my leather jacket, and I was glad the guy couldn't see my jeans. I was starting to look like an extra on a horror movie set.

Exhaustion started to set in at around three in the morning because anger could only fuel me for so long. There were two safe houses in Chicago, so I opted to go to one of them instead of returning to the command center. I was too tired to deal with Hamid and all his bullshit without following through on my threat to castrate him.

A warrior I didn't know opened the door and admitted me into the safe-house. He didn't ask why I was there instead of at the command center, for which I was grateful. I was not in the mood to explain my actions to anyone.

"I made a few kills tonight that require cleanup," I told him wearily. "You think you could send someone to take care of that?"

"Yeah. It's been a slow night."

"Not for me." I told him where all my kills were located, and his eyes widened. Then he pointed me to the shower and a bedroom I could crash in.

"Thanks."

I always carried a change of clothes in my saddle bag, so at least I had something clean to sleep in. Amazingly, I was out not long after my head hit the pillow.

I half expected to wake up to Hamid beating down the door like a caveman, but I woke midmorning to a quiet house. In the kitchen, I found cereal and milk and had a quick breakfast before I decided I should turn on my phone.

I winced when I saw all the missed calls and texts from Sara and Beth. Taking off without telling them I was okay was a shitty thing for a friend to do, and I was going to have to do some groveling when I saw them.

Instead of reading their messages, I sent off a quick group text letting them know I was still alive and I'd see them soon. I didn't ask about Hamid. There were missed calls from him, too, but he didn't deserve a reply from me.

It was almost noon when I finally returned to the command center. I heaved a sigh of relief when I didn't feel Hamid's presence there. I was going to have to face him eventually, but I was happy to put off that meeting as long as possible.

I could hear voices in the control room, but I encountered no one as I walked to my room. Good. I'd rather not talk to anyone until after I showered and got out of the clothes I'd slept in.

I was getting out of the shower when I felt Hamid in the building and coming closer. I dried off in record time and pulled on a pair of worn jeans and a soft T-shirt. I didn't bother to check if my door was locked, because that wouldn't stop him if he was determined to have it out with me. I sat in the middle of my bed with my back to the headboard and waited.

The jerk didn't even bother to knock. He opened the door and walked in as if he owned the place. His expression was darker than a thundercloud, and he stood in the middle of my room with his arms crossed, looking like he was the one who should be pissed off.

I opened my mouth to tell him what I thought of him, but he cut me off.

"No," he growled. "You will not speak a word until you hear what I have to say."

"I don't want to hear anything from you," I shot back.

The furrows in his brow deepened, and his voice hardened in warning. "If I have to, I will hold you down and make you listen to me. After what you put me through last night, you're lucky I don't put you over my knee."

I sputtered furiously. What *I* had put *him* through? "I'd like to see you try, you whoring –"

The next thing I knew, I was flat on my back with Hamid straddling my hips. I tried to buck him off, but he was immovable. I punched him in the chest, and he grabbed both of my hands and trapped them in one of his.

Someone knocked on my door and opened it. "Hey, I heard you were back and..." Sara's voice trailed off, and her mouth formed an O at the sight of Hamid sitting on top of me. "I can see you're busy. I'll come back later," she said with a little grin as she shut the door.

Great. I glared daggers at Hamid while he took his time getting around to saying whatever it was he'd come to say.

"I'll get to that stunt you pulled last night in a bit," he said in a tight voice. "First, we are going to talk about what you thought you saw at the witch's house."

"No explanation is necessary. I know what I –"

His free hand covered my mouth, silencing me. "You saw me kissing another woman, and I know it must have looked bad."

I scoffed loudly under his hand. If that was just kissing, I'd hate to hear what his idea of second base was.

"What you don't know, because you took off before anyone could tell you, was that I had no idea who I was kissing. Seraphine used a spell to glamour me and tricked me into it."

I stared at him, stunned. A spell?

"She was flirtatious when I interviewed her, but nothing that crossed the line. I remember walking to the door to leave, and the next thing I knew, I was on the couch and Sara and Nikolas were there, telling me what happened."

A big part of me wanted to believe him, but a niggling voice in my head said a witch's glamour couldn't possibly trick a Mori into touching someone it wasn't bonded to.

"Likely story," I mumbled into his palm.

Hamid expelled a frustrated breath. "Seraphine is a powerful witch who specializes in love spells. She can pull faces from your memories and make you see anyone she wants you to see."

I moved my head to indicate I wanted to speak, and he lifted his hand from my mouth.

"Oh, really. And what face did you see that made you so ready to drop your pants?"

He leaned down until his face was inches above mine. "Yours."

15

My mouth fell open, and I searched for something to say, but my mind had deserted me.

Hamid lowered his head, and his lips brushed my bottom one with a tenderness I did not expect, based on our one and only kiss. I didn't breathe as he tasted my lip a second time before gently tugging it between his teeth. He released it and soothed it with his tongue, sending a delicious shiver through me.

Needing more, I lifted my head to fit my mouth to his. He released my hands and rested his forearms on either side of my head, caging me in. Then he kissed me long and deep, his tongue dancing with mine as my body arched beneath him and my arms curled around his neck, holding him in place.

His lips left mine, and I made a sound of protest that was quickly muffled when his mouth began to explore my jaw. I tilted my head to one side to give him access to my throat, and he accepted my silent invitation.

He shifted his body as his lips blazed a trail over my collarbone and to where the bottom of the V in my neckline rested between my breasts. The scratch of his soft beard against my skin had me gasping with each brush of his lips.

I was acutely aware I wasn't wearing a bra, and his low growl of appreciation told me he'd just discovered that. My blood felt like it was on fire when he rose up enough to hook the bottom of my T-shirt and push it up, baring my breasts to him. The moan I'd been holding back was ripped from me when he dipped his head and took one of my nipples into his mouth.

A small part of my brain told me I had to stop this, but the desire burning through me drowned it out. All I could think about was getting rid of these clothes between us and feeling his hard, naked body against mine. Just the thought made me writhe against him, moaning his name.

Hamid lifted his head, and his eyes were dark with lust when they met mine. "Tell me you want this," he said huskily. "If we go any further, I'm not going to stop until I have all of you."

It took several seconds for his words to sink in, and cold pricked me when I realized what I'd almost done. If he hadn't spoken up, I would have given in to my desire and bound myself to him.

I closed my eyes and let out a ragged breath. "I can't."

He pulled my shirt down and rolled off me. The only sound in the room was our heavy breathing as we lay beside each other.

For the first time in my life, I wasn't sure what to do. I didn't know if I should get up and leave or wait for him to go.

Hamid wasn't in any hurry to leave. After five minutes of staring at the ceiling, I turned my head toward him and found him with an arm over his eyes. Guilt made my throat tighten. Twice, I'd let things go too far between us, and then I'd pushed him away. What was wrong with me?

"I'm sorry," I said in a low voice.

He lifted his arm and looked at me without a trace of the resentment or anger I'd expected to see in his eyes. "You have nothing to apologize for."

I swallowed hard. "I shouldn't have led you on."

"I kissed you first," he said roughly. "You don't have to lead me on to make me want you."

My chest constricted at his admission, and I faced the ceiling again so he couldn't see the effect his words had on me. "Don't say things like that."

"Why? Because you don't wish to hear that I want you, or you're afraid to admit you feel the same for me?"

I shook my head. "No, I mean...yes, I want you, but it's just the bond making us –"

His strong fingers touched my chin and forced me to meet his eyes. "Are you saying you did not desire me before we bonded?"

I thought back to the first time I'd laid eyes on him, and I flushed at the memory of how many times he'd starred in my fantasies since then. I cleared my throat. "Physical attraction means nothing. Neither of us wants a mate, remember?"

His gaze burned into mine. "Don't we?"

What was he saying? A month ago, he couldn't stand me, and now he wanted to have me as his mate?

"*I* don't want a mate," I said in a rush.

"You fear what you think you'll have to give up if you take one." His thumb stroked my jaw, distracting me. "Answer me this. Would you have been as upset about what you saw at Seraphine's if all you felt for me was a physical attraction?"

I twisted out of his hold to look away before he saw the truth in my eyes. Seeing him with that woman had gutted me because I did care about him, more than I wanted to admit to myself. In my heart, I knew he was the perfect mate for me, but a part of me refused to let go of the future I'd always envisioned, the one that didn't include a mate.

Hamid's sigh was barely audible. "It's okay if you're not ready to answer that yet."

I sat up, keeping my back to him, and would have stood if he hadn't captured one of my hands with his.

"We still have one thing to discuss," he said, tugging me back down to the bed.

I tried to pull my hand away to no avail. "What?"

He rolled to his side to face me. "I understand why you were upset and angry yesterday, but staying out all night like that and going after those kills alone was reckless. And then you threw away your trackers and turned off your phone." He sucked in a breath and let it out. "Nikolas and I spent most of the night looking for you because you wouldn't answer your phone and we had no idea if you were in trouble. It wasn't until you showed up at the safe-house that we stopped searching."

My brows pulled down. "How did you know I was at the safehouse?"

"We sent word to every warrior in the city to keep an eye out for you and to contact us the minute you were spotted."

"Great. You make me sound like a runaway child."

"You were behaving like one," he retorted. "You're lucky Nikolas talked me out of going to the safehouse after you. The mood I was in, I really would have put you over my knee."

The promise in his voice told me he would have done just that. A little thrill shot through me at the image my mind conjured.

"Now that we know we are up against Alaron, we have to be more vigilant and careful," Hamid said. "We have no idea where he will show up. You angered him when you stood up to him, and he would take pleasure in torturing and killing you."

The anguish in his voice made my chest feel like it was in a vise as guilt and shame pressed down on me.

His fingers flexed around mine. "We kept your disappearing act from the Council, but if they get wind of it, they will demand a security detail for us, or worse. They are already on edge since learning about Kai and Alaron."

I swallowed dryly at the thought of being locked away for my own protection. And my actions didn't only affect me. Where one of us went, the other had to go. I couldn't do that to him.

I turned on my side to face him. "I'm so sorry I put you through that," I said hoarsely. "It won't happen again."

His free hand cupped the side of my face. "I'm sorry you were hurt. I would never do that intentionally."

"I know."

We gazed at each other until I broke our stare. "Um, I should go get started on the reports for last night." The last thing I wanted to do was write up reports, but it felt too good lying here like this with him and it wouldn't take much for us to pick up where we'd left off.

His smile told me he knew exactly why I was in a hurry to go. Anyone who spent more than a day with me knew I'd rather clean toilets than do reports.

He let go of my hand, and I rolled off the bed like it was on fire. I ignored his low chuckle as I went to the closet to find shoes – and a bra. Behind me, I heard the bed creak and then the sound of the door opening.

"I'll be in meetings most of the afternoon," he said. "I'll see you later."

"Okay," I called without looking at him.

The door clicked shut.

I sank down to the floor with my head in my hands. "I'm so screwed."

"Hamid was livid when he realized what happened," Sara said as we sat in the living room, catching up later that afternoon. "Seraphine was cowering in the corner, and I had to calm her down while Nikolas kept Hamid from losing it."

I sneered at the mention of the witch. "She would have been unconscious if I'd known the truth, so it's better for her that I left when I did."

Sara nodded. "I think she knows to never mess with another Mohiri warrior, especially a bonded one. And I told her if I ever hear of her seducing men against their will, I'll make sure she never does magic again."

"You can do that?"

"Yes. It's something Eldeorin taught me for after the baby comes. He said she'll have trouble controlling her power at first, so I'll have to bind her to keep her from hurting anyone. It works on anyone with magic."

"Too bad we can't use something like that on Alaron," I said, thinking how binding him from doing magic would erase that threat. "Not even Orias, Ciro, and Bastien working together could bind him."

Sara tapped her fingers on the armrest. "Warlock magic is strengthened by their demons, so it makes sense they'd have trouble going up against an archdemon."

"What about Eldeorin? Doesn't Fae power cancel out demon magic?"

"Not an archdemon's." She smiled ruefully. "I already asked him about it, and apparently, it's a bit of a sore subject with him."

"Oh," I said, deflated.

"But he said he'll try to make us a weapon to use against Alaron."

Hope flickered to life inside me again. "A Fae weapon? How would that work against an archdemon if Fae power won't work?"

"I'm not sure. I don't even know if it's possible." Sara's face clouded, and she placed a hand over her bump. "Nikolas is afraid for me and the baby. He wants me to promise to go to Faerie if the worst should happen." Tears sparkled in her eyes. "How could I ever leave him here to face that alone?"

"You won't have to," I promised fiercely. After everything she and Nikolas had gone through to be together, I wouldn't let some demon destroy their happiness. "We know who we are dealing with now, and if he could have brought the barrier down, he would have done it already. We'll find him again and send him back to hell before he knows what hit him."

She gave me a watery smile. "I really wish I could hug you right now."

"This from the girl who hated PDAs a few years ago," I teased. "When all this is over, you can hug the crap out of me."

"I'm going to hold you to that." A laugh slipped from her.

"Let's talk about something less depressing," I said, glad to see the worry leave her eyes.

Her smile turned devious. "Why don't you tell me why Hamid was pinning you to your bed when I walked in?" She made a face. "Sorry about that, by the way."

I waved it off. "That was just his way of making me listen to him while he explained what happened at Seraphine's."

"Well, you did punch him in the face and then threatened to castrate him," she reminded me cheerily. "It's no wonder he wanted to restrain you."

I grinned. "I did, didn't I?"

"Are things better between you and him now?"

"As good as they can be I guess," I said vaguely, remembering my conversation with Hamid earlier. "I no longer want to cut off his body parts."

"I'm sure he's relieved to know that," said Nikolas, whom we hadn't heard come in. He grabbed a bottle of water from the fridge and turned to me. "You look like you're in better shape than Hamid was this morning."

"I know, I know. He already read me the riot act."

"Good." Nikolas held up two fingers an inch apart. "You were this close to getting your own security detail."

I groaned. "Don't remind me."

Nikolas grew serious. "You had a lot of people worried last night. Sara wouldn't go to bed until I told her you were at the safehouse."

My gaze shifted guiltily to Sara. She could barely stay up past ten these days, so she must have been worried sick to stay up that late. "I'm so sorry," I said, my voice thick with remorse.

"I know how difficult this is for you, and I did my share of running away." She smiled at Nikolas before looking at me again. "But I had you, Roland, and Peter at my back. It scared me to think of you out there alone and upset, especially when you wouldn't answer my calls or texts."

I hung my head. "I'm officially the worst friend ever."

"You're the best friend ever. Just promise to let us know you're okay next time you feel like going off alone."

"I will. I promise."

Nikolas fixed me with a hard stare. "And if you ever pull that again, I'll take you off patrols so fast your head will spin."

I gulped because he did not make idle threats. I'd be spending my nights doing paperwork and manning the control room. I shuddered at the thought.

"You two are worse than parents," I said to Sara.

She grinned. "We're practicing for the real thing."

I sank back into the cushion. "It's a good thing that kid will have Auntie Jordan to bring all the fun."

Sara's and Nikolas's eyes met, and they smiled before he left us. Mated couples could communicate through their bond, and I had a feeling a whole conversation had taken place between them in that moment.

"What did he just say to you?" I asked her.

She chuckled. "He asked if we could live in Russia until our daughter is twenty."

"Hey!" I yelled after him, knowing he could hear me. "Would you rather have me or Eldeorin teaching her the facts of life?"

Sara snorted. "He said to tell you our home is your home."

I nodded smugly. "That's what I thought."

Hamid was holed up in the conference room with the Council team that afternoon, and I made sure to keep my distance from all of them. I'd planned to go to the wrakk, but when I mentioned it to Nikolas, he suggested it might be a good idea for me to wait until tomorrow.

"You scared him last night," Nikolas said when I asked why I needed to wait. "I wish I could explain what it feels like when a bonded male doesn't know where his mate is or if she's safe. It's gut-wrenching, and it can take our Mori a while to calm down even after we know our mate is okay. Hamid needs to feel you nearby today even if he doesn't see you. Does that make sense?"

"Yes."

It made all too much sense to me. Despite our intentions to stay away from each other, Hamid and I had done a poor job of following through on it. Some of it had been beyond our control, but the sparring sessions, the kissing and touching, and sharing a hotel bed had been our doing. Because of it, our bond had grown to the point where we could barely keep our hands off each other when we were alone. The thought of him touching another woman made me want to kill something, and he was so protective he needed my presence to calm his agitated Mori.

I spent the rest of the day trying to keep busy, but I started to get stir-crazy as the hours passed. I had no idea how Sara could stay here day after day without going out of her mind with boredom. I was climbing the walls by dinnertime, and I cringed at the thought of the long night ahead. Nikolas had pulled me off patrol tonight as punishment for removing my trackers and turning off my phone last night. I knew I deserved it, but that didn't make it any easier to bear.

I hadn't laid eyes on Hamid since he left my room, but I could sense him no matter where I went in the building. It was another indication of how much the bond had grown – not that I needed more proof.

When he didn't make an appearance around our usual sparring time, I figured he wasn't going to. I went to my room and changed into workout clothes anyway. There would be no sleep for me tonight if I didn't get in a good training session.

The gym was empty when I entered, and my gaze immediately landed on a long, dark wooden box lying on the weight bench. I went over to it and ran my finger along the glossy wood. The size and shape of the box told me it held a sword, and I was dying to take a peek inside.

I chewed my lip indecisively for a minute before curiosity got the better of me and I lifted the lid. "Oh," I breathed at the sight of the beautiful katana laid on a bed of yellow satin. The blade was flawless, and it looked brand new, like it had never been used.

My fingers itched to wrap around the handle and see how the sword felt in my hands. The last time I'd wanted to touch a sword so much was when I'd found my old one in that weapons room in Los Angeles.

"Go ahead. Pick it up," Hamid said from behind me.

I spun to see him filling the doorway. I'd been so enraptured by the sword I hadn't heard or sensed him approach.

He tilted his head toward the box. "Tell me what you think."

I didn't need any further urging. My hand grasped the handle, and I lifted the sword reverently from the box. It was lighter than it looked and felt like it had been made for me. I sliced it through the air and did a pattern of strikes to get a feel for it.

"Perfect," I murmured as I examined the blade, almost forgetting I wasn't alone.

"It was given to me by a little-known swordsmith named Hiroko Tao when I lived in Japan."

I tore my gaze from the sword to look at Hamid. "This is yours?"

He walked over to me. "It was. Now, it's yours, if you will accept it. It's not a *Muramasa*, but it is a fine sword and worthy of you."

I ran a finger along the flat side of the blade. "It's beautiful." His words registered, and I stared at him. "Why would you give this to me?"

His hand came up to caress my cheek, sending a familiar heat through me. "You need to ask?"

"I..." I faltered, unsure how to respond. I looked down at the sword, because the tenderness in his gaze made it hard to form words. "This is the most incredible gift anyone's ever given me."

Hamid dropped his hand but didn't move away from me. "I've had this sword at my home in Egypt ever since Hiroko gave it to me. Ammon asked why I never used it, and I told him it didn't feel right in my hand, like it belonged to someone else. After you lost your sword protecting me from Alaron, I knew this one was meant to be yours."

My hand went to my chest. "I...don't know what to say."

"That is a first," he teased. "I should give you weapons more often."

I scowled at him, but there was no anger in it. He smiled back, looking all too pleased with himself.

"Do you want to try out your new sword?" he asked.

"On patrol?" I suggested hopefully.

He chuckled as he walked to the other side of the room to get a sword for himself. "Nice try. You'll have to settle for training with me tonight."

"Fine," I grumbled as a thrill shot through me. I could pretend to be put out, but there was nothing I enjoyed more than sparring with him.

I smiled to myself. Well, maybe there was one thing. And based on my hot make out sessions with him, I knew he would be an insatiable and skilled lover. My belly quivered in anticipation.

I knew another truth as well, something I'd been living in denial about for days. Hamid and I were past the point of no return. There was no going back for us. No breaking this bond. He knew it, too, and he'd said as much in my room this morning. I'd just been too afraid to admit it.

My heart gave a little flutter, either from excitement or fear, I wasn't sure. I wasn't quite ready to take that final step. I needed a little more time to get used to the idea of me with a mate. With Hamid. Forever.

I inhaled deeply and forced myself to focus on sparring, because I couldn't think of any of that other stuff now, or my head would explode.

But later? Yeah, later, I was totally going to freak out.

16

The next three days were quiet compared to all that had happened in the previous week. I went back to patrols and my self-defense classes at the wrakk, and Hamid spent most of his time with the Council team and in conference calls. There hadn't been a sign of Alaron since our run-in with him in Tallahassee, and everyone was on alert, waiting for him to strike again.

Hamid and I still made time to train together every night, and those sessions were the highlight of my day. We kept our hands and mouths to ourselves, but there was a current of anticipation that seemed to grow between us as the days passed. Though neither of us spoke about our relationship, we both knew where this was headed, and I think he was giving me the time I needed to be ready for it.

Beth and I had been taking turns giving the class at the wrakk, but today we were pairing up to demonstrate some fencing techniques. It was a special treat for our students, who were progressing nicely in their training, and I was looking forward to it as well. I had a bag of wooden training swords strapped to my bike, and I couldn't wait to see Lem's and Jal's faces when I gave them their swords.

We parked our bikes beside each other in the parking lot, and I frowned as I put down my stand. The wrakk was usually bustling with activity this time of day, but there were only two cars in the lot and not a person in sight. I'd never seen it this quiet here.

"Do you think it's closed?" Beth asked, coming to stand beside me.

I stared at the building. "Wrakks never close." Wrakks were like the demon version of Walmart and open twenty-four-seven all year long. It would take something pretty serious for one of them to close.

We walked up to the main door, and I tried the handle. Locked. Something was definitely up here, and my spidey sense was tingling.

It could be more Gulaks seeking retribution for the death of the group that had attacked me. I wouldn't put it past them to take it out on the innocent patrons of the wrakk.

"Come on." I started around the building to the hidden door in the back. The secret entrance wasn't generally known to anyone other than the demons who worked in the wrakk, but Beth and I had been taken into their confidence since we'd started giving lessons here.

Beth caught up to me and grasped my arm. "I don't think we should go in there alone."

"You're right." I'd promised Hamid and my friends that I would be more careful and less reckless from now on. Pulling out my phone, I called the command center for backup. Nikolas and Chris were out, but Hamid was there. He said to wait by our bikes and he'd be there soon.

Twenty minutes later, he arrived with Orias and Ciro. I didn't ask why he'd felt the need to bring the warlocks. Secretly, I was glad they were there.

Orias walked up to the building and came back shaking his head. "The demon wards are too strong. I can't see through them."

"We'll have to go in then," Hamid said.

"There is a secret door in the back," I told them. "We can use that."

Beth and I led the way to a tall stack of pallets at the back corner of the building. There was just enough space between the pallets and the building for Hamid's large body as he followed me to the door cleverly disguised as a patched section of the wall. I eased the door open and stepped aside so he and the warlocks could go ahead of Beth and me.

"Stay behind us until we know what we're dealing with," Hamid said to me. I nodded, and he entered the building.

As soon as I passed through the demon ward, I knew something was very wrong. It was always noisy inside the wrakk, but silence greeted us today.

Hamid looked back and motioned for us to be quiet, and the five of us moved stealthily down the small, dark hallway to the main area.

I gripped my sword while hoping for the first time that I wouldn't need to use it. I'd gotten to know many of the demons who worked and shopped here, and I'd hate for any of them to be hurt.

Orias, who was beside Hamid, stopped suddenly. "He's here," he whispered. No one needed to ask who *he* was.

Hamid stiffened and spun to face me. "You and Beth leave now," he ordered in a low voice.

"You're not going in there without me," I argued. He was no more a match for Alaron than I was, and he knew it. Together, we stood a chance, if Orias was right about the spell protecting us.

Hamid opened his mouth to say something, but a child's terrified scream cut him off. The sound turned my blood to ice.

I grabbed Hamid's hand with my free one, praying the contact was enough to protect us from the archdemon's magic. "Together," I whispered urgently.

He nodded, and we quietly followed Orias and Ciro into the open area that made up the marketplace. Stopping behind a baker's stall, we took in the scene before us.

At the center of the building, stalls had been destroyed and pushed back to form a wide circle of debris. In the cleared area, a familiar summoning circle was painted in blood on the concrete floor, with the smaller circle inside of it.

Alaron stood just inside the inner circle with his arms raised as if he was prepared to start the ceremony. Everything looked exactly as it had in the gym except for one thing – the dozen or more demon children huddled together at his feet.

Bile burned its way up my throat. He was going to use the children as blood sacrifices to open the barrier.

My gaze moved over the tearstained faces, and I sucked in a breath when I found Jal holding a little Vrell female, who couldn't be more than five. The girl clung to his neck as he rubbed her back and whispered to her. I could see no sign of Lem, and I sent up a silent prayer that he was safe.

Tearing my eyes from the children, I looked around for the adults and found them standing against the far wall, hitting and pushing against some kind of force field. Their faces were masks of horror, and their screams were silenced by the magic that held them prisoner.

I started forward, but Hamid held me back.

"Wait," he mouthed. He inclined his head toward the two warlocks, who were moving away from us, positioning themselves on either side of Alaron. The demon seemed to be so focused on his work he didn't notice our presence.

Alaron began speaking in demon tongue, and the crystals around the outer circle started to glow. I craned my neck to see where Orias and Ciro were. If they didn't do something soon, it might be too late. I was not going to stand here and watch children be slaughtered.

My grip on Hamid's hand tightened when Alaron lowered his hands and looked down at the children as if deciding which one to kill first. What was taking Orias so long?

I felt Orias's magic a few seconds before his deep voice began to chant in what I now knew was Navajo. Farther away, Ciro's voice rang out as his own chant filled the air.

Alaron straightened and threw off his hood with a growl to reveal a face that was starting to resemble that of a demon mummy. As Orias had said, Kai's body was deteriorating from the stress of being possessed by an archdemon. Alaron was running out of time.

The demon flung out his arms, and a wave of magic hit us. I felt the pressure, but it didn't burn like it had that night at the school. Behind us, Beth gasped in pain because she wasn't immune to the magic.

Hamid half turned to look back and motioned for her to go outside. I heard her softly retreating footsteps as she followed his order, and I exhaled in relief. Hamid and I were protected by the spell, but Beth was vulnerable. I should have thought of that when Orias told us Alaron was here.

I couldn't see Ciro, but Orias was in my line of vision. I watched him standing strong, seemingly unaffected by Alaron's magic as he countered with his own spell. He began to walk around the outer circle, keeping plenty of space between him and Alaron. He moved farther away from us, and Ciro came toward us, his voice growing louder as he mimicked Orias's. I couldn't tell if they were chanting the same spell or doing their own thing, but whatever it was, the demon was not happy.

Alaron roared and threw more magic, this time focusing on the two warlocks. Ciro wavered for a few seconds under the force of the magic, but his chanting never faltered. Instead, it grew louder and more insistent.

The light in the crystals flickered and dimmed. Whatever the warlocks were doing, it was working.

The demon was fully enraged now and flinging spells at Orias and Ciro like he was throwing knives. Each time the magic hit them, they flinched, but they never stopped their chant.

Movement behind Alaron drew my gaze to the children. Jal was on his feet with the little girl in his arms as he quietly herded the other children out of the inner circle.

I held my breath as they stepped over the pattern of symbols drawn in blood, but whatever magic had held them there was gone. Alaron was using it in his battle against the warlocks.

As soon as the children were free of the first circle, they ran in all directions. Alaron spun and bellowed when he saw his captives escaping. His murderous eyes locked on Jal, who had fallen behind, carrying the little girl.

"Jal," I choked out, already moving toward them.

Hamid released my hand, but before I could take another step, he was gone in a blur and a small gust of air. My heart lodged in my throat when I saw him appear next to Jal and scoop the boy and girl up in his arms.

Alaron roared, turning his rage on Hamid. He threw a spell, but Hamid was already speeding back to me.

I felt the pulse of magic in the air just as Hamid reached me. He threw his arm around me and bent over me and the children to protect us from the blast.

Just as it had before, Alaron's magic bounced harmlessly off us. I refused to think of what might have happened to Hamid if he hadn't gotten back to me in time.

Hamid set Jal and the little girl on the floor, and the children scampered behind the stall. Standing together, Hamid and I faced Alaron, who was once again battling the warlocks and looking like he was about to explode with rage. He had to be getting desperate, and we'd just foiled another attempt to open the barrier.

Alaron hit Orias with another spell as the warlock walked in front of us. The attack was strong enough to make Orias stagger, but he stayed on his feet.

Even though Kai's body was weak, Alaron was still very powerful. I shuddered to think what he would be like if he ever succeeded in bringing his own body across the barrier.

The demon looked past the warlock, and his black eyes met mine. "You!" He snarled like a rabid beast, and spittle flew from his mouth. Lifting a hand, he shouted something unintelligible.

Hamid drew me close to him, and we clasped our hands together. I had to close my eyes against the tide of magic that flowed around us. It didn't hurt, but the prickling sensation all over my body was not at all pleasant. It was ten times worse than this when Orias or one of the other warlocks did one of their tests on me.

Alaron looked ready to lose it when he saw his spell hadn't hurt us. If Orias and Ciro hadn't been there, I felt certain the demon would have come after us. The spell protected us from his magic, but physically, he was a match for Hamid.

The warlocks moved closer to Alaron, their chants growing louder and more urgent. He swatted away their spells like they were annoying gnats, but his stare was still fixed on Hamid and me.

The hair on the back of my neck stood up as I looked into the face of pure evil. For the first time in my life, I felt real, bone-chilling fear.

After what felt like an eternity, he turned his attention back to Orias and Ciro. Hamid squeezed my hand reassuringly, and I started breathing normally again.

When Alaron spun away from the warlocks, I knew he'd abandoned the fight and was about to make his escape again. I kept my eyes glued to him, waiting for him to disappear any second. There was nothing Hamid or I could do to stop him. It was all on Orias and Ciro now.

The demon whirled back to face us, his arm moving so fast I couldn't see it.

In the next instant, Hamid was in front of me, spinning me around so he shielded me with his body.

His body jerked, and he hissed in pain. At the same time, there was a bright flash behind us and the room erupted in shouts and cries. I knew without looking that Alaron had left.

I waited for Hamid to let me go, but his hold didn't lessen. If anything, he seemed to be leaning into me more.

"I think it's safe." I patted his arm when he didn't respond. "If you're trying to cop a feel, you're going about it all wrong."

He chuckled, but it was immediately smothered by a cough. His arms fell away from me and I turned to see him sway on his feet and fall to his knees.

I caught him under the arms before he hit the floor. "What's wrong?"

Alaron's magic shouldn't have been able to hurt him, and I had no idea what to do. My mouth went dry as fear for him swelled in me.

"Orias," I shouted.

The warlock ran over. "Are you two in a competition to see who can sustain the worst injuries without dying?"

I snarled at his flippant remark. "Help him."

"I'm not a medic, but I'll do what I can," he replied calmly. "Knife wounds are not my specialty."

"Knife wounds?" I repeated in confusion. I followed his gaze and gasped when I saw the knife handle protruding from Hamid's back.

"Oh, God!" I looked down at Hamid's head resting against my chest. "Hamid, talk to me."

"Mmmm," he murmured.

Relief washed over me, but it was quickly replaced with fear. He was alive, but his sluggish response told me he was badly hurt.

"Help me lay him down," I said to Orias. "I need to call for a healer."

Beth appeared by my side. "They're on the way. I called them as soon as I went outside."

She took one of Hamid's arms, and together, we lowered him to his stomach on the floor. I pulled off my jacket and placed it under his head before I turned my attention to the knife in his back. The handle was made of what looked like onyx, and its location put the blade frighteningly close to his heart.

A warrior his age could survive a hit to the heart if the damage wasn't too bad, but I had no idea what Alaron had done to the knife. It could be spelled or poisoned. We were not invincible, no matter how much I wanted to believe it in that moment.

"Orias, can you detect any magic on the knife?" I asked him.

He held a hand over it and then carefully touched it with one finger. "It's clean," he said, taking his hand away.

I let out a shaky breath. "Good. We need to remove it and give him some gunna paste."

"Shouldn't we wait for your healer?" Orias asked.

"No. Hamid's Mori should already be trying to heal him, and the knife will slow it down. The gunna paste will help it along."

My paste was in my jacket under Hamid's head, so I looked at Beth, who handed me hers. Every warrior carried a small tin of the medicine in the field.

Laying the tin of paste on the floor, I knelt over Hamid and grasped the knife with both hands. One quick, hard pull and the blade came free. He grunted but made no other sound even though it had to hurt like hell.

I tossed the bloody knife a few feet away and asked Beth to put pressure on the wound while I gave him the paste.

I opened the tin and scooped out a generous amount. Leaning down, I cupped Hamid's face, and his eyes flickered open to meet mine. His olive skin was paler than normal, and the clench of his jaw told me he was in pain.

"You need to eat this," I said as I put my fingers to his lips. "Xavier will be here soon."

He dutifully took the gunna paste and closed his eyes again. "You're sexy when you take charge," he slurred, earning a chuckle from Beth and a smile from me.

I sat on the floor to cradle his head on my lap. "You remember that the next time you try to boss me around."

Orias stood. "It looks like he'll survive, so I'm going to help Ciro deal with the rest of this mess."

I looked around for the first time since Hamid had been hit. The adults had been freed and were holding their children like they'd never let them go. The happy crying was a welcome sound after what had almost happened here.

Orias went to join Ciro in studying the circles, and after a minute, Beth left us to see to some of the injured demons. I stayed where I was, content to let them handle everything. My only concern was making sure Hamid was okay.

He groaned softly, and I gently rubbed the back of his neck. "What can I do?"

"You're doing it," he said without opening his eyes. His hand came up to rest on my thigh. "I should take a knife to the back more often if it'll get me this treatment."

My hand stilled, and I glared at him. "Don't even joke about that."

A smile curved his lips. "I'll stop if you will stop pretending you don't care for me."

"That's emotional blackmail."

"Only if you don't care, which you do. Why are you so afraid to say it?"

I swallowed. "I'm not afraid."

His hand lightly squeezed my leg. "For such a skilled warrior, you are a terrible liar."

Warmth flooded my chest. "You think I'm skilled?"

Hamid rolled onto his back so he was looking up at me. He lifted one hand and caressed my cheek. "You are the fiercest female warrior I've ever known, and my heart fills with pride to know you are mine."

My stomach dipped wildly at the open adoration in his eyes, and it took me a moment to find my voice. "I didn't say I was yours."

"Not yet, but you will." He slid his hand behind my head and pulled me down for a brief kiss that left me hungry for more. "Soon," he murmured against my lips before he released me.

I sat up, trying to control my pounding heart, and Hamid wrapped one strong arm around my waist as if he expected me to flee. But I wasn't going anywhere, not after he'd just turned my legs to Jell-O with his words. No man had ever spoken to me that way, and from anyone else, I would have hated it. But coming from him, I liked it.

Oh, who was I kidding? I loved it. The confident way he spoke and the possessive gleam in his eyes made me want to crawl into his arms and tell him anything he wanted me to say.

Everyone left Hamid and me to ourselves until Xavier and a half dozen other warriors arrived. They'd barely entered the building when a door slammed open, and I smiled when I heard Chris shouting Beth's name. I got it now. I understood the protectiveness mates had for each other because I felt it for Hamid just as he did for me.

Hamid tried to sit up, but I laid a hand against his chest to hold him. "Not until Xavier checks you out."

He sighed and settled down again, although it wasn't like I could stop him if he was determined to get up. Even injured, he was ten times stronger than I was. I secretly liked that, too, not that I'd ever tell him. The man was arrogant enough.

I looked for Xavier and saw him talking to Beth, who pointed in our direction. The healer hurried over, carrying a duffle bag, and knelt beside Hamid.

"How is he doing?" Xavier asked me.

"He is fine," Hamid answered grumpily, suddenly the surly patient. "It's not like I've never been cut before."

I glowered at him. "You were stabbed by an archdemon, and I'm pretty sure the blade nicked your heart. So, you're going to let Xavier do whatever is necessary to help you."

Hamid's scowl transformed into a smug smile. "You do care about me."

I lifted my eyes to meet the healer's amused ones. "Do you have anything in that bag that will knock him out?"

Xavier laughed and examined Hamid. "Your vitals all look good, and you seem to be healing well. I'd like to do a scan when we get back to the medical ward, just to be sure."

Hamid nodded and sat up with a little help from me. I was relieved to see his color had improved, even though he was still weak.

The healer stood. "I have a stretcher in the van if you –"

"No stretcher." Hamid's lip curled in disgust. "I can walk. And I need to stay here to oversee everything."

I got to my feet. "Chris is here along with Orias and Ciro, and I'm sure the rest of the team will be along soon. They will handle it."

Hamid started to argue, and I tried another tactic. "Are you really going to make me follow you around all day worrying because you didn't take time to heal?"

He fell silent. No bonded male could stand to see his mate emotionally distressed, especially if he was the cause. It was a low blow, but I'd just pulled a knife from his back for Christ's sake.

"I'll go back to the command center," he said at last. "But you are coming with me."

I smiled. "Someone has to keep you in line."

Xavier and I helped him to his feet, despite his protests that he could stand on his own. I caught Chris's eye, and he came over.

Chris grinned at Hamid. "Stabbed by an archdemon. Always the over-achiever."

Hamid grimaced. "Next time, you can have the pleasure."

"No, he cannot," Beth called from nearby where she was tending to an older Vrell demon with a gash on his cheek.

"We're going to the command center," I said to Chris.

He looked from me to Hamid. "Probably a good idea. I'll take care of things here and keep you updated."

I shot Chris a grateful look, and then Hamid, Xavier, and I left the building through the loading doors someone had opened. Hamid refused Xavier's help, but he allowed me to take his arm as we walked to the van parked behind the building. It was a two-seater van, so Hamid took the passenger seat, and I climbed into the back, repressing a shudder at the sight of the stretcher across from me. I couldn't remember much of what had happened after the Gulak attack, but I was pretty sure this was the same van that had transported me.

At the command center, Xavier parked in the loading bay, and we went directly to the medical ward where Sara was waiting anxiously for us.

"We're okay," I assured her as Hamid walked to the same bed I'd been in for several days. "Hamid wanted to play patient today."

Sara wrung her hands. "When Beth called, I was so afraid one of you would be hurt. I can't believe Alaron went to a wrakk in the middle of the day, especially now that he knows we're onto him."

"He has no way of knowing the demon community has a relationship with us," Hamid said. "I think we were the last people he expected to show up there."

"But why a wrakk?" Sara asked. "What could he gain by hurting children?"

Hamid lay back on the bed. "I don't know, but I'm sure Orias and Ciro will have some ideas."

Xavier changed into his white lab coat and rolled a cart with a scanning unit over to the bed. Our mobile scanner wasn't as thorough as an MRI or CT scan, but it gave healers enough to see what was going on in a body. We couldn't get cancer or other human diseases, so we didn't need all the big diagnostic equipment used in hospitals.

Sara excused herself when Hamid began to unbutton his shirt. Xavier turned on the machine, and with a steady hand, he held the scanner an inch above Hamid's chest, running it slowly up and down Hamid's torso while keeping his eyes on the monitor. When he got to the heart, he stopped and studied the picture for a minute before completing the scan.

"There was some damage to the heart, but it's healing nicely," Xavier said once he'd finished. "Fortunately, you have a very strong Mori. A younger one might not have been able to save you."

Hamid's eyes met mine where I stood at the foot of the bed, and I knew he and I were thinking the same thing. If he hadn't moved so fast to cover my body with his, I'd probably be dead now.

Xavier went on, oblivious to our silent exchange. "I'm ordering you off duty for the next twenty-four hours. Other than that, you are free to go."

Hamid sat up. "Thank you, Xavier."

"Anytime," the healer said with a smile.

Hamid stood and walked over to me. Wordlessly, he took my arm and led me out of the medical ward.

"Where are we going?" I asked when we entered the deserted living area.

"To my room."

A thrill zinged through me at the thought of being alone with him in a room – with a bed. But before I had time to think too much about it, we were at his door.

We entered the room, and he closed the door with a resounding click. The room looked exactly like mine, except for the few personal belongings on top of the dresser.

"Make yourself comfortable," he said, grabbing a change of clothes from a drawer. "I'm going to clean up, and then you and I have things to talk about."

"What things?" I asked, though I already knew the answer. It hit me that for the first time, I wasn't spooked by the idea of discussing my feelings with him.

Hamid stopped at the bathroom door to give me a fierce look that made my insides quiver in the best way. "Don't make me come look for you."

I couldn't speak as he shut the door. All I could think about was the promise in his eyes and how much I wanted him to chase me – and catch me.

I'd known days ago where this was going between us, but almost losing him today had made me see how stupid I was. I'd always believed in living life to the fullest, but here I was holding back when I could be with the man I'd fantasized about for years. More than that, he was the only one I could imagine spending my life with. The only man I had ever loved.

I suddenly felt lighter and oddly free. I loved Hamid, and I suspected he felt the same way for me. I was pretty sure that was what he wanted to talk about after his shower, but I didn't want to wait. Not one more second.

Smiling, I grabbed the bottom of my shirt and pulled it over my head.

17

I walked away from the pile of clothes on the floor and opened the bathroom door. Through the shower glass, I could see Hamid's muscled back and rounded ass, and my mouth watered at the sight of him. I took a few seconds to admire him, and then I opened the shower door.

Hamid turned to face me, and I sucked in a breath when I got my first look at his naked body. "There is a God," I breathed, letting my eyes devour him before lifting my gaze to meet his smoldering eyes.

I entered the shower and closed the door. Wordlessly, I reached up and pulled his head down to mine. Our mouths met in a hungry kiss, and his arms wrapped around my waist, pulling me to him. The feel of his hard body against mine without the barrier of clothes made my brain short-circuit a little, and I almost lost the ability to think.

When we came up for air, he tucked my wet hair behind my ears. "I think we're violating your rule number two."

"I never liked rules anyway." I stroked the hard planes of his chest up to his shoulders. "I forgot to tell you something."

"What was so important you couldn't wait to tell me?" His sensual smile made my knees weak.

My gaze held his. "That I love you."

His mouth crashed down on mine, and I responded with a need that rivaled his. I clung to him as he deepened the kiss, taking everything I had to give. And I gave it all. I was done holding back with him.

Eventually, the kiss became gentler, sweeter, until he pulled out of it. "So, you do care."

I rolled my eyes at him. "You want to go there now?"

He let out a sexy laugh, and I felt it rumble in his chest, which was pressed to mine. His hands rested on either side of my neck, and his thumbs stroked my jaw. "I love you, too."

I gave him a saucy grin. "I know."

"Is that so?" he asked huskily.

"Mm-hmm." I traced the muscles of his lower back to the curve of his ass. "I had another reason for coming in here."

His voice grew deeper. "What?"

I stepped back and picked up the bottle of body wash, pouring a generous amount into my hand. "I thought with your injury, you might need some help washing. I don't know if I ever told you, but I make a great nurse."

His eyes were heavy-lidded as he watched me work up a lather and start running my soapy hands over his shoulders and chest. I kept my gaze locked with his as my hands moved downward, sliding over his ribs and hard stomach and lower still. He tensed and hissed out a breath when I took him in my hands and slowly stroked his length.

"Do you know how long I've wanted to touch you like this?" I asked, my voice hoarse with desire. "Ever since the first time I laid eyes on you at that command center in Santa Cruz." My grip tightened, pulling a groan from him. "Since that night, it's you I think of when I –"

Hamid let out a low growl and pulled me to him for another searing kiss. Then he was behind me, his hot mouth grazing my neck and shoulders as he fondled my breasts. I moaned and leaned back into him, inviting him to touch me more.

One of his hands slid down my slippery skin to my aching sex, making me writhe. Holding me against him, he whispered wonderfully wicked things to me as he made me come apart under his hands and mouth.

I was floating in a blissful haze when he turned off the water and carried me to his bed. He laid me down on the soft sheets and claimed my mouth again before we began to explore every inch of each other's bodies. He was an amazing lover and clearly intent on making me forget my own name before he was done. But I enjoyed giving pleasure as much as receiving it, and I loved every moan and growl I pulled from him.

"You are going to be the death of me." Hamid raised himself over me, his face covered in a fine sheen of sweat. He settled between my legs, and anticipation built in me when I felt him at my entrance.

I ran my fingers through his damp hair. "But what a way to go."

"My beautiful mate." He lowered his head to brush my lips with his.

"Not yet," I reminded him breathlessly. "There is one more thing we need to do first."

He smiled, and it amazed me that he could still make my stomach quiver after all we'd just done to each other. "You've been mine since the moment we bonded. This just makes it official."

"Then let's make it official," I said roughly, lifting my hips and making both of us moan.

He pressed forward, and I took him into my body with a happy cry. My Mori sent a burst of pure joy through me as Hamid and I moved in a timeless rhythm to bind us together forever. As the tension inside me crested, a new awareness blossomed in my mind until I could feel him there, joined with me in every way. *My mate*, growled his voice in my head as we fell over the edge together.

We made love over and over, unable to get enough of each other as the daylight hours faded into night. I asked him once if he wanted to rest because of his injury, and he answered by kissing me senseless until I forgot the question.

Late into the night, our stomachs started to growl from hunger, and Hamid left to get us some food from the kitchen. I dozed among the rumpled sheets until he returned and fed me. I'd never thought of myself as the romantic type, but he showed me I could be soft and feminine with him and still be the warrior I wanted to be.

"What will you do when there is no more Alaron to chase after?" I asked him as I sat propped up on pillows, nibbling on a piece of cheese.

He cut a slice of apple and handed it to me. "There is always a job somewhere that needs me."

"Do you intend to keep working for the Council then?" I tried to hide how much that possibility did not appeal to me, but I failed miserably.

Hamid laid down the apple and knife. "Only if that is what you want. We're partners now, and we'll decide these things together."

"You won't miss it?"

"There are plenty of jobs to be found outside of working for the Council." He gave me a teasing look. "I have a feeling life with you will be an adventure no matter where we go."

I licked apple juice from my fingers. "Talk like that will get you lucky."

He laughed, but I caught the flare of desire in his eyes. The man was insatiable, and I was a happy, happy girl. Something told me I wouldn't be needing any more of those late-night runs or workouts to help me sleep.

"Before you say no to working for the Council, I want you to consider the perks that come with the job," he said. "We would travel the world in our own plane, doing jobs a young warrior would rarely get to work on. You would see and do things you only dreamed of."

"You make a great sales pitch." I set down my plate and crawled over to straddle his lap. "Does that plane come with a bed?"

His arms slid around my waist, and he trailed kisses along my jaw. "No, but I'm sure I could arrange for one."

"And can I take my bike with me? I'm not leaving that behind."

"Of course."

"Okay. I'll consider it." I pushed him onto his back and leaned down to taste his lips, which were sweet from the apple he'd been eating. "Mmmm."

He rolled us, and suddenly, I was under him. "Are you still hungry?" he asked huskily.

"Not for food."

A sexy smile spread across his face. "I think I can help you with that."

Hamid and I didn't emerge from his room until early the next morning. I would have been happy to stay in there a few more days, but we had a job to do. Alaron wasn't going to wait around while we got our fill of each other. Not that I could ever get enough of him.

It amazed me how different the world looked today, even though the only thing that had changed was our relationship. We were still facing one of the greatest threats to our world. We had no idea where Alaron was or when he'd strike next, or if we could even defeat him. But despite all of that, I was ridiculously happy to the point of bursting.

We went straight to the control room. Chris briefed us on the wrakk situation and told us the Council team had finished their investigation there last night. Since we'd interrupted Alaron at the start of the ceremony, there was nothing new to report.

"A few of the demons had injuries, but miraculously, no one was killed," Chris said. "Nikolas is there now with a team, helping them get up and running again. The plan is to keep two of our warriors there for the next day or two as a precaution."

"You think Alaron might come back?" I asked.

Chris shrugged. "It's hard to predict what he'll do next."

Hamid looked up from the report he was skimming from yesterday's incident. "Do we know why he was going to use the demon children for this one? The bodies at the previous sites were all human adults."

"From what the witnesses said, Alaron hoped demon energy would strengthen his spell to open the barrier. Orias said there is no evidence to suggest it would work, but Alaron might be getting desperate."

I puffed out a breath. "Just what we need, a desperate archdemon."

The door opened, and Orias came in. "Good, you're both here," he said when he spotted Hamid and me. "We need to run some tests to make sure the spell is still stable after Alaron's attack."

Some of my earlier happiness dissipated. Orias knew just what to say to put a damper on my good mood.

"It won't take long," Hamid reassured me as we followed the warlock to the conference room where the rest of the team waited.

Orias wasted no time getting down to business. As soon as we sat, he placed his hands on either side of Hamid's head and began the now familiar chant.

A minute later, Orias's brow creased and a puzzled look entered his eyes. He dropped his hands and moved to do the same test on me. Again, he appeared bemused by whatever he was seeing. He pursed his lips and stepped away from me.

"Is the spell intact?" Bastien asked when Orias only stared thoughtfully at Hamid and me.

"I think so. It's changed," Orias said. "Look, and tell me what you see."

Bastien and Ciro came over, and each of them performed the same test on us. I could tell by their surprised expressions they were as mystified as Orias.

"It's not the same spell that was there a few days ago," Ciro said to Orias. "I can see your magic but no trace of the demon's."

Bastien nodded. "And there is something new I can't identify. It's very strong, whatever it is."

Hamid and I looked at each other and shared a smile. Something had definitely changed all right.

"You completed the bond," Charlotte said astutely, her smile wide. "Congratulations."

"Thank you," Hamid and I said together.

Orias stroked his chin. "Fascinating. It looks like your mating has completely reworked the structure of the original spell."

"Is the spell compromised?" Marie asked.

I held my breath as I waited for one of the warlocks to answer. The last thing I'd thought about yesterday was how our mating would affect the spell.

"If anything, I'd say it's stronger," Orias replied.

"But you might no longer be protected from Alaron's magic," Ciro warned us. "Perhaps we should study it more to make sure there is none of the demon magic left."

I balked at the idea of more tests. "No need for that. Sara can detect demon magic."

"That is true," Ciro conceded. "And it would be much faster. Is she here?"

"I'll check." I stood and hurried out of the room before they changed their minds.

I found Sara exactly where I expected to – in the kitchen making breakfast. Beth was there, too, brewing her morning cup of coffee. When they saw me, they gave me expectant looks.

"Are you here to give us some special news?" Beth asked eagerly.

I leaned my elbows on the island and pasted on an innocent smile. "Whatever do you mean?"

Sara scooped scrambled eggs onto her plate. "She means that based on the sounds coming from Hamid's room all day and night, he was doing more than recovering from his injury."

I couldn't contain my grin. "We did a little physical therapy. It's amazing what that can do for the body."

"Indeed," Beth said seriously, and then the three of us cracked up.

"Well?" Sara asked when we'd stopped laughing. "Tell us already."

I looked from her to Beth and nodded.

Beth squealed and hugged me. "Oh, my God. I'm so happy for you."

"It's about time," Sara joked. She gave me a teary smile. "And I can't even hug you. This sucks."

Her comment reminded me why I'd come looking for her in the first place. "Maybe not. It turns out that completing the bond changed the spell on Hamid and me. None of the warlocks can detect demon magic on us now, and I came to see if you can."

Sara's face lit up, and she came around the island to stand near me. She placed her hand a few inches from mine on the countertop and slowly closed the distance until our fingers were touching.

"I'm happy to report there's not a trace of demon magic on you," she said before she threw her arms around me and squeezed me like we hadn't seen each other in years.

"When did you become such a hugger?" I teased her.

She sniffled. "It's the baby hormones."

"That reminds me." I squatted in front of her. "Hello, little one. I'm your auntie Jordan, and I can't wait to meet you."

Sara let out a delighted laugh. "She likes you."

"Of course, she does." I patted her belly. "We're going to have so much fun together."

"Well, this is an interesting picture," said an amused male voice.

I stood and faced Eldeorin, who had appeared in the living room.

The blond faerie smiled devilishly. "Don't stop on my account. I'll just stand over here and watch."

"Lech." I glared at him. "Only you would make something dirty out of this."

"It's nice to see you again, Jordan. I believe you get more ravishing every day."

"And you're still not getting into my pants," I retorted.

He chuckled. "Someday."

"Never," growled a deep, angry voice that made my stomach flutter.

Hamid strode angrily through the door and came to stand behind me. One muscled arm circled my waist possessively and pulled me back against him. The old me would have punched him in the junk and asked him what the hell he thought he was doing. The new me was incredibly turned on by this alpha side of my mate.

I'm glad you like it, he said in my mind. The wave of desire that came across the bond told me I'd accidentally sent him my carnal thoughts. Oops. I definitely needed to work on that.

Eldeorin ignored Hamid and smirked at me. "A mate, Jordan? I must say I'm surprised. You never struck me as a one-man kind of woman."

"Eldeorin," Sara scolded. "Stop trying to cause trouble."

"Me?" He put a hand to his chest. "Why, Cousin, I'm shocked you would think that of me."

She scoffed and walked over to him. Eldeorin might be a good mentor to her, but I had no idea how she could spend so much time with the arrogant faerie. It drove Nikolas nuts, but he tolerated it for Sara's sake.

"I didn't expect to hear from you again so soon," she told Eldeorin.

"I come bearing gifts." The air in front of him shimmered, and a small sheathed knife appeared between them. Plucking the weapon from the air, he laid it flat on his palm and held it out to Sara.

She accepted it and turned it over in her hands. "What is this?"

"That, dear cousin, is the weapon you asked for."

My heart began to thump in excitement. Hamid needed no urging when I started forward, tugging him with me.

Sara pulled the knife from its plain wooden sheath and held it up for us to see. The handle was made of the same dark wood, but the jagged four-inch blade was made from a shimmering white metal I'd never seen before. It seemed to glow from within, and even from several feet away, I could feel power emanating from it. I was overcome with the feeling that I was in the presence of something so sacred and pure it was not meant to be touched by one as unworthy as I was.

"It's beautiful," Sara said softly. She held the knife out for Hamid to take, but Eldeorin snatched it and held it away from him.

"Do not touch the blade," the faerie warned us. "This will kill any demon, even yours."

"Sara touched it," Beth said.

Eldeorin gave her an indulgent look. "Sara is half Fae, and her power shields her demon. Ideally, she would be the one to wield this, but her pregnancy prevents her from fighting."

Her pregnancy and Nikolas, I quipped to Hamid, who grunted softly in reply.

Sara reached for the knife again and studied the blade closely. Her eyes reflected its unearthly glow. "I've never seen metal like this. Is it from Faerie?"

"It was not forged in Faerie, but this piece has been in our possession for many millennia. When you said you needed a weapon to defeat an archdemon, I almost didn't remember this because it's been hidden away for so long."

I leaned in as far as Hamid would let me for a closer look. "If it's not Faemade, why is it dangerous to us?"

"Because this" – Eldeorin ran a finger along the flat part of the blade – "is a shard from the sword of an archangel."

I gasped as shock punched the air from my lungs. Next to me, Beth made a choked sound. Sara was so startled she dropped the knife, and Eldeorin caught it. Hamid remained stoic, but I could feel his surprise across our bond.

"An...angel's sword?" I asked, needing him to say it again so I could process it. In my heart, I knew he was telling the truth because I'd sensed there was something special about the blade the moment I got near it.

"An archangel," he corrected me.

"How...?" Sara trailed off, at a loss for words.

"How is it you are in possession of such a holy relic?" Hamid asked with more composure than Beth, Sara, and me put together.

Eldeorin sheathed the blade with a reverence I'd never seen from him. "Fae lore says our ancestors were the offspring of angels who fell to Earth. They were unhappy in this realm, so they created their own paradise, away from humanity, and no one left it for thousands of years. Over time, we became a new race with no real memory of our origins, except for what is in our lore."

"You're descended from the Nephilim?" I asked incredulously. Faeries weren't exactly known for being chaste and moral, something Eldeorin took great pride in.

"According to the lore, some of the angels' offspring chose to stay in this realm. We believe they were the ones who came to be known as the Nephilim."

Hamid inclined his head at the knife in Eldeorin's hands. "And the blade?"

"It came from the battle that happened when the angels were cast down to Earth," Eldeorin said. "There are other artifacts, but this is the only sword fragment."

Sara put a hand to her forehead. "This is...too much. I can't wrap my head around the fact that you have a piece of an archangel's sword in your hands."

I wondered what her reaction would be when she worked out the part where she might be descended from angels. She was looking a little pale, so I decided not to mention it. Better to let her connect those dots on her own.

"That is a powerful weapon," Hamid said to Eldeorin, not hiding his suspicion of the faerie and his motives. "Why would you give it to us?"

"Because Sara asked me for help and we always take care of our own. And because this world has many delights I would miss if it were gone."

Sara gave him a tremulous smile. "Thank you. I knew you would come through for us."

I raised a hand. "I hate to rain on our parade, but who is going to use the weapon if none of us can hold it?"

"You can hold it as long as you don't touch the blade." Eldeorin held the knife out to me, but Hamid's reach was longer, and he got to it first. I held my breath fearfully as his fingers closed around the handle.

I started breathing again when nothing happened. Hamid didn't do anything but hold the knife as Eldeorin continued to speak.

"The handle and sheath are made from the wood of the fura tree, which only grows in Faerie. The wood is impervious to fire and magic, and it will protect you from the power of the blade. The sheath will also prevent the demon from sensing the blade if he gets close to it."

"So, all we have to do is catch Alaron trying to open the barrier again and hit him with this?" I asked skeptically.

"Not quite," Eldeorin said. "The blade must be used on the demon's physical body in order to kill him. And touching an archdemon with it won't be enough. You'll need to pierce his flesh."

I threw up my hands. "The whole point of this is to keep him from opening the barrier to bring his body through. If he gets into his own body, nothing can kill him."

Hamid held up the knife. "Nothing except an archangel's sword."

"A whole sword, wielded by an angel," I argued. "Alaron will be too powerful for anyone to get close enough to use that little thing."

Eldeorin's smile was almost apologetic. "I did not say it would be easy."

Hamid's arm slipped around my waist and squeezed it reassuringly. "We will figure out a way."

I leaned into him. *We're warriors. It's what we do.*

18

I tossed my coat on the foot of the bed and kicked off my boots. "Well, that was fun," I said without enthusiasm.

Hamid didn't answer as he walked across the hotel room and stared out the window at the Miami skyline. He'd been distracted and moody lately, and today hadn't helped. Chasing down our second false lead in three days hadn't put anyone on the team in better spirits.

It had been over a week since our run-in with Alaron at the wrakk, and the longer we went without a sign of him, the higher tensions ran through everyone involved. Foremost on our minds was what he was up to and where he would strike next.

Some people speculated that Kai's body might have finally deteriorated too much to host the demon and he'd gone back to his dimension. I wanted so much to believe that, but Hamid didn't think we'd seen the last of the archdemon yet, and I trusted his instincts. So did the Council. They had so much faith in Hamid they had decided he would keep the angel blade with him. He carried the weapon on his person at all times, except for when we were in our room.

At the moment, however, Alaron wasn't my main concern. The only thing I cared about was easing the stress of my mate, who bore the weight of this investigation on his shoulders. They were very strong shoulders to be sure, but I was determined to relieve them of their burden, if only for a few hours.

Pulling off my shirt, I let it fall to the floor. Next came my jeans, leaving me in the matching Victoria Secret set I'd put on this morning with this moment in mind.

"I'm going to grab a shower. Want to join me?"

Hamid's head turned in my direction. Lust blazed in his eyes as he took in the blue lace bra and panties that left little to the imagination. He abandoned the window and prowled toward me, the intensity of his stare sending my pulse racing.

His hands framed my face, and he gazed down into my eyes with so much love and desire it stole my breath away. "You are a temptress, my mate."

Only for you, I said as his mouth covered mine in a dizzying kiss, his hands roving over my body until my legs were too weak to support me.

Backing me up until I lay on the bed, he bent to press scorching kisses to my stomach that made me nearly mindless with need.

"Shower," I gasped.

His fingers slipped beneath the low waistband of my panties. "Later."

Much, much later, I lay in the bed and drowsily listened to Hamid ordering room service. I could have taken this little break from our lovemaking to get that shower, but my body had all the strength of a limp noodle. I was content to just lie there and let him feed me. Maybe if I asked nicely, he'd wash me, too. I smiled lazily because he wouldn't need a lot of coaxing.

As soon as he hung up, his cell phone rang. I was used to people calling him, so I didn't pay attention until I heard him say, "We'll be there by morning."

I sat up. "Where are we going?"

"Los Angeles. Raoul said they've had unusual activity at Fisher Middle School."

"What kind of activity?" Tossing the covers off me, I got out of bed.

Hamid's gaze slid over my naked form as he hit the call button on his phone. "Have the plane ready to take off within the hour." Pause. "Los Angeles." He hung up and met my eyes. "Grab a quick shower while I let the others know we're leaving."

I rooted in my bag for a change of clothes. "What kind of activity are they seeing?"

"The janitor saw a strange light in one of the classrooms. He was spooked and called the command center. Raoul checked it out, and they found nothing out of the ordinary, but he wants the team to go over it."

"I don't blame him after what happened there last time." I headed to the bathroom. "I'll be out in five."

I was drying off when Hamid came into the bathroom and entered the shower. I forgot what I was doing and watched him standing beneath the spray of water as I thought for the thousandth time what a lucky girl I was.

He turned to face me, wearing a knowing smirk, and made a show of washing his front.

Keep it up, big guy, and we're going to be late for that flight. I left the bathroom to the sound of his deep laughter.

We joined the rest of the team in the lobby ten minutes later. Some of them looked bleary-eyed from lack of sleep, but a familiar current of excitement ran through the whole group as we drove to the airport.

On the plane, I grabbed my usual seat in the last row. Hamid spent the first hour talking to the others, but then he made his way down to sit with me.

"I thought you'd be asleep by now," he said.

I yawned and rested my head against his shoulder. "I tried, but I can't stop thinking about what we'll find in L.A."

"You won't be finding anything but a bed if you don't get some rest," he admonished lightly. He reclined our seats until we were almost lying down and tugged me over so I was on his chest. I tried to lift my head, but he held me in place. "Sleep."

"Don't think you're going to make a habit of bossing me around," I said grumpily as I shifted to get more comfortable.

He stroked my arm laying across his stomach. "I wouldn't think of it."

"I don't want to be coddled either." I yawned again and let my eyes close.

"What if I just need to hold my mate?"

I smiled sleepily. "I'll make exceptions for that."

The sun was rising when Hamid gently shook me awake to let me know we were about to land at LAX. We taxied into the hangar, and I was delighted to see Raoul standing beside one of the waiting vehicles when I stepped off the plane.

"Welcome back," he said warmly as he gave me a quick hug. He shook hands with Hamid. "Thanks for coming so soon."

"Have there been any new developments?" Hamid asked him.

Raoul opened the back door of the SUV for me. "No, but we have people posted at the school. Thankfully, it's the weekend, so we didn't have to worry about closing it down."

We drove directly to the school, and Raoul showed us the classroom where the janitor had seen the light. The warlocks went to work, doing whatever it was they did to check for the presence of other magic. It didn't take them long to confirm traces of Alaron's magic in the room. What had he been doing there if he hadn't been trying to reopen the barrier?

We trailed after Orias, Ciro, and Bastien as they went from room to room, testing for magic. When we entered the gym, I stopped and took in the place where two life-changing events had happened in one night. Life-changing for me, anyway. It was here that I'd witnessed the barrier being opened for the first time. And here that Hamid and I had bonded.

How differently would our lives have played out had he not tackled me that night? We might have gone our separate ways without ever knowing what could have been. I would have lived a happy and exciting life, because I didn't believe in living any other way. But deep inside, would I have known a part of me was missing?

I watched Hamid talking to Raoul, and as if he felt my eyes on him, he looked at me. A few months ago, all I'd wanted was to be free of this man. Now, I couldn't imagine life without him.

Everything okay? he asked.

I smiled. *You know how much I love all this magic business.*

The warlocks finished their tests in the gym and informed us there was no sign of the spell used to open the barrier.

"We'd like to stay a bit longer to see if we can discern what other reason Alaron would have to be here," Orias said.

"Call me when you're done," Hamid told him. "We'll head to the command center."

Raoul drove Hamid and me to the house I used to live in. It was weird being back, and the house felt different somehow. It took a few minutes for me to realize what had changed was me. I wasn't the same person I'd been when I left here.

We entered the control room as Mason walked out of the weapons room with a big smile on his face. "Look who finally decided to come home. And just in time, too."

"In time for what?" I asked.

He pointed at the large computer screen on the wall that displayed an interactive map of Los Angeles. Colored dots represented our people out in the field, and there seemed to be more active warriors than usual for the middle of the day.

"Already today we've had Lamprey demons infesting a nursing home, an incubus attack at a mall, and two separate vampire attacks in the subway. I don't know what's going on, but something has the demons riled up."

Hamid and I exchanged a look. Alaron had been at the school last night, and he could still be in Los Angeles. Having an archdemon in the vicinity was bound to cause problems in a city with such a large demon population.

"We need to reach out to all our demon contacts in the area," Hamid said to Raoul.

Raoul nodded. "I'll call Kelvan and Adele. If anyone has heard something, it will be them."

"What will we do?" I asked Hamid because I knew he wouldn't stand around and wait to hear something.

He hesitated, and for a few seconds, I thought he was going to tell me to stay at the house. I was preparing myself for an argument when he took out his phone and said, "We'll visit the local wrakks. I'll ask Orias to accompany us."

There were three wrakks in the greater Los Angeles area, and it took the better part of the afternoon for us to visit all of them. We found a lot of frightened demons whispering about the archdemon that was supposedly in the city. Peaceful demons such as Vrell, Mox, and Quellar demons were afraid for their families, and some were planning to leave the city.

The city quieted down by early evening, leaving us to wonder if Alaron had left already. I had mixed feelings about that. As much as I did not want to see him again, I wanted all of this to be over with, and that was going to happen in one of two ways: either we killed him, or he ran out of time and went back to the other side of the barrier.

Hamid and I had dinner at the command center with Raoul, Brock, and Mason, while Orias went out to eat with the team. It was great catching up with my friends, even though I endured a lot of ribbing from Mason and Brock when they found out Hamid and I had mated. They had fun reminding me how much he and I had butted heads in the beginning.

"I think we actually feared for your life after you suggested putting her on day patrols," Brock told Hamid. "You are a braver man than I am."

Hamid nodded gravely. "I have a healthier respect for her temper since she threatened to castrate me."

Everyone laughed, and I winked at him. *I'm glad I didn't. That's one of my favorite parts.*

Our dinner was interrupted a few minutes later by Caleb, who was manning the control room. "The LAPD is getting calls from all over the city about strange sightings and vampire attacks," Caleb told Raoul, who was already standing. "Our teams are responding, but there are too many incidents for us to deal with them all."

"What kind of sightings?" Hamid asked as we all stood.

"Based on the calls we've monitored, at least one Drex demon, some Ranc demons, and a sheroc demon," Caleb said. "Nothing we haven't seen before, just not this many at once."

"Call in anyone who isn't working," Raoul ordered Caleb as the five of us hurried to the control room.

Hamid called in the Council team that had decided to check into a hotel instead of staying at the command center with us. He hung up with them and called the Council to let them know what was going on. I left him to that business and went to Raoul to ask what I could do to help.

"Help Caleb monitor the calls," he said in a rush. I frowned, and he smiled. "Just until we get organized. Don't worry. We'll all see some action tonight if this keeps up."

Hamid found me a short while later. He sat on his haunches beside my chair, his mouth set in a grim line. "If I asked you to stay here, would you do it?"

"Are you asking as a senior warrior in the field or as my mate?" I could sense the worry and agitation coming off him, and I knew he was feeling protective, but he couldn't keep me from doing my job because of that. We'd discussed this very thing in great detail since our mating, and he'd promised he would never hold me back.

"Both," he answered honestly. "This house is protected by Fae wards, which makes it the safest place in the city."

I spun my chair to face him fully. "Did you ask Mason and the other junior warriors to stay here?"

Hamid didn't answer immediately, and that told me what I wanted to know. I scooted my chair closer to him and placed my hand over his heart. "It's my duty to protect humans, and they need me now. Please, don't ask me to ignore that and to hide while you and everyone else put yourselves at risk. I don't think I could stand it."

He sighed heavily, and I saw the internal struggle in his eyes. One of his hands came up to cover mine. "Promise me you will follow my orders. And if it gets too bad out there, you'll come back to the house if I tell you to."

"I promise."

Raoul walked over to us. "We have twenty-eight warriors in the city, plus you two and the Council team. Having Orias and the other two warlocks will be a big help, but I've asked for backup from San Diego, Las Vegas, and San Francisco. It'll be hours before most of them can get here, so we might be in for a rough night."

Hamid stood. "It's better for you and me to lead separate teams. I will take Jordan, Charlotte, and Marie, and ask Orias to join us."

"I'll take Caleb and Brock with me," Raoul said. "Mason is staying here to man the control room."

I looked for Mason and found him near Brock, looking none too happy.

Raoul followed my gaze. "Someone has to stay here to monitor everything, and he's the youngest."

I looked away, not wanting to meet Mason's gaze and see his disappointment. I knew what he was feeling because I'd feel the exact same way if I'd been ordered to stay behind. We were warriors, and this was what we lived for. Being left out of the action was like an athlete going to the Olympics and being forced to stay on the sidelines and watch everyone else compete.

Hamid and I armed ourselves to the teeth while we waited for the others to arrive. I was strapping on the sword he gave me when Orias and the others walked in. Hamid brought them up to speed, and then we headed out in one of the SUVs.

We'd barely been on the road for five minutes when Mason asked if anyone was near the Santa Monica Pier. Something was attacking people on the beach. Everyone else was engaged, so Hamid told him we were on the way.

The pier was crowded with onlookers trying to see what was going on down below, while uniformed police officers attempted to keep anyone from getting too close to the beach. We parked behind one of the police vehicles, and Hamid went to speak to the nearest officer. They appeared to be arguing until Hamid handed the man his phone. The officer spoke to the person on the other end and quickly nodded.

I didn't have to ask Hamid what that had been about. Government officials, including the police commissioner's office knew about us and what we did. But police officers weren't privy to this information. Hamid had likely called someone on the commissioner's staff to let the officer know we were authorized to be there.

Hamid came back to us. "Witnesses said something came out of the water and grabbed a teenage girl. A boy tried to help her, and whatever it was took the two of them under the pier. The first police officer to respond went in and never came back."

"Description?" Charlotte asked as she adjusted her knife harness.

"Too dark for anyone to see clearly, but people said they smelled ammonia and heard clicking sounds."

Marie frowned. "A Gargan? Impossible."

A Gargan was a water demon that lived near the equator. Resembling a giant black lobster, they fed mostly off fish and other sea creatures. When hunting, they excreted a dark, oily venom that paralyzed their prey and smelled strongly of ammonia, and they made a distinct clicking sound when they fed. There had been some recorded attacks on humans, usually fishermen, but gargans rarely came ashore. And they preferred much warmer waters than the North Pacific.

"As impossible as an archdemon trying to open the barrier?" Orias asked dryly. I didn't agree with him on much, but he had a point. We'd seen enough in the last two months to know anything was possible.

Hamid studied the inky blackness beneath the pier before he looked at Orias. "We will handle this. Can you create a glamour to conceal us? We need to contain this as much as possible."

Orias nodded. "I can do better than that. I have a spell that will make the humans forget what they see here. It won't fix anything that's already been recorded and uploaded on their phones, but from what you said, it's dark and they didn't see much."

"Thank you." Hamid turned to the rest of us. "I'll go first to see what we're dealing with. If it's a Gargan, I can take care of it. If I need backup, Charlotte and Marie will assist me."

"What about me?" I asked, feeling a pang of disappointment.

"You will stand this one out," Hamid answered decisively. "You are not strong enough yet to take on a Gargan."

I opened my mouth to tell him what I thought of his assessment of my abilities.

He spoke before I could. "You promised to follow my orders out here."

"Fine." I took in a frustrated breath and let it out. Why the hell had I made that promise?

He smiled and turned away, his voice filling my mind. *There will be other fights.*

I know. Be careful.

I watched him run to the pier and quickly make his way along it toward the water. My breath caught and held when he ducked between the pylons and out of sight.

For a long torturous minute, I could hear nothing above the waves and the sounds on the pier, even with my demon hearing. I wanted to ask him what was happening, but I couldn't risk distracting him.

Just when I didn't think I could stand it any longer, Charlotte and Marie started forward at the same time. They were gone before I could ask if Hamid was okay.

As soon as the two female warriors disappeared beneath the pier, the distant sounds of fighting reached my ears. I moved a dozen or so yards closer, trying to hear what was going on while staying at a safe distance.

I was so focused on trying to see what was happening beneath the pier that I didn't notice the dark shape emerge from the water until it started to scuttle across the sand toward me.

At first, I thought it was too small to be a Gargan because they were over ten feet long. But as it got closer, I could pick out the lobster-like shape and the large pincer claws that could snap a man in half. Based on its size, it had to be a young Gargan. I hoped it was a lot weaker than an adult because I was the only one between it and the hundreds of people on the pier.

Lifting my sword, I ran to intercept the demon. It lunged at me as soon as I was within a few feet of it, but I evaded its snapping pincers. It might be fast in the water, but on land, I had the advantage.

Staying out of its reach, I ran around the Gargan and struck out at the six legs on its left side. My blade sliced easily through the softer shell, and the demon staggered as two of its legs fell away. It made no sound as it steadied itself and came at me again.

One of the Gargan's long antennae whipped in my direction, and the stinging smell of ammonia reached my nose. I threw myself to the side as venom sprayed in my direction.

I hit the sand and rolled to my feet, my blood boiling. My sword whistled through the air and removed the remaining four legs on the Gargan's left side.

"Try shooting that shit at me again," I ground out as the demon fell over, wriggling on its side and exposing its soft underbelly.

Jordan, Hamid said through the bond. *There were three Gargans, but we got them. We'll be out shortly.*

Make that four, I replied as I severed the two antennae so they couldn't shoot more venom at me.

Four? he echoed.

I didn't respond. I was too busy gutting the demon at my feet.

I felt Hamid coming before the Gargan shuddered its last breath. Hamid stopped in front of me so suddenly that sand sprayed my legs. His lips pressed together in a thin line as he looked from me to the dead demon and back to me again.

I took in his appearance, noting the rip in his jeans and the black blood on his clothes. I'd fared much better in my fight.

"I ordered you to stay back," he said angrily.

I put my hands on my hips. "I did stay back. But what was I supposed to do when this thing came out of the water? You guys were a little busy."

He stared at the ocean and let out a ragged breath. "You're right. You did what any warrior would have done."

I watched his handsome profile. "And?"

Charlotte appeared beside him and looked down at the Gargan. "Good job, Jordan!"

"Why, thank you, Charlotte," I said in an exaggerated drawl.

I started to walk away, but Hamid's hand on my wrist stopped me. I looked over my shoulder and saw the pride in his eyes.

"You did well. Not many warriors can say they have killed a Gargan, even a young one."

My chest warmed because Hamid didn't bestow his praise lightly. As a warrior, his approval meant a lot to me.

I smiled. "Thanks. I seem to be having a lot of firsts lately."

Marie interrupted our little moment. "How are we going to dispose of four gargans with every warrior in the city engaged elsewhere? And then there is the matter of the three half-eaten human bodies under the pier."

Hamid released my hand, all business again. "We'll pull this one under the pier with the rest, and I'll ask Orias to glamour them until we can get rid of them."

"And the humans?" I asked.

"I'll let the proper authorities know where they are, and they can spin their own story for the media," he said, sounding like he'd done this before.

While Hamid dragged the dead demon to the others, Charlotte, Marie, and I scoured the beach on either side of the pier to make sure there wasn't another Gargan lurking nearby. We didn't find anything, but that didn't mean more wouldn't come. Who knew what would show up here tonight?

Orias had done an impressive job of spelling the onlookers. Not only did they forget what they'd witnessed, they all had the sudden urge to go home, which made our job easier.

After Orias hid the bodies under a powerful glamour, we piled into the SUV and let Mason know we'd handled the situation at the pier. He sounded harassed as he filled us in on the mounting violence all over the city.

"I can't keep up with the calls," he said, frustrated. "It's like the city is under siege."

"Do what you can," Hamid told him calmly. "What do you have for us?"

Mason listed off half a dozen incidents, and we took the closest, which was at Douglas Park. We were too late to save the middle-aged couple who had been out walking their dog, but we took care of the two vampires that had killed them. Once again, Orias used a glamour to hide the vampire bodies, while Hamid let the authorities know about the two human bodies in the park.

The body count continued to pile up as the night went on. Our team killed eleven vampires in the subway tunnels, plus another eight in other locations. We took out Incubi, Ranc demons, Gulaks, and two separate Lamprey infestations.

"It's like the demons are no longer afraid of humans learning of their existence," I said after Orias had spelled a family to forget the two Gulaks that had tried to take a teenage girl right from her home.

"We have observed that certain demons – the aggressive ones – will respond to the presence of a stronger demon," Maria said. "An archdemon would definitely trigger their aggressive tendencies."

I climbed into the SUV. "Why haven't we seen this in other cities where Alaron has been?"

"He could have shielded himself to avoid detection," Charlotte said as she sat beside me in the back. "I think he is deliberately riling up the demons here."

I thought she was right. The question was why? The obvious reason was to keep us all occupied and out of his way. He had to have something big planned, and that prospect scared me more than any demon we'd face out here.

Throughout the night, Mason kept us apprised of the other teams' statuses, and I tensed each time he mentioned a warrior getting hurt. A heavy silence fell over our group as we learned a member of Jon's team had been killed by vampires.

An hour later, we lost a warrior from the San Diego team. Mason didn't know the details, but that didn't make us feel the loss any less. After that news, Hamid wouldn't leave my side, and I was surprised he didn't order me back to the house. I was tired and filthy, but I wanted to be with him. I'd go insane not knowing where he was or what kind of danger he was facing.

Just after four in the morning, our team responded to a false alarm out near the San Bernardino National Forest. We were walking back to the road where our SUV was parked when Mason told us the calls were dropping off at last. I was irritated about coming all the way out here for nothing, but relieved we could finally be seeing an end to this crazy night.

"I can't wait to get a shower," I said wistfully when Hamid told us we were returning to the command center. "And then I plan to stay in bed until noon."

"You'll need your sleep because we'll be spending the next few days cleaning up from tonight," Charlotte said from behind us.

I groaned inwardly at the unpleasant job ahead of us. I had no problem doing the killing, but I hated the cleanup.

Then I had an even more horrifying realization. Every job we'd done tonight had to be written up in a detailed report. The thought of spending hours doing field reports made my steps falter.

Hamid immediately reached out to steady me. "You okay?"

"I'm great. And I'll be even better if you tell me I won't have to write up any of the reports for tonight."

Everyone but Orias laughed. He was too busy walking ahead of us, muttering to himself. No matter how much time I spent with warlocks, I still found their behavior weird at times.

Orias stopped abruptly and held up his hands, motioning for us to stop, too. Everyone went still. It was then that I noticed how quiet the woods were.

My skin prickled, and it took me a few seconds to register the sensation. Magic.

The warlock shouted something in Navajo. At first, nothing happened. Then the darkness around us began to dispel as a purplish shimmer filled the air. Farther away, I thought I saw indistinct shapes moving through the trees, but I couldn't focus on them.

Do you see that? I asked Hamid.

Yes. He moved closer to me, and I could feel tension radiating off him. *No matter what happens, don't leave my side unless I tell you to run.*

What are they?

Not human, was his less than comforting reply.

Orias threw up his hands and began chanting so fast the words sounded like gibberish. The purple light changed until it was bright green, and it grew brighter until I could make out the forms a little better. They were shaped like people, and they formed a wide circle around us.

My heart rate spiked, and my knuckles whitened around the hilt of my sword. *It's a trap.*

Hamid's voice was calm in my mind. *They're hidden behind a glamour.*

What is Orias doing?

I think he's trying to erect a shield around us.

My mind spun from the possibilities of what could be out there. After what we'd seen tonight, it could be anything.

The thrill of pending battle filled me, along with a healthy dose of fear as I remembered the two people we'd lost tonight. Their deaths were a stark reminder that none of us was invincible, not even the big warrior beside me.

The woods were eerily quiet, except for Orias's chanting. Charlotte and Marie were so still behind us that I wondered if they were even there anymore. I didn't dare turn my head to look for them, afraid to take my eyes from the faceless beings standing outside the ring of light.

Orias jerked as if he'd been shot, and the green light dimmed. I sucked in a breath when I saw a few of the shapes move toward us. This was it.

The warlock straightened and resumed chanting, and the light brightened again.

I let out my breath.

He motioned with one hand for us to follow him, and we began a slow trek to the road that couldn't have been more than thirty yards ahead of us. I could see the glint of moonlight on the SUV through the trees. If he could maintain his shield a little longer, we might actually survive this.

The thought had no sooner entered my mind when the glamour obscuring the beings surrounding us disappeared. The bottom fell out of my stomach when I saw what was out there.

Vampires. Dozens of them, maybe fifty. Unless they were new vampires, we didn't have a prayer of fighting them all.

And they knew it. Malicious smiles spread across their faces, baring their long fangs to us. A few bolder ones took steps in our direction and hissed in pain when they came up against Orias's shield. I'd never been so happy to have the warlock on our side.

Hamid's free hand slipped inside his coat.

Hamid, no, I said urgently. *You can't.*

He wasn't supposed to use the angel blade on anyone but Alaron. It was our only weapon against him, and we couldn't tip our hand. But I also knew he would do anything to protect me.

His hand stopped moving, and a wave of primal rage and fear surged across the bond. *I will not let you die.*

A light flared from somewhere behind the line of vampires. Orias gasped and fell to his knees. "It's him," he choked out as if he were struggling to breathe. "Too...strong."

In an instant, I was surrounded by vampires. I heard Hamid's voice in my head, calling my name as I struck out at them. I wounded several vampires before I was subdued and my sword was wrenched from my hand.

Jordan, Hamid shouted in my mind, his voice full of impotent rage.

I'm here. I struggled in my captor's hold, trying to see Hamid. *Where are you?*

I'm on the ground. There's some kind of spell binding me. I can't move.

I looked down and spotted his feet through the mass of legs. *I see you.*

The relief at knowing he was close by was pushed aside when magic wrapped around me. It encased me from head to toe until I feared it would smother me. I couldn't move, and I tried not to panic as my lungs became starved for oxygen.

I can't breathe.

I know, he said calmly, sounding weaker than he had a minute ago. *You're going to pass out soon, but your Mori will keep you alive.*

What about you?

I'll be here with you.

The male vampire holding me from behind pressed his nose against the side of my throat and inhaled deeply. "Mmmm, young Mohiri."

"She's not for you," growled a female vampire.

Their voices sounded far away as darkness filled my vision.

Hamid? I called frantically, but there was no answer.

I love you, I said before my world went dark.

19

A sharp pain in my side pulled me back to consciousness. Swallowing a moan, I forced my heavy eyelids open. I had to blink a few times for things to come into focus, and I wished I hadn't when I saw the vampire standing over me, his foot poised to kick me again.

"About time you woke up," he said sullenly, looking disappointed he didn't have to deliver another blow.

I didn't speak as I cleared the last of the cobwebs from my head and took stock of the situation. Twenty feet above me was a ceiling of uneven rock, which meant we were in a cave of some kind. The cold ache in my body told me I was lying on the floor of the cave, and when I moved my legs, the clink of a heavy chain alerted me I wasn't going anywhere. A shackle wrapped around my left foot, and a chain connected it to a thick bolt in the floor. My boots were gone, along with my coat.

I whipped my head to the left and then to the right, releasing a breath when I saw Hamid lying on his side, facing away from me. *Hamid?* I called to him.

He didn't respond. Rolling over, I got to my knees and crawled to him.

"Stay where you are," barked the vampire.

I ignored him and kept crawling. Because of the bond, I knew Hamid was alive, but that didn't mean he wasn't badly hurt.

Pain shot through my ankle and up my calf as the vampire yanked hard on the chain, making the shackle bite into my leg.

I fell onto my bruised side and snarled at him. "Touch me again and I'll rip your balls off and shove them down your fucking throat."

The vampire took a hasty step back as a deep, grating laugh echoed off the cave walls. The sound made my stomach lurch, and I didn't need to look to know who the laugh belonged to.

"She's got fire, that one," Alaron boomed in a voice laced with amusement. "It's too bad I won't have any use for her when I'm done here."

Swallowing my fear, I sat up and got my first real look at my surroundings. The cave was large – maybe forty feet in diameter – and it was lit by torches. Through the wide entrance, I could barely make out a dark rocky landscape, but I had no problem seeing the ocean of stars in the night sky.

My mind worked furiously to figure out where we were. Definitely not Los Angeles. I shivered, and my Mori immediately sent warmth through me. Based on the temperature and the fact that we were in a cave, my guess was somewhere in the desert.

I forced myself to look at the archdemon, who stood in the center of the cave, and I could only stare at his grotesque face. The flesh was rotting and split open across his forehead and cheekbones, and there was no skin at all on the bottom jaw, allowing me to see the bone and decomposing muscle. At the corner of his eye, something moved, and I nearly gagged when I saw it was maggots.

Alaron's mouth formed a twisted semblance of a smile. "Not my best look, I know. These human bodies are so frail." He waved a hand at the body hidden beneath his robe. "Millions of years of evolution, and this is all they could come up with."

I didn't respond, sensing my participation in the conversation was not required. All I wanted was for him to turn his attention elsewhere so I could go to Hamid.

A female vampire walked over to Alaron, carrying a wooden bucket. He took it from her, and the contents sloshed. My nostrils flared at the coppery smell of fresh human blood that made my stomach turn.

Alaron knelt and dipped his fingers in the blood. He began to draw a symbol on the floor as if I wasn't there.

I shot the vampire near me another look that promised a messy death, and then I crawled to my mate. *Hamid?* I called, getting no reply.

His eyes were closed, but his breathing was deep and even. I rolled him gently onto his back and checked him for injuries. Finding none, I sat and cradled his head on my lap as I tried to think of how we were going to get out of this alive.

I studied the heavy iron shackle around my ankle. My first thought was that Hamid could break our chains when he woke up, but then I felt something I'd been too preoccupied to notice until now. There was a faint uncomfortable tingle in my foot that could only mean one thing – magic. Alaron would not have gone through all the trouble of capturing us only to make it easy for us to escape.

I would never give up as long as there was a drop of hope, but I had to admit our situation looked bleak. I counted ten vampires in the cave with us, and I suspected there were more outside. Hamid and I were shackled with no weapons, and his coat was gone, too. That meant the angel blade – the one weapon that might have saved us – was lost to us. And we had no warlocks to help us this time. I saw no sign of Orias, Charlotte, or Marie, and I didn't want to think of what had most likely happened to them.

My gaze went back to Alaron, who was painstakingly creating more symbols in what was clearly an inner summoning circle. I didn't know how long it took to set up a summoning site, but my gut told me I didn't want to be here when this one was complete. I had a sinking feeling that Hamid and I were not brought here to be spectators.

Jordan?

I'm here. I looked down at Hamid, and his eyelids flickered and slowly blinked open. He looked up at me, and his blue eyes were the most beautiful sight I'd ever beheld. He opened his mouth to speak, but I placed a finger over it to stop him. *We're not alone.*

His eyes stared past me at the cave ceiling. *Where are we?*

I don't know. Somewhere in the Mojave, I think.

The others?

I pressed my lips together. *I haven't seen them.*

A wave of reassurance came through the bond. *Okay. Let's just focus on the immediate situation. Tell me what you know.*

I told him about Alaron, the vampires, and the magic infusing our shackles. It was a relief to be able to share it all with him. He'd been in a lot of tight situations before, and if anyone could figure out how to get us out of here, it was him.

I can't do this lying down. He sat up and leaned against the cave wall beside me, taking one of my hands in his.

Alaron looked up from his drawing. "Ah, you're awake. I've been waiting for you to join us."

"Maybe you should not have knocked us out," Hamid replied without an ounce of fear. "Why have you brought us here?"

"Right to the point. I like that." The demon studied his work before looking at the vampires, who watched him silently. "Leave us."

He waited until the last one had left to speak again. "Vamhir are useful soldiers, but they've gotten too far above their station since they came here. I'll set that to rights as soon as I'm restored to my body."

"*If* you are restored," I wanted to say, but I didn't think it would be smart to anger an archdemon in close quarters.

Dipping his fingers in the bucket of blood, he resumed his drawing. "You two have proven to be a... What do you call it? A pain in the ass. Always showing up and interrupting my work. I've spent hours entertaining myself with what I'd do to you when I caught you."

I tried to block out the thoughts of what horrors an archdemon could inflict on a body. My body would give out, but Hamid was strong. He would endure days or weeks of torture before Alaron finally tired of him.

"I can't tell you how annoyed I was when you found that farm and ruined a perfectly good lair," Alaron said without looking up from his work. "And then you didn't die from my spell, which should have turned you into ash. That sent me into a bit of a rage. At first, I blamed the warlocks. I thought they were shielding you from me. It wasn't until our last meeting that I started to put it all together."

He stood, wiping his bloody fingers on his robe. His black eyes regarded us, but it was hard to make out his expression with his face rotting off.

"You were there at the school when I opened the barrier. I would have finished what I set out to do if you and the warlock hadn't interfered. He was more powerful than I expected, but my magic would have soon overwhelmed his. Or so I thought."

Fury blazed in his eyes. "I was so close that night. I finally had the spell right, and I could feel my body on the other side, waiting to come to me. And then something happened to tip the balance of power away from me, and it was as if the spell was no longer mine."

He started to pace, his steps growing more agitated with each pass. "After that, none of my spells to open the barrier worked. I could manage a small hole, but nothing the size of what I need. As time passed, it got more difficult to breach the barrier. I couldn't understand why my spells were failing. Nothing I tried worked.

"And then you showed up at the wrakk, and once again, my spells had no effect on you. What was more, you appeared to know you were shielded from my magic. It wasn't until later that day that it all made sense to me."

I clenched Hamid's hand tighter, and his thumb stroked my palm soothingly.

"I don't know why I didn't see it sooner. The only way my spells wouldn't work against you was if you were already protected by my magic. But there is no way I would have cast a protective spell on you."

Alaron stopped pacing to look at us with a triumphant gleam in his eyes. "It took me a while to make the connection to the first time I saw you at the school. You two fell between the warlock and me, and you got hit by our spells. Somehow, you caused the spell to change, and it created a protection around you. I don't know how you did it, but that's not important. All that matters is I know what I need to do to open the barrier."

I couldn't stop myself, I had to ask. "What?"

The archdemon attempted a smile, and his left ear fell off. He didn't seem to notice it as he answered me. "I designed a new spell to undo the one I created in the school and to open the barrier. And you will bear witness to the greatest moment in the history of this world."

"You mean the destruction of this world," Hamid said coldly. "Once the barrier comes down, there will be nothing left of this place."

Alaron shook his head. "I am not going to destroy the barrier. This world is teeming with life, and I don't plan to share it with anyone. Once I have my body, I will rule this realm and the humans will be my slaves – and my food."

I swallowed back the bile rising in my throat. "The angels came the last time demons threatened this world. What makes you think they won't come after you?"

"Angels," Alaron spat as if the word left a bad taste in his mouth. "Have you seen what the humans do to each other and to this place? Why would the angels want to save the likes of them? They'll probably thank me for taking care of the problem for them."

My heart felt like it was made of lead when I thought of the lost angel blade. The odds of us being able to get close enough to Alaron's body with the knife had been slim, but at least there'd been a chance. It had given us hope that we could defeat him.

"So, you brought us here just to be witnesses?" I asked bitterly. "Excuse me if I don't cheer."

The demon laughed, and the sound made my skin crawl. "Not exactly. The new spell won't work without part of the original spell, which is where you come in." He pointed at Hamid. "Actually, where he comes in."

My heart began to thud painfully. "What do you mean?"

"The spell requires living blood. You are too weak to survive long enough for the spell to finish, so I will use him instead."

"No," I shouted. I tried to stand, but Hamid's arm came around my waist, holding me back.

Stop, he ordered gently. *You can do nothing now but anger him.*

"Don't be distressed," Alaron said with mock kindness. "You will have your part in all of this." His black tongue came out to lick his teeth. "My body will be hungry after the joining, and you'll make a good meal."

Hamid let me go and lunged forward with a vicious snarl. The chain stopped him before he could close a quarter of the distance between him and Alaron. He strained against his shackle like a wild animal caught in a trap, which only served to amuse the demon more.

"You Mohiri males are a protective bunch. I shouldn't be surprised, though. Mori are ridiculously possessive of their mates. Looks like that hasn't changed here."

Hamid growled something unintelligible in a voice that didn't sound like his. I went to him and stood behind him with my arms around his waist. "I need my warrior back. I can't do this without you."

A shudder went through him. He spun and hugged me so tightly I felt my bones creak. I rubbed his back and whispered soothing words to him until he calmed enough to loosen his hold.

"How touching," Alaron mocked. "Now if you'll excuse me, I have a ceremony to prepare for."

Hamid led me back to our spot at the wall. He sat and pulled me down to sit on his lap, encircling me with his strong arms. His movements were calmer, but his eyes still had some of the crazed look. At least, when he spoke to me in my mind, it was his own voice.

I have to get you out of here, he said desperately.

I stroked his hard jaw. *Even if I could escape, I'm not leaving without you.*

He gritted his teeth. *Don't fight me on this. I can face my death if I know you will live.*

Fury rose in me, and I slapped his face. *Don't you ever talk like that again. We either leave here together, or we die together. Where you go, I go.*

And where you go, I go. He watched me with tortured eyes, and I leaned in to kiss the red spot I'd made on his cheek.

"I love you," I whispered, needing to say the words aloud because I didn't know how many more times I would get to say them.

He brushed a kiss across my lips. "And I love you."

We sat like that for a long moment until Hamid lifted his head to sweep his gaze around the cave.

What are you looking for? I asked.

Anything we can use to escape. There's still time. He stared at something at the back of the cave where there were no torches, and I could sense his sudden excitement.

What do you see?

He narrowed his gaze. *Our weapons and coats and...Orias. He's bound and gagged, but I think he's alive.*

I didn't know what to be more excited about, the presence of Orias or our coats. If Hamid's coat was here, there was a chance the angel blade was still tucked away in the inside pocket. The knife was small, and it might have been overlooked when they were disarming us.

Do you see Charlotte and Marie? I asked hopefully.

Only Orias. I don't see his satchel, and I don't think he will be much help without his demon.

I sagged, deflated. Warlocks had natural magic, but their real power came from the demons they summoned. Without his demon, Orias was as powerful as a hedge witch.

We were on our own, which meant nothing had changed. But if we could somehow get to the coats and find the knife, it could tip the odds in our favor.

"You two are awfully quiet all of a sudden," Alaron said, his black gaze fixed on us. "You wouldn't be plotting something, would you?"

Play along. Hamid's hand squeezed my arm. "My mate is afraid, and I am comforting her."

"Afraid? That one?" Alaron abandoned his work to walk over to us. "Are you frightened, female?"

His amused tone made me want to tell him to go to hell, and I glared at him before I could stop myself.

He laughed. "That's what I thought. I can't have you trying anything foolish and disrupting my work." Raising the hand that wasn't covered in blood, he started speaking in demon tongue.

I wasn't prepared when the same paralyzing spell hit me, choking the air from my lungs again. Panic rose in me, but it wasn't out of fear of dying. If we were knocked out, there'd be no way for us to get to the angel blade before Alaron carried out his plan. I'd be forced to sit here and watch Hamid die.

Hamid, I called. I was in his arms, but I could no longer feel his touch.

I'm with you, he said as the blackness came once more.

***

I awoke to the feel of the cold stone floor under me instead of Hamid's warm body. I bolted upright and frantically looked for him. I was in the same spot as before, but Hamid was gone.

Hamid! I called to him over and over until his weak voice spoke in my mind.

I'm still here.

I scrambled to my feet. *Where are you?*

I found him before he could answer me. My hand flew up to cover my mouth when I saw him chained on his back a dozen feet from me. His clothes were gone, and there were shackles on his arms and feet, as well as a band of metal over his torso to hold him down. His left arm was resting above a groove that had been cut into the rock, and there was a shallow furrow in the floor that ran from the groove to the center of the now complete summoning circle.

"Oh, God." I ran toward him, but my chain wouldn't let me go far.

"God has left the building," Alaron taunted as he approached Hamid, carrying a knife. He stopped to smile at me. "You joined us just in time for the main event."

"Leave him alone," I shouted at the demon. "Use me instead. I'm strong enough."

"No," Hamid bit out.

Alaron knelt beside Hamid and unceremoniously slashed the inside of his left elbow. Blood poured from the cut and into the groove. Within seconds, a stream of blood began to flow along the furrow toward the circle.

"No!" My scream echoed off the cave walls. I strained futilely against my shackle as Alaron stood and walked to the inner circle. The cave was empty, except for the three of us. He must have sent all his vampires outside while he did the spell.

Facing away from us, he raised his hands and began to speak in demon tongue. One by one the torches along the walls went out until the cave was plunged into darkness.

Hamid, I called, feeling real bloodcurdling terror for the first time in my life. Not even when I'd nearly been beaten to death by Gulaks did I feel this level of fear. My mate, the other half of my soul, was alone in the dark, bleeding to death, and I could do nothing to help him. I couldn't even hold him and let him know he wasn't alone.

Shhh, he said gently as the crystals around the summoning circles began to emit a soft glow. The light grew stronger until I could see Hamid's face. He had his head turned toward me, and his eyes were fixed on mine. His face looked paler, and I didn't know if it was because of the light or from blood loss.

He smiled regretfully. *I'm sorry. If I had listened to the Council and taken you to a secure location, you would not be here now.*

I wouldn't have stayed there, and you know it, I argued. *None of this is your fault.*

Alaron's deep voice rose, and his tempo increased. The air in the cave felt charged with static electricity, making the hair on my head lift. The crystals glowed ever brighter until it hurt my eyes to look at them.

The demon bent and dipped his hands in a pool of blood at his feet. My stomach lurched at the sight of his hands dripping with Hamid's blood.

He straightened and lifted his bloody hands in the air. A pit opened in my stomach because I knew what came next.

I couldn't let this happen. If I didn't do everything I could to stop this horror from being unleashed on the world, I'd carry that stain on my soul for the rest of this life and into the next.

Turning, I scanned the floor of the cave near me, looking for anything I could use to try to break the shackle. Maybe if Alaron used all his magic to open the barrier, it would weaken the magic on my shackle. It was a slim possibility, but I had to try.

What are you doing? Hamid asked when I sat and picked up a fist-sized rock. His voice was fainter now, and it terrified me.

Trying to get out of this thing. I gritted my teeth and brought the rock down on the shackle. It barely scratched the metal.

Alaron didn't even glance in my direction as I struck the shackle with the rock over and over until I was panting from the effort.

I hung my head. *It's no use.*

Don't give up. Look for a bigger rock.

The last thing I would do was let him see me give in to my despair. I could be strong for the both of us.

Crawling, I felt along the floor and wall, but the pickings were slim. I made my way over to where Hamid had been chained earlier and found a larger rock near the wall. Holding it in both hands, I smashed it against the shackle again and again, but all I managed to do was bruise my ankle.

Above me, a purplish glow filled the cave, and a pulse of magic hit me, knocking me backward and sending needles of pain through me. Gasping for air, I could only lie there for a minute before I forced myself to sit up and grab the rock again. I would not give up. I'd tear off my own foot to get to Hamid.

Raising my hands above my head, I brought the rock down on the metal with all my might. There was a grinding sound, and I stared in shock at the shackle lying open on the floor.

Precious seconds passed before my brain registered that I was free. I looked at Alaron, but he was too busy shouting and gesturing at the far wall of the cave to pay attention to me. He must have focused so much of his magic into his spell to open the barrier that it had weakened the magic on the shackle.

Jordan, Hamid called as a crackling sound reached my ears. I lifted my head to see a tear forming in the air on the far side of the cave. Ice formed in my gut. It was starting.

I'm coming. I picked up the rock and crawled over to where he lay.

I had to swallow back a cry when I saw him. His skin was ashen and covered in a sheen of sweat, and his eyes were dull. Even his lips had lost all their color.

You're free? Surprise and joy filled his voice in my mind.

I wiped the moisture from his brow and kissed him tenderly. *It will take more than an archdemon to keep me from you.*

I ripped the bottom from my shirt and wrapped it tightly around his bleeding arm. He'd already lost a lot of blood, but his Mori could regenerate it as long as he didn't lose more.

I need to get you out of these shackles. I moved to one of his feet and struck the metal hard with the rock. I expected the shackle to fall open like mine had, but nothing happened. I hit it three more times, the knot of fear in my stomach growing bigger with each unsuccessful blow.

It's not working. I crawled back to his head. *I need to find something else to get them open.*

No. His eyes pleaded with me. *You can get out of here while he's distracted.*

Forget it. Anger blazed through me. How could he think I would abandon him to save my own life?

I sat up and scanned the cave for something to use on the shackles. My gaze landed on the shadows at the back of the cave, and I sharpened my sight until I could make out the pile of coats. What if the angel blade was still in Hamid's coat? Did I have a prayer of using it against the demon? Maybe if I could wake Orias, he'd be able to hold Alaron off long enough for me to go after Alaron's body.

Excitement and hope blossomed in my chest, and I stole another glance at Alaron to make sure his back was still to me. Standing, I moved swiftly along the cave wall, my stockinged feet making no sound against the stone floor.

The first thing I did when I reached the back of the cave was check on Orias. He was alive but unconscious, and no amount of shaking would wake him up. I finally had to accept that he couldn't help us. We were on our own this time.

I pulled Hamid's jacket to me and stuck my hand into the inside pocket. My whole body trembled when my fingers closed around a wooden hilt. I couldn't breathe as I cradled the knife in my hands as if it was the most precious object in the world.

A distant roaring reached me. I stared at the tear in the barrier, which was now half a foot wide.

Gathering up the knife, my sword, and my combat boots, I cast a regretful look at Orias and hurried back to Hamid. I hated to leave anyone behind, but I couldn't save them both. I'd feel guilty about it later – if Hamid and I somehow got out of this alive.

Hamid's head was turned toward me, watching me approach. *Orias?* He asked when I knelt and quietly laid the weapons and boots beside him.

Alive but I couldn't wake him up. I turned my back to Alaron and held up the knife for Hamid to see. *But I have this.*

Hope filled his eyes, and he closed them for a moment. Then he fixed me with a determined stare. *Take the knife and use it to escape.*

Blood loss must be addling your brain because you know I'm not walking out of here without you. Excitement built in me as an idea began to form. *Lie very still. I'm going to try something.*

I glanced over my shoulder at Alaron whose attention was riveted on the tear in the barrier.

Keeping my back to him, I grasped the sheath and uncovered an inch of the blade. I didn't dare unsheathe it completely for fear the demon would sense its presence.

Ever so slowly, I brought the knife down until it was inches from the shackle on Hamid's left wrist. Hamid grunted, and my hand stilled.

Are you okay? I asked him.

Yes. Do it.

I inhaled deeply. Moment of truth.

I lowered the blade to the shackle. Before it had even touched the metal, sparks flew. Hamid's body jerked and convulsed, and his eyes rolled back in his head. I laid the knife down and leaned over him. My heart nearly stopped when I saw he wasn't breathing.

Hamid! I covered his mouth with mine and forced air into his lungs. On the fourth breath, he inhaled, and I nearly collapsed on top of him.

The roaring in the barrier grew louder. I lifted my head to see the hole was over two feet high and expanding quickly.

Hamid wheezed. "You have to leave."

I looked down at the open shackle. "No. I can do this."

"You can't free me without killing me." He coughed weakly and looked at me with pleading eyes. "Please."

I shook my head fervently. My heart felt like it had been ripped in two, and I gasped from the physical pain in my chest at the thought of losing him.

"Yes!" Alaron shouted triumphantly.

I stared at the hole to see it was almost as tall as me now.

"Look at me," Hamid ordered. I did, and he reached up with the hand I'd freed to cup my cheek. "We are almost out of time. You have to leave me."

"No. I won't." My chest tightened painfully. I just needed to think about it, and something would come to me. I had always excelled at escaping traps in training. This was no different.

Hamid turned my head to make me look at him. "I love you, my fierce mate, and I will carry your love with me from this world. Someday, we'll see each other again, and we will have eternity together."

"Don't talk like that." I pounded his chest as hot tears scalded my cheeks and dripped onto his skin.

He smiled tenderly as he wiped away my tears with his thumb. "I thought you never cry."

I sniffled. "If you tell anyone, I'll deny it."

His hand slipped behind my head and pulled me down for an achingly sweet kiss that was over too soon.

"It's time for you to go," he said hoarsely. "The world will need warriors like you in the days ahead."

There was a loud sucking sound and a pop, followed by the howl of wind. I looked up and forgot to breathe when I saw the window had grown into a doorway that was six feet wide and at least fifteen feet tall. Beyond it, shapes moved in the ghostly netherworld light, but none of them tried to come through the hole like they had the first time.

A huge shape caught my eye, and when I got my first look at Alaron's body, I knew immediately why the other demons were staying back.

Covered in red scales with legs the size of tree trunks, the archdemon was as tall as the doorway and just as broad. Large horns curled on either side of its head, and a pair of massive wings were half unfurled from its back. I couldn't make out the facial features, but I saw enough to know I couldn't let that abomination enter our world.

I shoved my feet into my boots and laced them up in a frenzy. I gazed at the face of the man I'd come to love more than my own life. Leaning down, I kissed him hard, pouring every ounce of my love into it. Then I got to my feet, clutching the sheathed knife in one hand and my sword in the other.

"What are you doing?"

I gave him a watery smile. "Saving the world, of course."

I drank in his handsome face one last time, memorizing every feature. And then I turned and sprinted for the hole in the barrier.

Alaron didn't spot me until I was halfway across the cave. "Stop," he bellowed as if I would obey. When he didn't come after me, I realized he couldn't. He had to stay where he was, doing his spell to keep the barrier open.

I stopped in front of the hole and felt the coldness pulling at me. From here, it was like looking through a shimmering waterfall. Only there was nothing pretty waiting for me on the other side.

I tossed a grin over my shoulder at Alaron, who was staring at me with a mix of shock and rage. "I'll see you in hell, demon."

And then I dove through the barrier.

20

Hell was – for lack of a better word – a shithole. I landed on some kind of coarse black sand, and all around me jagged black rocks protruded from the ground, making me glad I'd taken the time to don my boots. There were no trees or vegetation, just rocks and sand as far as I could see, and the sky was blood red. It was also freezing here. I thought hell was supposed to be an inferno, but this place was colder than Idaho in February.

And oh God, the smell. If you mixed sulfur, roadkill, and sewage together, it still wouldn't be as bad as the putrid stench in this place. It was no wonder demons wanted to leave here.

Speaking of demons, about half a dozen of them waited for me, including a Drex, a Kraas demon, something that looked like a giant gray squid, and others I couldn't identify. A few distant shapes swirled in the sky, and from here, they resembled pterodactyls. Whatever they were, I hoped they stayed away. I had more than enough to deal with here.

And then there was the archdemon that looked twice as big up close. His face was as monstrous as the rest of him, with a wide bony brow lined with spikes, glowing red eyes, and a snout like a boar. The other demons were giving him a wide berth, even though he was just standing there. Was the archdemon's body even cognizant of its surroundings while its essence was possessing another body?

Someone shouted, but it sounded garbled and distant. I turned to see Alaron through the hazy window into my world. He was holding out his arms and making frantic summoning motions with his hands, but his body seemed to be in no hurry to comply.

A noise behind me drew my attention back to the demons to see every one of them, except the archdemon, focused hungrily on me. A few of the braver ones rushed at me, the lure of fresh meat clearly overcoming their fear of the archdemon.

I brought my sword up and assumed a fighting stance with the sheathed knife in my other hand. Once I bared the angel blade, everyone would know it, and I wasn't ready to tip my hand yet.

The squid demon was one of the first to reach me, and one of its barbed tentacles went straight for my throat. My blade sliced through the tentacle, and the demon hissed loudly when the clawed tip fell to the ground.

The demon withdrew its injured limb as it lashed out at my legs with another tentacle. I jumped back and tripped over a protruding rock. I managed to keep my grip on my weapons as I fell backward and rolled to my feet.

I came up swinging, my blade taking two more tentacles from the demon that had rushed in for the attack. It hissed again and pulled back behind the other demons waiting for their chance.

A Drex demon came next, bellowing at me as it charged, shoving aside or trampling other demons in its path. I didn't wait for it to reach me, running out to meet it halfway.

My aggression must have baffled the Drex demon because it stopped mid-stride to stare at me. Taking advantage of its confusion, I struck fast and hard, driving my sword deep into its stomach where its heart was located.

I pulled my sword free and retreated as the demon let out an agonized sound and toppled over. Its body was still twitching when the remaining demons descended upon it, ripping into it with teeth and claws.

Now that they were busy with their meal, I turned my attention to the real reason I was here. Alaron's mindless body was slowly lumbering toward the hole, its dragon-like tail dragging behind it.

I took a deep breath and switched the knife to my sword hand before I slid the blade free of its sheath. "I hope you're as good as they say."

The knife thrummed in my hand as if it knew it was in the presence of evil. I could feel its divine power in every fiber of my being as the blade cast a white glow around me. My Mori whined piteously and shrank away from it. The other demons must have felt it, too, because they stopped their frenzied eating and watched me warily.

I looked from them to the massive demon and mentally prepared myself for the fight of my life. I couldn't think of Hamid or what could be happening in the cave right now. My only priority was to stop the archdemon from crossing the barrier.

"God, please let me be worthy of this weapon," I said before I took off after the demon.

Running toward the thing, I scanned it for a soft spot between the scales where I could stab it. Its armpit looked promising, but I had no way to reach it.

Catching up to it, I took a swing and tried to pierce the scales on the back of its knee. The blade glanced off the diamond-hard scales without leaving a mark.

I grunted as the demon's tail slammed hard into my midsection and sent me flying. I slammed into the side of a large rock and slid down to the ground. Blood trickled down the side of my face from a cut on my head, and I had some new bruises, but I'd seen worse. At least, I hadn't lost my grip on my weapons. And my question about whether or not the demon was cognizant had been answered.

Pushing up off the ground, I looked at the rock and shuddered. I'd hit the flat side of it. If I had landed on top of it, I would have been impaled and it would be game over.

I turned back to the archdemon. Before I could take a step, something landed on my back, knocking me to the ground.

I rolled, trying to shake the thing loose, but claws dug into my back and arms, holding it in place. I couldn't use the angel blade on it while it was attached to me or I'd die, too.

I managed to get to my knees and push myself up to my feet. Then I rammed my back against the same rock I'd hit.

Teeth bit down on my shoulder and I screamed at the pain, but I didn't stop. Two more times I bashed the demon into the rock until I was able to dislodge it.

As soon as I pulled free of its claws, I heaved it over my shoulder. It was a Kraas demon, and it was stunned but not dead. I ran to it and touched the angel blade to one of its flailing legs.

The demon let out a horrible shriek as its skin turned gray and glowing cracks formed in the surface. It thrashed wildly and tried to scuttle away, but it didn't get far before it exploded into a million pieces.

I brandished the knife at the other demons that had crept closer to me during the fight. The knife cast a white glow around me, and the demons cringed away from it as if it burned them. I took a step toward them. "Who else wants some of this?"

They all turned tail and ran.

I bent to retrieve my sword, which I'd lost when the Kraas demon had tackled me, and I winced when pain shot down my arm from my injured shoulder. Dropping the sword, I tightened my grip on the angel blade because it was the only weapon that would work against the archdemon anyway. At least, the Kraas demon hadn't bitten my sword arm, or I'd be in even worse trouble now.

I ran at the archdemon again. The tail slashed at me, but this time I expected it and I leaped out of its path. Every time I tried to get near the demon, the tail kept swatting me away. And with each step the demon took, it got closer to the hole.

My stomach hardened with desperation when I saw we were less than twenty feet from the barrier. On the other side, I could see Alaron beckoning his body, his voice raised in excitement.

I raced ahead of the demon to an outcropping of rocks and climbed them. The sharp edges cut into my hands, but I kept going. I made it to the top just as he came abreast of the rocks, and I flung myself onto his back.

His tail swiped at me, and it would have dislodged me if I hadn't grabbed one of his thick horns. Clinging to him with one hand, I raised the other and stabbed at his shoulders and neck over and over to no avail.

Is there no goddamn way to kill this thing? What if Eldeorin was wrong and the blade couldn't hurt an archdemon?

The demon stopped walking. One of its hands came up and grabbed my calf, and agonizing pain shot through my leg when claws pierced my flesh to the bone. He wrenched me from his back and dangled me upside down before him.

I slashed at him with the knife, but he held me out of reach. Being close to the angel blade didn't even faze him. Things were not looking good for me.

And they were about to get a lot worse.

The demon lifted me higher and flung me away from him. I sailed through the air, and fear squeezed the oxygen from my lungs when I saw the glassy spikes I was headed for.

A loud screech came from above. I barely registered the sound of flapping wings before claws wrapped around my waist. I was yanked upward, seconds away from hitting the deadly rocks.

The ground fell away as the flying demon rose into the air. I didn't need to look to know it was one of those huge pterodactyl things I'd seen when I got here. I also knew I was dead if I didn't get away from it in the next few seconds.

I looked below me and saw a stretch of sand. Gritting my teeth, I braced myself. Chances were this was going to kill me. But at least I'd die on my own terms.

I touched the blade to one of the claws digging into my stomach. My body went rigid as a current of electricity shot through me. Stars exploded before my eyes as my numb fingers lost their grip on the knife and it fell to the ground.

A second later, I was falling, too. By some miracle, I landed on my feet, but as soon as I touched the ground, my legs gave out and I crumpled to the sand. I lay on my back, struggling for the breath that had been knocked out of me as ash floated down around me.

Distant shouting forced me to my feet. I looked for the archdemon and saw I was at least a hundred yards away from him. The hole in the barrier looked smaller from here, but I could hear Alaron calling to his body.

I scoured the ground for the knife and found it buried to the hilt in the black sand. As soon as I pulled it free, the glow surrounded me, filling me with renewed strength.

Limping on my injured leg, I ran to the demon that was slowly moving toward the hole again. He was nearing the last group of rocks, and after that, there was nothing but sand and no way for me to jump on him.

I put on an extra burst of speed, ignoring the burning pain in my leg. This was my last chance. If I didn't stop him now, he'd reach the hole.

Sprinting past the demon, I scaled the rocks just in time to jump on him as he passed. I grabbed onto one of his curled horns and used my momentum to swing me around to his front. Dangling from his horn, I found myself face-to-face with him and choking on his rancid breath.

Red eyes burned into mine. I didn't know if there was any intelligence in the body, but for a fleeting moment, I thought I saw some recognition there. I also saw the weakness I'd been searching for.

Tightening my grip on his horn, I raised the hand holding the knife.

"No!" screamed Alaron from the other side of the barrier.

I looked over my shoulder and saw him running toward the hole he'd created.

"Fuck you," I shouted at him as I turned back and thrust the angel blade deep into one of the glowing eyes.

A blast of white light from the knife blinded me as a jolt of power hit me square in the chest and sent me flying backward. I landed hard on my back, unable to breathe as convulsions seized my body.

An explosion rent the air, and the ground shook. I opened my eyes in time to see bits of archdemon raining down around me, and I covered my face with my arms to protect it.

Rolling to my stomach, I forced myself to my hands and knees. When I'd come through the barrier, I'd known it was probably a one-way trip, but now that the end was near, I wasn't ready to die.

I was surrounded by a sea of demon parts that smelled worse than this place. I gagged and started to stand when I saw a wooden handle amidst the gore a foot away. I grabbed it and staggered to my feet, fighting off the waves of dizziness that assailed me.

"Jordan!" Hamid bellowed from far away.

I spun and found the doorway was half its original size and getting smaller by the second.

My steps were uneven as I ran for the barrier with every ounce of strength left in me. It was Hamid's voice calling to me that gave me the final burst of energy I needed. I reached the doorway and dove straight through it a second before it closed with a loud popping sound.

I tried to hit the cave floor in a roll, but I was all out of slick moves and I did a crazy tumbling thing instead. The knife fell from my hand and skidded across the stone floor, and for once, I didn't have the energy to care.

"Jordan," said a deep voice I never thought I'd hear again. Warm hands touched my face, and I looked up into worried blue eyes.

"I know you." I smiled, or at least, I think I did. My body wasn't exactly cooperating at the moment.

Hamid brushed aside the hair that was sticking to my face. I must be quite the sight covered in demon guts.

"Let me guess; I look like crap," I joked as his face began to blur.

"You're beautiful."

My eyes were too heavy, so I let them close. "Liar."

He tapped my cheek. "Jordan, stay with me."

"Just going to take a quick nap," I murmured. "It's been a hell of a day."

Voices and light filled the cave when I next awoke. I was sitting on Hamid's lap with my head resting against his chest inside the cocoon of his arms. "Mmmm," I said as I breathed in his comforting scent. I'd never been much of a cuddler, but I could get used to this.

He lowered his head. "Are you awake?"

"Yes," I said through a yawn. "Sorry I fell asleep. Was I out long?"

The muscles in his arms flexed. "Five hours."

"Five hours?" I tried to sit up straighter but fell back with a groan. My body felt like it had been run over by a large truck.

"Easy. You're still healing from your injuries."

I frowned as I tried to clear the cobwebs from my head. "How did you get free?"

"When you killed Alaron, the magic on the shackles died with him."

"Oh." I looked down at myself and was surprised to discover I was wearing different clothes. I put a hand to my hair, which felt grungy but not full of demon gore. My eyes met Hamid's again. "Who cleaned me up?"

He raised his eyebrows as if I'd asked a ridiculous question. "I did. The healers brought the clothes and cleaning supplies."

"Healers? Who else is here?" I craned my neck and found people everywhere I looked, but no one I knew.

"Tristan and two of the other Council members, a few dozen warriors, and Ciro and Bastien."

"Council members?" I wasn't surprised Tristan was here, but I'd never heard of the other Council members going out into the field.

He smiled. "I don't think you realize the magnitude of what happened here last night, of what you did. There are lot of people who want to talk to you."

I laid my head against his chest again, suddenly weary. "How did they find us?"

"Tristan said they suspected Alaron had us when we didn't check in, but they couldn't pick up anything from our trackers. Alaron's spell on us and on the cave blocked our signals, but when he died, our signals were visible again."

"Did they find Charlotte and Marie?" I asked, not wanting to hear the answer.

"Yes. They didn't make it."

My chest ached at the loss of the two women. I had gotten to know them in the last month, and I'd like to say we had been friends. We were different in our pursuits, but I'd respected their quest for knowledge and their complete dedication to their work. And though they'd been more at home in a library than in the field, I had seen their fighting prowess last night.

I lifted my head again. "What about Orias?"

"He's a little banged up but okay. He's upset because Alaron sent his demon home, and now he'll have to summon a new one."

I frowned. "That should be easy for him."

Hamid chuckled. "Apparently, he was very attached to the one he had."

Footsteps approached us, and I looked up to see Tristan with a Latina female and a blonde male. The authoritative way the newcomers carried themselves said they had to be Council members.

Tristan's concerned gaze met mine. "Jordan, how are you feeling?"

"Better than the other guy."

His face relaxed into a smile. "Hamid told us what you did. I've always known you would do great things, so I can't say I'm surprised you would take on an archdemon. But crossing the barrier, knowing there was a good chance you wouldn't come back, took incredible courage and selflessness. I can't tell you how proud I am of you."

My eyes misted, and I blamed it on my weakened state. No way had I survived a trip to hell and back just to tear up over every little thing.

The blond warrior stepped forward. "Jordan, my name is Friedrich Voigt," he said in a German accent. "The Council is deeply grateful for what you did here. On a personal note, I am in awe that one so young as you not only went up against an archdemon but defeated him."

Before I could respond, the woman spoke. "I am Camila Pérez, and I am honored to meet such a brave, young warrior. Tristan speaks very highly of you, and I now see the reason for his praise."

My gaze darted to Tristan, who smiled encouragingly. I'd never sought the Council's approval, but his faith in me meant more than he'd ever know.

"Thank you," I said to all of them. "I'd like to be able to say I did it all on my own, but without the angel blade, last night would have ended a lot differently."

Hamid shook his head. "Don't try to diminish what you did. The blade did not wield itself."

"He's right," Tristan said. "It's the warrior, not the weapon, who wins the battle."

"Where is the knife now?" I asked, feeling a little overwhelmed by all the praise. I liked being the center of attention as much as the next person, but this was a bit much. I'd done what I had to do to save the people I loved.

Tristan pointed to some spot off to our left. "It's over there. We decided it should go back to the Fae for safekeeping. Sara is contacting Eldeorin to ask him to come retrieve it."

The two other Council members nodded, but the unhappy set of Friedrich's mouth told me not everyone agreed with that decision. I was with Tristan on this one. The angel blade was a weapon of immense power, but it belonged with the Fae.

"Jordan, can you tell us your side of what happened?" Camila asked. "Hamid told us some of it, but he had a limited view of the fight."

Hamid rubbed my back. "Can't this wait until she is fully recovered?"

"It's okay. I don't mind." I took his hand and threaded my fingers through his. Then I related the events that had taken place, from the moment I'd crossed the barrier to when I'd returned.

Friedrich and Camila peppered me with questions about the other dimension and the demons I'd seen there. Even Tristan asked a few questions. They were all particularly interested in the archdemon and how I'd killed him. It wasn't hard to remember every detail of the experience. I doubted I'd ever forget a second of my time in hell.

"Incredible," Friedrich said after I'd described my fight with Alaron's body for the second time. "Our scholars will want to talk to you at length as soon as you're up to it. You are the only person to ever enter the demon dimension, and everything you saw and experienced must be recorded."

Camila smiled. "And the tissue samples you brought back on your clothes will be invaluable to our scientists and scholars. They are already clamoring for the chance to study actual archdemon DNA. There is so much we can learn from it."

I thought about Charlotte and Marie and how much they would have loved this. Sadness pricked at me again. The whole team had worked so hard on this job, and it wasn't right that they weren't here to celebrate our victory.

"The Council is always looking for people to join our investigative teams," Camila told me. "Normally, we wouldn't try to recruit a young warrior, but you have proven to be more than up to the job. I hope you'll consider working for us – partnering with Hamid, of course."

"Hamid's already told me about some of the perks of the job." I shared a smile with him. "But we'll need to discuss hazard pay."

Everyone laughed, and Hamid squeezed my hand. *I think you could ask for anything, and they'd agree to it.*

Good to know. But right now, there is only one thing I want.

I smiled at Tristan and the others. "Would you guys mind if we continued this later? I'm a little tired, and I'd really like to spend some time alone with my mate."

Friedrich looked like he was about to object, but Camila cut him off. "Of course. There will be plenty of time to talk later." She took his arm and led him away.

"Take all the time you need," Tristan said before he followed them.

Hamid unclasped our hands so he could put both arms around me again. "Sleep. We'll be here a while longer."

I leaned back to look at him. "I'm not really tired. I just wanted them to go away."

He chuckled softly. "You still don't have much tolerance for the Council."

"That's not it. I really want to kiss you, and I thought it would be rude to make out in front of them."

"Good call." His gaze fell to my lips, and then he lowered his head to claim my mouth in a slow, sensual kiss that made me wish we really were alone. Once we got out of here, the two of us were taking a well-earned vacation to some secluded location where all there was to do was eat, sleep, and make love.

"I like this plan," Hamid said against my lips, letting me know I'd been projecting my thoughts again. "How about a private oasis in the Kalahari where there is nothing else but desert for hundreds of miles?"

"Can we go now?"

"I don't think you're going to get out of talking to the scholars first," he said, bursting my bubble.

My mouth turned down. "Oh, God. They're going to make me write up a huge report on this, aren't they?"

Hamid's laugh rumbled in his chest. "I think we can convince them to wait a few days for it. You did just save the world."

I perked up. "That's true. There needs to be a rule that people who save the world are exempt from writing reports."

"Sounds reasonable." He nibbled on my bottom lip. "Didn't you say something about making out?"

"I did." Grinning, I moved off his lap and straddled him. "How's this?"

"Much better," he said huskily before he kissed me again.

All too soon, the world intruded on us again.

"Hamid," Friedrich called. "We received a tip about a large *heffion* drug ring in India. Vivian said she'll go unless you want this one."

Hamid looked at me. "It's up to you."

I'd always wanted to see India, but I had a feeling I was going to get plenty of chances to go there. Hamid had promised to show me the world, and he was a man of his word. Plus, my mind was too full of images of that oasis in the Kalahari to think about anything else.

I pulled his head down to mine. "We'll get the next one."

EPILOGUE

3 months later

I lifted my head and peered down at the narrow road from my position atop the rumbling old truck. The headlights cut through the darkness, showing nothing but trees and more trees. According to the GPS on my phone, this road didn't even have a name. Where the hell were we going?

A muffled cry came from inside the truck, and it was immediately cut off by a slap and a shout. I pressed my lips together and forced myself not to react. There were at least two Gulaks in the back with the dozen or so human girls they were transporting. I could take the Gulaks, but I couldn't risk harming the girls by fighting in such close quarters. As soon as this truck stopped and those scaly bastards showed their faces, it was game on.

My phone vibrated, and I saw Hamid's name on the screen. Holding it to my ear, I whispered, "Hey."

"Hey. I wanted to let you know I got a lead on a shipment for that slaving operation. I know you wanted to be there to take them down, but I had to act on it."

"I'd do the same," I replied, keeping my voice low.

"You sound off," he said. "Why are you whispering? I thought you and Ana were having dinner together."

I bit my lip. "It's kind of a funny story, but you have to promise not to yell."

"Why would a funny story make me yell?" he asked warily.

"Well," I drawled. "I was on my way to meet up with Ana, and there was this truck parked in an alley that didn't look right. So, I left my bike on the street and went to check it out."

"Jordan." I didn't need to see him to know he was pinching the bridge of his nose, something he'd been doing a lot in the last few months.

"Don't worry. They didn't see me."

His tone sharpened. "Who didn't see you?"

"The Gulaks. They were too busy loading the girls into the back." I paused as the truck slowed going around a curve. "I slipped on without them having a clue I was there."

Hamid swore. "Do not tell me you climbed into a truck with a bunch of Gulak slavers."

I scoffed softly. "Of course not. Give me some credit. I'm on the roof of the truck."

He growled something, and I heard another male laughing. It sounded like Mario, one of the warriors we were working with on this job, along with his mate, Ana. We'd been in Panama for two weeks, at the request of the government, to locate and shut down a human trafficking ring. But this one was a lot more sophisticated than any other Gulak operation we'd encountered, and they'd managed to evade us completely. Until now.

"This is not a funny story," he said in an exasperated voice. "Where are you now?"

"I'm not quite sure. We were on Route One, but we took a right turn off the main road after..." I brought up the map on my phone. "What was that town called?"

"Chepo?" Hamid asked.

"That's it. How'd you know that?"

He sighed heavily. "Because we are about five minutes behind you."

I grinned at the starry sky. "What do you know? We are so in sync it's downright scary sometimes."

"Terrifying," he muttered.

The truck slowed and took a sharp left turn onto a dirt road. Up ahead, I could see lights and the outline of what looked like a house.

"Looks like we've reached our destination," I whispered urgently into the phone. "You boys better hurry, or you're going to miss all the fun."

"Stay out of sight, and do not engage them until we get there," Hamid ordered.

"Oops. Gotta go," I said when the truck lurched to a stop in front of the two-story house. "Love you."

I hung up and stuck the phone in my back pocket. Keeping my head low, I peered around the bare dirt yard, which was dimly lit by a single light over the front door of the house. There were lights on in the downstairs windows, but the second floor was dark. I hoped that meant there was no one upstairs to look down and see me on top of the truck.

The truck doors opened, and two Gulaks got out of the cab. The driver walked around the front of the truck to the passenger side and handed the second Gulak a set of keys.

"Unlock the cellar, and get the cages ready," he ordered in a deep voice that grated on my eardrums. "I'll help Brok and Gand unload the cargo."

"When do we meet up with the buyer?" the second Gulak asked.

"Tomorrow night."

I clenched my jaw at hearing them refer to the girls as cargo. God only knew how many humans they'd brought here and where those people had ended up. I was going to take great pleasure in shutting this operation down and burning this place to the ground.

The second Gulak hesitated. "The buyer asked for ten girls. What will we do with the other two?"

A nasty laugh rumbled from the driver. "Those are for us."

Fury blinded me for several seconds. In the next instant, I was on my feet and leaping off the truck.

I landed silently behind the driver, and before his friend could shout out a warning, my sword sliced through his thick neck. The other Gulak could only watch as the driver's head landed on the hood and rolled off the other side.

His shocked gaze swung back to me, and he fumbled for the short sword at his waist. I let him slide the sword free of its sheath, and then I struck.

He bellowed when my blade severed his sword arm at the elbow. He stared in disbelief at his hand and weapon lying on the ground at his feet. Clamping his remaining hand over the stump, he turned to flee, his leathery wings unfurling from his back.

I caught him before he'd made it past the front bumper of the truck. A single hard thrust between his wings was enough to pierce his heart. He made a choked sound and fell facedown into the dirt.

Banging came from the back of the truck. I found the keys on the ground and ran to the double doors that were padlocked together. I inserted the key into the lock and tossed the padlock on the ground. Then I swung one of the doors open, making sure to stay behind it and out of sight.

"It's about time." A Gulak jumped out of the truck. "What the hell took you so long?"

I stepped around the door. "They were a little busy dying."

"Who...?" he sputtered, his reptilian eyes wide.

Any other time, I might have played with him a bit, but I had a truck full of human girls to protect and another Gulak to deal with. I drove my blade through his chest, and he collapsed without another word.

I looked at the open door of the truck, but there was no sign of the last Gulak. From inside, I could hear whimpers and the sounds of bodies shifting.

"You have nowhere to go," I called as I wiped my blade on the pants of the dead Gulak at my feet. "If you make me come in there, it's not going to end well for you."

"If I come out, you'll kill me like you did Brok," the Gulak shouted.

"No, I won't." I wasn't lying. I needed to keep at least one of them alive to tell us about the rest of the operation. It was too big to be limited to this one location. "But if you don't come out before my team arrives in the next minute or so, I promise you they will not be as nice as I am."

As soon as the words left my mouth, I heard the distant sound of a vehicle. "I hear them coming now. Better decide soon."

The Gulak growled in desperate rage, and I thought he was going to choose to go down fighting. Seconds later, he appeared in the doorway and tossed his sword to the ground. He jumped out of the truck and put his hands up in surrender.

"Lie facedown on the ground," I ordered as I felt the first tickle of awareness in the back of my mind that told me my mate was near.

The Gulak complied without another word. Keeping my eyes on him, I called to the girls in Spanish to let them know they were safe. One petite blonde peeked out, and tears spilled down her dirty cheeks when she saw me.

"Are...you American?" she asked in a southern accent.

"Yes."

"Oh, thank God!" She jumped down despite the plastic ties binding her wrists. "Please, get us out of this hellhole."

Before I could answer her, a black pickup roared up and skidded to a stop next to the truck. The passenger door opened, and Hamid was beside me in an instant, wild-eyed and looking like he'd been running his fingers through his hair.

"I told you to stay out of sight," he said sternly as if the girl wasn't there.

I shrugged unapologetically. "I was going to, but the situation necessitated me taking immediate action."

Hamid narrowed his eyes. "And that required you to take out all four Gulaks by yourself instead of waiting for us?"

"Not all of them." I pointed at the one that had surrendered. "I kept one alive for interrogation."

Mario chuckled as he walked past us to my prisoner. "Thanks for leaving us one."

"Anytime." I let my sword drop to the ground and reached up to loop my arms around my scowling mate's neck. He was unhappy, but he let me pull his head down to mine. As soon as our lips met, he kissed me hungrily like we hadn't seen each other in weeks instead of hours.

One thing I'd learned about Hamid in our months together was that danger and fighting turned him on as much as it did me. I traveled the world, hunting the bad guys, and spent each night in the arms of my insatiable and hot-as-sin mate. Yep, I was officially the luckiest girl on the planet.

After the big showdown with Alaron, Hamid and I had spent a week at Westhorne with the entire Council and a whole team of scholars and scientists. I was poked and prodded and asked questions, until I nearly had a meltdown and started yelling at everyone who came near me. That was when Hamid put his foot down and said we were done. If they needed to know anything else, they could watch our recorded accounts of the events. We were taking a well-earned vacation.

We left Westhorne and spent two glorious weeks alone on the remote oasis in the Kalahari that he had promised to take me to. We spent our days swimming naked in the tiny lake or relaxing in the shade, and our nights making love on the sand beneath the stars. It was as close to Heaven on Earth as I could imagine.

Since then, I'd been settling into my new job working for the Council. As long as Hamid dealt with them, I was happy, and I loved being able to travel the world with him. So far, we'd been to Thailand, Pakistan, Spain, Italy, and Panama. Life was good.

"Get a room," Mario teased.

I smiled against Hamid's mouth and pulled back. "Duty calls."

We got down to work. He and Mario took the Gulak and made him show them around the place while I saw to the girls. Some of them had a few bruises, but nothing worse. There were three Americans in the lot, college friends who had been visiting Costa Rica. I had a feeling none of them was going to be planning more trips to Central America anytime soon.

The rest of the Panama City team arrived an hour later in Jeeps and two large vans that would carry the girls back to the city. Once they were checked out at the hospital, arrangements would be made to see them all home safely. They were all a little traumatized by their ordeal, but they'd been spared from a much worse fate.

Hamid's phone rang as we watched the last van leave to take the girls to the hospital. Figuring it was someone from the Council, I strolled away, tuning out the conversation like I usually did.

"Jordan," Hamid called to me.

I looked back to see him holding his phone to his chest to muffle it. "Friedrich wants to talk to you."

Frowning, I walked over to take the phone from him. "What's up, Friedrich?"

"I hear you cracked that human trafficking ring," he said jovially. "Well done! Once again you have proven to be a wonderful addition to our team."

I rolled my eyes at his effusive praise. He did that whenever he wanted something and expected resistance from me. "Thanks, but you didn't have to call to tell me that."

He chuckled. "Well, I do have another reason. Now that you're almost finished there, I have a job in Australia for you two and –"

"Sorry, no can do." I shot Hamid a dark look and caught him smirking at me. He was in so much trouble.

"But this is possibly an active Lilin," Friedrich rushed to say. "You can't pass that up."

"Normally, I'd agree with you, but I promised my family we'd be home for Thanksgiving. And I'm not missing the birth of my first niece."

"Niece?" he said, confused. "But you have no siblings."

I waved a dismissive hand. "Semantics. Anyway, I need to get back to work if we're going to finish up here this week."

"But..."

I didn't hear the rest of his protest because I handed the phone back to Hamid with a glare that promised retribution. He knew I didn't have the patience or diplomacy to deal with the Council, except for Tristan.

I walked over to one of the Jeeps and grabbed a bottle of water from a cooler in the back. I was taking a long drink when Hamid joined me.

"I think we're done here for tonight," he said, taking a bottle for himself. "We'll head back to the hotel soon."

I looked down at my blood-splattered clothes. "I could use a shower. And I want to pick up my bike along the way."

He set his bottle down on the bumper and pulled me into his arms. "You were amazing tonight."

I gave him a saucy smile. "You haven't seen anything yet."

His eyes darkened with desire. "Is that so?"

"Jordan, Hamid," Mario called to us from his truck. "Our new Gulak friend just told us where to find two more holding facilities. Feel like taking another ride?"

I looked at Hamid as the thrill of the hunt began to fill me again. "What do you say? I'll even let you kill a few this time."

"If it makes you happy, you can have all the kills." He pressed a quick kiss to my lips.

I sighed dreamily. "You say the sweetest things."

~ The End ~

BONUS SCENE

If you have jumped ahead to read this scene before Hellion, I encourage you to read the book first. The events in the bonus scene take place after Hellion, so the scene will be much more enjoyable after you've read the book.

A soft thump pulled me from the reports I was reading, and I frowned at the stairs that led to our bedroom on the second floor. Sara was napping before dinner, and if those imps woke her, they were going to get an earful from me. She was almost full-term, and she barely slept through the night anymore. Fae pregnancies were twelve months long, and the last quarter of Sara's had been hard on her. She needed all the rest she could get.

The noise came again. I laid my tablet on the couch and quietly climbed the stairs, ready to chuck the little fiends out the window. It wouldn't hurt them, but it would give me a small bit of satisfaction.

Our bedroom door was open, and I stepped inside, my eyes scanning the room for the source of the noise. But there was no sign of the little demons. My gaze landed on the bed, where I'd left my tired mate an hour ago, only to find it empty.

I felt a moment of fear that Sara had jumped to the middle of nowhere again like she had last Christmas. I quickly came to my senses when I realized I could still feel her. Besides, Eldeorin had put a ward on her to make sure that didn't happen again during the pregnancy.

"Darn it," said her muffled voice.

I walked to the nursery I'd built on to our bedroom this summer, smiling when I found her bent over trying to reach a bottle of baby powder on the floor. Her belly was too large to allow her much agility, and she couldn't quite get her fingers around the bottle.

"You're supposed to be resting," I scolded as I crossed the room to her. I picked up the bottle and set it on the dresser next to the changing table. Then I took her in my arms and kissed the top of her head.

"I couldn't sleep. I keep feeling like I'm missing something." She sighed and rested her head against my chest.

"Between my mother and yours, we have everything a new baby could need. If either of them sends us one more thing, I'll have to build another addition onto the house."

She yawned. "You're right. I'm being silly. Stupid pregnancy brain."

"I love your brain and every other part of you."

She tilted her head up and made a face. "My belly is the size of a whale. I can't even touch my toes anymore."

Laughing, I carefully lifted her into my arms and kissed her pouting lips. "You've never been more beautiful to me."

"You're supposed to say that," she said as I carried her back to the bed and tucked her in. When I started to stand, she grabbed my hand and tugged me down beside her. She rolled onto her side, and I spooned her. It was the only position that was comfortable for her these days. I placed my hand over hers and laced our fingers. She sighed and snuggled closer to me.

"If you're too tired to go up to the stronghold for dinner, we can stay here," I said against her hair.

"And miss Thanksgiving? No way."

I smiled at her vehement reply. Sara loved holidays and being surrounded by family and friends. Thanksgiving and Christmas had been quiet for her growing up, and she was determined to make up for that now. She would have been at the stronghold all day if I hadn't insisted we stay here until dinner. Otherwise, she would have worn herself out and fallen asleep before the first course was served.

The baby moved under our joined hands, and Sara shifted slightly. "She's restless today."

"Are you uncomfortable?"

"I'm perfect as long as you hold me like this."

Contentment filled me as I held close the two people I loved more than my own life. Listening to Sara's breathing even out, I thought briefly of the reports I was supposed to go through and quickly dismissed them. Nothing was more important than Sara's welfare, and right now, she needed to rest.

Two hours later, I gently roused my sleeping mate and told her it was time to go. I helped her up, and in less than ten minutes, she was dressed and ready to leave.

Outside, Hugo and Woolf lifted their heads from where they were dozing on the porch. Their tails wagged, but they didn't jump up and rush at Sara like they used to. The hellhounds had been subdued ever since we came home in September, and I wondered if they could sense she wasn't strong enough to play with them now. If anything, they'd become even more protective of her, rarely leaving the porch when she was in the house.

I moved to pick up Sara and carry her to the SUV, but she waved me off. "The walk will do me good." She took a deep breath of cold air. "Hmm. It's going to snow soon. Day after tomorrow."

"How much?" I was used to her weather predictions now, and she was never wrong.

"Just a few flurries but it feels like we're going to have a lot of snow this winter."

Smiling, I took her arm and helped her off the step. "I'll make sure we have plenty of firewood on hand."

Escorted by the hellhounds, we took our time walking along the path by the lake that led to the clearing where the SUV was parked. As we rounded the lake, a reflection in its glassy surface drew my gaze to the small white domed structure on the far side. The faeries called it a birthing hut, and Eldeorin had erected it a few days ago in preparation for Sara's delivery. When the time came, only Sara and the faeries would be allowed inside the hut, which was specially warded for her delivery.

My stomach clenched every time I thought about not being with Sara when she brought our baby into the world. According to Eldeorin, she would be unable to control her power or the baby's, so I had to be content with staying outside until it was safe to go in.

The ride to the main building of the stronghold was short, and we had a welcoming party waiting for us on the front steps. Before I'd pulled to a complete stop, my mother and Madeline were at the passenger door of the SUV, ready to help Sara out of the vehicle. Sara didn't like everyone fussing over her, but she smiled sweetly and let them assist her.

Sara's relationship with her mother had improved a lot in the last year. When Sara found out she was pregnant, Madeline had been there to offer the guidance and advice that only a mother can give. She was trying hard to make up for the lost years and the pain she'd caused her daughter. And Sara, whose capacity for love and forgiveness was boundless, had opened her heart to the mother she had been estranged from for most of her life. They weren't as close as my mother and me, but I could see them getting there eventually.

I followed the three of them into the main hall, which had been decorated for the holiday season. Music and laughter spilled from the dining room, and I entered it to find Sara already surrounded by Nate, Tristan, Chris, Beth, and our parents. Other Westhorne residents stood around the room talking amongst themselves.

"You look tired. Are you getting enough sleep?" asked Nate, who was visiting from his home in Asheville, North Carolina. He'd traveled quite a lot the last few years until he found a place this summer where he wanted to settle down again. Sara didn't like him being so far away, but she understood his need to be around other humans and people who didn't look half his age. He seemed happy there, which was all that mattered.

Sara laughed softly and hugged her uncle. "You sound like Nikolas. And yes, I'm well-rested. Nikolas made sure of it."

"You never tell a girl she looks tired, Nate," chided a voice from behind me. I smiled when Jordan nudged me with her elbow as she went by.

Hamid stopped beside me as Jordan squeezed between Chris and Nate to get to Sara. I'd known Hamid a long time, but I'd never seen him look so relaxed. It wasn't exactly the state of mind I would have expected from Jordan's mate.

"Where are you off to after the holiday?" I asked him.

"Australia," he said absently, never taking his eyes off the blonde who had just said something to make the people around her laugh.

I chuckled. He had that newly-mated look, the same one I'd probably worn for at least a year. He was so fixated on his mate that he was barely paying attention to anyone else in the room. I'd been surprised when he and Jordan had bonded, but seeing them together, it was clear they were a perfect match.

Hamid tore his gaze from Jordan to glance at me. "The Council wants us to go to Australia. I have made plans to go to Japan after that."

"Japan? I haven't heard of any trouble there."

"There isn't. I've arranged for Jordan to train with Daigo for six months."

"Ah." I nodded as understanding dawned.

Daigo Matsui was one of our oldest living samurai warriors. I'd trained with him a long time ago, and Jordan had asked me about him during our sparring sessions. I knew it was her dream to train with one of our samurai someday.

"I'm surprised she's not bouncing off the walls with excitement," I joked.

Hamid's gaze went back to Jordan. "She doesn't know about it yet. It is to be a surprise."

"You know her well." I smiled, imagining Jordan's reaction when he told her. Warriors waited years to get to train with Daigo. Hamid must have called in some big favors to get her in so quickly.

Chris left the others to join us. He and Beth had gotten home yesterday from Alberta, where they were setting up the first of the three new command centers we were establishing in Canada. Sara and I hadn't seen our friends since we'd finished the Chicago command center in August.

"How are things coming along in Canada?" Hamid asked him.

"Good. We're ahead of schedule, actually. I think we'll have all three centers set up by next June at this rate."

With half an ear, I listened to them talk about the new command centers as I watched Sara to make sure she wasn't showing any signs of fatigue. She tired so easily these days, and I knew she wouldn't listen to her body in all the holiday excitement.

She looked my way, and our eyes met. I could feel the warmth in her gaze, even without the connection between us.

Stop worrying, she scolded lightly across the bond.

I'm not worrying, I lied. *I'm just wondering how long I have to share you tonight before I can take you home to our bed.*

Pink tinged her cheeks. I loved that I could still make her blush, even with our child growing in her belly, and I hoped I never lost that ability.

I excused myself from Hamid and Chris and went to Sara. Taking her hand, I led her over to a loveseat that normally sat in one of the common rooms. I had expressed my concern about Sara being on her feet tonight, and Tristan had moved the couch in here for her. The fact that she didn't complain about me coddling her said she was more tired than she let on.

We weren't alone for long. Within minutes, our family and friends had drifted over to surround us.

Jordan sat on the arm of the couch next to Sara. "You didn't invite the wolves?"

Sara nodded. "I did, but Roland's mom wanted them to stay home this year. Emma's parents and sister are visiting them. And it's the first Thanksgiving for Peter and Shannon's little boy, Caleb, so they wanted to spend it with their family."

Jordan quirked an eyebrow. "I wonder how that conversation went when Emma told her family she was mated to a werewolf."

"It couldn't have been more shocking than finding out Emma used to be a vampire," I said.

"True." She looked at the faces of the people around us. "It's crazy how much has happened in the last four years. Did you guys ever think we'd be friends with werewolves and ex-vampires?"

"Yes," Sara answered immediately, earning laughter from everyone. "Well, yes to the werewolves."

"Seriously, though." Jordan held up a hand and started ticking off her fingers. "People in this room have killed a Master, a Lilin, and an archdemon just in the last few years. That's insane when you think about it."

Chris squeezed Beth, who was leaning back against his chest, and smirked at Hamid and me. "What I'm hearing is that our mates are total badasses and we need to up our game."

I smiled at Sara. "I think you may be right."

"Are you saying you wish to take a break from work?" Hamid asked Jordan with a glint of amusement in his eyes.

The glare she shot him was comical. "Don't even joke about that."

I opened my mouth to tease her just as a dull pain shot up my arm from the hand that was holding Sara's. I looked down at our joined hands to see hers glowing faintly. It wasn't an unusual sight these days, but it was the first time her power had shocked me during her pregnancy. Her lack of reaction told me she wasn't aware she had done it.

She sighed softly and shifted as if she were uncomfortable.

"Feeling okay?" I asked her.

"Yes." Sara rested her head on my shoulder. "I think our daughter is getting a little impatient to come into the world."

I put an arm around her. "Soon."

Tristan glanced toward the kitchen and back to us. "I believe dinner is ready to be served."

Sara lifted her head. "Perfect timing. I'm famished, and the turkey smells amazing."

I stood and reached down to help her to her feet. At the last second, she yanked her hand back as it began to glow brightly.

She shrunk back against the cushion, away from Jordan and me, her eyes wide with panic. "Stay back."

"What's wrong?" I asked more calmly than I felt.

"I-I can't pull my power back in. Oh..." She looked down and then up at me with a shocked expression. "I think my water just broke."

Madeline and my mother rushed forward, but Sara held up her hands. "Don't come near me! It's not safe."

"It is for me." Nate came to sit beside her, and Sara clutched his hand like it was a lifeline. I was glad she had him, even though it killed me that I couldn't offer her physical comfort during her time of need.

"What do we do?" Beth asked.

"Nothing," Sara said shakily. She closed her eyes briefly and sighed. "Eldeorin and Aine are coming."

No sooner had the words left her mouth than Eldeorin appeared in front of me. Ignoring everyone else in the room, he knelt before Sara and laid a hand on her belly. I held my breath as I waited for him to speak.

At last, he lifted his head to smile at Sara. "We need to get you to the birthing hut. Aine is there now, preparing it for you." Without another word, he stood and scooped her into his arms. In the next moment, they were gone.

I ran from the building and sped down the road to the lake. In less than a minute, our cabin came into view, but I passed it and headed straight for the faerie hut. I got within five feet of the structure and came up against a wall of Fae magic that caused my skin to prickle painfully. I couldn't feel Sara through the ward, but its presence told me she was in there with the faeries.

Sara? I called as I took a step back.

Nothing.

I paced helplessly. Tristan arrived, followed shortly after by my parents, Madeline, and our friends. They all gave me expectant looks, but I had no news for them. I was as in the dark as they were.

Nate got there five minutes later, having driven one of the vehicles over. "How is she?" he asked when he ran up to me, out of breath.

Before I could answer, a smiling Aine appeared in front of us. "Sara is doing well," the red-haired sylph assured me. "She knew you would worry and asked me to come to you."

"Can I talk to her?" I asked.

Aine nodded. "As soon as we bind her power, we'll reduce the wards so you two can communicate."

Relief flooded me. Not being able to physically be with Sara for our daughter's birth was hard enough, but being cut off completely from her was sheer torture.

"I must return to her," Aine said softly and disappeared.

It was another ten agonizing minutes before my Mori began to flutter in excitement. My entire body relaxed when I felt Sara's presence. It was a little muted because of the ward but strong enough to soothe my anxious Mori.

Nikolas? Sara called through the bond.

I'm here. Are you okay?

As good as any woman can be in labor, she said with a smile in her voice. *How are you holding up out there?*

As good as any man whose mate is in labor, I replied.

A wave of love came across the bond. *I wish you could be in here with me.*

I do, too.

I –

Her words cut off, and I sensed rather than felt her physical pain. My jaw clenched. I would give anything to take her pain into me. But this was one time I couldn't share my Mori's strength with her.

Contraction, she said after the pain passed.

Can't they do something to ease the pain?

It's not that bad, she assured me. *And Aine said Fae births are much faster than human births. Before you know it, we'll be holding our baby.*

Madeline approached me, her eyes dark with worry. "Are you talking to Sara? How is she?"

I realized then that I was surrounded by people, who were watching me closely, waiting for some word about Sara.

"She's doing well," I told them, not knowing what else to say.

For the next hour, I paced and talked to Sara as the time between her contractions shortened. I tried to distract her from the pain, but I could tell it was getting worse. I'd been in countless dangerous situations in my life, but not one of them had made me feel as impotent as I did now.

When are we telling Jordan she's going to be the godmother? I asked, watching the blonde warrior who was talking quietly with Hamid. Jordan had been hinting for months that she wanted the job, and we'd been waiting until the baby came to surprise her with the news.

Sara laughed. *You can have that honor when we present our daughter to her.* She grew silent for a long moment. *You're still okay with Eldeorin being her godfather, right?*

Yes. Aine had explained to us that our daughter should have at least one Fae godparent. As much as I disliked Eldeorin, he was powerful and he cared for Sara. And Sara cared for him and trusted him with her life.

When we have a son, you can choose – She broke off abruptly, and I sensed her pain as a contraction hit her. This one seemed to be longer than the previous ones, and I thought I felt a trickle of fear from her.

I clenched my hand into a fist. I knew she was in the best possible hands, but I hated that she was going through this without me.

Without warning, a wall slammed down between us, and I couldn't feel Sara anymore. I spun to face the hut, but everything there looked the same. A knot of fear formed in my gut. Something was wrong.

Sara? I called, but silence answered me. It took all of my self-control to not try to push past the ward keeping me from her.

Tristan was suddenly beside me. "What is it?"

"I don't know. We were talking, and now I can't hear or feel her."

My fear must have shown on my face because he laid a hand on my shoulder. "I'm sure we would have heard if something was wrong."

"You're right," I said without conviction. I looked around, and my gaze landed on Nate, who stood a few feet away talking to Chris and Beth. "Nate," I called.

He hurried over to us, his brow furrowed in concern. "Is something wrong?"

"I can't hear Sara anymore. Can you see if you can get through the Fae ward and reach the hut?"

Nate turned away without another word and started toward the hut in long strides. He walked straight through the ward without pausing and went up to knock on the side of the hut that had no visible doors or windows.

It felt like an hour had passed before Aine appeared, although it had only been minutes. I couldn't hear what she said to Nate because they were inside the ward, but the tightening of his mouth made fear claw at me.

They walked toward us. Aine, who normally wore a serene expression, looked troubled as she approached me. I tried to brace myself for whatever she was going to tell me.

"There is a complication," Aine said gently when she reached me. "Sara's body is ready to deliver, but the babe refuses to come."

"What does that mean?" I demanded.

"Sara's contractions have stopped, and the babe's magic is preventing us from removing her from the womb without causing her injury."

I stared at the sylph as I tried to make sense of what she was saying. "She's an infant. How can she match Eldeorin's power or yours?"

"Her magic is pure, and she is drawing from Sara's magic. Until she is bound, she is extremely powerful."

"There's nothing you can do?" I asked as blood started to pound in my ears.

"No," Aine replied. "But do not be alarmed. Sara says something has distressed the babe, and she is trying to calm her."

I dragged a hand through my hair. Sara was very good at soothing our daughter when she was restless or excited, which tended to happen a lot when carrying a Fae baby.

Aine's head tilted slightly as if she was listening for something. Her eyes widened, and she blurted, "I must go," before she did her disappearing act again.

The moment she left, everyone surrounded me, wanting to know what was going on. I filled them in and went back to pacing. I didn't know how many minutes passed because each one felt like an eternity.

Nikolas. Sara's voice in my head was accompanied by a wave of intense joy.

Sara? I called as a doorway formed in the side of the hut and Eldeorin appeared.

Eldeorin's eyes found me, and the look on his face could only be described as wonder. "You may come in now."

I hurried over to him. "How are they?"

"They...are well." The faerie smirked at me. "Come see for yourself."

He stepped aside to give me room to enter. The interior of the hut was softly lit, and the walls were draped in filmy white cloth. Aine was off to one side doing something, but I only had eyes for Sara, who lay in the bed in the center of the room. She was propped up on pillows and holding a tiny wrapped bundle to her chest. I hadn't thought it was possible for her to be more beautiful, but the sight of her with our daughter stole my breath away.

Sara's green eyes sparkled with tears when they met mine. "Nikolas," she breathed as if she was too overcome to say more than my name.

I went to her and kissed her tenderly. Then I sat beside her and gazed down at our daughter. Her eyes were closed and her tiny face was puckered, but I could already see Sara in her. She had a shock of thick black hair that could only have come from me.

"She's beautiful," I said hoarsely, touching her soft cheek with my finger.

Sara sniffled. "Yes, he is."

I sucked in a sharp breath and lifted my eyes to Sara's. "What?"

"Nikolas, meet your son." She smiled, and happiness radiated from her.

Shock rippled through me as she laid the baby in my arms. "My...son? But how? Eldeorin said we were having a girl."

"And you did," said a soft voice behind me. I looked up as Aine walked over, carrying a second baby, whom she gently placed in Sara's waiting arms. "This is your daughter."

Unable to form words, I stared down at my son and daughter. A wave of protectiveness, unlike anything I'd ever experienced, washed over me as my heart expanded until it felt like it would burst.

"Twins," I finally choked out. "How...? Is he...?"

Sara reached out with her free hand to smooth our sleeping son's hair. "He's full Mohiri like his daddy, and his sister is half Fae like me. We thought she was protecting her Mori from my power, but it turns out she was also shielding her twin. That's why none of us could sense him."

Dazed, I struggled for the appropriate response. All I managed to say was, "I have to build another addition on the cabin."

Sara laughed and clasped my hand. "I think the nursery will do for now. We can easily fit a second crib in there."

I sat beside her with my son cradled in one arm and my other around Sara and our daughter. We stayed like that in our own little cocoon of happiness until Eldeorin spoke.

"Your family and friends are asking to see you. I've removed the wards, so it's safe for them to come in if you are ready."

Sara nodded. "Yes. Oh, wait!" She looked at me. "We need to give our son a name first."

"True."

When we'd discovered Sara was pregnant, she had asked if we could name the baby Danielle after her father, Daniel. It saddened her that he would never meet his grandchild, and this way, our daughter would carry a part of him with her. We had never once discussed a boy name because neither of us had expected to have a son this soon.

"We can name him after someone in your family," she suggested.

I thought about it. "My grandsire's name was Dimitri. How about that?"

Her face lit up. "I love it. Danielle and Dimitri. They sound good together."

"Then Danielle and Dimitri it is." I kissed her temple. "Are you ready to introduce our son and daughter to everyone?"

She rested her head in the crook of my shoulder. "I just want to stay like this for a little bit longer. Something tells me it's the last rest we're going to get for a while."

"If Danielle is anything like her mother, I may never sleep again."

Sara scoffed. "Don't forget I've heard all your mom's stories about what you were like when you were a little boy."

"At least our life will never be boring."

"Never." She sighed happily. "I love you, Nikolas."

I kissed the top of her head. "I love you, *moy malen'kiy voin.*"

ABOUT THE AUTHOR

When she is not writing, Karen Lynch can be found reading or baking. A native of Newfoundland, Canada, she currently lives in Charlotte, North Carolina with her cats and two crazy lovable German Shepherds: Rudy and Sophie.

Made in the USA
Coppell, TX
22 December 2020

46956204R00163